RICOCHET

L.K. REID

Cover Design by Opulent Swag and Designs
Editing by Maggie Kern at Ms. K Edits
Formatting by Black Widow Designs

To those who have both light and dark in them.
This one's for you.

PLAYLIST

The playlist for Ricochet has more than 80 songs, and while I did try parting with some of them, I just simply couldn't. Each one of them holds a small part of this story, but the four that have marked my whole journey with Ricochet are *Crawling* by Linkin Park, *Insanity* by Kaizer & Alex Cheef, *Darkest Part* by Red and *Higher* by Sleep Token.

If you would like to hear what I've been listening to while writing this book, head on to Spotify.

AUTHOR'S NOTE

While Ricochet isn't the darkest book ever written, it still is a dark romance and I would like to ask you to proceed with caution. If the themes such as abuse, torture, rape, suicidal thoughts and/or attempted suicide, as well as substance abuse are something that triggers you, I need you to be aware that all of these are mentioned throughout the book. It is not recommended for readers below eighteen.

While it has been dubbed as Mafia Romance, I would like to mention that the Mafia part of the book is not the main focus. This is not a fairytale.

It is a love story, but it might not be the one you are expecting to get.

FOREWORD

"The monsters in my head always knew that I would lose you in the end."
David Jones

PROLOGUE

"Where the fuck am I?" I mumbled. A sudden movement on my right side sent a jolt of fear mixed with excitement through me, making me realize I was not as alone as I thought I was.

"Hello." The chilling feeling in my bones had nothing to do with the actual temperature of the house anymore, but everything to do with my emotions skyrocketing. "Is anybody here?"

A million and one thoughts about human trafficking and horrors I could be facing ran through my head. I expected shit to happen, but I preferred to know what I was getting myself into.

"Please," I whispered. Nothing brings men down to their knees like a damsel in distress. "What is this place?"

Was I hallucinating? No, I saw somebody, I was sure of it.

I stepped inside the room the shadow disappeared to, and gawked at the sight in front of me. This whole place should've been on a magazine cover or something. The whole design looked like something my mother would've used in her house. The white curtains were linen—the kind of white devoid of dust or any kind of human touch. The room reminded me of a hotel foyer with its size and artwork. Two beige couches stood on the opposite sides of each other, right in front of the fireplace, accompanied by a sofa chair of the same color.

What had me excited, however, wasn't the size of this room nor its brilliant setup. I didn't give a fuck about the architectural beauty or the interior design. I inched closer to the fireplace, tipping my head to look at the picture above. They say snakes won't attack unless provoked. I knew some that would.

The Nightingale emblem stood there in all of its glory. An imposing snake wrapped around the gleaming sword, looking ready to attack. I didn't have to be a genius to figure out who owned this house.

And who brought me here.

This was no coincidence, and that little voice in my head told me Theo had his hands in this. Just how I suspected, just what I wanted. He thought I was heading into the trap. Poor little toad. After all these years, he should've known that nothing and nobody could surprise me anymore, especially not him.

Okay, alright, it was showtime. I just wondered why they didn't lock me up like they did before? Had they grown a conscience somewhere along the way? How fucking sweet of them for not chaining me to the fucking wall this time around.

I took a few steps back as deep laughter resonated somewhere behind me. The usual reaction I would have to that sound, to those voices, couldn't be used right now. Oh no, they had to think they had me.

My hands started shaking, the keys dropping to the ground.

You can run, but you can never hide, little bird.

The threatening words *he* repeated so many times resurfaced again. I didn't want to turn around. I didn't want to face them.

I didn't want to face them because I knew I would want to

kill them, one by one—claw their fucking eyes out, carve up their hearts, rip their throats out. I could be creative.

I'd been waiting for this moment for the last four years.

It kept me awake, it kept me moving, and it kept me motivated.

Keep your fucking cool, Ophelia. No messing around this time.

Helpless little lamb, that's what you are.

Their steps echoed around the room, taunting me, closing in. There was nowhere to go now. My hands felt clammy, the urge to run overtaking my whole body. I just didn't know if I wanted to run away, or run to them. I knew what was about to happen. My mouth was parched and my throat constricted. I hadn't cried in so long, I forgot how it felt. My tears threatened to spill over my cheeks, and it wasn't because the shithead I was related to betrayed me. I wanted to cry because I couldn't kill them, right here and right now.

"Hello, birdy," one of them marveled. The walls were closing in... tick tock. "You're not going to greet us? Not that we mind the view from here." Instinctively I grabbed the hem of my shirt, trying to pull it lower, remembering my lack of pants. Oh well, what the hell.

Taking a deep breath, I turned around, facing my demons head-on.

Kieran, Cillian and Tristan Nightingale.

The three brothers, the three musketeers, and my worst nightmare. Oh no, wait. I think it was the other way around.

I was their worst nightmare, they just didn't know it yet.

They stood side by side, all three dressed in black. How fucking lovely—they were now wearing matching clothes. If I had my phone with me, I would've snapped a picture. While they were dressed for my funeral, I planned for theirs. Tristan and Cillian wore amused expressions on their faces, but I could see the darkness swirling behind their eyes. They were going to enjoy every second of this, whatever it was they had planned for me.

Kieran stood between the two of them, his dark hair disheveled, a few strands falling onto his forehead. Unlike the other two, he didn't smile. His face was like a marble statue, devoid of any emotion. But I could see it.

His anger, his hatred, his pain. It was all there, showing through his obsidian eyes. He cocked his head, meeting my gaze head-on. I knew what that was.

A challenge.

An invitation.

He wanted me to fight this. To scream and shout, demand to be let out. He wanted me to entertain them, but I wasn't going to do that. They thought they lost everything that night, but they weren't the only ones.

The difference was, I knew the truth. They didn't.

"Did you miss us, little bird?" Cillian took a step closer, while I took two back. He laughed, pushing me closer to the fireplace with every new step. "Because we sure as hell missed you."

1

OPHELIA

Seven Years Ago

"What do you mean, you're breaking up with me?"

I stood in front of Ronan Carson, his voice grating on my nerves. Why did I ever think dating him would be a good idea?

"I just don't think this is working out," I told him. "And with summer break coming, I might be going out of the country."

I glanced around the stadium, making sure we were still alone. The last thing I wanted to do was make this a public spectacle because his ego was hurt. Ronan didn't love me. He was simply infatuated with me and everything I represented—status, money, fame in this little town. For most of my life, I was invisible to people like him, but without Theo and his friends at school scaring the ever-loving crap out of everybody, and Maya going away, I was the last Aster left to conquer.

And they tried.

The moment I started school last year, they swarmed around me like locust. They invited me to their parties, football games, you name it. Two months ago, I finally succumbed to Ronan, and I liked him. He was fun to be around when he wasn't talking about football—he was the quarterback and all—or when he wasn't trying to arrange a hangout with the Nightingale brothers… Okay, maybe he wasn't as fun as I thought he was, but he was harmless.

"Is there somebody else?" My eyes snapped to his face, unease rolling through me.

"No." *Yes*.

Did I feel awful about lying to him? Yeah, yeah, I did. Ronan wasn't a bad-looking guy, and half of the girls at our school told me how lucky I was to have his attention. But his sandy-blond hair never did it for me. Neither did his blue eyes, no matter how many times I tried to forget the onyx ones.

And every time he kissed me, I imagined somebody else's lips on mine. It wasn't fair to him, and it wasn't fair to me. I could see he wanted more from me, but I wasn't willing to give him something that belonged to someone else.

"I really am sorry, Ronan." I stood up and waited for him to say something. Anything at all, but it never came. "I'll see you around, okay?"

I could hear the bell ringing, and I knew these bleachers would be filled with students in the next couple of minutes. When he kept staring out at the stadium with a very visible tick on his cheek, I took it as time to go.

I passed a group of cheerleaders sneering at me, and I couldn't even imagine their behavior once word of our breakup got out. The last two months, the jocks and their girlfriends were, I could say, civil toward me, but I knew it was only because I was dating one of their own. Next year was going to hurt. I could already feel it.

I wasn't going to dwell on that right now. I was adamant on making this the best summer of my life.

School was officially over for the year, but everybody still lingered around, talking about their summer plans, parties they were going to attend, people they were going to meet. I had no interest in any of it.

Instead, I walked by the main building of our school, heading for the cliffs overlooking the ocean. If I looked to the left side, I could almost see my house down in the valley, nestled next to Nightingale Hill.

I always wondered which presumptuous prick named the house as if it were a small town in an already small town. Half of the town already had their names plastered on shops, billboards, and whatnot. Even Ava always joked that her ancestors must have been compensating for something else, if you know what I mean. In my opinion, both of our families were just a bunch of assholes controlling this town.

Hers more than mine, but still.

I took a deep breath, inhaling a familiar scent of the Atlantic Ocean, reveling in the sound of crashing waves against the cove beneath the cliff. Families were milling on the beach, taking advantage of the warm weather. June was always a tricky little bastard. It would be sunny in the morning, and then suddenly, a wave of rain would sweep through the town in the afternoon, confining everybody to their houses.

I loved both, but I preferred the sun over the clouds on any given day. Summer solstice was upon us in ten days, and half of the town would be filled with tourists, running away from their cities, seeking some sun and ocean. I still didn't know what our plans were, but I had no doubt they involved the Nightingales and some sort of a resort for at least a week. It didn't really matter as long as I had Ava with me.

"Phee!" Speak of the devil. I turned around, seeing a flustered Ava walking toward me. She always reminded me of Snow White, with her black hair, and round blue eyes, a complete contrast to her pale skin. Some people in school called her an elf, thinking it would bother her. If anything, she reveled in the nickname. I couldn't recall how many times she made me watch *The Lord of the Rings* with her, fawning over Legolas and later on his father when *The Hobbit* came out.

"I've been looking everywhere for you," she huffed, plopping down on the stone next to mine. "What are you doing here? I thought you were with Ronan."

"I was with him." I chuckled at the scowl on her face. For a person that got along with almost everybody, she hated Ronan's guts. "We broke up, you psycho, so you can remove that look on your face."

"Oh, thank God. I was going to punch him in the face."

For such a little thing, she was one of the fiercest people I knew. When she loved somebody, she loved with her whole being, giving them everything. But if she didn't like you. Jesus, just run away.

"Why do you seem sad, though?" She sobered, her eyes zeroing in on mine. "I thought you wanted this."

"I did. Trust me, it had to happen."

"Then what's the problem?"

Wasn't that the million-dollar question? What was the real problem? What started as a mere crush years ago, turned into a full spectrum of feelings I had no control over. Her brother was the problem, or well, my feelings for him.

"Is it—"

"I don't want to talk about that, Ava. Today is really not the day."

Not that I wanted to talk about it ever, at least not with her. She never made me feel weird about the whole situation, but I didn't want to see that pity in her eyes, both of us knowing that nothing would come of it. I was his sister's best friend. His friend's little sister, and no amount of feelings from my side would change that. I just had to get over it.

"You know what?" She suddenly jumped in front of me, hauling me up. "I know what will make you feel better."

I laughed at her excitement, "What?"

"Sally's Burgers. And you know what today is?"

I waited expectantly for her to tell me, because truth be told, I only knew it was Thursday.

"It's Shroom's Day, and being your best friend—"

"Basically, my only friend," I chuckled.

"Semantics." She waved me off, pulling me toward the parking lot. "I know how much you love their mushroom and swiss burger. So, move your ass woman. I am hungry."

I t was almost nine in the evening when we finally pulled in front of my house, with Ava chattering about the summer days ahead, and her brothers coming back from college. My foul mood had been forgotten as soon as we'd entered Sally's Burgers, and whoever said that food couldn't fix anything, obviously didn't have a nice, juicy burger in their life.

"So, pick you up at seven tomorrow?" she asked, almost yelling over the sound of the music. *Doomsday* by Architects was blasting at full force, the car vibrating from the sound.

"Seven-thirty," I responded. "I need to wash my hair in the morning."

"Fine, princess." I smacked her on the arm, her bubbly laughter echoing around the car. "I'll see you tomorrow. Don't be late."

She slapped my butt as I exited the car, the tires screeching not even a second after I closed the door. One day she would end up in a ditch somewhere with her reckless driving.

Noticing my father's car in the driveway, the nerves I hadn't felt for days skyrocketed. I thought he was still on his business trip with Mr. Nightingale? The foyer of our house was dark, not one person in sight. Our main maid, Cassandra, was usually here, greeting me whenever I got home. But she was nowhere in sight tonight.

"Hello." I walked slowly toward the dining room, hoping to find somebody there. Squinting in the darkness, I could see the table set up, the dinner untouched, and chairs untucked from the table. Did something happen? "Is anybody home?"

Panic started taking over, and I fumbled with my phone, turning the flashlight on. I almost stumbled on a chair, jumping at the piercing scream coming from the back of our house. It sounded like a man, and before I could recover, another scream pierced through the air. With trembling knees, I exited the dining room, slowly inching toward the back area, where the entrance to the basement was.

The screaming grew louder, and I could hear somebody talking. Was that... Was that my father's voice?

For years these doors were locked. I never asked why, never even tried to check what was inside. For the first time, they were wide open, the light from below illuminating the hallway above. Should I call the police? What if somebody was trying to rob us? No, no, I needed to see what was going on first.

Turning the flashlight off, I slowly descended step by step. From this point, I could see silhouettes, the light casting a shadow on the floor. Finally reaching the bottom, nothing could have prepared me for the sight in front of me.

My mother stood there, her back turned toward me, holding a glass of amber liquid in her hand. My father, whom I hadn't seen in months, stood behind a man tied to a chair, with a knife pressed against his throat. There was so much blood on his body, cuts and bruises visible on his face. His clothes were disheveled; his shirt ripped across the chest, caked in blood.

Mom laughed at something, and I couldn't hear exactly what they were talking about because of the buzzing in my ears. Who were these people? My parents or serial killers?

My father inched lower with his knife, slicing the man's nipple off. The phone slipped from my hand, and as I reached for my face to cover the gasp threatening to escape from my mouth, I felt wetness on my face. I hadn't even realized I was crying.

Oh God, I was going to be sick.

Both of them turned at the same time, my mother taking a step toward me.

"Nikolai, look. It's Ophelia." I wasn't sure if she was drunk or high, or maybe even both, but I didn't recognize the person in front of me. "Did you come to join us, baby?"

She was smiling, while my father carved this man like a pumpkin. Did I somehow step into a parallel dimension? Her eyes were glassy, unfocused, and the fear I had never felt around her started creeping in.

Did I come to join them?

Was she serious? Nikolai, my father, stepped away from the man, taking a cloth from the nearby table, and wiping the knife clean. He didn't seem fazed by my presence. As a matter of fact, he looked so cold; colder than what he usually was. His blue eyes narrowed at me, the same look on his face whenever he wasn't pleased with something I did or said.

The one just before the beating.

"Hello, *doch'*."

Daughter.

Never Ophelia, never with affection, just the Russian word for daughter. The Aster family used to be Asterov, immigrating from Russia shortly after the Nightingales settled here. Almost three hundred years later, and he still insisted on us knowing the language, as if I was ever going to use it.

"Hi, Papa." My voice sounded small, timid. I could feel fear coursing through me. How many slaps did I get throughout the years for answering fully in English? Hundreds. So I learned.

I learned Russian better than my brother and sister. I learned because there was no stopping him when he wanted to hurt me, and me knowing his beloved language at least pleased him a little bit. He stepped in front of me, and I flinched involuntarily when he raised his left hand toward my face. The hand that had just held a knife at another man's throat.

The hand coated in blood.

"I won't hurt you, *dorogoy*. You are just in time." *Darling*. He never used terms of endearment with me. His hand caressed my cheek, and the metallic smell of the blood traveled up my nose. I gagged, holding the food I had earlier in my stomach. I didn't want to find out what would happen if I vomited all over the floor.

Breathing through my mouth, I met his eyes, the mirror of mine, and asked, "In time for what, Papa?"

"For your initiation to the family, of course," my mother squealed, the amber liquid sloshing in the glass as she jumped around. "Your brother and sister already went through theirs."

Theo and Maya knew about this? Why didn't they tell me?

"I wanted to wait until your eighteenth birthday, but we can do it now."

What are we going to do? Was this a sick joke? Ha-ha, let's pull a prank on Ophelia.

"Papa, what are we doing?"

He walked away from me, and only then did I notice an array of instruments on another table, further inside the room. Knives, screwdrivers, clamps, a gun, they all laid there, ready to be used.

"Did you know that our ancestors shared the same bloodline with the Romanov family?" He looked at me. "The last Russian Dynasty?"

"Yes, Papa. You told me this story when I was a child."

"But I never told you why we ran away. My great-great-grandfather was a leader of one of the largest crime syndicates of that time, and when he found out they were going to attack us, he moved the whole family to the States, starting anew."

Crime syndicate? I'm sorry, what?

"Everybody feared him, as they should have. His name was Alexei Dimitri Asterov. Now, he didn't want his family to be weak, and since only boys were part of the syndicate up to that point, he decided to include females as well, bringing them deeper into the family. Guess what?"

"What, Papa?"

"They were better assassins than his sons. We continued his legacy, our empire growing with each year, and now we control most of the States as well as Eastern Europe. Our friends, the Nightingales," he smiled at me, "they were one of our allies here in the United States."

The Nightingales were involved in this?

"I thought we owned a real estate business—"

"Oh we do, *moy dorogoy*. We have several legal businesses around the globe, but that is just a small part of what we are."

I was going to faint, or puke, or maybe even both. What was going on here? This was madness, all of it. My father was a madman.

I took a deep breath and asked him, "What is the initiation, Papa?"

He looked at me, then at the man who looked almost dead, and smiled. "You get to kill this *izmenik*. If you succeed where your siblings didn't," he held the knife out to me, "everything you have ever wanted to have will be yours."

"And if I don't?"

"You can ask Maya. I'm sure she will be more than happy to provide you with details."

I was seventeen years old, for fuck's sake. People my age were fighting with their parents about curfew, their grades—mine were asking me to kill somebody. I wasn't a murderer. I hated violence, but the look in his eyes was serious. He would make my life a living hell, I was sure of that. I gnawed at my bottom lip, contemplating my options—refuse him or do what was asked of me? Could I really do this?

How was it possible that I never saw this level of darkness in him? Had I missed all the signs? Was I that naïve? I had a feeling that my whole life was one gigantic lie. I looked at the dagger in his hand, its blade shining in the light. Glancing at my mother, I noticed her swaying, almost dancing to nonexistent music, and I knew she wasn't going to help me. I always knew she had a drinking problem, but this… This was so much worse than what I expected.

"We don't have all night, Ophelia." I snapped my eyes to him, a small smirk dancing on his face. Did he want me to fail? The sadistic bastard probably did. There was no love in those eyes, only a darkness I never saw before. What a good actor he was.

Something numbed inside of me, my fear subsiding, and a newfound resolve taking over my body.

"I'll do it," I said to him. "But if I do this, I want to know everything."

"Of course."

I walked toward him, snatched the dagger from his hand, and turned toward the man.

"You're saying he's *izmenik*. A traitor?" I trained my eyes on the man's brown hair. He couldn't have been much older than me, a couple of years maybe.

"That's correct."

I stepped in front of him, bending down so that we were face-to-face. His right eye was swollen shut, and I could see that he wasn't going to live much longer with the wounds that had already been inflicted. I grabbed his hair, tipping his head up as I stood. He mumbled incoherently, but I didn't have time to listen to his pleas.

He was a dead man, with or without me. So what difference did it make what killed him in the end? It was either him or me, and if I thought my father was already cruel, I couldn't even imagine the horrors he would set on me if I didn't do this.

"Everything, Papa." I didn't turn around as I repeated his promise to me, but I needed another confirmation.

"Everything, *moy malen'kiy*."

His little one.

Maybe he would get better if I did this. Maybe I would finally have a father instead of a dictator inside this house. He hadn't called me his little one since I was five years old.

I gripped the handle tighter, breathing through my mouth, and preparing myself for my next step.

"I am sorry," I whispered to the man when his one eye snapped open to look at me. There was no fight there, no will to live. He knew, just like I did. This was the end.

I watched a movie once where the serial killer kept slitting people's throats. It looked so easy.

Bringing the blade closer, he suddenly muttered, "Thank you". My hand shook, but I didn't stop. The sound of skin slicing, the meat breaking beneath the blade, almost made me vomit. As the blood rushed through the cut, I pressed harder, hearing the crunching sound of his larynx breaking, and he started choking on his own blood.

I don't know how long I stood there, staring at the red rivulets of blood on my hands, at his head hanging loosely, before my father approached me, hugging me as if it was the most natural thing in the world.

"*Ya znal, chto ty moya doch'.*"

He knew I was his daughter. Of course, I was.

I was a monster.

2

OPHELIA

ynthia Larson was staring at me from across the football field. She either had a death wish, or was too stupid to realize I was five minutes from ripping her eyes out of their sockets. She's been doing that a lot lately, staring. Well actually, since I broke up with Ronan, she thought it would be a good idea to open the hunting season on me. Their petty thoughts and insignificant lives were of no interest to me. She always had something against me, and with all the other shit I had going on around me, Cynthia's bullying was the last thing I needed.

But she was pissing me off. Since my initiation night, one month ago, it was as if something snapped inside of me and the parts I never knew existed came to the surface, taking over my mind. My tolerance levels were almost nonexistent. The sinister thoughts were almost constant these days.

I just didn't know anymore where the good ones ended and the bad ones began. During dinner yesterday, I caught myself imagining my father bleeding out from wounds I caused. I imagined his body mauled and destroyed beyond recognition, and I was the culprit. I was gripping the handle of the knife so tight, I could still feel the steel digging into my hand. Was this darkness always inside of me?

I caught Ava's worried eyes on me, and I managed to fake a smile, trying to erase the murderous glare I was no doubt sending in Cynthia's direction.

"What the fuck is wrong with you lately?" I should've known she wouldn't let it go. Ava knew me too well, and after I tried avoiding her for the first two weeks, she knew something was up.

I just wasn't ready to talk about it. What would I say, anyway?

Oh, darling, I've been initiated into something called Syndicate, run by my father. Saturdays are stabbing days, you know, to slice somebody up. Also, did you know that if you cut someone's jugular, it takes them less than ten minutes to completely bleed out? A piece of art, really. Oh, and your family is in on that business. I am basically part of the Russian mafia now, so no, I can't go shopping for a prom dress because there's another person to kill.

Yeah, I couldn't exactly tell her that. I wasn't even sure if she would ever be privy to that information, and the less she knew, the better it was. If my pretending to be a distant bitch meant she gets to live in ignorance, free of the chains they put on me, so be it.

"What do you mean?" My voice pitched, trying to sound cheerful, trying to show her that everything was okay. The scowl on her face told me I was failing.

Majorly.

"Don't act coy with me, Ophelia. I know something is wrong. You've been avoiding me lately. You're not going out, you don't speak to me, you've become withdrawn... what the fuck is going on?"

Her tone increased with every word spoken, and I felt like the shittiest person ever to walk on this Earth.

"Is it," she lowered her voice, "Kieran?"

I flinched at the mention of his name, and her eyes widened thinking she got it.

"It is, isn't it?"

"No—"

"You don't have to see him tonight. We can go and do something else."

But I actually wanted to see him. I wanted to talk to him about the things that were haunting me day and night. I needed to hear how he functioned with all of this; how did he cope with this shitshow? I had to talk to somebody, otherwise I would go mad.

The fact that I was in love with him, or whatever this ridiculous feeling was, didn't even pass my mind. I just had to know I would be normal again. Well, as normal as I could be.

There was nothing normal in being a seventeen-year-old in training to become a killing machine. Father was happy with my progress, and my cold demeanor and indifference I showed with every guy he brought to me.

Truth was, I was screaming inwardly, begging to be released, hoping this was all a nightmare I would wake up from. This darkness clawing at my chest, begging to be released was a heavy burden. Maybe I was always a monster—a dormant one, but a monster, nonetheless.

"No, no, I want to welcome them home. I haven't seen any of your brothers for almost a year and I miss their stupid faces."

"Are you sure? They would—"

"Yep." I smiled at her. I could only imagine how deranged I actually looked—like a walking bipolar disorder. One minute I was lost in my thoughts, imagining somebody's death, the next I was smiling like a lunatic.

How do people do this?

How do they shut down all their emotions and manage to kill without remorse? How is it possible that I never saw any difference in the way Kieran and Cillian were behaving, or my brother for that matter?

Theo didn't pass the initiation, but he was still part of the organization. Why the fuck would our parents put us up for this shit? I hoped, and hoped, and hoped my father would change his mind. Maybe I wasn't good enough, maybe I wasn't strong enough.

But with each passing day, with every glance at him, I knew he wasn't going to let me go. God fucking dammit, I just needed somebody to talk to. Someone who would understand what I was going through.

I really hoped Kieran would have answers to some of my questions.

Like, why the fuck he never told me what our families were involved in? Not that we were best friends or anything, but they all knew, and not one of them said anything to me. I was pissed at my parents, I was pissed at myself, and I was pissed at all of them for keeping this from me. My chest hurt. My mind felt like a distorted picture, and I didn't know who I was anymore. Two months ago, I was a daughter, a friend, a sister, but now... Now I was what the darkest nightmares were made of.

"Are you even listening to me?" Ava's voice pulled me from the fog enveloping my mind, an impatient expression visible on her face. "Or are you just ignoring me? Again?"

I shouldn't have come here today. My mind was already a mess, my attention span even worse, and she didn't deserve it. "I'm sorry. I guess I got distracted."

"You know what," she stood up abruptly, knocking the milkshake cup in the process, "screw this. You don't want to tell me what's wrong? That's fine. But I think I at least deserve you to be fucking present here—"

"I am present."

"No, you're not. Your body's here, but your mind is somewhere else. You know where to find me once you decide I am worthy of your time and attention."

"Ava!" She started walking away, and I pulled myself up, catching up with her. "What the fuck, dude?"

"You're asking me what the fuck? Are you for real right now?" She turned to me, her angry eyes slicing through me. "First," she lifted her finger, "you ghost me for two weeks. No texts, no calls, it was like you disappeared. Second," another finger added, "your whole behavior is very much doom and gloom, which I would understand if I fucking knew what was wrong. And third, you're completely distracted, when I could really use a friend right now."

"Ava—"

"No, I'm done. Find me when you start being you again."

I had nothing to say to her because I knew she was right. I was distracted, I was somewhere else. But as I said, if being a bitch meant she gets to stay safe and ignorant of all this bullshit, then so be it.

"So, that's it? You're just gonna stand there and say nothing?"

My eyes were burning from the tears wanting to spill over my cheeks, but this was one sacrifice I would gladly make.

"You're unbelievable."

I could see the slight quiver in her chin, but just like me, she swallowed her emotions, and with one last look at me, she left the field. We attracted quite the attention from the teenagers milling around, enjoying the summer day. I wished I was one of them—gushing after boys, deciding what to wear, even gossiping about other people, but I wasn't.

I was me.

And tonight, I had to survive dinner at Nightingale Hill without killing one of the people I shared blood with.

∼

"Ekaterina!"

Sitting in front of the mirror and applying makeup, I almost stabbed myself in the eye with the brush, flinching at the sound of my father's voice. I wasn't Ophelia to him anymore; I was Ekaterina because, "*I had to embrace my true Russian heritage*". I was already stabbing people left and right, what more could he want from me? Should I start chugging vodka morning, afternoon and evening to completely accept my heritage?

Oh, I know. I should probably follow in my mother's footsteps. A little bit of lithium, a couple of shots, and I would be good to go. Even she stopped calling me Ophelia, using Ekaterina every step of the way.

Couldn't they let me have at least a small semblance of who I used to be?

A year ago, I read *The Flowers of Evil* by Charles Baudelaire, and I was so captivated by it that I kept rereading it over and over again. The way he described his beloved city, the decadence of what was once beautiful, but was now like rotting flesh, destroyed from the inside out, it reminded me of me, of my family, of this world I thought I knew. I thought was beautiful, but was nothing but rotten.

The place I once called home was unrecognizable to me. Even the people I loved were practically strangers. My dreams and hopes disappeared with one single act that night. With the blade of my knife slicing through that man's throat, it sliced through everything that was me. We all kill pieces of ourselves.

One piece at the time.

One dream per day.

One hope per second.

All of them shattered, lying on the pile of what we once used to be.

"Ekaterina!" His voice sounded angry now, and I didn't want him to come in here.

"*Da*, Papa?" Was that a quiver I heard in my voice? Of course, it was. Even a monster had another monster it feared, and I feared him.

"We have to go. The boys have already arrived."

Boys.

Kieran and Cillian.

He refused to call them by their names. For him, they were just that, boys. I guess I should've felt happy because he called me by my name, even if it wasn't the one I wanted him to use.

But happiness wasn't what I felt every time he called for me.

It only meant that he owned me, body and soul. After the tenth person he brought to me, I stopped counting the number of people I killed in his name. I stopped counting the number of people on which I imagined my father's face instead of theirs.

"I'm coming, Papa."

I dreaded seeing anybody tonight, but I needed answers. I pulled a small dagger Father gave me and put it inside the small black bag I decided to take with me tonight. I tried to cover the dark circles around my eyes, but it was futile trying to cover the despair I was feeling. You could see it in my eyes. You could hear it in my voice.

My chestnut brown hair cascaded below my shoulders in waves, and with the tight black dress enveloping my body and boots of the same color, I would fit in better at a funeral, than at a family dinner.

Though, knowing what I knew now, our family dinners might just turn into one.

I walked down the staircase leading to the foyer and saw my mother sitting with her legs crossed on one of the sofa chairs, a faraway look on her face. I didn't know how I never noticed it, or maybe I just wasn't paying attention, but my beloved mother was an addict. All those times when I thought she was in a bad mood, she was just coming down from her latest high. Even now I could see she was on something.

It didn't matter if it was drugs or alcohol, or maybe even both, she was too far gone for me to help her. Besides, how could I help somebody who didn't want my help. How could I stop her from destroying herself when my father was the one supplying her with everything? I guess it made her more compliant, quiet and invisible.

I honestly couldn't even blame her.

We all had our ways of coping with reality, and if this was hers, who was I to stop her. After all, this whole circus we called life, was enough to drive me to the brink of insanity. How did she feel being in all of this for most of her life?

I just couldn't understand one thing. My father loved her. My God, that was the only thing that man was truly honest about. I could see the way he looked at her, the way he listened to her even when what she was spewing was complete and utter nonsense.

Then why did he keep feeding her that shit?

"You look lovely." The Devil in disguise walked in just as I reached the ground. His eyes scanned over me, and with a satisfied nod, he finally smiled at me. "Just like *chernaya vdova*."

A fucking black widow.

I shuddered from the attention directed to me and turned around just as he bent down to kiss my mother. She giggled at something he said, and for a moment, I could imagine us as a perfectly normal family.

Parents with their daughter, going to dinner at their friend's house. I would talk about school and my plans for college with my mom. My dad would be interested in my extracurricular activities, and I would have a close relationship with my siblings.

But none of that would ever be true.

"Thank you, Papa."

Thank you for the shadows in my eyes.

My mother kept gazing at my father as if he put the stars in the sky, as if I wasn't standing in front of her. Why did I still hold hope that one day she would wake up from the world she drugged herself into and see what was happening around her? Maybe because she was my mom. She was supposed to protect me from this, because if she wouldn't, who would?

I should've been feeling warm, it was summer after all, but the mere thought of tonight's dinner kept sending shivers along my skin. I talked the talk, but I wasn't so sure I would be able to walk the walk and ask Kieran everything I needed to know.

Fuck it.

I just tortured a grown-ass man yesterday, and now I was afraid of a conversation between me and somebody I've known for most of my life. *Grow a backbone, Ophelia.*

"Papa, Mama," I started, stopping them from mauling each other in front of me. "It's already eight o'clock. Shall we?"

Did I deliberately stop their little ménage a deux? Of course, I did. I didn't want to see my parents going at it right in front of my eyes. When my father looked at me, that fear I felt lately whenever he was around started crawling up my spine, seeping into my bones, and I expected him to reprimand me.

Another hit meant nothing to him. Another degradation was but a 'good morning' for him.

I straightened my shoulders, but when his hand connected with my cheek, pain never followed. In its place was a feathery touch to my face and a look in his eyes I couldn't decipher.

He almost looked proud.

With a smile I rarely saw, he walked toward the door, opening it for both of us. Maybe tonight wouldn't be so bad. Maybe I would be able to forget who we were and just enjoy dinner.

But my father has played this game for far longer than I have, and just before we exited the house, he gripped my arm, stopping me in my tracks. The smile was gone, replaced by the sinister look I was familiar with.

There he was. The dragon. The devil. My nightmare.

Faster than it started, all the hope I had diminished with his words.

"There will be some," he cleared his throat, "revelations tonight. I need you to work with me and not ask too many questions. Can you do that?"

Two oceans were clashing in the staring match between the two of us. I hated his surprises. He was planning something, and whenever the wheels in his head were turning, I ended up with yet another person to kill and a body to bury. It wasn't like I could say no, or run away. The things he showed me were enough to strike fear into my heart, and to understand that no matter what, the Syndicate would always find me.

I nodded like an obedient little child, and the pleased look on his face told me I was out of trouble. For now, at least.

"Good." Placing his arm around my shoulder, he started walking to the car where my mother already sat inside. "You're good."

Good? What the fuck was that supposed to mean? I kept glancing at his satisfied face. He looked like a cat that ate the canary. What was he up to?

I sat next to Mom, trying to ignore the twitch in her right hand, and the looks she kept throwing at my father. I knew those looks—she was due for her next fix. Nope, not my problem anymore. If she could give me to the wolves like this, I wouldn't care about her disease.

Absolutely not my problem.

The Nightingale house was only ten minutes away from ours, but it felt like an eternity, being trapped with the two of them inside the car. Nobody spoke. Hell, I almost held my breath trying to be as quiet as possible. Ava was pissed at me, my father had something planned, my mother was high as a kite, and I had another assignment tomorrow.

We pulled in front of the large, mahogany doors where like an entourage, the Nightingale family stood, including the twin brothers. Tristan was nowhere to be found. Was he not joining us tonight?

My breath hitched as my eyes raked over Kieran's body, my heart racing inside my chest. Both of the twins started walking toward the car with Ava trailing after them. My door opened in the next second, and I found myself in an embrace so tight, my air supply started cutting short.

"Kieran," I wheezed. "I can't breathe."

"Little bird." He squeezed me tighter, almost lifting me off the ground. His lips connected with my temple, and I felt that kiss all the way to my toes. "Look at you." He took a step back, holding my hands in his. The smile on his face hurt my heart because in the next second his eyes connected with mine, and whatever he saw there banished the happiness he was enveloped in. He kept glancing between my father and me, a scowl marring his face.

"You know," he started, lowering his voice. "Don't you?"

Swallowing a needle in my throat, I carefully nodded, inching closer. "We need to talk."

I noticed Ava standing behind him, a puzzled look on her face. She was still pissed off, and she had every right to be, but dealing with her emotions would have to wait—at least for now.

"After dinner, little bird?" Kieran asked.

"Yeah, sure."

I didn't miss the worried look he sent my way, or how he tightened his hold on my shoulders. Ophelia from one year ago would revel in his attention, even if it was for all the wrong reasons. Today, his attention was the last thing I needed.

I just needed to know how to move forward.

"Let's go inside, yeah? They should be serving dinner soon, and the sooner we get that over with, the sooner we can talk."

3

KIERAN

"Son, why don't you take a seat next to Ophelia?" Nikolai Aster said to me as soon as we entered the dining room, while my father took a seat at the head of the table, a smug smile on his face. I wanted to punch both of them and get the hell out of here.

They were the monsters parents warned their kids about. The greatest nightmare any of us could have, and I had to call them family when I wanted nothing more than to see them suffer for everything they did. I couldn't even imagine what Ophelia was going through living with Nikolai and her deranged mother. That look on her face earlier told me everything I needed to know.

She was in.

I always knew she would end up being part of this darkness, this madness consuming us all, but I never expected it to happen so soon. Just last year she was saying goodbye to Cillian and me, sending us back to college, excited about what the future would bring her. Some things were inevitable, but I thought she had time—the time to be a normal teenager, to be free of all of this, because once you were in, you weren't just committing yourself to the job.

No, you were selling your soul to the Devil.

And in our case, Nikolai Aster and Logan Nightingale were Abaddon and Beelzebub reigning on Earth. My father was a cruel man, but Nikolai… that man put everybody else to shame. The depravity swirling in the pit of his soul, if he even had one, and the chilling detachment he acted with—he was everything I never wanted to be.

And now, Ophelia… She was just a kid. An innocent girl. What sick fuck could make his seventeen-year-old daughter kill a man? The one standing next to me, obviously. If she passed the initiation, he was already training her, shaping her to become like him, to become like all of his soldiers—a psychopath, an assassin, a cold and emotionless human being.

She kept her eyes trained on the table in front of her, the only thing moving was her chest with every breath she took. It was never easy killing another, taking their life into your hands and destroying their soul. With each stab, each gunshot, each wound you inflicted, you weren't just killing the person in front of you. You were destroying yourself, piece by piece, until the only thing left inside of you was the hollow space where your soul used to be. They never wanted us to just kill. They wanted us to enjoy it, to strive for it.

People said killers were born that way, but I refused to believe that. I think they were made by the circumstances of their lives, by people that made them who they are. Psychopaths on another hand, the ones like my father and Nikolai, they were born deranged.

I tried catching her eyes, but it was no use. Ophelia seemed completely detached from the world around her. I looked at her father, plastered the brightest smile I could muster, and walked to the other side of the table where she sat. She was here, but she also wasn't. Her mind was somewhere else, somewhere far away from this place, and as she played with the napkin in front of her, ignoring the rest of us, I got a sudden urge to take her away from here. Something inside of me wanted to protect her, to remove her from this whole situation. Ava hadn't said a word to her since they got here, just threw a few cautionary glances her way.

"So, how are your studies going, Cillian?" My attention snapped from Ophelia to Cillian, another mess at this table. I pulled the chair out and dropped down, carefully watching my twin brother and his reaction. Nikolai Aster had a smirk on his face, and the knife in front of me looked like the perfect weapon to erase it, or maybe to carve it further up. Cillian hated going to the university. He fucking despised it, and I had a feeling that the only reason he was still there and tried to appear as a normal member of society, was because I was there.

He was like a bomb, waiting to explode. One wrong step could send us all up in flames, and this whole break from the university could be that step. I knew he stopped taking his meds. I also knew he stopped going to his therapist, but I didn't have enough fucking time to deal with all the clusterfucks surrounding me at the moment. I needed Theo to get his ass home, so that we could think about what to do next. If Ophelia was initiated, that meant Ava was next, and I didn't like it.

Not one bit.

"Oh, it's peachy, Mr. Aster. My favorite part about this whole experience are the college girls. Especially Freshman. They're just..." Cillian picked up the glass of wine in front of him, and took a sip before continuing, "Juicy. So ripe, full of fire, eager to please…"

"Cillian!" my mother exclaimed from the other side of the table, her eyes narrowed at him. "Language. We are about to have dinner for Heaven's sake."

"I'm sorry, Mom." He lowered his head, feigning innocence but his grip on the edge of the table never loosened. During moments like these, I wished twins could read each other's minds. Not that I was necessarily keen on being inside of his head—God knows what kind of a mess resided there—but it would have been extremely helpful to stop him from making stupid and rash decisions. Though, I didn't need to be a mind reader to know that my brother wanted nothing more than to jab the fork he started turning in his hand, in Nikolai's neck.

A laughter coming from my right side made me turn my head. Ophelia was staring at the empty wine glass in front of her, chuckling at whatever she found funny. What I saw in her eyes earlier bothered me.

Emptiness.

Coldness.

Darkness.

If what was happening to her happened to Ava, I would've wanted her to have somebody.

But you don't think of her as a little sister, do you, Kieran?

That annoying voice in my head started. My fucking subconscious toyed with me, just like it has been doing since the last time I saw her. I wasn't feeling this way out of sheer courtesy or because she was my sister's friend. I tried to deny it, I tried to fight it, separate myself from it, but there was something about Ophelia that started calling to me. Like a siren's song to a sailor, she had been haunting me for a year now.

"That's alright, Leanora." Nikolai's voice tore through my thoughts and I looked up only to see him smiling at my mother. A snake's charm, that's what this man had. "Boy is only joking. Isn't that right, Cillian?"

One day, one fucking day, I would burn this man down, destroy him inside out, peel his skin, piece by piece. He did this every time—fucked with Cillian's head, criticized everything I did, sneered at Ava, and my father did nothing. Just like a pussy of a man, he just sat there, nodding, while the other asshole insulted his family. Some people killed serpents; we were feeding them. For a moment, I could see myself holding Cillian down, or even attacking Nikolai myself, then a loud crash echoed through the room, halting me momentarily. All eyes turned to Ava, who started getting off of her chair, and crouched next to the table.

"I'm so sorry." She stopped whatever she was doing as all other noise in the room ceased to exist. "My glass just fell off. Too much caffeine today."

She tried to downplay it, but I knew better. Her eyes connected with mine, and I knew that this wasn't an accidental slip. She could feel the tension, and reading Cillian was always much easier for her, than for me. Ironic really, considering that we shared a womb for nine months. Ava didn't need a verbal confirmation that something was going on. Something she didn't know about, and I didn't want her to know. I didn't want her to be involved in any of this, because hers was one of the souls I wanted to see off to Heaven rather than Hell.

"Are you okay, honey?" Mom asked her. A hand gripped my knee, sharp pain traveling through my body, awakening all of my nerve endings. I tried prying Ophelia's hand from the spot, but her grip got stronger, her nails biting into the meniscus. A thousand sharp jolts spread from the spot.

"It's fine, Mom. I'm not hurt." I could hear Ava's voice, but I focused on the girl next to me, trying to wrestle her off of me.

"What the fuck, Phee?" Her ocean blues clashed with mine, sparkling with amusement. She knew what she was doing, and even when I pulled her hand away and squeezed harder, the smile didn't disappear from her face. If anything, it only increased as if she enjoyed the pain. As if it was some kind of game she was playing with me. Who the fuck was this girl sitting next to me? She seemed so quiet, so timid on the outside. What happened in the span of a couple of minutes?

"Ophelia?" I asked her again, and from the corner of my eye, I could see my father observing us, that familiar calculating look on his face.

"Do you like pain, Kieran?"

Did I like pain? What kind of a question was that? Our little wrestling match didn't go unnoticed by the rest of our families, and as soon as she sat back on her chair, Ava narrowed her eyes on us. Yeah, I got it. She wasn't the only one confused by Ophelia's behavior.

"No, I don't like pain."

"You should." She moved back, ridding me of the sweet vanilla scent she always had, and lifted the knife from the table. "Because pain is all we will ever know. It can set you free."

Fuck, fuck, fuck... There it was, the darkness rising. "Why would I need it to set me free?"

I looked around the table, but everyone seemed to be too distracted with their own conversations. Well, everyone except for Ava who still kept sending daggers Ophelia's way. That was another mess I would have to deal after this forsaken dinner was finished.

I inched my chair closer to Ophelia's, hoping no one would be able to hear us that way. She ignored me, seemingly lost in thoughts.

"Phee," I whispered, hoping to bring her back from wherever she went.

"Is this what madness feels like?" she suddenly asked, looking straight at me, the smile she wore just a second ago diminished. It was like watching a manic episode in person, only this one was going from the highest high, to the lowest low in a span of seconds.

"What do you mean?" I prayed to everything possible in

this universe that she wasn't on drugs. I checked her pupils, but they were the normal size. Dealing with Cillian's addiction, knowing her mother, I wasn't really sure what to think about her erratic behavior. This world we were thrown into, this strange, dark world, didn't allow you to be weak. You were either a hunter, or you were the one being hunted. There was no in between, no blurred lines and gray areas.

Hide your emotions, they warned us.

Show them your teeth, they told us.

What did they do to her? Why was she asking me all of this? This world didn't allow friends, didn't allow love—only lust and hatred.

"There is… something inside of me. It's crawling, trying to get out. It's dark. So, so, dark..." She shuddered as if the mere thought scared her. "I am just like him, am I not? Just like my father. A monster, a murderer. I can't. I can't…"

Her breathing got frantic, her eyes unfocused. I gripped her hand, pulling it into my lap.

"Phee," I started soothingly. "Look at me."

She started pulling her hand from mine, but I just gripped her tighter, placing my other hand around her shoulders.

"Phee, look at me. Please."

She finally focused on me. Her body relaxed but the sight of tears in her eyes gripped at my chest. I hated it, hated seeing her like this.

"You're not a monster, okay?" I stroked her knuckles with my thumb. "If you are, then so am I. Do you think I'm a monster?"

She started shaking her head. "No."

"Then you aren't one either."

My heart was jackhammering inside of my chest at the mere thought that this girl, this beautiful, strong girl, was looking for reassurance from me. Maybe, just maybe, the demons we both had could dance together, thrive together, instead of destroying us. Even if I was probably just the first person she saw she could talk to, it didn't matter. My chest hurt for her, my instincts urging me to protect her. She thought there was something inside of her, something dark, sinister, but it was in all of us. All of us learned how to tame our darkness, how to control our demons, and I was going to teach her. I was going to show her that not all of those demons would eat us from the inside out.

I never did drugs, I didn't know the feeling of a high when it came, but her presence alone was the best opium I could ever have. The best kind of high I could ever experience, and goddammit, I wasn't going to allow anyone to take it away.

"Kieran."

At the mention of my name, I extracted myself from her, turning toward Cillian.

"Is everything okay?"

He kept glancing at Ophelia, then back at me, but we didn't have time to discuss all of this now. We had to survive this whole dinner without any casualties first. I nodded, and before he could ask another question, the devil himself spoke again.

"I am so happy to see you getting along so well with Ekaterina, Kieran." She stiffened next to me, but didn't look at him. Was it my turn to get aggravated now? "Isn't it perfect, Logan?"

Nikolai chuckled with my father. "It sure is Niko."

I was getting confused with the whole dynamics of this dinner. They usually were fucked up, but this one... this one took the number one spot on the list. My father hated Nikolai with everything he had, but he wasn't strong enough on his own. The Asters always craved more. They wanted the world to be at their feet—not just to own it, but to burn it down. Logan

Nightingale might represent himself as a strong man, but everyone could recognize a follower when they saw one.

And that's what my father was—a blind follower.

"This just makes everything so much easier."

What makes everything easier? Me being nice to Ophelia?

"Logan and I wanted to wait a little bit with this news, but seeing as almost everyone is here, why wait?"

I looked at our mother, but she kept staring at our father, a confused look on her face. Did she not know either?

"Kieran," my father started, "you will soon be twenty-one, am I correct?"

"Yes." But where the fuck was he going with this?

"And Ophelia, you are going to be eighteen soon?"

"In November," she replied quietly. My mind was trying to figure out what they were planning, but nothing, none of my theories could prepare me for what Nikolai announced next.

"Well," he stood up from his chair, taking the glass filled with wine in his left hand, "seeing as we are basically a family, Logan and I have decided to truly strengthen those bonds."

Ava paled at his words, and I found myself fidgeting in my seat. Did she know something? She told me she had to talk to me, had to share something with me, but we didn't have time. Was this it?

"My son isn't here yet. He is late as per usual." The disgust in Nikolai's voice was hard to miss. "Nevertheless," he continued, "he will find out later. Ava," he looked at my sister and unease started rolling in my gut, "you're almost like a third daughter to me, and I cannot wait to officially welcome you to the family."

What the fuck was he talking about?

"What's this all about?" Cillian asked, his knee bouncing again, no doubt as confused as I was with all of Nikolai's babbling.

37

"This, my boy, is me officially announcing that Ava will be marrying Theo in a couple of months—"

"You can't fucking do that." Cillian jumped from his chair, knocking it to the floor in the process. I was in shock, but I kicked my ass into action when Cillian started rounding the table. I stepped in front of him before he could reach Nikolai, the sound of sobs slicing through the air.

Ava.

"Go back to your seat, Cillian." Our father stood next to me, taking a hold of Cillian's arm, but he wasn't having it.

"Are you fucking serious, Dad?" His eyes were unfocused, the madness taking place. This whole dinner was going to turn into a bloodbath, and we didn't even get to the appetizers. "You're just gonna sell her to him. Just like that."

"Kill—"

"No, no, no," he repeated, "I won't allow it."

"It's not up to you, Son."

"The hell it's not. That's my sister, you sick fuck," he screamed at our father.

"I wasn't finished, Cillian." Nikolai spoke again. I tried turning around, but holding Cillian in one spot, didn't allow for any additional activities.

"Kieran and Ophelia will be getting married on the same day as Ava and Theo."

I'm sorry, what? I turned around this time, just in time to see the knife flying toward Nikolai, missing his shoulder by an inch. Ophelia stood, her full focus on him, her hair disheveled around her shoulders. Nikolai chuckled, taking the knife from where it fell, and placed it on the table.

"You missed, *dorogoy.*"

"What the fuck?" She slammed her hands on top of the table, sending a couple of glasses to the ground. Ava gaped at her as if she was seeing her for the first time. Goddamn, she looked hot when she got angry.

"I told you—"

"You didn't tell me shit."

"Ekaterina—"

"Ah," she groaned. "Stop calling me that. I am not marrying Kieran." Did my heart just stutter at her refusal. "And Ava isn't marrying Theo. We aren't living in the old country anymore, for you to have arranged marriages ready for us."

"Ophelia." He spoke with a warning clear in his voice. The vein on his forehead became visible, and I didn't know if I should hug her for standing up to him and waking up from whatever stupor she was in, or take her upstairs and spank her for the same reason. I've seen what this man could do, and he didn't give a shit if he shared blood with you. "I suggest you lower your voice and sit down."

The calmness with which he spoke sent shivers over my skin, and I rushed toward her, pulling her away from the table.

"Are you crazy, birdy?"

"Oh, you've no idea." She tore away from my grip, again taking the same spot. "I am mad, so fucking mad. I would love to pull his eyeballs out of their sockets and feed them to the dogs."

Okay then, it just got worse.

"*Dorogoy*, we will discuss this at home."

"*Ya khochu obsudit' eto seychas.*" Was that Russian? Since when did she speak Russian?

"*Dorogaya, prekrati eto.*"

Before I could stop her, a glass went flying over the table, crashing on the wall behind Nikolai and her mother. Ava sat frozen, still gawking at her best friend. I wasn't sure if she completely lost her mind, or if this was the delayed reaction to everything that was going on around her.

"You think I'll miss? Ah, Papa, you trained me." Aaaand, there was another knife in her hand. Just brilliant. "I never miss."

I would forever remember this night as the beginning of the true fuckery our lives ended up being. A fitting setting if I might say. A couple of glasses broken, some knives thrown, and all of a sudden, Theo Aster strolled in, as if we weren't in the middle of an almost fight between Ophelia and Nikolai.

"Holy shit. What is going on here?"

"Didn't you hear, brother?" She looked away from Nikolai to Theo. "You just got engaged."

4

OPHELIA

Six Years Ago

One...
   Two...
      Three...
Four...

I counted every whip on my back. My teeth rattled in my head, knocking against each other, as I tried to keep all of my whimpers within my chest. I couldn't hear anything but the blood rushing in my ears. I couldn't feel anything but my skin opening.

Raw.

Broken.

You're a broken little girl.

"Count, *grebanaya suka*!" my executioner yelled when the whip connected with my back one more time. *Motherfucking bitch.* "Count!"

"Fifteen," I yelled out. "*I, yedinstvennaya suka zdes' eto ty,* Sergei."

"What did you just say?" He yanked my head back, pulling my hair.

"I said," I tried to focus on his face, "the only bitch here is you, Sergei."

My head went flying as he landed a punch to the side of my face. There was a ringing sound in my ears, and it took me a moment to refocus on the dark wall in front of me. My knees were bleeding from the concrete floor I was thrown to, and I knew it was only a matter of time before I lost consciousness.

The human body could only take so much.

"I'm going to—"

"Sergei!"

The new voice echoed around the room, sending shivers all over my skin. I could feel blood trickling over my naked back, the cold air of the room hitting me in unpleasant ways. My stomach churned, but even if I wanted to puke, there would be nothing in there to throw up. An acidic taste filled my mouth, and I wondered if this was the way I would finally go.

Finally leave this sick world I never wanted to be a part of.

This Devil's playground—a fucking misery I had to wake up to every single day, never knowing what the next thing would be they threw at me. The hushed voices of Sergei and my father barely reached my ears, but I was already too far gone to pay attention to anything they said.

Insubordinate, they said.

Reckless.

Wild.

My father thought sending me to Siberia would fix the problem. That this barren place would finally break me, leaving a clean slate for him to build on. Daddy dearest didn't know that there was nothing left to build on. In the year since I became a part of this fuckery, I killed, maimed and attacked.

After the first fifty of them, the faces became distorted and their screams haunted me.

When I closed my eyes, I could see theirs, pleading with me.

When I sat at the table, instead of my mother's voice, I always heard the other women. They begged me, and then they were cursing me—cursing the ground I walked on, wishing the worst on me and my family. Poor things didn't know that I didn't have family, not really. So when I started screaming back at them, when I started killing people who shouldn't be killed, I was sent to the end of the world.

Where winter never ended, and the torture was served for breakfast, lunch and dinner.

"*Dorogoy.*" My father kneeled behind me, his presence almost soothing. He was the only connection to Croyford Bay. "You're so strong, aren't you?"

Was that awe I could hear in his voice? Was he finally proud of me?

I hated the man, but some fucked-up part of me always wanted to please him. Always wanted him to see what I could do. I wanted to make him proud as much as I wanted to defy him. I hated myself for being this way. For being this weak in the presence of a man who wanted nothing more than to break me. His touch on my neck felt both like hellfire and holy water in one.

Before I could answer him, blinding pain went through my body as he dragged his finger through the wound on my back, pushing harder, scratching at the raw skin. I felt the wound open wider with his strokes.

"Papa!" I cried out, my voice echoing in the room, but he didn't stop.

Have you ever watched a butcher slice a piece of meat?

That slicing sound at the skin removal, the smell of blood in the air. The sick satisfying look the butcher had on his face.

Well, my father was my butcher.

His breathing, my screams, the ripping and slicing, those were the only sounds you could hear. Do you know how it feels when your body is trying to heal itself, to close the wound, but something is stopping it?

"Can you feel that, *moy malen'kiy drakon*?"

He still thought I was his little dragon? Papa loved me, he still loved me.

"Can you feel your skin trying to close down? I can almost see it beneath my fingers."

"Papa, please!"

"No, goddammit." He pressed into the other wound, my whole body coiling from the pain. "I asked you a question. Can you feel it?"

More pressure, more pain, I couldn't take it anymore.

"Papa," I yelled. "I can't. I can't."

"Answer me!" he roared out, punishing me with his hands. "You better answer me, Ekaterina, or you are not coming out of here alive."

He would kill me. I knew he would. Papa always kept his word.

But he loved me, he really did. I was his favorite, his little dragon, his heir. But I had to be stronger than this. I had to be stronger than my mind.

"Yes, I can feel it," I finally answered. My mouth was dry. The lack of water for the last three days was insufferable. My lips were parched, breaking apart. I could taste blood from them, but I didn't know if I was the one who broke through the soft tissue or did it happen when one of the guards hit me in the face.

"Your body will always want to heal itself, but you have to

let it. Can you let it heal?" my father started again. "Can you accept who you really are?"

Could I accept myself? Could I accept the monstrosities I committed? Could I run away from the voices in my head, from all the faces haunting me in my sleep?

"You need to let it go, *dorogoy*. You need to fucking let it go."

"But they are here," I cried out. "They are everywhere, Papa. They're calling me, haunting me, screaming my name—"

"Then let them scream. Let them shout, and beg, but they are not here." He turned me around, finally releasing my back. "You are."

He cupped my cheeks, the blood on his hands smearing over my skin. I couldn't focus on his face. I couldn't focus on anything but pain.

Pain in my body would have been bearable, but the pain in my head was tearing me apart. I didn't want to accept what he was saying. I didn't want to see the truth that's been there all along.

I was my own destruction, and I was my own pain. I was the bearer of everything bad, and I had to let it go. I had to let this misery go, this sorrow in me. The guilt over everything I've done was going to eat me alive, and if I couldn't learn how to control it, I might as well be dead.

"Ekaterina." His voice was distant, as if I was underneath the water—floating, drowning.

Our wounds would never close if we continued poking them, if we continued slicing the same spot, over and over again. The human mind was a fragile thing, but it was also stronger than most of us thought. Was I going to be a little bitch and cry over the lives I'd taken, or was I going to put my big girl pants on and be what I was supposed to be?

An assassin.

I was their biggest nightmare, and the sweetest dream, and if I couldn't carry the burden of our family, of this life, somebody else would.

Did I really want to be remembered as the girl who couldn't handle the pressure? Who couldn't control her demons?

My demons were my own, and if I allowed those bitches to take over my life, I would never live life fully. I could never be free if I couldn't accept who I really was.

A murderer.

A monster.

Maybe a psychopath.

But that was me. That was what this life made me, and I could let it control me. I really could. Let it take over me, let my fear and my doubts be the two things leading me through life. Except, I wasn't born for that.

I was born to be this. This darkness I feared so much. I wanted to run away from it, but the truth was, I was running away from who I really was. Some people were destined to become doctors, lawyers and politicians. I was destined to become an assassin.

The best one the Syndicate ever had.

What was I thinking, allowing my feelings to get involved? Wasn't that the first thing Papa tried to teach me? *No remorse, no pain, death comes to all of us anyway.*

And who gave a fuck if you died today or in fifty years?

If you got involved with the Syndicate, you knew what you were signing up for. There was no mercy, no salvation for those who wronged us. And if I had to be the one who would bring justice, I would be the last thing you saw before your soul became eternally damned.

All of us would burn in Hell, we just had to choose which kind of Hell we wanted to have while on Earth.

"Ekaterina?"

I snapped my eyes open, suddenly annoyed with the name he continued using with me. All this time I've tried splitting myself into two different people.

Ophelia, the girl my friends knew. The one who could walk with her head held high.

Ekaterina, a murderer my father created.

I had to come to this point to realize that there was no use in me splitting those two. Lying to myself and trying to be somebody else would never have worked. I was who I was.

I was both good and bad.

I was both lover and murderer.

Ophelia and Ekaterina were the same person and it was about time I started acting like that. It was about time I stopped acting like a child.

"My name isn't Ekaterina, Papa." I leaned toward him, looking into those blue eyes—the color almost the same as mine. "My name isn't *only* Ekaterina."

"No?" He smiled at me. "Then what is it?"

"My name is Ophelia Ekaterina Aster."

"And are you ready now, Ophelia?"

For the first time in my life, he called me Ophelia. Not Ekaterina, not darling, not a little dragon, but by my name. A name given to me by his father, which he never wanted to acknowledge. Was I ready? I almost didn't want to answer, but if I were to start being who I wanted to be, I had to suppress my fear.

If I were to take him down one day, I had to stand tall and face everything he was throwing my way.

"For what, Papa?"

"To be who you were always meant to be."

I lifted my head, the last atoms of strength slipping from my grip, but I wouldn't fail now. I wouldn't bow my head to him. Not now, not ever again.

"And who is that?" I asked. "Who am I meant to be?"

He touched the crown of my head, a faraway look in his eyes. If I didn't know better, I would dare to say that he looked wistful. Almost human.

"A true leader, *dorogoy*." He removed the strands of hair falling on my face. "A leader of Syndicate."

His form was blurring in front of my eyes. My head felt heavy, the wounds on my back throbbing, and I just wanted to sleep. I needed to rest.

"Papa—" I started, but he cut me off before I could say what I wanted to say.

"I have a job for you."

My eyes snapped open, the aggravation rising up in me. Did this man see what I looked like right now?

"You will leave tomorrow morning to St. Petersburg and they will give you all necessary information there."

"And if I don't want to?" I retorted. What if I didn't want to do his bidding this time? What if all I wanted to do was to go home?

The sinister smile spreading across his face told me I wouldn't have much choice.

"You want to know where Maya is, don't you?" My interest piqued up, the anger rising up in my chest. He had a knowing smile on his face. How did he know I was looking for her?

I slowly nodded, concealing my emotions. He was my father, but he was also the monster that made me this way. He was the monster who sent Maya away, and the only one that knew where she was.

"If you do this," he started, "I promise to tell you where she is."

~

The apartment building in front of me was almost falling apart. It was as if this part of St. Petersburg was completely forgotten, left to rot in its misery, in its poverty. While the masses celebrated on the main streets, while the rich stole from the poor, there were people living in here, forgotten by everybody else. It probably made me a hypocrite, knowing how my family came into the money we had, but we at least never pretended to be angels God sent. We were more like demons, you know? Nightmares, really.

A young girl ran from the building, and from my spot on the sidewalk, I could clearly see how malnourished she was. Her blond hair was tied into a messy ponytail, and the clothes on her body probably did nothing to protect her from the awful winter weather. I wanted to believe that maybe one day she would be able to afford something better, but I've seen what this kind of life does to these kids. The peace she might be looking for could only be found seven feet below the ground. Never mind, the girl was of no concern to me.

I walked toward the entrance, the door already missing, making my task so much easier. The informant from the center told me Svetlana Avramova lived on the first floor, in apartment 12B. Thank God, because I wasn't keen on dragging my ass up to the higher floors, seeing as there was no elevator.

My back still ached with a dull pain from the little ordeal back in Siberia, and I just hoped that the painkillers they pumped me with would last through this whole thing. I still wasn't at my full strength, and while a single woman with her child wasn't the biggest threat, you never knew what a mother would do when her child was in danger.

The stairs creaked beneath the soles of my boots, the remnants of cigarette butts, used needles and condom wrappers all over the place. I understood why they lived here. It was easy going off the grid, because a sane person would never step foot in this building.

Scratch that—they wouldn't step a foot in this neighborhood.

The old Soviet buildings usually had only a few apartments per floor, and it didn't take me long to locate 12B, standing just at the end of the hallway. I looked around to make sure that nobody else was there with me and taking a deep breath, I prepared myself for what was to come. I ran my hand through my hair, trying to appear more disheveled, but I hoped that the dark circles around my eyes, courtesy of the time spent in Siberia, would at least give away the sight of a person with a very bad life.

Acting like a damsel in distress never really worked for me, but I had to try.

"*Pomogi mne, pozhaluysta,*" I banged on the door, faking a panic in my voice. "*Pozhaluysta! On ub'yet menya.*"

It always worked with women, telling them somebody else was after you, especially the women who already went through something similar. In those moments, they tended to forget everything about their own safety. Only the urge to help another poor woman was there, coursing through their bodies.

"*Pozhaluysta.*" I continued knocking, pushing the tears at my eyes. "*Pozhaluysta, otkroyte dver'.*"

Just as I was about to decide to knock the door down, and fuck everything else, the sounds of chains being removed traveled to my ears, and I knew I had her. But, seriously, who would open a door like this?

A woman I already saw in pictures stood there just a head shorter than me. Her dark hair framed her face, and the compassion on her face almost made me laugh. If she only knew.

"*Bednyazhka.*" She opened the door wider. "*Zakhodi.*" *Get inside.*

The interior of the apartment, if this could even be called an apartment, was almost barren. A lone couch sat on the other side, closer to the windows and a little boy stood just in front, looking at me with curious little eyes. His hair was the same color as his mother's, but his eyes definitely belonged to his father.

Ocean blue.

I scanned my surroundings, seeing a chair next to the table on my right side. Perfect.

"*Kto*," Svetlana spoke, but just as she locked the door, I turned to her and grabbed the back of her neck with my hand.

"*Privet*, Svetlana," I whispered in her ear as I pushed her onto the wall. "Do you know who I am?"

She started struggling, trying to break free, except that won't work with me. I pressed my index finger and thumb on the sides of her neck. She started whimpering and stopped immediately.

"*Ne delay nam bol'no.*" *Don't hurt us*. It always fascinated me how hopeful these people still were, even after they saw the executioner with their own two eyes.

"I know you speak English, Svetlana, so cut the crap and stop pretending." I turned her to me and slammed her head on the wall, her eyes closing with impact. "Do you know who I am?"

She opened her eyes, the blood vessels breaking from the impact with the wall.

"You're a devil." What did I just say? She does speak English.

"Oh my God." I faked the excitement. "How did you know my nickname? Are we going to be besties now?"

She sneered at me, and I smiled at the sheer bravery this woman was showing. She still didn't answer me, but living this life, being with that man, meant she knew more than she was showing. She knew who I was and why I was here.

She kept glancing toward the little boy who stood still in the same spot. If only she knew. I pushed her onto the chair and pulled out the two zip ties I stored in the pocket of my coat. I started tying her hands together, tightening the hold. I pulled the other chair and sat across from her, resting my elbows on my knees.

"For the last time, Svetlana." She looked at me again. "Do you know who I am?"

Her lower lip trembled, but the scowl on her face, and no doubt, her pride, prevented her from crying in front of me. Well, maybe I could admire her before taking her life. Most men would start crying as soon as they saw me.

"I don't know who you are," she spoke. "But I've heard of you. We all have."

Fascinating.

"Oh yeah? Tell me, I wanna know."

"You're *Baba Yaga.* Death, destruction."

Baba Yaga? Now, that was a nickname I could get behind. The other ones usually sounded too boring. Murderer, psychopath, assassin, people really weren't creative enough.

"And do you know why I'm here?" I stood up and slowly walked toward the boy. I sat on the couch and tapped the spot next to me. "*Prikhodit'.*"

"Please don't hurt him." I looked at her, panic written all over her face. *Weakness.* This little boy was her biggest weakness, and what did I do with those? I exploited them, took them and made their hearts bleed when what they wanted to protect the most was torn away from them.

"I won't," I lied. "If you answer my questions."

"You want to know about Evgeniy, right? You want to know his location."

I quirked an eyebrow at her, and the little boy climbed on the sofa, sitting right next to me. "Yes."

He had hair as dark as midnight, and a curiosity of a little dog. I pulled a knife out of my pocket and handed it to him, the blade shining under the sunlight coming through the windows. I was hoping it would rain.

It sets the whole mood up.

"Keep talking, Svetlana."

"Please don't hurt him. Please." Sobs wracked her body, but she didn't move from the chair. I knew she could if she tried, but we both also knew that this would be over much faster if she did so. "Misha is my whole world."

"Ah." I touched his head. "Misha."

He lifted his head, his attention going from me to the knife in his hands. As soon as I saw the red handle in the safehouse, I knew I had to have this knife. Maybe I could put it with the rest of my collection.

"I don't know where Evgeniy is!" she yelled at me, and I tightened my hold on the boy's head.

"Careful now, Svetlana." I laughed. "We don't want this to be over even before it starts."

"I am begging you. Please let us go."

"But I can't do that, love." I stood up, taking the boy's hand in my own, and walked closer to her. "Because I know you have the necessary information. I know he contacted you just yesterday, and judging by those suitcases," I pointed to the two suitcases stationed next to the door. "You also know where you'll be going."

"Please." Tears cascaded down her face freely. I kneeled behind Misha, looking at her over his shoulder.

"Where is Evgeniy, Svetlana?"

"I don't know!" she screamed.

I blew a raspberry on Misha's cheek, and his laughter vibrated around us.

"Are you sure about that?" I stood up and placed my hands on Misha's shoulders. He craned his head back, and looked at me with a childish smile, not a worry in the world. I caressed his cheek as Svetlana started pulling at zip ties, trying to break free.

"Where is he?"

"I don't fucking know!" Her body went limp in the chair, her eyes as well as her face, red from crying. "Just let us go."

"You see," I took the knife from Misha, and a small frown started at his face, "I think you just need an incentive to talk."

"What?" Her eyes followed my every movement. I pulled Misha closer to me. "What are you going to do? You aren't going to kill a child?"

She smiled—a forced smile—because even she knew I would do everything in order to get what I wanted.

"Maybe," I brought the knife closer to his face. "Maybe not."

"You're a psychopath!"

"I prefer creative. Now," I pulled the little boy's hair, exposing his neck to my blade, "for the last time, where is he? Where is your husband?"

Her eyes frantically jumped from me to the door, but even if she managed to run outside, she would have to leave her son behind, and that wasn't going to happen.

"Where is Evgeniy?" I yelled at her. "I promise you, if you give me his location, no harm will come to either of you. You have my word."

"He's in Volgograd!" she suddenly screamed. "He's in Volgograd and yes, he contacted me, but only to tell me to leave the city and go somewhere safe. Please, please," she sobbed.

"That's all I know. He never said his address or anything like that. I just know the city he's in."

"I believe you—"

"Please, let us go."

"I believe you, okay?" She stopped struggling for a moment, her breathing calming down.

"Thank you."

"But that doesn't help me, which means," I smirked at her, "that this was just a waste of my time."

"What—"

The Syndicate had one rule that had to be followed no matter what. One rule, that if broken, could cost us all our lives, freedom and our families.

No witnesses. It didn't matter if they were young or old, children or adults, they had to be removed. We couldn't have all these people running around trying to destroy us.

And this boy... This boy could be one of them if kept alive.

Before she could finish the sentence, I sliced the blade across the boy's throat. Blood rushed out immediately, and the gurgling sounds of him choking echoed around us. She screamed, but I could only see red coating his blue shirt. His eyes lost focus, and I grabbed his throat, squeezing the blood out. Misha's little body collapsed to the floor, his blood coloring the white carpet red.

"Misha!" I wiped the blade of the knife on the back of his shirt. I really hated it when they bled so much. Who would've thought that a toddler could have such an amount of blood? I mean, I didn't cut through his artery.

"Murderer!" She continued her screaming. "Psychopath! What have you done?" Her full body was shaking, and I understood where she was coming from. Not that I cared, but still. I noticed a tray on the kitchen table filled with what seemed to be chocolate cookies.

"Oh." I stepped around the body and walked toward them. "Are these chocolate ones?"

"I am going to kill you, you fucking bitch!"

They seemed like chocolate ones. The ones with raisins were always disgusting to me, so it was chocolate or nothing.

"Can I take one?" I asked her as she struggled to get free. "I will take one. I hope you don't mind, but I haven't had chocolate in quite some time."

"I am going to gut you like an animal. Slice your chest open and watch you bleed."

I bit into the cookie, the softness melting in my mouth. I almost moaned from the attack on my taste buds. It was really tasty.

"You killed my baby." She started crying again. "You killed the sun of my life. My sunshine, my little bear."

Should I take another one? Maybe one more, just for the road.

"How could you do this?"

I strapped the knife inside its holder, and pulled the gun already equipped with a silencer. I took another bite, and lifted the gun with my left hand, pointing it at her.

"You're a devil!"

And everybody else was a saint. Yeah, yeah, I've heard the story before.

"You will burn in Hell!"

"Lady," I swallowed, "I am already in Hell." Her head flew backwards as I released the bullet from the gun.

"Jesus fuck." I placed the gun on top of the table. "She was talking too much."

Just as I took another cookie, my phone rang, the display showing my father's number.

"Funeral services," I joked. "This is Ophelia speaking."

"Cut the crap," he barked out. "Is it done?"

I bit into the cookie and started chewing. "Yep."

"Are you eating?"

"Yep." This thing was really delicious. Shit, I needed to find out which recipe she was using.

"You're unbelievable."

"But it's really tasty, Papa. I need to find the recipe for this." I stuffed my pockets with two more cookies and remembered. "Oh, wait. Shit. He's in Volgograd. You want me to go there?"

"No, just get your ass in front of the building. Dmitri will pick you up."

"Yes, boss." I snickered. "And Papa, don't forget what you promised me."

There was silence on the other end of the line before he started again, "I won't."

"Good," I replied somberly and bit into another cookie. "These are honestly amazing."

"Cookies," I heard him murmur. "I'll see you at home."

5

KIERAN

Five Years Ago

My hands became numb approximately fifteen minutes ago, but was I retreating back into the house, and throwing away the cigarette I was holding between my fingers? Abso-fucking-lutely not.

I guess freezing your ass off was a better option than being in the same room as my family, where my mother faked happiness, my twin hid the twitching in his hands—itching for the next fix—and my sister didn't have the saddest eyes this world could've ever seen. Tristan was supposed to arrive tomorrow, and we could all then descend into the beautifully woven lie of a happy family. It didn't really matter that my eyes kept flickering to the house at the bottom of the hill. That my soul wanted to be with hers.

I needed to see her, touch her. I needed to know she was still alive.

Because she wasn't here. She hasn't been home for a very long time and nobody was fucking telling me anything. It's been almost a year since the last time I held her. A fucking year and not a single word from her. Theo told me she was on an assignment, but all of my senses screamed that he was lying. I just needed to know she was alive, that's all.

Nothing else and nothing more.

What a fucking disaster our lives have become that I would be happy if she was at least alive. Not hurt, but alive, because I knew that wherever she was, she didn't stay unscathed. The last time I saw her, she was sinking deeper, drowning in the despair, and I didn't know how to help her.

I thought... I fucking thought showing her that somebody cared about her, that somebody loved her, would pull her back. That the voices and all of the faces would quiet down if she could find a piece of her mind by clinging to me. It would, however, seem that kissing her in the middle of the road, wasn't the best idea. She thought I lied to her, that I showed her affection just because we were technically engaged now.

I mean, there was that, but the idea of her being with me forever, and me belonging to her did something to my chest. Didn't she know that my blood danced inside my veins every time she was nearby? Did I somehow read the signs wrong? The way she looked at me, the way she talked to me, she felt it.

This.

Us.

She must have felt it, otherwise she never would've kissed me back. She still ran away, but I knew that there was something there. My heart didn't beat like this for anybody else. Then why the fuck was she hiding away from me? And not only from me; even Ava hadn't heard a word from her, and that alone was putting a thousand crazy thoughts in my head.

It was her birthday three days ago, on February thirteenth, and all of my hopes went flying through the window when I realized that she wouldn't be coming home yet. If she was alive.

I fucking hoped she was alive. I needed a chance to make all of this right, to make all of us right. I needed Cillian to stop snorting coke every five minutes, and to actually be sober for a change. I had to take her away from this world, or to destroy the monsters that were destroying us. I just needed time, and I needed her to come back.

The cigarette in my hand almost burned down to the filter, and I threw it into the snow, immediately reaching for the packet in my coat pocket, taking another one out. Smoke filled my lungs, the burning sensation in my throat warming me against the bitter cold.

"Those could cause cancer, Brother." I turned around at the sound of Cillian's voice. He was leaning on the wall, his arms crossed against his chest.

"Because snorting coke is much healthier, isn't it?"

"At least I get to forget this shit for a little while." He shrugged. "Pass me one." He crossed the short distance between us and took the packet of cigarettes from my hand.

"And what happens when the reality hits again?"

"Then," he lit the cigarette up, the tip brightening up as he pulled the smoke. "I take another hit. And another, and—"

"Another," I cut him off. "And what happens when the hits aren't enough?"

"Then I'll find something else that can hit me harder, faster, because being fully present through this fuckery that is our life, truly isn't worth it."

"Kill," I warned.

"I'm fine. It's fine."

But it wasn't fine. Nothing about this fucking situation was fine. My twin brother was a drug addict who, by the way, didn't want to admit that he was one. My sister was just a kid, forced into an engagement with a person she couldn't stand. My mother was behaving as if our father saved baby turtles on a daily basis, and Tristan tried to fuck his way through North America. I didn't need a mirror to see my demons dancing around me. I could feel them without one.

"What are you doing here?" my brother asked. What was I doing here? Hiding, sulking, thinking. His dark hair fell over his eyebrow as he looked at the same spot I was focused on before. "Do you think she's okay?"

"She fucking better be."

"But what if she isn't?

"No."

"But Kieran—"

"I said, no. She is okay. She has to be okay."

My chest burned, but it must have been the cigarette, right? It was the heartburn because I didn't eat anything. It wasn't choking me because I was thinking of her lifeless body somewhere, all alone, thrown to the wolves. No, no, it wasn't that.

Cillian kept quiet, but I could feel his eyes on me. Truth to be told, I didn't know what I would do if she really was dead. The radio silence from the Asters was making me uneasy. Even Nikolai hadn't passed by in a very long time, and I wasn't sure what his arrangement with my father was anymore. Both of them held power over two very strong criminal organizations, but there was no doubt that Nikolai held the reins of a much stronger horse.

"Are we expecting anybody today?" Cillian asked, and I turned toward the pathway leading to our house. The evening fog was slowly settling onto the bay, but I could clearly see the lights of a car, driving up to our gate. I couldn't see the plates nor the type from the front porch where we stood, but with our house being the only one on the hill, they were most definitely coming here.

"Father's associates maybe," I murmured, but Father never brought his business here, unless it was Nikolai and his goons.

For all of his mistakes, he never wanted our mother to know the true span of monstrosities he was capable of.

The gate opened slowly, and neither of us moved a muscle, awaiting to see who was coming. They weren't a threat, that's for sure, otherwise the guards would have alerted us already. Was it somebody familiar? The windows of the black Audi were tinted and I couldn't see who was sitting inside, nor did I know who this car belonged to.

Cillian reached for the gun on his hip as the car slowed to a stop on the roundabout in front of our house. A heartbeat, or maybe two, and I slowly walked down the stairs, leaving my brother behind me. It looked like a bad scene in a horror movie. Birds couldn't be heard, the impending doom in the air at the arrival of an unknown person, and I halfway expected us to start getting attacked by Hitchcock's ravens to come out of nowhere and attack us here.

The engine of the car quieted down, but nobody exited. I could almost feel the nervous energy radiating off of my brother in spades, and after the fucking circus of a year we had, I completely understood why. The unknown in our world was an extremely bad thing.

Know your enemy and all of that bullshit.

I stood at the bottom of the stairs, my hands gripping the insides of my pockets. Father would've told us if we were having guests, especially with our mother's constant need for perfection.

The door lock clicked, and the one on the other side of the car slowly opened, revealing the back of a person, their head covered in what looked like a hoodie. A leather jacket hugged their body, but they couldn't be taller than five foot eight. This person looked slender, tiny… feminine.

He or she stood at the open door for a moment, as if taking in the surroundings. My pulse spiked, the familiarity creeping inside my bones, then the door closed and the person slowly turned around.

A sledgehammer to my chest would have had less of an impact than the sight in front of me.

The ocean eyes I've been looking for, I've been praying for, connected with mine, sucking the breath out of me. Her skin was paler, her face gaunt, but the smile that appeared erased all of my worries from before.

"Ophelia," I croaked. She ran around the car toward me, throwing herself into my arms. I only had a second to pull my hands out of my pockets and grab her, as she circled her legs around my waist, and clung to me like a monkey. "Phee," I whispered in her hair as the cap of her hoodie fell off. I squeezed her tight, holding her to me.

She was alive.

She was here.

My heart was going a million beats per minute as I held her, as I tried to tell myself this wasn't a dream. She was laughing, and it sounded like a fucking symphony to me. A perfect symphony to calm my racing heart.

"You're here."

If I could, I would've hidden her inside of me, next to my heart, so that she could never disappear again.

"You're really here."

"I'm here." She leaned back, her arms still around my neck. "I'm really here, K."

"But how... Why... Where—"

"I'll explain everything." She kept smiling, and I couldn't control my need to kiss her. I pulled her head to mine, our lips clashing in the process. It was as if life had finally returned to me. I hadn't felt this alive for almost a year.

The taste of her, the feeling of her body in my arms, it was the best ecstasy.

"Ahem," Cillian sounded, and I almost forgot that he even stood there. Fuck, I needed to get us to a room somewhere, alone.

"Hey, Kill." She pulled away from me and greeted him over my shoulder. "You look well."

"I would probably say the same, but I can't exactly see the rest of you since my brother decided to hide you from the world, apparently."

A full belly laugh erupted from her, and I couldn't remember the last time I heard her laugh like this. Was it that summer before we went to college?

Quite possibly, considering the shitshow that started in the year after.

"Should we go inside?" What I meant was, should we go to my room, but I couldn't exactly word it like that when I hadn't seen her for almost a year. Besides, Ava would cut my head off if I hid her best friend from her.

She started shaking her head, playing with the hair at the nape of my neck, sending shivers all over my body.

"Nope." God, she was beautiful. "I'm here to take you away, actually."

"Take me where?" My own voice sounded lighter, pulled by her cheerful tone. Not a single thought of the situation we were in filtered through my head.

None.

Zero.

"You'll see." She dropped her legs to the ground and took my hand in hers, pulling me toward the car. "See ya, Kill. I'll talk to you later."

She waved to my brother, but I was too transfixed by her sheer presence to look anywhere else but at her.

"So, you're not staying for dinner, K," Cillian yelled after us, amusement obvious in his tone.

"Apparently not." I finally turned to face him and saw the subtle shaking of his shoulders, probably trying not to laugh out loud. "Just tell them I'll see you guys later."

She opened the door and let me enter first, before sliding in after me. A driver sat in the front seat, his hair graying at the ends, watching us in the rearview mirror.

"All ready, Ms. Aster?"

"Yes, Jonas. All done. We can head to the parlor now."

Parlor? What parlor?

Seeing the confused look on my face, she laughed again and crossed the small distance between us, settling herself in my lap. Her knees dropped on the sides of my hips, and I slid lower grasping her hips in my hands.

"We are getting a tattoo, baby."

"We are?" I mean, I had nothing against tattoos, but the first one I got was the bloody present from my father. A symbol of our Outfit.

"Of course, we are." She dropped her head to my neck and started kissing the trail from my ear to my chest.

"Oh God," I groaned. I could almost feel her lips on my dick, every caress sending shivers through my body. She ground on me, awakening all of my senses at once, blurring the lines between them. I gripped her hips harder, pushing against her center, both pain and pleasure dancing through my body as my pants became tighter and my dick grew harder.

"Phee—"

"I missed you so much..." Kiss. "So, so much..." Bite. And with every new touch, my resolve was slipping from me, the need to fuck her here growing stronger.

"Phee," I moaned against her mouth. "We need to stop."

We needed to stop, because the first time I took her body, wouldn't be in the backseat of an Audi with her driver in front.

"But I missed you." She pouted.

"I know, baby." I removed the hair that fell on her face. "And I missed you too, but the first time we have sex won't be like this."

"But you do want to fuck me, right?"

"I don't know," I pulled her harder against me, against my aching dick, "you tell me."

She grinned like a kid on a Christmas morning, and my own smile intensified immediately. With her snuggled against my chest, the soft rumble of the engine made me sleepy even with the raging situation in my pants. I entwined my hands in her hair, feeling the silky softness, and trying to forget the past year she was away.

"So, why are we getting tattoos?"

She kept quiet for a moment, and I looked down to see her playing with the loose thread on my coat. When I saw her earlier, I expected to see the same shadows in her eyes. The same monsters fighting inside, but there was nothing. I needed to ask her where she had been for almost a year. Why did she disappear like that, only to return behaving like a completely different person?

"I wanted us to do something together." She looked up at me and continued, "And I want to do something that will make me remember them."

"Remember who?" I asked, confusion lacing my words.

"Them."

"Who are they, Phee?" She snuggled closer to me, burying her face in my shirt.

"Ophelia." I took a hold of her arms, and pulled her up, our faces on the same level. "Who are they?"

"I did what I had to." A sinister smile spread over her face, and for the first time tonight, I could see it.

The emptiness.

The coldness.

It was all there—the lack of emotions on her beautiful face.

"What did you do, Phee?" I asked carefully, almost wishing she wouldn't give me an answer.

"I killed my demons." She took my hand in hers, a satisfied smile on her face. "I killed them all."

6

OPHELIA

Four Years Ago

Snow.

There is something so beautiful, yet so tragic in it. It's so temporary, and just when you think you got used to its beauty, it is gone, faster than it ever came. Kieran was my snow, and I could feel him slipping away. Bit by bit, day by day, we were becoming strangers.

Somewhere deep inside, I always knew we would end up here. Two people connected by our hearts but disconnected in every other part of our lives. He wasn't coming to me anymore, and for some reason, he wasn't the first person I sought after every mission.

But he was still mine, and I was still his. We were Kieran and Ophelia. We were meant to be together. Right? We were. I knew he hated the life I led, and everything I did, but fuck it, he wasn't letting me go.

Then why did it hurt so much when I couldn't see the same spark in his eyes? Or when he didn't feel the urge to see me for days on end? Did he even love me anymore?

Fuck, of course he loved me. My insecurities can fuck the fuck off right now, because I knew that what we had, people rarely found.

I needed to do something, maybe surprise him. Yeah, that's it. I just needed to pull us out of this crazy funk we found ourselves in. We've just been stressed out about everything going on around us, and busy with our assignments.

And then, there was Ava, who wanted to either kill my brother, or just run away. I wasn't sure that either of those options were plausible, given the fact that with both of them, she could end up dead. Unfortunately, I would probably end up being the one sent to kill her, and that was one thing I could never do. Not in a million fucking years.

I would rather die than harm her.

I was a terrible, terrible friend, and despite all of that, she still loved me. She still stayed by my side, even though the Ophelia that came back wasn't the Ophelia that left Croyford Bay. Hell, I could even see Kieran recoiling from me sometimes, but Ava never.

During those nights when the blood was too thick to wash, when the ghosts were too much to handle, I could see it in his eyes. He couldn't stand the sight of me.

He couldn't handle me at my worst anymore, and I had a feeling the only time either of us was resembling anything close to what we used to be, was in our bed. He was still the boy I used to love—a man now—and I was still a girl with peace in my mind, and without any of the demons haunting my dreams.

I think that a part of me always knew we would end up here. There was an impending doom written in our stars, I was just too stupid to realize that. I always knew he would start pushing me away or was it maybe me who pushed him away?

The two of us... We weren't born to love. We were born to destroy.

Was I too blinded by my love for him to see that he was slowly slipping away? Did he even notice it, or maybe he didn't even care? I sometimes dreamed of running away, taking him away, his brothers, Ava... But those were just dreams.

The reality was much harder to deal with, and the knowledge that there was no escape from this life we were thrown into was eating me alive.

I hated to admit it, to admit what he didn't want to hear, but I didn't resent who I was and what I did. The adrenaline, the excitement I felt every single time the life would leave somebody else's body, it was keeping me alive, and I clung to it like a newborn child to its mother.

Sometimes I felt like one, if I was being honest. At least my father started behaving more like a father, and less like this stranger who just made me. Ever since that night in Siberia, ever since the jobs I did in Russia, he involved me more. He wanted my opinion, he wanted to hear how I would do things.

And no matter how much I hated him, no matter how much I hated what he made of us, I loved the way he made me feel.

Like I was loved. Like I was important to him, and if that made me a psychopath, so be it.

He was my father, and even Kieran's refusal to acknowledge that what we did wasn't that bad, I wasn't going to stop loving somebody who's my blood.

Jesus fucking Christ, when did all of us become such a mess?

This wreckage of our lives was pulling us beneath the water, and the only difference between Kieran and me was that I stopped fighting the current.

I used to hear that phrase "*If you can't beat them, join them*", and wasn't that the truth. I didn't want to beat my father anymore. I didn't want to see him suffering, because somewhere, deep down in me, I knew he went through the same things I did, he did the same things I did, and I refused to believe that Nikolai Aster was born a bad man.

More often than not, bad people were made. Or well, what somebody else thought was bad, but for others was normal.

The only difference between my family and other families was that instead of going to the church on Sundays, we attended meetings in Syndicate, taking assignments and discussing which target bled more.

Mine usually bled the most, and I could always see the proud gleam in my father's eye, appreciating everything I did for our group.

If only he would tell me where Maya was.

But hell, one disaster at the time. Right now I had to deal with Kieran and the clusterfuck our relationship ended up being. I didn't want to marry somebody I didn't know anymore.

Somebody I couldn't trust.

Somebody who didn't want to be with me anymore.

I just couldn't understand when we became virtual strangers; hiding things from each other, pushing each other away, destroying our hearts and everything we ever worked for.

I knew he struggled with the reality of our actions. He never really accepted this world, and seeing me embrace it with open arms, I knew it never sat well with him.

What was I going to do?

I tried figuring out a way to bring us back together to the way we were. What if I surprised him in Ventus City?

I didn't exactly need his permission to enter the apartment building he usually stayed at, and looking at the clock, I knew he was going to be home in the next three hours. It was the perfect amount of time for me to get ready and get my ass there from Croyford Bay.

I had to check if Ava would want to visit the city as well. She didn't want to be anywhere near Theo, but he was here and she could use some time alone with me, away from all this madness.

She had questions, I knew that. I also knew that I wouldn't be able to hide shit for much longer. She was getting suspicious, seeing my bruises, seeing me disappear for days on end, and she wanted to know.

I would rather be the one to tell her what was going on, than to have somebody else kick her mind into overdrive.

"Ophelia." A knock on the door pulled me back from my thoughts, and I turned around to see a nervous looking Ava standing there. "May I come in?"

Since when did she ask for permission to enter my room? Well, technically it was Kieran's room, but I guess with the amount of time I was spending on Nightingale Hill, it was becoming my room as well.

"What's up?"

She slowly walked toward me, the floor creaking beneath her feet. Judging by the expression on her face, I had a feeling I wouldn't like whatever she came here for.

"Do you have time to talk?" Her eyes looked everywhere else but at me, and I could feel my heart picking up speed, because well, I didn't know a person that liked hearing "can we talk" sentences.

"Of course." I sat on the bed, patting the spot next to me, and waited for her to finally come to me. This was the first time in our life that I'd seen her nervous about talking to me. She was always so open to me, always willing to share everything with me, and in these last couple of months, I could see that there was something bothering her, I just never pushed enough to find out what it was.

Or, well, I was a shitty friend too consumed with everything going on in my life to stop and take some time to talk to her like I used to.

She chewed at her bottom lip, but still kept standing a few feet away from me, worrying me.

"Ava?" I didn't like the sight of her like this. I didn't like it at all. "What happened?"

Her nervous energy was clogging the air in the room, and I fucking needed to know. Did she kill somebody?

If she did, I was going to get rid of the body. The universe knew I was an expert at getting rid of people, regardless of their living status.

"I-I," she stuttered. "I did something."

Okay, alright. Progress.

"What did you do?"

Let's be honest, whatever she did couldn't be worse than what I did for a living.

She finally looked at me, and the unshed tears in her eyes pulled at my soul. What in the ever-loving fuck happened?

"Ava? What did you do?" I got up and stood in front of her. I didn't notice how skinny she'd become, but I could see her collarbones sticking below the shirt. She seemed frail, weak, and a thousand different scenarios ran through my head.

Motherfucker, I was going to kill my brother.

"Is it Theo?" A sob tore from her, and the first tear rolled down her cheek. "It is, isn't it?"

Her body shook, and tears kept cascading down her face.

"I am going to fucking kill him." I went to move past her, but she took a hold of my arm, stopping me immediately.

"It wasn't Theo." Her voice shook with every word spoken. "It was me, and I am scared you will never want to talk to me once you hear what I did, and what I want to do."

There was something so vulnerable in her eyes, her whole posture screamed "weak", and the urge I always had around her was there.

Protect her.

Save her.

Take her away from the darkness.

"Hey, hey." I turned and pulled her into a hug. "Whatever it is, we will figure it out together."

Her body shook in my hands, and she tied her hands around my waist, gripping, holding onto me.

"I'm scared, Phee."

"Shhh," I murmured. "It'll be okay. I am here for you, and no matter what, I will always be here for you."

I started pulling her toward the bed, her pale face streaked with tears—a sight I never wanted to see again.

"Talk to me," I urged her. "I can't help you if you don't tell me what's wrong."

Hey gaze was flickering from me, to around the room, and coming back to me.

"Av—"

"I'm pregnant," she blurted out. I would have been less shocked if she told me she killed a man.

"I-I'm sorry," I stuttered. "What?"

"I think I'm pregnant."

"You think, or you know?"

She hesitated for a second, before answering, "I think, but I'm not quite sure."

"Okay, okay." I tried wrapping my mind around this. "We can find out for sure. We can go to the pharmacy, and tell Theo, and—"

"No!"

I pulled back, confused by her reaction.

"No? What do you mean, no?"

"I mean," she lowered her voice, "Theo can't know. Please, please, please Phee, promise me you won't tell him."

"But he has to know. He has to take responsibility."

"Phee." Another waterfall of tears started. "It isn't Theo's"

Oh fuck me sideways and every other way. I had a feeling my eyes were going to pop out of my head.

"What do you mean it's not Theo's?"

Did somebody hurt her?

"Exactly what I mean. Theo isn't the father. We haven't slept together for months."

"Then whose is it?" How did I never notice this? I needed to seriously work on my friendship skills. "Did somebody, um, do something to you?"

She flinched as if I pinched her. "Oh no, God no. It wasn't anything like that, but there is so much I need to tell you, and I tried postponing this as much as possible, but I guess the cat is out of the bag now."

"So," I started, confusion lacing my words. "You're trying to tell me that there's somebody else? Someone who isn't my brother?"

"Please don't hate me." And here we go with tears again. "You know I never loved him, I never even wanted to be with him. And Theo is awful, Ophelia. I've never met a more self-centered person than him."

"I could never hate you, silly." I should probably slap some sense into her, considering that what she was doing was a betrayal of our families. "Tell me, who is he?"

The brightest fucking smile appeared on her face, and I knew.

She loved this man.

She loved him more than anything, and if he made her happy, I was happy for them.

Ava fidgeted in her seat, but the nervous energy from before wasn't what radiated from her anymore.

It was happiness, a pure joy, and I really wanted to know who this person was.

"His name is Nathan," she started. "He actually works for your father."

The happy little feeling I started having in my chest evaporated when I realized who she was talking about. Ah fuck, she couldn't have found a nice little accountant from the town to fall in love with?

She had to fall for one of our assassins.

"Nathan Iverson?"

Please, I never prayed for anything, but now I was praying it wasn't him. He was an amazing soldier, but he was still a soldier, and that was one thing I never wanted for her. At least Theo didn't have any involvement in the bloody side of our business.

"Yes," she squealed. I could almost touch the excitement in the air, and I hated that I couldn't be as happy for her as I wanted to be. "Do you know him?"

"I've heard of him." Well, I've heard of him decapitating people, and leaving their limbs lying all around the place, but you know, I've heard of him.

"Oh, Ophelia, he is absolutely amazing. So kind, just perfect for me."

Fuck, fuck, fuck.

Was there another word in the English language to describe my state of mind, because fuck just wasn't cutting it anymore.

"I'm so happy for you, Aves." And I was happy for her, I really was, I just wasn't happy with her choice.

Goddammit, I needed to talk to him, and see what all this was about. If somebody was using her to climb the ranks, the decapitating he was doing to other people would be child's play for what I would do to him.

"Does he know?" I asked her. "Does he know you might be pregnant?"

"Yes." She nodded. "And he is so excited. But, Phee, it's a

dangerous game we're playing here. I don't know what it is you guys are involved in, but Nathan told me it's dangerous."

Son of a bitch!

Was he a fucking idiot, or what? She wasn't supposed to know. She wasn't supposed to be involved, for fucks sake.

I lied to her so many times to keep her away from all of this. Kieran, Cillian and Tristan did as well, This wasn't good, this wasn't good at all, and I needed to talk to Kieran.

We had to figure out how to solve this whole mess.

"What did he tell you?" Ice dripped from every word I spoke, but fuck it. He jeopardized her safety, and if he told her anything she wasn't supposed to know, I was going to cut his gut open and let the dogs feed on him.

"Oh." She was visibly uncomfortable with my mini interrogation, but it was too late to pull back now. "Just that it tends to be dangerous, and that he can't tell me anything more than that."

Well, he had at least half a brain.

Was the world intentionally fucking with me these days, or what? I mean, this kind of information was something I didn't want to have thrown at me right now. My head was a mess without the added worry for her safety, and what her idiot of a boyfriend would tell her.

"Are you mad at me?" she asked timidly, and I could only imagine what I looked like.

"No, of course not." I squeezed her hand in mine. "I am happy for you, even if it means that I have to find a way for you to get out of here, but I am happy. I am just pissed off at Nathan for telling you anything, and I am sorry even I can't tell you more than what you already know."

"That's okay." She smiled. "I don't even want to know. I just want to be happy with him, and if I am pregnant, this baby. That's all I'm asking for."

Oh, Ava.

If she was pregnant, we were going to have to fight the forces we probably weren't strong enough to fight. Our families wanted to be joined by our marriages, and our feelings weren't the ones they cared much about.

I was lucky enough to be betrothed to Kieran, but Ava hated Theo. It was like watching fire and ice trying to coexist together.

"And you'll be happy. Everything is going to be just fine."

I lied to her. I lied because I didn't want to diminish that gleam in her eyes, but I still lied.

"Are you going to tell my brother?"

"No, not for now, but I do need to go to Ventus City tonight."

"Oh." She seemed disappointed.

"What's wrong?"

"Oh, nothing, I just thought you might be here tonight to meet Nathan."

Well, fuckety fuck.

"I'm sorry, babe, but I really do need to go to Ventus. There's something going on with Kieran, and I need to try and salvage what's left of our relationship."

"I understand." She stood up, and I followed suit. "Do you want to go with me to the pharmacy tomorrow or the day after? I would really like to find out if I am pregnant or not, and I don't want to have any of the guards breathing down my neck."

"Of course." I pulled her to me, hugging her. "I would be glad to go with you."

She hugged me back, rubbing circles on my back.

"Thank you, Phee. Now," she pulled back, "go and kick some sense into my brother."

∾

H*ere we go.*

The tall building in front of me felt imposing, and for some unknown reason, I felt nervous knowing I would see Kieran in less than five minutes. He's been avoiding me for the last month, and we'd only managed to see each other one time.

Honestly, that one time would've been better if it never even happened.

The wind was howling on the streets, and I hugged my coat tighter around me, heading to the entrance of Kieran's building. The key he gave me felt heavy in my hand, and I just hoped he was actually home.

But hell, even if he wasn't I could still surprise him once he came back.

A couple exited the building, and I used the momentum to slip inside, passing next to the security desk that stood empty. I guess I'd be able to just slip in without anybody noticing me. The elevator was already open when I came to it, and I pressed the button for the twentieth floor, leaning against the wall as I started ascending to my destination.

"Please be home, please be home," I murmured to myself.

Well, unless the secretary in his office lied to me, he should definitely be here.

The doors opened, and I started slowly walking toward his apartment, my steps echoing in the hallway.

There it was, *210B*.

I pushed the key into the lock, turning it around, the clicking sound of the door unlocking, breaking the silence around me.

I always loved his apartment. The floor-to-ceiling windows on one side of the living room made sure that the sunsets here looked like something out of a fairy tale.

I unfortunately felt as if I stepped into a nightmare, as my eyes zeroed in on a disposed bra on the sofa that definitely didn't belong to me. My heart thundered in my chest, as a female moan came from the location of the bedroom.

No, no, no...

I followed the trail of disposed clothes on the floor. The pants and the shirt were definitely Kieran's.

A camisole, a skirt... I was ready to kill them both.

Taking a deep breath, I walked toward the bedroom—our motherfucking bedroom. The same one where he told me he loved me for the first time. The one where he officially asked me to marry him, and this fucking asshole dared to bring somebody else here.

The door was left open, and I shouldered my way in, the scene in front of me enough to bring me to my knees.

But this bitch didn't kneel. Not in front of a tragedy, and definitely not in front of a man.

Kieran's hands were gripping the hips of a redhead I knew way too well, grunting as he thrust into her from behind. He seemed lost in pleasure; lost in everything they were doing.

He was with Cynthia, fucking her where I laid my soul bare to him. Taking her where I left my heart and never even thought of taking it back.

With each thrust, each grunt, I could almost feel my heart shattering into a million tiny, little pieces.

Was this my punishment for everything I did? Taking away the one thing I loved, breaking my trust, breaking my heart.

The person I loved more than anything in this world was fucking somebody I hated with a fiery passion, and I was pretty sure I was the last thing on his mind.

Her head was bent down as he fucked her from behind, the bed creaking with their weight. They didn't talk, but that didn't make the pain any less.

He dared to betray me like this? He dared to break me like this, use me, push me away?

Was I not enough anymore? Was I just another one of his puppets?

A sound escaped my mouth, and our eyes met.

Those few seconds felt like an eternity, and I already knew what I had to do. I could forgive almost anything. I could forget the worst things a person did, but this... I killed people for this. I murdered them in their sleep, in their houses, with their families.

I destroyed their lives because they were traitors, and that was what Kieran was.

A bloody traitor.

"Ophelia." He finally closed his mouth and detached himself from Cynthia who scrambled back on the bed, hiding behind him. Her hand on his chest was another knife to mine, and I wanted to break each of her fingers.

Slowly.

Painfully.

He just killed me. He just killed everything we ever were, and there was no going back from this.

"How long?" I croaked. I needed to know how long this charade was going on behind my back. I needed to know how many times I was going to stab each of them once I get my hands on my knives.

I wanted to know how long I would let them bleed before ripping their throats out.

"Phee." He stood up, his hands in the air, fear evident on his face.

"How fucking long?" I screamed, the pain too heavy to keep inside.

"Phee, I can explain. This—"

"If you tell me that this isn't what it seems like, I am going to tear your dick off with my bare hands, Kieran."

He paled, the previous excitement he had on his face long gone.

"Please, Phee." He came to me, taking my hands in his.

Fear, there was so much fear in his eyes, and I loved every single second of it. You should be afraid of me.

You should fucking run away and take her with you.

I pushed him back, unable to stand his touch.

"Don't fucking touch me!" It felt like poison, scorching hot, and it was the last time he was ever going to touch me. "Tell me how fucking long."

"Three months." The whore he was fucking answered instead. His eyes flickered between the two of us, guilt evident.

"Three months," I murmured. "For three months, you've been screwing somebody else, while I only thought you needed some space to work out all the shit that's been going on."

"Birdy—"

"Don't fucking call me that!" I bellowed. "You just lost every single right to ever call me that."

I couldn't stand the sight of him, of the two of them together. I dropped the keys he gave me on the floor, and turned, walking toward the door. If I stayed a minute longer, one of them would end up dead, and I wasn't entirely too sure which one it would be.

"Ophelia!" He yelled after me, and I could hear his footsteps behind me. "Goddammit, you can't leave."

"Watch me."

"Stop." He pulled me back, turning me toward him. "Stop, goddammit, stop."

He took my face into his hands, and I stood still. I had to calm myself down.

"You're mine, dammit. She doesn't mean anything to me, but you do. You can't leave. You can't leave me, Phee."

And people said I was the psychotic one in this relationship.

Was he fucking delusional?

"Should I maybe join you guys, so we can have a three-some, huh? Do you want me to suck her tits while you jerk yourself off? Is that what you want, Kieran?"

"No, for heaven's sake, no. I want you to stay, because you are mine and I am yours, and this means nothing to me."

He started lowering his head toward me, and if he thought I would let him place his lips anywhere near mine after he kissed that slut, he had another think coming. I pushed him, his back hitting the wall, and grabbed his neck in my hand.

"I am not yours, Kieran," I whispered against his lips, a confused look evident on his face. His dick hardened between us, and I increased the pressure on his neck. I gripped the base of his cock with my other hand, and a moan escaped his mouth.

"Phee." Another moan, another delusional lie he was telling himself.

"I am never going to be yours."

"Ophelia." He opened his eyes, finally hearing what I was saying. "No."

"You should run, Kieran. You should fucking run to the end of the world, because I am going to kill you and that whore you just fucked in our bed. You should be scared of me, because the Ophelia you used to know doesn't exist anymore."

"Ophelia, please."

I dropped a kiss on his cheek and regretted it as the cheap perfume permeated my nostrils.

"You fucking reek of her."

"Baby girl, please."

I stepped back, nausea turning around in my stomach.

"You did this. You just killed me. Shattered my soul, stomped on my heart. And you should be fucking scared."

His eyes widened, understanding evident in them. The heavy feeling of loss settled over me. I just lost the one thing keeping me out of the dark.

I stumbled toward the door, but he didn't follow after me this time. He didn't do anything but kept standing as still as a statue as I walked out of his life.

7

OPHELIA

Present

I like control.

I like knowing the situation I am getting myself into —reading people, their emotions and their actions—so that I would know how to react to everything they say and do. Keeping everybody at arm's length prevents me from getting hurt, right? That's what I kept telling myself for years, but the truth is, I broke my own fucking heart. There was no one else to blame for the blade I stabbed my heart with, letting it bleed out. I ran when I should've stayed. I kept running until the lines between the truth and lies started blurring, and I started losing myself.

It is funny how our brain works. It blocks parts of our lives we so desperately want to forget, yet we still get flashbacks of those times.

Haunting us.

Destroying our souls, piece by piece, day by day, until the only thing that's left is a shell of the person you used to be.

Well, at least it destroyed mine.

I guess that when we bottle our emotions, when we seal them into a box we never want to open, we think we'll be able to forget about them. Unfortunately, what all of us fail to realize, *what I failed to realize*, is that you can never forget. You can pretend they're not there, you can try to run, try to hide, but reality is always the same. Whatever you were trying to run from always catches up with you, and it always feels like a sledgehammer to your chest when everything you were bottling up crashes into you full force.

For a very long time I've been blaming other people for the way I am, for all the choices I've made, but after a while I realized that it never was their fault. I could've fought what they tried to turn me into.

A monster.

A murderer.

They destroyed my mind, shattered my soul, and they built a world inside of me I didn't want. They opened the door to the darkness, but I invited it in. Emotions can be overwhelming and suffocating. It's easier to shut them down than to deal with the avalanche in your chest.

So that's what I did.

Instead of feeling everything and drowning in it, I shut it down and shoved it into that box. And deep down, I sometimes fear what will happen when everything spills out.

It gets tiring pretending that everything is okay, because nothing really ever was.

My wound was still bleeding.

Untreated.

Open.

Raw.

Everyone will tell you that an open wound has to be checked, otherwise it gets infected.

I never treated mine. There was no bandage big enough to

stop the bleeding, nor a doctor who could stitch it up. Sometimes I think it's healed. There are days when my mind isn't playing games on me, and it isn't burning me from the inside out. There are days when I wake up and think it'll be okay. I will be okay. But that shit never lasts.

Just like with every single wound, once you touch it, it starts throbbing, reminding you it is still there.

Maybe it is a memory, or somebody you used to know. It doesn't really matter because it always hurts the same.

I loved control. I thrived on it. With it, I could pretend to be a functional member of society. People react differently when you display emotions accordingly.

Did somebody tell a joke? Laugh Ophelia, remember to laugh. Move your lips and recall the sounds to go with it.

People can't hurt you if you're the one controlling them.

Waking up in an unfamiliar, dark room a couple of minutes ago took away all of the control I thought I had. The pounding in my head started inciting nausea. A croissant I had for breakfast this morning heavy in my stomach. Was it this morning, or was it yesterday? What time of a day was it now?

I pulled myself up, scanning the room, my mind still hazy from the sleep.

There were no windows in any of the walls, and the only light inside the room was a dimmed lamp, perched on the edge of a large mahogany desk, opposite the bed.

Where the fuck was I?

I glanced at the t-shirt, hugging my upper body, and frowned.

This isn't my shirt.

I could see my black pants and a sweater folded on the sofa chair, but who undressed me, and why?

I pushed the comforter off of me, and slid off the bed, my feet hitting the cold tiles beneath, evoking goosebumps all over my skin. Think, Ophelia, think. What is the last thing you remember?

I inspected my legs, arms and stomach, looking for bruises or cuts, but there were none. I wasn't hurt. I gripped the bed, pushing my mind to cooperate with me.

The house. The one Theo said Maya was staying at.

I was standing at the front door, knocking, and then... And then nothing. I abruptly stood up, a wave of dizziness almost knocking me off my feet. For fuck's sake, get a grip.

I looked to my left, noticing a door for the first time. Was it going to be unlocked? Time to find out if I was a prisoner or a guest.

I stepped around the bed heading toward the door and took additional inventory of the room. The walls were barren of any pictures. There were no books or any personal snippets, which told me that this room wasn't used very often. The air here had an earthy scent, reminding me of rainy days in Croyford Bay. Was I underground? Maybe some sort of a basement?

But the room looked too nice to be placed in a basement. The silky sheets I woke up entangled in must cost more than somebody's monthly wage. Even the pillow beneath my head felt heavenly. So why was I here?

The doorknob in my hand turned without any resistance, and relief washed over me at the small action. Maybe I wasn't a prisoner after all.

I swung the door open with my heart in my throat, expecting somebody in front of the door. But nobody was there —only an empty, illuminated hallway, stretching on both sides. I couldn't stay inside the room forever, and I needed answers. The eerie atmosphere reminded me of that scene in the movie *Resident Evil*, when Alice wakes up in the shower, with no recollection of her past. I was unfortunately very well aware of mine. Well, all except for the last couple of hours. I hoped it was hours, because if I had been knocked out for days on end, I would be majorly pissed off.

If anyone ever asked me what is one word to describe my life, I would say clusterfuck. And not a small one. Oh no. The Ragnarok proportions. And I didn't mean Marvel's *Ragnarok*, where we got a half-naked Thor and Loki in all of their glory.

No, my version was Odin being swallowed by the giant wolf, Fenrir. The end of everything.

If you didn't realize by now, I was Odin in this story.

I passed several doors, my head throbbing at my temples, when another memory resurfaced.

Theo had called me.

"You need to come to New York," he demanded. "Maya came back, and I need you here."

Maya was our sister. The sister we all failed. I've been trying to track her whereabouts for years now. She wasn't there when I went to the house. Nobody was.

I snickered because the fucker did what I assumed he would do.

He lied to me.

Four years ago, I ran away from our families, from the life I knew. I knew I could never return. That slimy little toad told me the Nightingales weren't in town.

"They're out. All of them are in Croyford Bay," Theo confirmed.

When I pulled in front of the house, I didn't see anything unusual. When you're running from the Nightingale family, you learn to keep an eye out for anything unusual—lone cars, suspicious people... you get the drill. But I didn't see anything.

I've managed to avoid all of them for the last four years. I cut all ties with my old friends. I didn't have social media accounts. I kept my head down and my mouth shut. Out there, I wasn't Ophelia Aster.

I was nobody.

And I waited. I waited until Theo called me, which I knew he would. I wasn't surprised Maya had been nowhere near the house. I also wasn't surprised that one of the asses he liked to kiss most probably had been.

My heart had put me in this situation, and while Theo was sure to scheme and use my one weakness against me, I just couldn't pass this opportunity. Even if it meant I would end up here.

I just hoped I was right.

The hallway ended with a staircase leading upstairs. I was right then; this was the basement. I stumbled up the stairs, my heart beating rapidly, threatening to jump out of my chest. Time stood still as I walked through the foyer of what seemed to be a massive house and scanned the area, looking for a possible weapon to take with me. Whoever stripped my clothes, took away my knives and my gun.

I saw a set of keys on one of the tables with a vase filled with white roses, and grabbed them, clenching them between my fingers. It wasn't like there were any guns or knives, so this would have to do. Maybe I could stab them in the eye.

At this point I wouldn't be surprised to stumble upon a couple of mutant rabbits, or zombies. Please, if there are zombies, please don't let them be the fast ones. I was a terrible runner. I would probably trip over my feet and die in the process. I walked toward the window, but the sight in front was unfamiliar to me. As a matter of fact, this whole house was unfamiliar to me. The whole area was covered in heaps of snow, glittering under the moonlight. I could see the fountain in the middle of a roundabout, and nothing else. October in Croyford Bay was cold, but not this cold. Not nine-feet-of-snow cold.

"Where the fuck am I?" I mumbled. A sudden movement on

my right side sent a jolt of fear mixed with excitement through me, making me realize I was not as alone as I thought I was.

"Hello." The chilling feeling in my bones had nothing to do with the actual temperature of the house anymore, but everything to do with my emotions skyrocketing. "Is anybody here?"

A million and one thoughts about human trafficking and horrors I could be facing ran through my head. What did I tell you before? A fucking Ragnarok. I expected shit to happen, but I preferred to know what I was getting myself into.

"Please," I whispered. Nothing brings men down to their knees like a damsel in distress. "What is this place?"

Was I hallucinating? No, I saw somebody, I was sure of it.

I stepped inside the room the shadow disappeared to and gawked at the sight in front of me. This whole place should've been on a magazine cover or something. The whole design looked like something my mother would've used in her house. The white curtains were linen—the kind of white devoid of dust or any kind of human touch. The room reminded me of a hotel foyer with its size and artwork. Two beige couches stood on the opposite sides of each other, right in front of the fireplace, accompanied by a sofa chair of the same color.

What had me excited, however, wasn't the size of this room nor its brilliant setup. I didn't give a fuck about the architectural beauty or the interior design. I inched closer to the fireplace, tipping my head to look at the picture above. They say snakes won't attack, unless provoked. I knew some that would.

The Nightingale emblem stood there in all of its glory. An imposing snake wrapped around the gleaming sword, looking ready to attack. I didn't have to be a genius to figure out who owned this house.

And who brought me here.

This was no coincidence, and that little voice in my head told me Theo had his hands in this. Just how I suspected, just what I wanted. He thought I was heading into the trap. Poor little toad. After all these years, he should've known that nothing and nobody could surprise me anymore, especially not him.

Okay, alright, it was showtime. I just wondered why they didn't lock me up like they did before? Had they grown a conscience somewhere along the way? How fucking sweet of them for not chaining me to the fucking wall this time around.

I took a few steps back as deep laughter resonated somewhere behind me. The usual reaction I would have to that sound, to those voices, couldn't be used right now. Oh no, they had to think they had me.

My hands started shaking, the keys dropping to the ground.

You can run, but you can never hide, little bird.

The threatening words *he* repeated so many times, resurfaced again. I didn't want to turn around. I didn't want to face them.

I didn't want to face them because I knew I would want to kill them, one by one—claw their fucking eyes out, carve up their hearts, rip their throats out. I could be creative.

I'd been waiting for this moment for the last four years.

It kept me awake, it kept me moving and it kept me motivated.

Keep your fucking cool, Ophelia. No messing around this time.

Helpless little lamb, that's what you are.

Their steps echoed around the room, taunting me, closing in. There was nowhere to go now. My hands felt clammy, the urge to run overtaking my whole body. I just didn't know if I wanted to run away, or to run to them. I knew what was about to happen. My mouth was parched and my throat constricted. I hadn't cried in so long, I forgot how it felt. My tears threatened to spill over my cheeks, and it wasn't because the shithead I was related to betrayed me. I wanted to cry because I couldn't kill them, right here and right now.

"Hello, birdy," one of them marveled. The walls were closing in... tick tock. "You're not going to greet us? Not that we mind the view from here." Instinctively I grabbed the hem of my shirt, trying to pull it lower, remembering my lack of pants. Oh well, what the hell.

Taking a deep breath, I turned around, facing my demons head-on.

Kieran, Cillian and Tristan Nightingale.

The three brothers, the three musketeers, and my worst nightmare. Oh no, wait. I think it was the other way around.

I was their worst nightmare, they just didn't know it yet.

They stood side by side, all three dressed in black. How fucking lovely—they were now wearing matching clothes. If I had my phone with me, I would've snapped a picture. While they were dressed for my funeral, I planned for theirs. Tristan and Cillian wore amused expressions on their faces, but I could see the darkness swirling behind their eyes. They were going to enjoy every second of this, whatever it was they had planned for me.

Kieran stood between the two of them, his dark hair disheveled, a few strands falling onto his forehead. Unlike the other two, he didn't smile. His face was like a marble statue, devoid of any emotion. But I could see it.

His anger, his hatred, his pain. It was all there, showing through his obsidian eyes. He cocked his head, meeting my gaze head-on. I knew what that was.

A challenge.

An invitation.

He wanted me to fight this. To scream and shout, demand to be let out. He wanted me to entertain them, but I wasn't going to do that. They thought they lost everything that night, but they weren't the only ones.

The difference was, I knew the truth. They didn't.

"Did you miss us, little bird?" Cillian took a step closer, while I took two back. He laughed, pushing me closer to the fireplace with every new step. "Because we sure as hell missed you."

8

OPHELIA

My father was a cruel and merciless man, but he was still my father. There was no love nor affection between the two of us, but there was something else. Respect and protection. He kept his promise and I kept mine. Everything I ever wanted was given to me, but there was a price.

I belonged to the Syndicate, and they belonged to me.

They taught me how to fight, how to survive, but nothing could ever prepare me for my death. I knew it was coming. That was why I was here, after all.

None of us moved as their eyes raked over my body, disgust rolling through me. These men were once my family, but I've learned the hard way that loyalty goes only so far. Trust is a fickle thing. It takes you years to earn it, and only seconds to lose it. They lost mine, and I lost theirs, and even if a thousand years passed, I knew we were never going back to the way we used to be before...

Before lies and deceit clouded our minds. Before they decided to condemn me, trusting the wrong people. You would think that after so many years of knowing each other, they would at least ask for my version of the story. But they never did.

Shoot first, and then ask questions. That's what Kieran told me the first time we were training together. When the black hole my father threw me into started swallowing me whole, he showed me light.

Lux Tenebris.

Light in Darkness.

That was what Kieran once was for me, but not anymore.

There were nights when I summoned him in my dreams, living the fantasy where he didn't hate me, and I didn't hate him. There were days when I could almost feel his lips on mine. The days when I was tired of running, tired of hiding, he was the first person I thought of. The days when I didn't dream of destroying everything he loved, as he had destroyed me. During those days, during those nights, I still loved him. I allowed myself to feel us. To remember what we used to be.

But seeing him now, seeing the hatred seeping from every pore of his body, I knew what it was and what it always would be.

A fantasy.

Cillian still stood only inches from me, his body rigid, waiting for me to run. But I wasn't going to, not this time. Once again, they didn't know everything. They didn't know that everything they ever believed in was a lie.

They were so consumed by their grief, by their blind trust, that they never saw what was right in front of their noses. They didn't know that they were keeping serpents in their gardens.

Some secrets are easy burdens, mine weren't. I put other people's safety before mine, thinking they would do the same. Papa always warned me to think with my head and not with my heart, but I always thought my heart was what made me human.

I was wrong, and it ultimately led to my downfall. It made me weak.

They wanted me to beg, to crawl in front of them, I could see it in their eyes. Except, I wasn't going to do that.

My father didn't raise a coward. A psychotic bitch, yes, but definitely not a coward. They were playing my game this time, and they weren't the puppet masters. I was.

"It took you boys long enough to find me." I smirked. "What's it been, four years already?"

Our hearts were our enemies. Unbeknownst to us, they'd lead to our downfall and this moment. Mine. theirs, my brother's. Mine, because I trusted too much. Theirs because they loved too much, and when that love broke down, they were left with nothing but hatred.

My brother's, because he wanted too much. He craved what wasn't his to crave, and I paid the price.

Tristan started walking toward me, but Kieran stopped him, shaking his head, that cold expression still on his face. If I closed my eyes, I could still see his smile. I could still see the boy he used to be; the boy this world decided to destroy.

They were blocking the only exit from the room, and I had no doubt in my mind that this estate was swarming with their bodyguards. I could take on two of them, but not Kieran and not the rest of their team. That asshole knew me too well.

I could feel the heat at my back from the fire dancing inside the fireplace. If Cillian took another step, I would end up like a roasted human marshmallow. Now that was an idea.

Human marshmallows.

No, thank you. Interestingly, they didn't attack. At least not yet. Oh, they thought scaring me would work this time around, but I wasn't the girl they used to know. Maybe I should give it to them. Show them my fear, the tremble in my chin, the pleading in my eyes.

These fucking psychopaths wanted me broken. But didn't they know that it was already too late? I was beyond repair, and breaking me again simply wouldn't work. Broken things couldn't be broken again. Death wasn't something I feared anymore. Some days, it felt more like an old friend.

So whatever they had prepared for me, I couldn't wait to see it. I just hoped they would get fucking creative for once.

My hand brushed against a cold item, and I looked down noticing the fire iron. Bingo. I gripped the cold handle, and pulled it in front of me, almost grazing Cillian's chest. Aww, would you look at that surprised look on his face? He probably thought I was going to attack him already, but I wanted to enjoy the show. Men were always so predictable.

They always needed to feel powerful. Invincible. Unbreakable.

Cillian was the same. He had to feel stronger than me, and I was going to give it to him. For now. Some sick part of me always knew I would end up getting hurt. It was always there, simmering beneath the surface, waiting, haunting. Until the other shoe dropped, and the life I knew went out in flames.

I was being hated for something I didn't even do, but I was sick and tired of trying to explain myself.

When I wanted to talk to them, they chained me to the wall like an animal, waiting for an execution. When I cried, kicked and screamed, they sliced my skin with their blades, and broke my heart with their words.

"Are you going to kill me, little bird?" The idiot in front of me sneered. And to think we were once friends. "Are you going to stab me like you stabbed her?"

Her.

Ava.

The pain I buried for so long sliced through me, freezing me in place. When you lose someone you love, it stays with you.

The bad memories were not what caused me pain. It was the good ones that drove me to the brink of insanity, knowing I will never get new ones.

Faster than my eyes could follow, the fire iron was snatched out of my hand, and my head hit the floor as Cillian threw me down, his legs pressed against my sides, his eyes crazed, hands squeezing my neck. I coughed, wheezing for air, but the grip he had on me just tightened. Black dots started dancing around his head, and I knew I was minutes from passing out.

"Fight me, little bird," he mocked, his lips next to my ear sending shivers all over my skin. "Or do you just want to die like the sad little bitch you are?"

I was running out of air, and no matter how hard I tried to move his hands away from my throat, they just squeezed harder and harder. I was panicking, out of control.

I could hear somebody shouting, but my mind was so far gone, that the only thing I could see were his eyes. Blue just like the ocean, and as cold as the Northern Seas.

Ty doch' drakona, Ophelia. Ty ne klanyayesh'sya, ty pobezhdayesh'.

You are the daughter of a dragon.

I was the daughter of a dragon. Yes.

You do not bow. You conquer.

How many times did my father say that to me? I snapped my eyes open.

I wouldn't bow, I wouldn't cower. They wanted me dead? They wanted to play the game?

"Cillian!" somebody shouted. "This is not what we talked about."

"I'm just having a little bit of fun, Brother." *Then let's have some real fun.*

With the last atom of strength I had in me, I pulled my legs up, connecting my knee with his back, causing him to stumble forward and loosen his grip on my neck. I was going to show them so much fun, by the time I was finished with them, they wouldn't want to go to an amusement park ever again.

"Shit," he exhaled.

I pushed my torso off the ground, wheezing from the sudden onslaught of air in my lungs. Unfortunately, I didn't have time to recover. I had to get out from underneath him, and I had to do it fast.

With one hit to his throat, Cillian started wheezing, clutching his neck and rolling off of me. My hands were sweaty, my lungs still trying to catch up with the air finally coming inside. On unsteady feet, I pulled myself up, stumbling away from him. My knees were shaking, and wave after wave of dizziness kept hitting me, trying to knock me down.

If I lost consciousness now, there was no guarantee they wouldn't kill me immediately, or do something even worse. I looked away from Cillian toward the other two. Tristan looked ready to attack, while Kieran kept his usual composure. What I wouldn't give just to see a chink in that cold armor of his.

It was inhuman seeing how little all of this affected him.

I frantically searched for my previous weapon, and once I spotted it lying next to the couch, I lunged forward, my hand once again gripping the steel handle.

"Impressive," Kieran drawled lazily, his hand around Tristan's arm, holding him in place. "So, you aren't as useless as I thought you would be."

"I am going to kill you, you bitch." I looked at my attacker again, still kneeling on the floor, sneering at me.

"You asked me if I wanted to kill you." I coughed, my throat constricting. "It would seem that I do."

"An eye for an eye." I turned, and my nightmare stepped closer. "A tooth for a tooth." He continued prowling toward me.

Cillian stood up, joining Tristan who seemed frozen in his spot, looking at me.

Kieran smiled, his gaze never wavering from mine. "Leave us," he requested.

"Dude, no," Tristan protested.

"I said," he turned toward them, "leave us. Don't make me repeat myself."

Vicious. That was how you could describe him.

Cold, dangerous, unrelenting. Even with all the shit going on in our lives, he used to be lenient, loving, caring. The way he was talking to his brothers now, I could see it was all long gone. Or was he locking his emotions up the same way I was?

"No! We are supposed to do this together, remember?"

"She won't die today." I won't? "But I do need to talk to her. Alone."

I couldn't take my eyes off of him. His dark hair was longer, falling over his forehead. Those calculating, obsidian eyes raked over my face, my chest, my naked legs. My cheeks were burning, a thousand memories slamming into me.

Our first touch.

Our first kiss.

Our first time.

There is a very thin line between love and hate. Sometimes it's hard to decipher which emotion you are feeling more, and I wonder how long it took him to erase me from his heart. Was it seconds, minutes, days, or was it years? I wonder what he saw when he looked at me. What did he feel every time he thought about me?

I wasn't sure what hurt more -the fact that he didn't know me at all, or that he could disregard me as if I never meant anything to him.

As if we were nothing.

He was always tall; much taller than my five foot five, but

the animalistic, raw energy emanating from him now, made him look larger than life. His shoulders were broader, muscles straining against the black shirt he wore. Was I ever going to wake up and not be affected by him? He seemed calm, too calm for the situation at hand, but I knew better.

There was hell hiding inside of him, waiting to be let out. Cillian and Tristan weren't happy with his decision, but if there was one thing I learned about him over the years, it's that he just simply didn't give a fuck. It didn't matter if he loved you or hated you. Kieran Nightingale just couldn't be bothered with other people's feelings. What he wanted, he always got, in one way or another.

I knew it firsthand. I had been on the receiving end of his recklessness not so long ago. All he cared about was the power he could get, and it didn't matter that I was the collateral damage. That the people I loved were the ones that got hurt.

No. When he had his sights set on something, he just took it. No questions asked.

He advanced toward me, while I stood still. Frozen in place.

"Little bird, little bird," he started in a singsong voice, caressing my neck with one hand, his eyes focused on the skin there. "Why did you fly away?"

"You know why." My voice was shaking, and the grip I had on the fire iron started loosening. Why was I letting him affect me this way? His scent was everywhere around us -the smell of wood and a fresh spring day.

"What are you doing?" His lips skimmed over my jaw, tasting me. His other hand snuck into my hair, tugging at the loose strands. "Kieran?"

That's right, K. Show me what you want to do to me. Show me, because the destruction you showed me once wasn't enough to erase you from my memories. Give me pain, Kieran, because that was the only thing you were good at giving.

His grip became tighter, almost painful, tipping my head up. The soft touch of his lips was replaced with his teeth, biting and marking.

"I am tasting you." He continued his onslaught, moving to the other side. "I always wanted to know the taste of death, and your skin is reeking of it."

Death. Such a funny concept. It was supposed to be the place of eternal rest, but what about those left behind? We never found peace when death came to those we loved. And this poor thing, he wanted me dead.

I mean, that made two of us, but all in due time.

I slammed my hands on his chest, pushing him from me. His chest was rising and falling with each breath, matching my own.

"You're a piece of shit." *Slowly, Ophelia. You aren't supposed to rush this. Savor it, savor him, remember him and all he did.* I had to remember the pain, because if I didn't, I might as well sign my own execution and it was still too early for that.

Eternal rest wasn't in the cards for me. It probably wasn't in the cards for any of us.

I wiped my jaw angrily, trying to lose the tingling feeling he left behind. I had to pace myself, I had to control myself because emotions, good and bad, could kill you if you weren't the one controlling them.

"Don't pretend you didn't like that." Smug bastard.

"Why the fuck am I here," I asked. "Why don't you just kill me and get it over with?"

"Where would the fun be in that?"

I wanted to wipe the stupid smirk off his face, stab him in the neck, find his brothers and do the same, but I couldn't. *Just, deep breaths, Ophelia. Deep fucking breaths.*

"Since when do you wanna have fun?" I glanced toward the

door. I had no idea where we were, but I had to check the grounds. I had to see their security details here, and staying inside playing dead wouldn't help with everything I had planned. Oh no, we were going to have fun, all of us. We were going to dance.

"Don't even fucking think about it," he gritted. "These grounds are filled with our guards. Besides, you wouldn't last a second outside."

Kieran, Kieran, Kieran… so pretty, yet so dumb.

"I'm sure that dying in this cold is better than being here with you."

"Ophelia!"

I laughed, dashing to the door, my heart racing in my chest. Come on, chase me baby. We loved to play this game. Cat and mouse, yin and yang, that's what the two of us always were. Two opposites, light and dark, chasing each other for years now. Come on, give me the thrill.

I had no idea if the front door was unlocked, but who gave a fuck anymore? I didn't. Even if it was, I hoped their security detail this time around would be capable of getting me first. I really didn't want to freeze my ass off here, wherever here was.

"For fuck's sake." I could hear him behind me, inching closer, but the thundering roar inside my head urged me to run faster. Adrenaline rush, the thrill, I hadn't felt this in years.

The door was just a couple of inches from my reach, when a strong arm wrapped around my midsection, pulling me back. Oopsie daisy, I got caught.

"Where do you think you're going?"

"Let me go." I struggled against his hold, but I knew my efforts would be futile. "You're going to kill me anyway. What difference does it make which way?"

Truth be told, if I really had to die, I preferred for it to happen in a real battle and not this way. But, he had to believe me. He had to believe I was helpless, that I was at his mercy. I urged my chin to tremble, my eyes glossing over.

There they were. Emotions.

He pushed me against the wall, his body heavy behind mine. "The difference is that I will be the one who gets to slice you up." He pressed harder into me. "The difference is that I will get to break you, piece by piece, just like you broke this family. If you thought my love was strong, my hatred is even stronger, little bird. Do not mistake my calmness for my weakness. I've dreamed about cutting you into pieces for years, waiting for this moment. Waiting for you to be back in my arms, just so that I could show you what real pain is."

He moved the hair from my face, pulling me closer to him.

"I told you already. An eye for an eye and a tooth for a tooth. You belong to us now, until I am satisfied with your punishment. Until you tell us everything we want to know. And then, and only then, will I kill you. You do not deserve to die peacefully. I will take everything from you, until the only thing that's left is a shell of who you used to be."

9

KIERAN

It's been four years, six months, and twenty-eight days since I last spoke to the little hellfire that kept my soul awake. Ophelia Aster used to be everything I desired. Now, she was everything I wanted to destroy.

Sometimes it felt like an eternity since the last time I saw her.

Sometimes like a second.

There were days when the pain became too much, when my heart didn't know which way to go. Did I hate her? Did I love her? But how could I love her, when she was the one who destroyed everything? I could see the hatred in her eyes, I could see the pain reflecting my own. I waited while Cillian and Tristan hunted. I was patient, waiting for her to come back, to tell me it was all a lie. That what they told me was just a bad dream. That she didn't do what they were accusing her off. That she didn't run away when they confronted her about it.

That she waited for me to come home. But none of the answers I needed ever came, and I was left with a pain that turned into something darker.

Something vicious. Something I have never felt before.

When my love turned bitter, when the resentment and anger consumed my whole being, I started believing everything my brothers told me. I became numb, and the only thing that kept me going was this insane urge to find her and make her pay for what she did. She shattered us all, leaving the broken pieces behind.

I've tried to understand what made her do it. A thousand scenarios ran through my head, but nothing could justify her actions. I've been waiting for this moment for what feels like forever, but now with her in my arms, I was torn, blinded by rage. I thought Cillian would kill her, but I wanted to be the one to turn those blue eyes lifeless. On the other hand, I didn't want her dead, at least not yet. I wanted her to suffer. I needed to own not only her body, but her mind. I wonder if she still bleeds the same; does she still taste the same?

My demons wanted to play with hers, just like they always did. It didn't matter if it was love or hatred, she always made me feel alive. What a shame really that she had to die.

Her chestnut-colored hair was tickling my face —the same scent, the same feeling —it felt like somebody shot me in the chest. I was breathing hard as I kept her pinned with her face pressed to the wall. She wanted to run from me, but I wasn't going to allow that. The animalistic urge to own her, punish her, keep her with me, was rushing through my body. She had to pay.

"Are you scared, birdy," I asked her as I ran my nose over her neck. Vanilla and almonds. She smelled good enough to bite. "Is your heart beating fast? Are your hands clammy, does your body know what is about to happen?"

Do you know I am going to kill you?

Her breath was coming out in short spurts, small puffs blowing against the hair that fell over her face.

"Can you feel that, Ophelia? Your chest caving in, your knees shaking... Do you know what that is?"

"Am I supposed to be afraid, Kieran?" She snickered. "Am I supposed to quiver under the hold of the great Kieran Nightingale? Do you feel like a man now that you have me in your clutches?"

I yanked her hair, tipping her head backwards. I could see the veins straining on her neck, but what unsettled me was the smile on her face. I squeezed her neck in warning, but she only smiled wider, her blue eyes dancing in delight.

Fucking psychopath.

"Careful now."

"Or what? You're going to kill me?" She beamed as if I wasn't seconds from snapping her neck. "Go ahead then, kill me. Get it over with. That's where this story is heading, isn't it?"

"Shut your filthy mouth."

"What would Ava say, Kieran?"

My hold on her loosened, a buzzing sound echoing in my head.

Did she just utter the one name that is forbidden to her? I turned her around, slamming my hands on the wall, caging her between my arms. The bitch enjoyed this. She wanted to rile me up, to make me lose control. Ophelia was always good at that— making me lose control, driving me crazy, pushing me to the brink of insanity. But not this time.

She started chewing on her lower lip, and I wanted nothing more than to bite on it as well. Instead, my hand took a hold of her chin, lifting her head closer to mine.

"You have no right to say her name."

"I have more right than you do," she whispered. "I have more right than any of you do."

Her laughter, lack of fear, lack of any emotions at all, irritated me. When she first saw us inside the room, she seemed terrified. Now she just seemed indifferent, as if she flipped a switch. Such a good little actor. Such a good little whore.

I took a better look at her and noticed the red marks already forming on her throat from Cillian's choking session. I didn't like the emotions threatening to erupt at the sight of those. Her health, her safety, none of those were my business. She didn't matter to me.

She looked exactly the same— the fucked-up girl, with nothing good to offer to the world. These ocean eyes of hers were such a contrast to her pale skin, and chocolate hair. To think that I once found her attractive, that I once loved her, made me sick.

She looked the same, yet completely different. There was fire in those eyes. Fire I never saw before.

I opened the doors of my soul to her once. I shattered my walls hoping she would be the one to save me from myself, and I would get to take her away from all of this. I let her in, allowing her to see every part of me.

What did I get in return?

A lifetime of regret and guilt eating me alive because I allowed the coldhearted bitch into my life. She loved her knives so much, she used them to stab us in the back. So what if she still looked like everything I desired? So what if I hated the redness on her neck, and how pale and gaunty her face looked? She wasn't my problem anymore, and the only thing I wanted from her was her pain.

Her misery.

Her destruction.

I would revel in seeing her completely broken. That defiant look in her eyes erased, leaving her begging for her end. She thought she had the right to utter Ava's name? I slammed her head against the wall, the echoing crack of her skull satisfying the beast inside of me. Her eyes closed at the impact and a frown appeared between her eyebrows. Her teeth clamped on her lower lip, ripping through it. Rivulets of dark red blood gushed down her chin, a stark contrast to her pale skin.

That's right baby, take all the pain. Feel it, because that's the only thing you'll be getting from me.

She looked more like a demon than an angel. I was a blind man once, failing to see just how much the darkness had consumed her soul. She would fall, and with her, their whole empire.

The syndicate and everything they had would be ours.

Maybe it wasn't such a good idea leaving her with me? But then again, it wasn't such a good idea leaving her with any of us. Cillian wanted to kill her as soon as he saw her. Tristan almost punched the wall when they brought her in. When I free this world from her, maybe the gaping hole inside my chest would finally disappear.

"Does it hurt, princess?" She opened her eyes, that fucking smile on her face again. Even with blood on her teeth and bruising on her neck, she still looked better than any other female I had ever met.

Our little Antichrist.

"I am not a princess, you moron," she sneered. Her knee connected with my groin, the sharp pain rendering me speechless. "I am a motherfucking queen."

I crouched in front of her, trying to break through the pain. Her fist connected with my nose; once, twice, three times.

"I don't enjoy pain. I. Am. Pain." Her foot hit the side of my face, sending me to the floor. "You want to break me, Kieran? You'll have to catch me first."

I tried to lift myself up, to reach for her, but my head snapped to the side when her leg connected with the other side of my face.

God fucking dammit.

She ran toward the front door, and this time, I wasn't fast enough to stop her. The cold December air filtered through the foyer as her petite figure disappeared through the door, leaving me on the floor.

"Cillian!" I boomed, hoping he would hear me. I would never hear the end of this. She was escaping thanks to me and my distracted thoughts. She was so pliant, so quiet and I wanted to feel her body against mine, then boom! Fucking idiot.

"Cillian!" I belted again, annoyed with the lack of response. I got myself up, wincing at the pain emanating from my head. A girl managed to knock me on my ass. Not that she hadn't done it in the past, but this was different. I thought I had control over her, when really she was just waiting for an opening.

Footsteps echoed behind me as I started toward the door.

"What the hell happened?" Tristan asked as I turned to see both of my brothers running toward me. "Is that blood on your face?"

"I don't have time to explain. She's running away."

"What the fuck, Kieran?" Cillian snapped. "I knew it was a bad idea leaving her with you. She was always your weak spot."

"Fuck off, Brother. I don't recall you being very successful in subduing her earlier either."

The scowl on his face would've been funny if it wasn't for the current situation. The snow crunched beneath our boots, making it harder to run. At least I knew she wouldn't be able to get too far away with this weather. A snowstorm was coming, and the temperature started dropping below zero as the night advanced. If she managed to pass through all of our guards, I was pretty sure we would be finding her body in a couple of days.

Whose fucking idea was it again to spend the winter here?

We could've gone to our beach house, but no, we apparently wanted to have our nuts frozen. I couldn't see her anywhere, and if we lost her now —well, if I lost her now —I was sure there would be hell to pay for kidnapping her. Ophelia was a vengeful bitch, and here I thought we would be able to scare her from the get-go.

"Call the gate, Tristan," I instructed. "I want her caught." I could barely see the roundabout and the fountain from the amount of snow that fell in the short period of time, and my ass wasn't appreciating the fact that I ran out only in my t-shirt.

"You couldn't have waited until we took our jackets, could you?" Cillian grumbled next to me, his teeth chattering from the cold.

"Oh, I'm sorry, Kill. Next time I'll make sure to ask her to wait for five minutes before she runs away, so that my brothers can catch up with us and get their motherfucking jackets on." I loved my twin brother, but sometimes... God, sometimes I wanted to smash his head on the wall. "Now, can you two actually move your asses? Tristan," I glanced at him, "I still don't see you calling the fucking guards. What are you waiting for? An official invitation to do it?"

"Jesus fuck, are you on your period today or something?" *Real comedians.* "I already alerted them. Alejandro is at the gate with the rest of the guys. She isn't going anywhere."

"I swear to God, Tristan, I'll cut your tongue off and feed it to the dog."

"But we don't have a dog," he snickered. "Besides, your psychotic asses would miss my lovely comments."

He probably fell on his head as a baby. There was no other explanation for the idiocy that sometimes came out of his mouth.

"Takes one to know one, Tris." Cillian said.

"Can you both just shut up?" The driveway was completely

empty, not one single guard around, and I started believing that he actually did what I asked from him. "I can't hear my own thoughts from all the jabbering going on."

"Hey, you aske—"

A female scream sliced through the air, all three of us stopping immediately. A sinister smile spread across Cillian's face and I could almost hear his thoughts. Every time I looked at my brother, only one word came to my mind.

Chaos.

Complete and utter destruction. A hurricane destroying everything in its path. Where Tristan was the coolheaded one, Cillian was the complete opposite. That thirst for blood was always there in his eyes. I often caught myself imagining what our lives would have looked like if this wasn't the path they had laid out for us. It wasn't like we ever had a choice, but imagining things that would never be possible sometimes helped me to get through the day. When your life was planned out even before your birth, there was almost nothing you could do to avoid it. I was born to lead Nightingale Outfit, and Cillian was born to be a killer.

When you have something beneath your skin, constantly pulling and pushing, calling and maiming, you eventually stop fighting. It takes over, creating something else.

Something different.

Something you never wanted to be.

Cillian never wanted to be this. My brother loved life, he loved people, but the same people he loved, were the people who destroyed him. There was a time when those dark orbs sparkled with happiness, instead of the infinite depth of darkness living inside of him. We all had our demons, but sometimes, for some of us, those demons won. His hands were twitching, almost reaching for the knife I knew he carried with him. I had no doubt that when the first opportunity presented itself to him, she would end up dead.

Unease washed over me, and I scowled, confused at my own feelings. I wanted her gone. I wanted to see her suffering, but the other part of me, the part that still loved her no matter what, that part wanted to protect her. That part wanted to take her far away from here, where I wasn't me, and she wasn't the object of our pain. But that part could also go fuck itself, because she wasn't getting any part of me. I wasn't going to lose my brothers over someone like her.

I already lost too much.

In the middle of a blizzard, with the cold hitting my cheeks, I recognized the figure walking toward us. I mean, it was rather hard not to, with the way he was built. Alejandro has been working for us for the last six years, and I could still remember the first time I saw him. The man resembled mini Hulk, minus the constant rage.

The constant rage part of the personality belonged to Cillian.

I snickered at the sight in front of me. Ophelia looked like a little child, draped over his shoulder, hitting him in the stomach with her legs. I couldn't see her face, but I could see her red panties covering her ass. And what an ass it was.

She was far skinnier than before, but the muscles on her legs were still visible. The result of hours and hours of grueling training all of us had to take. But those legs weren't just pleasant to look at. I knew firsthand that those were made to kill.

Jesus fuck, snap out of it.

I shook my head, trying to steer my thoughts in another direction. Hate, revenge, pain... I wondered if she still liked pain, and my cock hardened at the picture forming in my mind. Her, spread out on my bed, tied to the bedpost, completely at my mercy. Blood seeping from the wounds on her legs, on her chest, arms and stomach. Tristan stared at me, and I hated that knowing look on his face. He knew what I was thinking about. He always did when it came to her. He knew what I felt for her even before I did.

"What?" I snapped, rearranging myself, hating my body's reaction to her. He shrugged, smirking at me, and without another word focused his attention to her and Alejandro.

"Let me down!" she yelled at Alejandro. "Tell me, fucker, do you know what balls look like when you cut them off and skin them?" When he kept quiet, she continued, "Because I do. And trust me, I'll enjoy seeing your little Ping-Pong balls skinned. I heard that the omelet from those is pretty tasty. Have you tried it?"

Alejandro started smiling at her remarks until his eyes met mine and all the traces of his amusement were gone. I knew she would do it, given the chance. Her weapons of choice were always knives. Sharp, pointy little fuckers, and she knew how to use them.

"Gentlemen." Alejandro nodded at us, stopping a few feet away from our spot.

"Oh, is it the three assholes?" She tried pushing herself upward, but his arm tightened against her body, pushing her down. "Shit man, they can see my ass like this. Not that it isn't a lovely ass, but still."

She was a walking bipolar disaster. Just a couple of minutes ago, she'd been trying to run away, barely muttering a word, and now... All of a sudden, she couldn't shut up.

"Is Kieran here? Oh babe, if you're here, I hope you're enjoying the view, because this is the only time you'll be seeing my ass."

And just like that, the urge to take her over my knee, and see the red handprint on her ass arose inside of me. She had no idea what kind of a fucking carnival she was about to be part of. We had killer clowns, psycho maniacs and me.

"Should I restrain her, boss?" Alejandro asked, and only then did I notice the red streak traveling down his face. So, she still had her claws. Here I thought that this whole ordeal would be pure boredom.

"No, just lock her in her room."

"But it's my time to play," Cillian whined, his lips forming into a pout. "I still didn't get to cut her."

"Kill," I rubbed the spot between my eyes, "just, please... Not today, okay? You'll get your chance."

"Boss?" Alejandro asked again.

"Just to her room, Alejandro. I'll deal with her later."

He started walking away, when that little hellfire spoke again.

"Because the only way Kieran knows how to keep a woman is to either kill her or lock her up."

Alejandro continued walking toward the house while I stood there, unmoving, staring at her. That wild chestnut-colored hair seemed like it had a mind of its own, spilling all over the place. Her eyes met mine, but there was nothing there —just a bored, blank expression staring back at me.

No defiance.

No anger.

And, no pain.

She wanted a fight? I would give her war.

10

OPHELIA

Time.

We always think we have time, but that's just a lie we keep telling ourselves in order to feel better about wasted years behind us. I thought I had time to fix the shit I got myself into, to get Ava out of there, but life had other plans. Time is a fickle bitch. It tricks you into believing you have a bright tomorrow, but it never comes. The only thing you get is misery and years filled with regrets.

Even now as I was lying on the bed in a darkened room, my wrists tied together to the bedpost and my legs spread apart, chains on my ankles, I still thought I had time. Just enough time to do what I had to. I wasn't afraid of them, at least not in the way that most people would be.

I was afraid of what being this close to Kieran would mean for me. I was scared the emotions I kept buried would erupt, and that the avalanche would swallow me whole.

I was fucking terrified that for the first time in my life, I wouldn't be able to do the job I had to do.

The human body is an easy thing to break, but our minds are what keep us going, what keep us strong. I was afraid they would finally break my mind, and I very well knew that that was Kieran's plan. He wasn't going to let me go, not unless I was rolled out in a coffin. What they showed me yesterday was just the beginning of what they had planned.

The last four years have been like a walk through Hell for me, but the demon tormenting me didn't have claws and bright red eyes. My demon was a ghost of a girl with a human face, a kind smile and an exuberant laugh.

We had an angel connecting all of us, and we failed to protect her. I'm sure I wasn't the only one whom she haunted every night. It was there, visible in the eyes of her brothers.

The last four years gave me time to think. When you're running away from your past and from the punishment they wanted to inflict on you, the only things you're really doing are running and thinking.

But no matter how hard I wracked my brain about that night, I would always come back to ground zero. I had more questions than answers.

I started pulling on my restraints, but I knew it was futile trying to get myself out of here like this. I needed a plan, and if their bloodthirsty looks were anything to go by, I needed it fast. I didn't have enough time to mess around.

Get myself out of these chains, get some sort of a weapon, and do the job.

I had no idea what time it was, but my bladder was screaming at me, and if somebody didn't come soon, I'm pretty sure I was going to pee my pants. People seriously had to stop putting me in dark rooms knocked out and start facing me properly.

Oh no, wait. I know.

This was probably one of their lovely little mind games. I mean, they tried, I had to give them that. Isolated me, left me alone, I wouldn't be surprised if they tried to starve me.

"Fuckety fuck," I grunted. The skin of my throat was burning, thanks to Cillian's choking session earlier. I was still freezing from my little stunt outside, but I had no regrets. That was funny as hell, and thanks to that, I now knew that they had guards placed along the fence. Alejandro seemed like a cool guy, though.

Now if only somebody would come and get me, so that I could pee, it would be brilliant.

"Hello!" I yelled with as much strength as I could muster, but the only answer I got was the buzzing of the air conditioning and my shallow breaths. "Are you fuckers just going to leave me here? If this is your brilliant plan, I am highly disappointed."

Come on. I was getting bored, and I actually wanted to have some fun. I didn't haul my ass all the way to the East Coast for nothing. Their behavior yesterday—wait, was it yesterday?—was promising me a good time. Now they kept quiet. I didn't like it.

"Seriously? Is this all you've got?" I huffed, the chains on my legs rattling with every movement. "Cillian!" I chuckled. "Don't you want to play?"

I could bet on my collection of knives he wanted nothing more, but the party pooper, or well, Kieran, was probably stopping him. Cillian wanted me dead more than any of them, and I was counting on it.

He had a strong body but a fragile mind, and I wanted to pick it apart.

"Cillian! I know you want to see me bleed," I continued taunting. I wasn't a patient person, and I was pretty sure they knew it. Why wait? If they were going to fuck me up, they should've started already.

"You guys are all bark but no bite!" I wanted to feel their

teeth on my skin. I wanted them to cut through, because when I got my hands on them, I wouldn't be waiting to attack.

I was starving, freezing and if I fainted again, I would be extremely pissed. My stomach growled, and I had a feeling I would kick an elderly lady right now if she stood between me and food.

Just as I braced myself for another cheering-squad tryout with my yelling, the door slammed open, and I could see the dark shadow standing there. He was much shorter than the brothers, so it definitely wasn't any of them. With quick strides, he came inside the room, crouching right next to me.

The only other person I knew by name was Alejandro, the mini-Hulk who brought me in here after my escape plan failed. I'd be able to recognize a couple of guards I tried fighting, but this one... I've never seen him before.

His hair was cut short, almost to his scalp, and in the darkness of the room, I couldn't exactly see the color. His almond-shaped eyes started raking over my body, stopping at my hips and the bunched shirt around my waist. Ah, there it was, an interest. As he turned his head to check out my legs, I could see the tattoo of a snake extending from his neck, toward the side of his head.

I loved tattoos on men, but this one looked truly disgusting. I always hoped Kieran would get some more, sans the same snake tattoo on his arm, but he never did.

He was always Mr. Clean-Cut, and now that I thought about it, it was actually pissing me off. Over the years, I obtained several tattoos myself, and I couldn't wait to get some more.

A cold hand touched my upper thigh just above the skull tattoo I got years ago, and I immediately knew what this guy wanted.

"See something you like?" I used my sultriest voice, something I've learned over the years. Men were simple creatures, and whoever said otherwise just didn't know how to play them like the puppets they actually were. Show them a little bit of skin, some interest, and voila, you got what you wanted. You got them on their knees.

"Would you like to play, big boy?" Bile gathered in the back of my throat at my own words, but I swallowed it down, fluttering my lashes in the flirtiest way possible. I spread my legs further, the chains at my ankles clanking in the otherwise silent room. I wanted to play, and this one was a perfect candidate.

He kept glancing between me and the still open door, but I could almost see the wheels turning inside his head. Oh, he wanted this. He wanted me, and for a second there, I actually felt bad for the poor soul.

Come on, say yes. Play with fire.

"What's your name, darling?" He finally looked at my face, a sinister look in his eyes.

That's right. He definitely wanted this. He was a perfect pawn to bring the other three here.

His hand snaked over my ribcage, slow strokes caressing the skin there. I took a sharp breath, and his eyes sparkled in the dark, thinking I actually enjoyed this.

"You're a good little whore, aren't you?" He grabbed my chin, squeezing my face. "You want to play, whore?"

I smiled eagerly, trying to nod my head.

"You want to play with my cock?"

Oh, Jesus fucking Christ, the way he said it, you would think he sported a python in his pants.

"You want me to fill you up until you scream for everyone to hear?"

"Yes, yes, give it to me," I panted, leading him on. "Please... I've been a bad girl."

Insert vomiting right here, please.

"How bad?" He stood up and started unbuckling his pants. So fucking predictable.

"Very bad." I licked my lips when he finally dropped his pants, along with his underwear, and his 'big cock' appeared inches away from my face. I bit down on my lips, stifling the laughter threatening to erupt from my chest. Honestly, I've seen shrimps bigger than that.

"You want to suck it?" he continued, breaking through my daze. "Open your mouth wide."

Maybe I should've told him that it could've fit inside even if I didn't open wide. His tip slid over my lips, the precum gathered there sour on my tongue.

Seriously dude, there were ways to make it taste a bit better. I felt sorry for all the females that had to do this before me.

He groaned as I swirled my tongue over the head, and I knew that this one won't be eliciting my gag reflex.

Maybe if I was pixie sized?

He started groaning, moving his hips back and forth, his cock sliding over my lips. Eyes closed, his whole attention focused on the desire and need to come.

Humans are interesting beings. We can be serial killers, have serious control-freak issues, but, once desire took over, we completely detached ourselves from the here and now, succumbing to our deepest desires.

"Yeah, baby, just like that." *You would think I was deep throating him.* "That's it. Suck it."

I locked my jaw, applying pressure to his cock, as he gripped my hair, moving faster. I knew he was close to the finish line, and it was now or never.

While I sort of, kind of, alright, just a little bit, felt bad for him, I was gleaming because he would never have a chance to harass another female again. Did you know that human teeth can cut through most flesh, even some bone? I mean, cannibals didn't have shark teeth, but they still ate human meat just like we did animals.

This is why I knew I could do what I planned next. I've never tried it though, but I've wanted to, multiple times, in fact, over the span of the last eight or so years.

When his cock hardened even more, his grunts and gasps coming faster, I clamped my teeth around the bulbous head. They always told us it was like a lollipop, right? Well, I was the type to bite through lollipops.

He didn't stop at first, quickening his pace, but I wasn't going to be swallowing some bastard's cum, especially when it tasted so fucking bad. Just like a chicken leg, or lollipop, or a cucumber. I bit down just below the head, applying pressure and stopping his movements.

"What- the?" he stammered. "What the fuck, bitch?" He started pulling my hair, panic apparent in his voice. "Let go, psycho."

The sound of tearing flesh, him screaming above me… It sounded heavenly.

"Ahhh!" His scream penetrated the air, the pressure on my skull increasing. I was pretty sure there would be bald spots on my scalp. "Let go, let go…"

As he tried pulling me off of him, I locked my jaw harder, tasting a coppery liquid in my mouth. Oooo, we were finally getting to the golden mine.

"Help!" he screamed. "Somebody fucking help me!"

Just imagine what I would be able to do if my hands weren't tied. I couldn't look up to see the look on his face, but I couldn't stop either because stopping wouldn't get me to where I wanted. I drowned out his annoying voice and focused on the task at hand.

Let's be honest, I was hungry, cold, I needed a toilet, and some motherfucker thought I would give him a blow job free of charge. It was funny how pitched his voice got with every inch I bit.

"What the fuck?" the new voice echoed through the room. My teeth connected together finally, and the small head dropped into my mouth.

Nasty. But fucking cool.

My lovely bodyguard fell to the floor, screaming and shouting, holding his dismembered manhood. I spat out the part that used to be connected to him, and turned my head toward the intruder. Oh, peachy, just who I needed to see.

Tristan stood on the threshold, his face pale, disbelief in his eyes, taking in the scene in front of him. I grinned and channeled my inner *Carrie*. It wasn't pig blood, but I couldn't exactly choose, could I?

"Oh, Tris," I licked the blood from my lower lip, "did you come to join us?"

"What the fuck did you do, Ophelia?"

I tried to shrug, well, as good as I could being chained and all, while he approached the quivering mess of a man on the floor. Who knew that biting off a dick could cause so much blood? I should've used it in my torture sessions a long time ago.

Well, maybe with knives instead of teeth.

"Kieran!" he called.

"Oh, goody, more brothers for the party."

He turned to me, disgust written all over his face. "You're a psycho, you know that?"

"Ah, I am sorry, Tris. Maybe I should've let him rape me, or another poor woman in the future. Oh, I know, maybe all of you guys can suck each other's dicks while I watch. How about that? You can do what he was trying to make me do."

"You could've told us. We wo—"

"You wouldn't do shit, my friend. You wouldn't do shit and you wouldn't even feel bad about it." And we both knew it.

The coppery taste in my mouth wasn't going to go away until I washed my mouth, but seeing as none of them wanted to move me from here, I had to bite my tongue and wait.

I also needed a shower and a new shirt. My back was aching from the position I was in, and the moaning from Mr. Not-So-Big Cock was raking on my nerves.

"What the fuck?"

Why did all of them sound like a broken record? What the fuck indeed, leaving me with this idiot for a guard. Kieran just stood there, looking between me and the mess on the floor.

Oh, K. Look at him, hiring rapists for bodyguards. Must have been a coincidence. *Not.*

"What happened?" he asked in a calm voice, but I knew him. He was furious. It was his I-am-about-to-fuck-you-up voice, I just wasn't too sure if he wanted to fuck *me* up, or the man I already fucked up.

"Your dog here," I looked toward the guard who seemed to start losing consciousness, "thought it would be a good idea to show me how he treats girls. Or wait, what was that he called me? Ah yes, a whore. So, I decided to bite his dick off. You know, to show him what this whore can actually do to him."

He walked toward me and started smearing the blood on my cheek. "Jake," his eyes focused on me, "is this true?"

Not that Jake answered him. He was too busy fainting with his dick bleeding out.

"Call the doctor, Tris. I'll deal with him later."

Could I be there to watch at least? Maybe he could join him, seeing as both of them were cut from the same cloth. Such a fucking hypocrite.

My demons were singing loudly, wanting to play, begging to be released. There was one demon who called to my personal hell. Just like a moth to the flame, there was something inside of me that would always be attracted to this asshole.

Even when I wanted to strangle him.

Why was it that the thing we wanted the most, was the same thing that could destroy us?

"What are you going to do?" I couldn't take my eyes off of him, even when Tristan started talking again. "I am not leaving you with *her*."

I mean, seriously Tristan? I was quite literally tied to the bedpost. Harmless little girl.

"Kieran?"

My focus was solely on him, as he started pulling my shirt lower, covering my stomach.

"I am going to play, Brother."

11

KIERAN

Violent endings and violent beginnings. A disaster none of us could've predicted. Had I known the monster swirling in the pits of her soul, I would've never given her my everything.

I thought we would have a happy ending.

I thought she would be the one. I opened my soul to her, was so consumed by all this love I felt for her, and the only thing she gave me in return was sorrow and pain. I gave her my soul, my heart, and I would've given her my life. But she didn't want it.

She chose to betray me in the worst way possible. She chose to rip away everything from me.

I thought our love was strong, that it could withstand everything they were throwing at us. I thought nothing and no one would be able to destroy it.

Not a man.

Not a woman.

And certainly not death.

But I forgot who she was. I never even realized that she would be our ultimate demise, our destruction. I was so consumed by her, by the love I felt, and when the flames went out, the love I felt burned me from the inside out, until the only things left were ashes and hatred.

Hate.

Love.

Hate.

Love.

When did the lines get so blurred? Was it when she put that knife into Ava's stomach, or did we start hating each other long before, thinking it was love? I could only blame myself, because all the warning signs were there. Everything I should've paid attention to was there, but I was too blind to see them.

I ignored all of the warning signs, thinking I could save her from this shitshow. But Ophelia didn't need saving. No, she needed to die. She needed to be tortured, broken and thrown away. You can't save a person who didn't want to be saved. The apple doesn't fall far from the tree, and she was truly her father's daughter. A murderous, traitorous bitch.

Everything I needed to know was always there, I just never wanted to hear what everybody else was saying. Love makes you blind. It makes you weak, because the only thing you can see, the only person you think you can trust, is the one holding your heart in their hands. And she held mine.

Ophelia laid there, the oversized shirt she wore bunched at her hips, and that fucking psychopathic smile on her face. Jake's blood caked her lips, cascading over her chin and toward her chest. I wanted to fuck her, and I wanted to kill her, and not necessarily in that order. I wanted to fuck her out of my system, out of my blood, so that the only thing I would remember would be the lies she told me. The pain she caused us, and all of the suffering that came from me loving her.

I thought about the kid she used to be, before the darkness

took over. What was so bad about the life we had that she had to take the one good thing from us? Our plans, the feeling of her body in my arms, that sweet fucking smell of vanilla… My past had haunted me for so long, and now that it laid in front of me, I didn't know what to do.

"*Don't you dare fuck this up, Kieran,*" my brothers warned me the day before we finally took her.

"*Do you still love her?*" Cillian asked.

Did I?

Did I still love her? Would I still bleed for her, burn the whole world and stand on the ashes of what I've done? Four years ago, I would have.

I would've betrayed my whole family for the girl laying on this bed now, but not anymore. My eyes raked over her body, over the bruising at her neck… Jesus fuck, even looking the way she was, she was still the prettiest girl I had ever laid my eyes on. Her hair was splayed over the white pillow beneath her head. If it were up to my brothers, she would be inside the cage like an animal.

Not that she wasn't one.

The blood made her look feral, unhinged, crazy, and I used to love her crazy. I fucking reveled in it, because I knew that only I could tame her. The nights she would wait for me in our bed, teasing me, goading me, those nights were imprinted in my mind, not even a thousand different women could erase it. I never asked the questions I should've asked. She fed me lies, and I ate them like the idiot I was.

I sat next to her, the bare skin of her thigh brushing against my hip. I wanted to devour her, mark her, brand her skin. Make her remember how much I loved her, even though she never loved me. I needed to show her everything she'd lost, because even if she never loved me, I knew that there was a part of her forever connected to me. I wanted her hate more than I wanted her love. Because after all was said and done, the only thing we were left with was the dark abyss of hatred, swallowing us whole.

"Are you going to punish me, Kieran?" Her lashes fluttered against her cheeks, fake innocence transforming her face. But those eyes, those eyes weren't hiding the demons now. For the first time I could see her for what she was, and I hated what I saw in her. The reflection of myself.

A monster, a murderer, the two people shaped by the factors they had no control of. Fucked over by the family that was supposed to protect them.

I glided my hand over her thigh, stopping at the hem of the shirt. *My shirt*. Her breath hitched as I moved higher, over her hip, toward her navel, feeling the smooth skin beneath my fingers. The skull tattoo on her thigh pulled at me, bringing flashbacks of a time long lost.

Pax Aeterna.

Eternal Peace.

I touched the letters engraved on her skin, and I could still remember the day she had it done. The darkness I saw in her eyes then, has been haunting me for a very long time. The crown of thorns, the soulless eyes on the piece; I didn't know it was the representation of who she really was.

Did she ever think about the future we could've had together? The things we could've done, places we could've run to. Was I haunting her the way she was haunting me? She was still in everything. In every breath, in every day, in every memory I had, she was my personal demon.

I had no second thoughts over the plan we had for her. After all, she was the one who chose this. She chose darkness over light, over the opportunity for a better life. We could've left all of this behind, but she had to fuck it up.

I gripped her ribcage, the bones there biting into my hand. I wanted her to fear me, but all I got was a wider smile on her face. She licked her lips, removing the remaining blood there.

"Are you going to hurt me?" She squirmed beneath my touch. "Cut me, fuck me..." she trailed off. "Kill me—"

"You'd like that, wouldn't you?" I cut her off.

"Yes," she moaned, closing her eyes, throwing her head back.

"So eager." I leaned down and pressed a kiss on her collarbone. "You always loved the pain." I bit down. "Do you crave it now; do you want to escape from your head?"

I pulled the knife from my boot, bringing it between us. Her eyes widened, arousal sparkling in them. My little psycho really wanted this.

"Do you have any idea how many times I've imagined this?" I spread her legs, cupping her pussy in my hand. "How many times I've dreamed about you, just like this. Tied up, at my mercy."

Dragging the blade of the knife down her chest, I circled around her nipple, until the tip became visible through the white shirt. Her chest was rising and falling with steady breaths, her eyes focused on my hand. I kneeled between her legs, the heat of her pussy penetrating through the thin layer of cotton that separated my hand from her bare skin. I stroked my fingers through her folds, and the whimper escaped her lips.

"Kieran—"

"Shhh." I placed the blade on her lips, silencing her. "Just feel, baby girl. Let yourself feel."

"Please—"

I gathered the fabric of her panties in my hand, pushing them against her clit.

"I don't want to hear a sound coming from your mouth." I started moving the fabric up and down, the intoxicating smell of her pussy filling my nostrils. She started pushing into my hand, into the soaked panties. "That's right, let it go."

Her eyes closed and the redness started spreading over her chest. I slowly lifted the knife from her lips. Her eyes opened and connected with mine. I used to get so lost in those eyes — those traitorous eyes.

"You want to come, baby girl?" Goosebumps erupted over her skin as I pulled the knife from her mouth toward her cheek. "Should I let you?" I taunted. "Or should I leave you like this?"

The chains rattled against the bed with every movement of her legs. Her eyes rolled into the back of her head as I increased the pressure on her clit. Shaky breaths escaped her lungs, and my own started matching hers.

"Breathe." I caressed her neck. "Just breathe, Phee."

Eyes unfocused, she started pulling her hands, the ties digging into her skin. I could see the bruises already forming on her wrists.

Mine.

Mine.

Mine.

Body and soul.

I smiled at her, and without a warning, pushed the blade into the skin on her cheek. Blood spilled over the edge at the same time a moan escaped her mouth. I felt high from the sight of her blood, my own boiling in my veins. Without a sound, she pulled against the knife, cutting herself deeper, those hooded, ocean eyes zeroing in on me. She bit her lip, trying to push further, go higher, but the ropes held her in the same place, limiting her movements.

Mark her, destroy her, the voices in my head chanted. *Make her ours. Make her pay.*

It was only fitting to do so. Ophelia wrecked my soul, and now I was going to wreck her body.

I pushed at her chest, holding her on the bed, while her blood slowly trickled down her cheek. I leaned toward her, caging her head between my arms, the blade still in my hand. She pushed and pulled, but I could tell it was without a real fight. She wanted this.

She wanted to be destroyed, demolished, brought to her knees... And I, I was going to be the bringer of all of those.

"Do you like me now, baby," I whispered, hovering over her lips. "Do you like how it hurts?"

My tongue darted out, licking from her jaw, biting and soothing, toward the cut on her cheek. The taste of her blood was the best opium, but it wasn't enough. I needed more. So much more, and she was going to give it to me. With my lips coated in her blood, I licked the bloody trail, all the way to the wound already closing down.

But we can't have that, can we now?

"K," she whimpered. "Please."

"Are you wet for me, Ophelia?" I bit on her cheek, my teeth sinking into the wound.

"Argh," she cried out, her moans music to my ears.

My cock hardened as her pelvis lifted from the bed, meeting mine. The metallic taste of her blood drove me crazy, like an addict with the first shot of heroine. She was soaking through my pants, moaning in my ear, a masochist in disguise.

When all you ever knew how to do is bring the pain, you start craving your own.

I ground against her, pushing her on the bed, my cock straining against my pants. It was pain and pleasure mixed in one.

Bite.

Lick.

Rinse and repeat, but I wasn't stopping. This was only the start of our game.

"Your blood tastes like heaven, Phee." I gripped her hair in my hand, dropping the knife next to her head. "But it feels like poison running through my veins."

"Please, Kieran," she panted. "Please."

"That's right. Beg me. I want to hear you scream for me."

She threw her head back, exposing her neck to me. I clutched her hip in one hand and pulled her harder against me.

"Do you want me, my little psycho?" She trembled beneath my hand, her whole body shaking.

"Or," I took a hold of the knife once again and held it in front of her face. "This."

Her gaze flickered between the knife and me, but the hitch in her breathing at my suggestion told me everything I needed to know.

"You're a bad, bad bitch." I leaned down, licking the seam of her lips. "Aren't you?"

"Kieran…"

I bit her lower lip, pulling it to me. "What did I tell you? Keep quiet."

I kissed my way down her neck, biting and teasing, leaving my mark wherever I could. Her breasts were straining against the shirt, two round globes begging to be touched. Pulling the shirt all the way to her neck, I latched onto one nipple first, kneading the other one with my free hand. The mewling sounds coming from her as I played with her pushed me over the edge, and in the next moment, I was staring at her pussy covered by the soaked panties.

"A beautiful demon," I whispered and bit her clit through the fabric of her panties. "A beautiful chaos."

She was watching me with hooded eyes, her lower lip between her teeth. I lazily dragged the knife over her thigh, over that sinister tattoo she branded herself with, and toward her cunt. With precise cuts, I sliced the two lines on the apex of her thigh, just above the skull, marking her with an x. Her other leg bounced against the bed, but the chains forbade her from moving further. The blade of the knife cut through the fabric easily, exposing her completely to me.

Swollen, and so, so wet.

"Do you want my knife, baby?" I spread her lips with the blade and looked at her. "Or do you want my cock?"

She kept quiet, not a word from her, but this was one thing she had to answer.

"Tell me!" I cupped her pussy, squeezing the lips together. "What do you want?"

"K-Kieran…"

"Answer me!"

"Knife," she screamed. "I want the knife."

The muscles on my face almost hurt from the strength of the smile that spread over at her words.

Without a warning, I removed my hand and pulled her ass toward me, exposing her fully.

"Then that's what you'll get."

I dragged my finger from her clit to her opening, collecting the juices there. Turning the knife in my hand, I slammed the handle into her, pushing it to the hilt.

"Kieran!" Her whole body arched at the intrusion.

The blade glinted in front of me, a beautiful sight really. If she moved her legs, it would cut right through her skin. Flicking my fingers over the little bundle of nerves nestled there, I started pulling the knife out, holding it from the dull side.

"Does this feel good?"

She wasn't prepared for it, I knew it. The evidence was visible on the handle as I pulled it out of her. A bloody trail coated the green handle, and I could see her pussy clenching around it. I squeezed her clit between my fingers, evoking a loud screech from her.

"That's right."

"P-Please… Kieran!"

I started moving the handle back and forth, every time pinching her clit harder. Her panting got louder, and the squirming in her legs told me she was close.

"Are you going to come for me?" I increased my pace. "Are you going to come all over this knife, like the good little whore you are?"

"Yeeees," she drew out. "Faster. Please, please, please… F-Faster, Kieran."

I abruptly stopped at her pleas, my chest warming at the sight of a frown forming between her eyebrows.

"You don't get to call the shots now, remember?"

"Yes, yes I remember." She nodded, already lost in the pleasure I was bringing her, chasing her own delirium.

"Good." I continued with the punishing strokes. "I can see your pussy squeezing the handle. How badly do you want to come?"

"Fuck you, Kieran."

"Well, that's what you're kind of doing." I chuckled.

She started moving her hips, matching my thrusts. I wanted to throw away the knife, untie her and bend her over the bed as I fucked her with my cock, as I destroyed her inside and out.

But that would have to wait.

With two more strokes, she started shaking, her orgasm tearing through her body.

"Shit, shit, shit…"

I threw the knife on the bed, replacing it with three fingers, easily finding her little nub. I latched onto her clit, my tongue swirling around, collecting her juices. She tasted heavenly, pulling at my desire for her.

"Fuuuuck!"

I kept my ministrations, even after she started clenching around my fingers, her juices coating her thighs, my hand, my face.

"S-Stop. No more. Please."

"No. Gimme one more."

She tossed around the bed, her limbs flailing with their limited movement, but I didn't stop. If anything, I increased my pace until I could feel the second wave of her inner walls clutching my fingers.

"Fuuuuck!"

Her scream echoed around the room, and with one final lick through her folds, I removed my hand, licking my fingers clean.

"Mmmm, delicious." She glared at me, her eyes two daggers slicing through me. "This is going to be so much fun."

I chuckled as she tried to move from the position she was in.

"I am going to rip your throat out, Kieran."

"I think you would rather be sucking my dick." I kissed the corner of her mouth. "Get some rest, darling. This is just the beginning."

12

OPHELIA

Motherfucking piece of shit.

I didn't have enough words to describe what a fucking prick Kieran Nightingale was. Well, if I was being honest, I wasn't really sure if I wanted to stab him or to throw myself off the nearest cliff for once again falling for his antics. Stupid body, stupid hormones, stupid memories pushing me to him. How was I ever supposed to get out of here and get things done if he could disarm me with one single touch?

A knife.

I allowed him to fuck me with a knife. I allowed myself to succumb to my deepest desires, and even if it meant that what he did was out of hatred, I still did it. I craved his touch, his warmth, because for the longest time, he was the only light in the infinite darkness I was thrown into.

So what if the look on his face screamed revenge? I didn't need his love to feel good. Right?

Our hearts didn't matter anymore, because one of us… One of us won't be getting out of this alive. Over the years, I've imagined how our first meeting would go. At first, there were versions where Kieran found out the truth and sought me on his own, asking me to come back home. I quickly realized wishful thinking could only fuck me up more, and my messed-up head didn't need that. When the truth came to the light, the only version I had in my head was my knife sticking out from his chest.

No love, no regrets, just the end of the road for us. It was funny, really. I never questioned the tightness in my chest after every single touch, kiss or moment spent together. But now I know.

It was the impending doom our relationship was always sentenced to. Sometimes people make something beautiful, using all of the broken pieces. The two of us, we managed to turn those pieces into dust, killing our hearts in the process.

I always tried to understand his pain, the lies he was fed that clouded his mind. But how could a person promise his eternal love to you and then break your trust and your heart? I wanted to justify his actions, to try and find those little pieces of him I loved so much, but with every passing day, it became harder and harder to remember them. When my anger took over instead of the helplessness I felt, I knew we would be chasing each other until the end of our time.

They threw me into the darkness and expected me to find peace. They didn't expect me to survive, but I did. I came out smarter, better... What didn't kill me made me stronger. When every single person abandoned me, leaving me to my own devices, I became the darkness they all feared so much.

I became the dragon they thought I would never be.

He made me bleed, the wound on my cheek stinging with every movement I made. It wasn't the first time, and it sure as hell won't be the last. The cold I felt before was replaced with the fury emanating from my soul, spreading heat throughout my body.

Anger is the best fuel, at least that's what I've heard people say. He thought fucking me into submission would be the way to go. Silly little monster, he didn't know that his demons didn't scare me anymore. They were child's play compared to the things I've seen over the last four years.

The things they taught us were nothing compared to the depravity I saw. It didn't matter if you were old or young—the people I met would fuck you up and destroy the humanity you were born with. The world I was born into was full of privileges for people like me, but that one... They didn't give a fuck. The strongest ones survived, and the weak ones got eaten. The rules of the wilderness.

I felt sore, and I had no doubt that the idiot made me bleed in more places than just my cheek. After his little game, he just walked out of the room, leaving me half naked and completely exposed. My panties were ruined, the shirt was above my breasts and if I craned my neck, I could see the two symmetrical cuts he left above my tattoo.

My reminder.

My crown of fucking thorns.

I started shaking my head as if the motion would help me erase the memories of a different time. During my training, they told me to forget, to detach myself, and I did. But they never told me about the ghosts haunting you during the dark of the night when all of the distractions were away, when all you could think of were the people you destroyed. And you would do it again, and again and again. And you wouldn't stop.

I couldn't stop.

I clutched the ropes with my hands, trying to pull myself higher. My neck was pained from the position I was in, and my mouth was parched from the lack of water I hadn't had in God knows how long. My back screamed in pain as the chains on my legs pulled tighter with the small movement I made.

"Fuck," I groaned, my throat burning from the lack of water. I looked to my left at the open door Kieran had walked through. If I only managed to release one of my hands, I'd be able to do the same to the other one, as well as my legs.

I craned my neck and scanned the headboard the ropes were attached to. Taking a deep breath, I started yanking the ropes, thanking all of the possible gods and goddesses that they didn't tie it tightly.

One...

Two...

Three.

The headboard hit the wall with each and every pull, but these fuckers bought beds with sturdy headboards. The little hoops my ropes were tied through just rattled against it, but the headboard didn't break.

"God fucking dammit."

"You need some help there?" I froze and slowly turned toward the sound of a new voice. The youngest Nightingale, Tristan, stood there with a smile gracing his face. Of course all of this would be extremely satisfying for all of them. Seeing me tied, naked, bloody, I guess I was just happy it wasn't Cillian who came to visit me.

"What are you doing here, Tristan?" I let go of the ropes, the pain ricocheting through my wrists. I needed to stretch or kill something.

I was leaning toward the second option.

"I came to see how you're doing, of course." Cheeky son of a bitch. "And," he came closer, "I came to take you to the bathroom."

"You want to take me to the bathroom?" I asked with skepticism in my voice. "How fucking generous of you."

"Oh, birdy, don't be like that." The bed dipped as he sat next to me. "Wasn't I always your favorite one?"

He was, until he wasn't anymore, until he chained me to the wall and refused to believe me.

"Are we feeling sentimental, Tristan? You want me to hug you and kiss your boo-boos?" The smile disappeared almost instantly. "Do you want to know why you were my favorite one?"

He inched closer, his eyes flickering over my body. "Do tell, birdy."

"Because you were the weakest one." I moved my butt further away from him. "Because no matter what, you could never live up to the name your brothers created. Kieran was the calculating one, always on the lookout, always thinking about his next step. Cillian was the psychopath, a fellow loose end, and he never minded killing whoever stood in his way. But you..." I swallowed as his gaze clashed with mine. "You were nothing but a good little soldier. I could always use you, and abuse you, and you would never even know."

"You're a fucking bitch, you know that?" He traced his thumb over my cut cheek and pressed into the still bleeding wound. A moan escaped my mouth, when all I wanted to do was scream at him, but I wasn't going to give him that.

"Are you here to finish what your brother started, baby boy?" He scowled at the nickname and retracted his hand.

"Oh, I have something better for you."

I eyed him for a moment, as he retrieved the knife Kieran left on the floor and started cutting through the ropes. "You're going to love it, birdy." My hands fell above my head, all the strength I had suddenly leaving my body from the strain it went through. I lifted my head and saw him unlocking the chains from my legs as well.

"Why are you doing this?"

"I told you already, I have something for you." He leaned over me, his hand grasping my chin. "And after you see my lovely, little present, you're going to tell me everything I want to know."

I wanted nothing more than to remove that little smirk with my fist, but I was curious to see what he wanted me to see. However, my bladder decided to remind me that I needed to go to the toilet first and this little adventure would have to wait.

"Um, okay," I said as I shook my hands as soon as he freed me. "There's only one little catch here."

"Which is?" Tristan frowned.

"I kinda need to use the toilet first." He scowled at me as I cheekily grinned. "Unless you want me to pee on the floor, or on the staircase, or—"

"No!" He cut through my little monologue. "Just hurry up. We don't have all day."

I jumped from the bed and saluted him. "Yes, boss."

"Hurry the fuck up," he gritted again. I didn't wait another second and ran to the bathroom connected to the room.

I t felt as if another life had passed from that first time I exited the room until this moment, when in reality, it couldn't have been more than a day. I kept glancing at my bruised wrists, the skin chaffed, purple and yellow. They would've left me in that room until I completely lost the use of my limbs, or worse, until I froze to death. Tristan kept a hold of my upper arm, pushing me toward the staircase I now knew led to the foyer and the first level of the house. This was my opportunity to scan my surroundings properly, but the wariness coursing through my body had me constantly glancing at him, wondering what he was up to. But hey, at least I finally got to pee and wash my face.

"Don't worry, birdy," he looked at me, "I won't hurt you.

Just wanted you to have a quick walk, maybe eat something, and then we can talk."

"Why would you want to talk to me? The last time—"

"The last time I was hurt," he cut me off. "The last time we just found our sister lying in a pool of her own blood with you above her, holding that knife. Watch your step."

Watch my step?

"What—" My foot hit something, and I would've planted face first on the ground if it wasn't for his grip.

"I said watch your step."

The stairs were in complete darkness, the lights completely shut off.

"What the fuck?"

"I warned you. Now move your ass, there are places we need to see."

Was he on fucking drugs? What was he talking about? Places we needed to see?

His hold on me started getting almost painful the closer we got to the end of the stairwell. The blinding light coming through the windows hurt my eyes, and I squinted, trying to keep them open. The only thing I could see for hours was darkness, and the daylight now was a bit too much.

"All this money, and you couldn't have gotten some curtains." I squeezed my eyes shut, trying to avoid another migraine. He chuckled next to me and stopped abruptly after a couple of steps.

"Oh God, I missed your humor. But I need you to keep your eyes open for me."

"I can't."

"Yes, you fucking can. Open those eyes, Ophelia."

I could feel him in front of me, but my body wasn't cooperating with my mind.

"I told you, I can't."

A strong grip at the nape of my neck and the welcoming pain made my eyes open on their own volition. The blue orbs were right there, his face inches from mine, and another sinister smile taking over.

"You see," he clutched my hair tighter, "I told you, you can. Now come on, I need to show you something."

My head was screaming at me, the coiling in my stomach growing stronger—hunger and pain mixing together—but he kept pulling me toward another set of stairs. The muscles in my legs were screaming at me, tight from the lack of exercise, but the idiot in front of me didn't stop. He wasn't holding my arm anymore; it was my hand now imprisoned by his.

"Where are we going?"

"Shhh." He turned to me with a finger over his lips. "You don't want to wake up the wolves."

It was the middle of a fucking day. Who slept at this hour?

With his constant pulling, I was surprised I didn't end up falling somewhere in the middle of the grand staircase. We were now on the second floor, and he looked like a little kid the night before Christmas.

You know, the little kids whose families were celebrating Christmas in the proper way.

He was bouncing in front of me, and I had to admit, it was kind of funny seeing a grown ass man behaving this way.

"This way." He pulled me to the right corridor where several doors greeted us. All of them closed, except for one.

The one at the end of the hallway, the one from where unmistakable sounds of pleasure were echoing throughout the whole area.

"Tristan," I started. "What are we doing here?"

He ignored my question and kept pulling me toward the source of a female voice. I struggled to get free from his hold, but it was futile even trying. My captor, unlike me, at least had a proper meal in the last couple of days.

"Tristan," I seethed.

The female was getting louder now, the unmistakable pleasure ensuing in that room. Something coiled tight in my lower stomach.

"Look." He pulled me closer to where he stood, just at the entrance of the room, and as my eyes took in the scene in front of me, the previous coiling dissipated from my stomach, moving into my chest and leaving a trail of anger I felt only once before.

A redhead was on all-fours, right in the middle of the bed. A redhead I knew all too well, because, you never forget a face you wanted to smash into the wall.

Cynthia-fucking-Larson was moaning, screeching, and throwing her head back, as Kieran pounded into her from behind. Her full tits bounced with every stroke of his, and it was like a bad deja vu playing right in front of me.

Me coming to his apartment.

Me trying to surprise him.

Me seeing him fucking her once before.

Me leaving and my world falling apart.

He thought he could fuck me up, and then go and fuck the first whore he could find?

Red.

Red.

Red.

All I could see was fucking red.

"You like that, baby?" His voice was raspy, strained.

"Yees," she answered in a moan, as if she knew what he felt like. As if she knew what he looked like in the middle of the night, when the whole world fell apart, and he kept screaming for someone to save him from his own mind.

I had no control over my body, over my actions, but the next thing I knew, the gun strapped into the holster at Tristan's hip was in my hand, and I stood in front of the two of them. The shock on Cynthia's face, and the mild amusement on Kieran's were driving me crazy. He laughed at me, while Cynthia tried covering her naked body with a sheet beneath her knees.

Adrenaline, pure adrenaline was what got me through my actions.

"What are you doing here, whore?" the piece of shit who I wanted to kill since our high school days dared to ask. *What am I doing here?*

"Have you ever seen a demon, Cynthia?" I scratched my temple with the barrel. "You know, a human one."

"What are you talking about?" She turned to Kieran who kept smiling. "What is she talking about, babe?"

The twitching in my eye started at her words, the need to fucking strangle her grew stronger with every second.

"Yeah, babe," I mocked. "Can you explain to your bimbo what I'm talking about?"

"Kieran," she pleaded, but I had no more patience for the slut in front of me.

"What I'm talking about," I took a few steps closer to the edge of the bed, where she still kneeled clutching that fucking sheet, "is if you've ever seen a demon walking around in human flesh. I mean, you were fucking one, so I assume that you have."

"Ophelia, darling—"

"You don't get to call me darling." With one swift movement, I gripped her hair in my hand and yanked her off the bed. She was always a tiny little thing, save for her boobs and ass. Always shorter than me, always lower than me, and I regretted failing to shoot her all those years before.

"Kieran!" she screamed, but that fucker kept sitting there,

watching the scene in front of him unfold. Of course he would enjoy this. He would even try to make this whole shitshow as me being jealous of the whole scene, when the truth was much, much worse.

"He won't help you now. You see," I pulled the safety of the gun off, and placed the barrel on her forehead, "once you sell yourself to the Devil, somebody has to collect the soul."

"No, no..." Her lower lip trembled, her whole body started shaking. "Please. I'll do anything. Please God, please—"

"God doesn't live here anymore." I grinned at her. "This is my playground, my domain, and I want to see you bleed. I wanted to do this four years ago because you took everything from me. I have always wondered what the color of your blood was. Do you know?"

"I don't—"

Before she could finish the sentence, I pulled the trigger, and a loud bang echoed through the room. The white sheet fell at my feet, the remnants of her brain, her blood, splattered on the bed behind her. Her lifeless body dropped down, coloring the floor red, and as I kneeled in front of her, the joy I always felt after each kill spread through my chest. My heart pumped faster. My blood ran warmer. Her lifeless eyes stared at my feet, and I dipped one finger into the hole in her forehead.

"Huh." I lifted my finger coated in her blood. "It's too light. I expected it to be darker."

The sudden clapping had me lifting my head higher, the gun still clutched in my hand.

"There she is." Kieran jumped from the bed, his dick bobbing between his legs. He was still hard even after my little show. "I wondered when you would show us your true colors."

My God, I forgot how beautiful he really was. His chest glistened with sweat, dripping over his six-pack, and that delicious V, leading to his hips. I wanted to fuck him, and then cut off his dick for everything he did to me.

"Fuck off." I stood up and started retreating backwards toward Tristan, but when I turned, he was nowhere to be seen. That little—

"I was fucking somebody, and you ruined my fun." He was suddenly in front of me, and I gulped at the sudden nearness. Time, I still needed time.

"I'd say I'm sorry," I placed one hand on his chest, "but I'm not. Now if you'll excuse me—"

"Why in such a rush, birdy?" He took a hold of the gun, enveloping my hand and pulled it to his temple, the barrel resting there. "Didn't you come here to kill me?"

I swallowed hard, the fine line I walked blurring with the words he said.

"Come on, pretty birdy. Tell me why you're here." He lowered the gun, pressing it against his cheek. "Are you here to hurt me?" He pressed the barrel to his lips. "Or love me?"

"I-I..."

I fucking stuttered. The safety was still off, and he moved the gun, putting it in his mouth. A sick smile spread around the gun and if I moved my finger just an inch, I could end this. I would be free.

Free of him.

Free of *them*.

But my hand started shaking instead, and I couldn't bring myself to pull the trigger.

Just do it.

Pull it. Show him, show them what they made you do. Show him what happens to those who wronged you. But my heart and my mind weren't in sync this time, and no matter how much I tried pushing myself, I couldn't.

I couldn't kill him now.

He knew it, because in the next moment the gun was out of his mouth, getting knocked from my hand. He pulled me closer, his scent intoxicating my mind. "You owe me now."

"I don't owe you shit." I started struggling, trying to break free from his grip, but he only tightened his hold on me, pulling me even closer, until my chest started grazing his. My nipples were erect, hard, and if he slipped his hand toward my pussy, he would find out how much my body was betraying me whenever I was in his proximity.

"I think you do, baby girl. See," His lips grazed my cheek. The same one he cut earlier, "I don't want to take care of this by myself." He started grinding on me, lifting the shirt I had on with every movement. "And I don't want to have another girl shot in the head because you don't want to share."

"I don't give a fuck about other girls. But this one." I looked into his eyes. "This one had to die."

"Whatever you say."

"Kieran," I bit on my lower lip, "let go of me."

"Mhmm." He nuzzled my neck. "Do you really want that?"

"Y-Yes," I stumbled over my own words. His other hand traveled down the length of my body, over my boobs, toward my stomach and finally the place he knew so well. My body wasn't cooperating with my mind, and as he reached the apex of my thighs, my legs spread on their own volition, granting him easy access.

"Are you not wearing any underwear?"

"You destroyed it." My voice sounded breathless, and I hated and loved it at the same time.

"That I did."

His lips descended toward mine, a punishing kiss ensuing between the two of us. It was a battle of wills, neither of us wanted to succumb to the other one. As I entwined my hands around his neck, he entered me with his fingers, the pain and pleasure mixing in one.

"Is this for me? Are you this wet for me?"

With punishing strokes, he started fucking me, slowly increasing his pace.

"Or are you wet for somebody else?"

"N-No." My whole body trembled, the coiling in my belly intensifying with each and every stroke. "Please, Kieran. Please—"

"What do you want, birdy?"

"I want—"

"Yes?"

"I want you to fuck me." I dropped my forehead on his shoulder. "I want you to fuck me like you hate me."

With a sudden growl emanating from his throat, he ripped his hands from me, instead taking my hips in them and pulling me upwards. I locked my ankles around his waist as he carried me to the dresser at the other end of the room. I kept kissing his neck, licking his sweet spot just beneath his ear, the goose-bumps visible on his skin.

"You're gonna be screaming my name," he spoke against my hair. Holding me with one hand, I could hear the crashing of items he threw from the dresser, and in the next second, my back hit the wall almost knocking the air from me.

His chest was rising and falling with deep breaths, and the crazed look on his face fueled my own desire for what was about to come. He was mine once, and maybe, just maybe, I could pretend he was still only that.

Only my Kieran.

My ass dragged over the wooden surface as he pulled my legs closer to the edge, and without a warning, he entered me with one swift movement, burying himself to the hilt.

"Fuuuck." He hugged me to his chest, and all coherent thoughts left my body.

"Oh my God," I breathed against his skin. The scent was driving me wild, and when he stood there, frozen inside of me, I started moving my hips, looking for friction. "Please, Kieran."

"You want this?" He pulled out, and before I could protest, he slammed inside again, holding my hips in a punishing grip. "You want me to fuck you, baby?"

"Yes, yes."

"I can't hear you, Phee."

"Fuck me!" I screamed, "Please, give it to me."

"I am going to bury myself so deep inside of you," he kissed my lips, "so, so deep, you will never forget who you belong to."

"Just move, goddammit." He chuckled against my lips, and for a moment, I thought he would stop. But no. Kieran started fucking me, really, really fucking me. He pressed against my clit, sending wave after wave of pleasure through my body.

The dresser shook beneath me, hitting the wall with every onslaught he made on my body, but I couldn't care less. I imagined we were other people, just two lovers after a big fight, fucking it out.

I imagined he loved me and I loved him, and we would lay in bed after this, sharing stories from the previous day. He wasn't the man who betrayed my trust, and I wasn't the girl who destroyed his soul.

"Kieran!"

"Yes, that's right."

His dick should've gotten a fucking medal or something, because holy Jesus Christ, I could almost feel him in my womb. He rolled his hips, hitting that sweet spot, and between the pressure he had on my clit, and the strokes between my legs, my orgasm was building with a fast pace.

"I'm… I'm gonna—"

"Are you going to come for me?" he asked breathlessly, the sheen of sweat rolling over his temple.

"Yeees. Please, please, please," I chanted.

"Not yet." He bit my lower lip, "Not until I give you permission."

"Kieran… I-I can't."

"Wait."

"Oh dear Satan, fuck, shit…" My legs were shaking, the need to move away and come closer to him rushing through me.

"You feel so fucking good." He dropped his forehead on mine. "So fucking good. So fucking tight."

I squeezed my inner walls, trying to stop my orgasm, as he snarled and claimed my mouth once again. His hips pistoned against mine, and I dropped one hand to hold onto the dresser.

"Come for me, Phee. Come on."

"Oh. My. God!" I screamed as he pinched my clit. "I'm going to—"

"Yes, come on."

"Fuuuuck." My body started shaking as his hands enveloped around me, with his dick emptying inside me.

"Jesus fuck."

The black dots danced in front of my eyes, and all I wanted was to stay in his arms forever. In this cocoon of warmth, of happiness. But reality started creeping in, and we both stiffened at the same time, realizing what we'd just done. I could see Cynthia's lifeless body behind Kieran's back, staring at us, probably cursing me from the other side.

He detached himself from me, pulling his dick out. Warmth trickled out of me, and another frightening realization crawled into my mind.

"Did you just fuck me without a condom?"

He turned away from me, crouching in front of her body.

153

"Answer me!"

I jumped from the dresser and walked toward him. He stood, turning to me with a menacing glare. His hand shot out, taking a hold of my neck and backing me toward the wall.

"Are you forgetting yourself, little birdy?" he asked in a calm voice. "This isn't your home, and you're not my guest. I fuck a lot of girls, but only the good little whores like you get to have my dick with a full service."

13

KIERAN

Cillian glared at me from the other side of the table, but I just didn't have it in me today to entertain his fucked-up mind. He wasn't happy with me fucking Ophelia, but guess what buddy? I wasn't happy with myself either. It was as if I didn't have control over my own body, over my actions.

Truth to be told, I was horny as hell, and she looked like a fallen angel, standing in the middle of the room, with that pissed-off look on her face. For a moment there, I thought she would shoot me after Cynthia, but she didn't. There was something else in her eyes then, in her devil eyes.

Yearning.

Pain.

I knew it all too well, because it existed in mine, and no matter how much I tried, I couldn't let it go. We were all yearning for a better life, but our souls were too scarred to earn it. There was so much pain in all of our eyes, and if you looked closely, it was all the same. Pain from everything we'd lost and everything that would never be again.

Families.

Friends.

Lovers.

We all lost somebody, and even if it wasn't death that took them away, they were forever gone from us. Ten thousand missed chances for a better life, and we just threw it into the water thinking we could handle everything the motherfucking destiny was throwing at us. Were we all cursed, or was it all a part of a bigger plan?

A goddamn mess, that's what this whole situation was. I needed to kill her, but my heart wasn't cooperating with me. Why was it so hard separating who she was to me now, and who she used to be years ago?

I fucking knew what I had to do. I knew the plan; we went over it ten million times. Kidnap her, get the necessary information about the Syndicate and kill her.

Then why in the fucking hell was it so difficult to remember all those things when she looked at me with those ocean eyes? Cillian was pissed, which I could understand, but my head wasn't in the right space for all of this, and it made me furious.

I forgot how much I always craved her. How even during the darkest times I always sought her. Even when both of us were too lost to this world to even be considered as human beings, I always fucking wanted her. She was messing with my head, messing with everything we had worked so hard on over the years, and I couldn't let this infatuation I still had toward the little devil, this attraction, ruin it.

"Are you even listening to me, Kieran?" Tristan's voice tore through the haze in my mind, bringing me back from the endless stream of thoughts I simply didn't have time for at the moment.

"I'm sorry." I shook my head, as if that would help to get her out of my mind. "I drifted away for a moment."

"Or," Cillian interrupted, "you were too busy thinking about the bitch sitting in our basement."

He was awfully quiet while we sat here which was never a good thing when it came to him. That meant his mind was working overtime, either trying to come up with the best way to torture the information out of Ophelia, or he was plotting to kill us all.

"Cillian," Tristan warned.

"Shut the fuck up, Kill," I growled, but my brother just continued smirking at me.

"Why should I?"

"Dude!" Tristan exclaimed. "Cut it out."

"No, Tristan. I would really like to know why we are sitting here, blabbering around, when that piece of shit is just sitting there, for days might I add, chilling as if she's on vacation. He," Cillian pointed at me, "forbade me to go there, when I have the right to squeeze the life out of her with my own hands. You do too, or did both of you suddenly forget what that psychopath did?"

"Kill, we didn't forget—"

"Then fucking let me get to her!" He jumped from his chair and leaned over the table between us. "I want to hear her cry. I want to hear her beg for her life, and when I'm done, I want to see her bleeding on the floor. Those last moments, when her soul is leaving her body, I wanna be the last thing she sees before descending to Hell."

My hands clenched into the fists, a sudden need to protect her, to remove Cillian as a threat, rising inside of me. Would I attack my own brother, when everything he just said was true?

You know you would.

"Just imagine," he continued, "her broken body, echoes of her cries… Might even fuck her while I'm at it. I heard she's—"

157

He didn't get to finish the sentence. I advanced on him, seeing red.

Red.

Red.

Motherfucking red and nothing else.

Not my brother, not our plan, but just the need to kill him for talking about her in such a way. That monster inside me roared to life, begging to be released. Begging me to take his neck into my hands, to stop the intake of breath, to take his life. Tristan jumped behind me, pulling me backwards, as I struggled in his hold.

"What did I tell you, Tristan?" He sneered at me. "He would never be able to do it. Even after everything, he's still choosing her over his own family."

"Go to hell, Cillian."

"We are all already in hell, brother!" he screamed at me. "I can't even remember the time when we weren't in one. Why isn't she tied up, K? Huh? Why isn't she already dead? It's been five fucking days, and we've done nothing. What happened to our plan?"

"Let go of me, Tristan." I kept trying to get my arms free from him, but his grip just increased.

"What happened to cutting her guts out? What happened to making her fucking pay? Are you thinking with your dick or with your head?" Cillian kept shouting, his frantic eyes locked on mine.

My anger was rising with every taunting word he said. He was right, but also so, so wrong. I wanted her, I would never deny that, but I also wanted to see her neck broken. I wanted to see the same dagger she stabbed my sister with protruding from her, from that heart of darkness she was so fucking proud of. I needed to hate her because that was the only thing I learned in all of those years together.

But I needed more time.

I needed time to figure her out. I needed to know why she did it. Did she ever really love me, or was it all just a lie? The stolen moments, and all of the kisses, did she ever really mean them? Every single *I love you* embedded in my mind, and I couldn't trust a single one of them now. How foolish of me to think that a soulless could feel something.

"Will you both just cut the crap?" Tristan pulled me behind him, standing between the two of us. "We have serious shit going on, and you two are fighting like high school boys."

"We are not—" I tried.

"I don't wanna fucking hear it, okay?" Cillian kept his mouth shut as Tristan started pacing between us, lost in thought. I stood in the place, scowling at Cillian. Our youngest brother started again, "Father called."

Those two words were enough to redirect my line of thought from what was happening at the moment, to my innate need to erase said person from existence. When the people who were supposed to protect you from everything bad in this world, are in fact the same terrifying things they warned us about when we were kids, there was no other choice but to become like them. They shape you. They make you think what you're doing is the right thing, and you aren't as bad as everybody else thinks you are.

Truth to be told, our father was a fucking fairy godmother compared to Nikolai Aster, but the lesser evil didn't always mean a better one. The only reason why we accepted this job was because we wanted to see all of them pay. One big plus in all of this was getting our hands on Ophelia and getting our own revenge.

"What the fuck does he want?" Cillian asked. Out of the three of us, he was the one who hated our father the most, but he played along. He knew very well that you can't kill the king without going through all the pawns first. And the pawns, they were still way out of our reach.

"He wanted to know if the job was done, and—"

"What did you tell him?" I interrupted. If our father knew Ophelia was still alive, he wouldn't be a happy camper. In fact, I was halfway expecting him to barge in here and tell us how incapable we were.

"I told him we are working on it."

Cillian scoffed and went back to his seat. "You should've told him that his favorite son can't get his dick out of our prisoner, which is why we still have nothing."

"Go and suck a dick, Cillian. You would've killed her on the first day if it was up to you and your psychotic tendencies. And then what? We would've still been left with nothing."

"There's only one psychopath in this house, and she's currently downstairs. Probably munching on the food we are providing her."

Tristan started rubbing his temples, frustration more than obvious on his face. "Guys, we need to focus." He looked at me. "Did she tell you anything?"

"You mean, did he ask her anything while he was rearranging her womb with his dick?"

I chose to ignore my twin, and focused on Tristan instead, trying to think of anything.

"Not really, but looking at her, it doesn't seem that she is part of Syndicate anymore."

"That's a fucking joke." Cillian laughed. "The only way you can leave Syndicate is in a body bag, and I never saw her in one."

"That's right," Tristan started excitedly. "Which means that Nikolai might like her a lot more than we initially thought."

"Your point?" I was already getting tired of this whole conversation, and I just wanted to get out of here and clear my head. This whole house was suffocating me, especially with her holed up in here with us.

"My point is," he sat down, "our little psychopath might know a lot more than we initially thought. What if Nikolai kept her outside only to gather the information he wouldn't be able to get himself? Having somebody on the street means you have eyes and ears everywhere."

My attention perked up, because it was exactly what we needed. Syndicate was trying to spread into our territory, and we couldn't allow that. Four years ago our union fell apart, and the two families were at each other's throats. Well, apart from Theo who was the sneakiest son of a bitch.

That idiot wanted his father's empire, and if it meant he was playing double agent to get it, so be it. Couldn't really blame him, I would've probably done the same, given the fact that his father resented him and didn't want him anywhere near the main action. Then there was Maya... That was another shitshow I never wanted to think about, let alone have to deal with it. It was in the past, and that's where it should stay.

"So, what is the plan now?" Cillian asked, looking at me.

Maybe the only way for me to exorcise these demons was to kill them completely. If our roles were reversed, she would have never shown me mercy. No, that bitch didn't know what that word meant. I've seen her kill innocents without remorse, as if it was just another day of her shopping at Walmart.

"We start tonight." I smirked at them. "And we don't stop until we get what we want."

~

It was almost eight o'clock when I descended downstairs to her room. Riley stood in front of her door, eyes firmly fixed on the opposite wall. When he saw me, he straightened up and tipped his chin in a greeting.

"Where is Alejandro?"

"It's his break time, sir. Would you like me to give him a call?"

Dammit Alejandro. I already told him who can guard her, and who can't. That she-devil could trick the smartest man into doing her bidding, not to mention some of our guards who were just starting with us.

"No, that's fine, Riley. Give me ten minutes, I need to talk to her."

"Sir—"

"Alone, Riley."

He couldn't have been more than twenty, but even with his age, he knew the devil when he saw one.

"Got it, sir." He nodded. "I'll be back in ten minutes."

I took the keys from him, and started unlocking the door with my heart in my throat. Every single interaction with her was like a sucker punch to my stomach. We often heard stories of the antichrist, but we never quite believed them. Well, I didn't believe them until I saw it with my own two eyes.

She was our doomsday, the destruction, a wolf in a lamb's coat.

I opened the door, halfway expecting her to be right in front, ready to attack, but she sat on the bed, her legs crossed, and her eyes fixated on me.

"I was wondering when you'd be coming back." She spoke softly, endearingly, but I knew it was venom that coated her words.

"Did you now?" I closed the door behind me and crossed

the room. Unlike the first time I visited her here, the light was turned on and I could clearly see all of her tattoos on display. Some were new, some were old, but the one that always brought the most attention to me was the snake wrapped around her forearm, so similar to the one tattooed on mine.

"Missed me, baby?" she cooed as she spread her legs, bending them at knees, and showing me her center, covered in black panties. "Tristan brought me some clothes. How kind of you guys to take care of me while I'm here."

My hands clenched at my sides, but I wasn't going to give into her. She wasn't the one leading this game, we were.

"Aww, baby. You seem tense." With a smile on her face, she started tracing the path from her knee, toward her inner thigh, her fingers dancing on her skin. "Would you like me to help you?"

I would love to fuck her in ten different ways, but my desire for her couldn't cloud my judgement again. Ophelia lifted the hem of her shirt, showing me the smooth skin of her stomach, calling to me, begging to be touched. She didn't seem scared, and I wondered if she thought her only punishment would be this lockdown.

"I'm not here to entertain any of your sick ideas, Ophelia."

She pouted at me, but continued her descent toward her center, her gaze never wavering from mine. It would be so easy to fuck her like this, but when it was all done, I would just resent myself further, hate myself for succumbing to my desires.

"I came to tell you to be ready."

She perked up, immediately stopping her actions. "Are we going to play?"

Was she for real? Was she so far gone that even in the face

of danger she couldn't show at least a little bit of humanity? A little bit of the girl I used to know.

"We are going to play, but I'm not sure if you're going to like it."

"Oooh." She clapped her hands. "Are there going to be knives involved? Please, please, let there be knives."

This was the problem with her. I never knew where her mind would wander. When we just took her here, that first day, she seemed frightened, and now… Now she looked giddy from excitement, even though I was pretty sure she knew what 'playing' meant.

"Maybe—"

"And are there going to be ropes? I looove ropes." Of course she did. Knives were her favorite things to use, and ropes… She loved immobilizing her victims.

"Of course, you do."

I didn't even know why I came here tonight. It wasn't necessary to let her know what was going to happen, so what then? Was I expecting to find the girl I used to know beneath this shell? She wasn't emotionless, but she was also a manipulative bitch, and I questioned every single interaction I ever had with her.

I started retreating toward the door when her voice stopped me cold.

"Do you remember when I had just come back from Russia?"

Did I remember? Of course, I remembered. I remembered every single word spoken between us, every single touch, every single promise.

"Do you remember what you told me?"

I will get you out of this. That's what I told her. That's what I promised her, and I failed.

I am so sorry, baby girl. And I was, because after that trip, she was a different person. She was somebody unrecognizable.

"Does it ever haunt you how much you failed me? How all of you failed me?"

Her voice wasn't sweet anymore. Oh no, it was as cold as the winter night in the middle of the Arctic, freezing me to my bones.

"Because you did. And then you tried to destroy me because you couldn't control me."

I turned toward her, but she was still in the same position as before.

"All of my scars, all of my demons, they were weeping for you. I needed you to take me away, and what did you do? You pushed me further into the darkness, never giving a fuck about anything else but yourself."

She had no idea how wrong she was, but I wasn't going to entertain her crazy ideas this time.

"And when it all exploded, you fuckers threw me off the cliff. You drowned me. You killed the last bit of humanity I had left inside of me."

"That's enough!"

"Why, Kieran?" She laughed. "Is the truth too hard to swallow? It's so easy to make me look like a villain, when all you're doing is avoiding the person in the mirror. But I guess you had to do it, didn't you? You always needed your daddy's approval."

"I said," I crossed the room, and pinned her on the bed, holding her by her neck, "that's fucking enough."

"Go ahead, K." She licked her lips. "Hurt me. There's nothing else you could do to me that hasn't already been done."

"Are you sure about that, baby?" She tasted heavenly as I licked from her ear to her mouth. "Are you sure I can't do anything else to you?"

A sinister smile spread across her face, her eyes sparkling

with amusement, throwing me off balance. I squeezed her windpipe harder, and the bone chilling laughter emanated from her.

"Oh my darling. I would have to have a soul for you to hurt me again. But you took care of that, didn't you? You took it all away."

I kissed her cheek and released her neck, slowly walking toward the door.

"We will see about that."

14

OPHELIA

How do you kill the part of your heart that still loves the person that destroyed you? Sometimes it felt like another life, another me and another him, but the pain was always the same. I thought I parted with that piece of him embedded in my soul. I thought I eradicated every single particle of him I used to love. How was it possible to hate a person, but to want them so much, that I had a feeling my skin would catch on fire at the mere sight of him?

We used to be beautiful together, almost perfect, but we became so tragic, so violent. Were the two of us born to destroy, or were we made that way? Did our actions shape us, or was there something inside, pulling us to the darker side?

Destruction.

That's what we were. A pure and utter destruction, and we didn't know how to stop. I wasn't even sure anymore who pushed who to the brink of insanity. Was it ever love or was it just an innate need to possess the other one? To own them, body and soul, until the only thing left was a shell of a person they used to be. The Kieran I knew when I was a mere teenager wasn't the person standing next to his brothers, looking at my tied-up body. Actually, I probably never really knew him.

Truth is, he never knew me either.

He thought saving me from my demons would exorcise his. He thought he needed to save me, but I only needed him to accept me. When did we become so fucked up, we couldn't see anything else but our need for destruction? Not that I minded. Destruction and chaos were beautiful. So infinite, mesmerizing, it always gave me a power I never knew I needed.

But I never knew that my darkness would diminish his light.

Was I the instrument that finally pushed him over the ledge, into the black hole he was still living in? Funnily, he was the one that pushed me, so it would only be fair for me to be the one that pushed him. Right?

I almost wanted to laugh at the three of them, standing in front of me, looking like avenging angels. Men always thought they were smarter, more powerful, nondestructive, but the truth was always more bitter than what they could swallow. They were usually puppets controlled by somebody else.

And that's what Nightingale brothers became over the years. Just three sad puppets controlled by their father. Three sad excuses of humans that never really got rid of the shackles placed on them by their family. They looked so smug, so proud of themselves thinking they got me where they wanted me. If only they knew.

About an hour ago, Alejandro took me from the room, blindfolded, and I ended up here. What in the ever-loving fuck were they discussing for almost an hour, I had no idea, but I was getting fucking bored. My hands were getting numb. There was the spot on my nose I was dying to scratch, and well, drinking copious amounts of water before this didn't seem like a good idea now, because my bladder was killing me.

"So." I cleared my throat, and three sets of eyes zeroed in

on me. "Do I get a last meal or whatever it is they are giving to prisoners sentenced to death?"

Tristan rubbed his temples, and Cillian started pacing around, like a wild animal locked inside a cage. Well, I mean, he was kinda locked inside a cage, the only difference was, I was the wild animal. Kieran's eyes flashed with rage, and he closed the short distance between the two of us, leaning in my face.

Come on, baby.

Give it to me. Show me what you're made of. Show me what I made you —all of the shit you're hiding beneath that calm composure you're trying to fool people with.

"The only thing you'll get, little birdy," he swiped the hair from my face, and continued, "is a six-foot grave behind this house, and a world freed from your psychotic presence."

"Awww, baby," I licked my lips and grinned at him, "you didn't have to. Did you dig it yourself? Does it have flowers around it? It better not have any flowers, because you know how much I hate them."

"Fucking psycho," Tristan murmured loud enough for me to hear.

"What was that, Tris? A psycho?" I leaned to the side, looking behind Kieran. "Why, thank you. It took you long enough to figure it all out. I mean, not that I blame you."

"What's that supposed to mean?" Tristan snarled, asking through gritted teeth.

Kieran took a step back, but I could still feel the anger radiating off of him. Just a sad, little fuck who always had to control his emotions. Never reckless, never the wild one, I was surprised he didn't get constipated from all the self-righteousness he was trying to fake. When we were fifteen, Ava told me her brother loved girls with personality.

Lucky him, years later, he got me with multiple ones.

"I mean, darling, you were never the brightest one." *Come on, come on, come closer.* "I told you already, Kieran was the brain behind every operation, Cillian, my little fellow psychopath," I chanced a glance at him, and loved the turmoil on his face, "was the killing machine. And you," I let my eyes travel over his body, from head to toe, "were more like a lamb that could never get anything right."

"Shut the fuck up!"

He was suddenly in front of me, with his hands wrapped around my neck. What was it with all of these people trying to choke the life out of me? Don't get me wrong, I loved choking sessions, but, don't get me wet if you wouldn't do anything about it. This one, he was the only one that had some resemblance of a conscience, and I was planning on using it.

"Oh please, Tristan," I cried out, faking panic. "Please, please, please, don't hurt me. I didn't do it. I didn't do anything wrong. Please, I'm begging you. Don't hurt me."

Men.

They were always so easily manipulated when a female started begging for her life, and Tristan did exactly what I wanted him to do. He let me go, a shocked look on his face following the trail. This was why he sucked in executing orders. Feeling anything but cold indifference toward the person you were supposed to kill, could end up killing you, and why the fuck would you want that?

I never really gave a fuck who had to die and who got to live. Maybe in the beginning when I still thought what I did was wrong and there was something bad inside of me, but I learned, I improved, and I realized that no matter what, there would always be people who had to die. And they did. It didn't really matter if their death came today by my hands, or in fifty years by natural causes. All of us would end up in that coffin, or well, in the cold ground, six feet under, and there was no running away from that.

"She's fucking playing you." Kieran shook his youngest brother, who still seemed to be in some kind of shock. A killer my ass. If you couldn't kill a female who you thought destroyed your family, how in the hell would you kill somebody assigned to you.

"Weak, weak, weak, weak," I sang, laughing at their pissed-off expressions. "You all are weak. No wonder my father didn't want to do business with your family anymore."

"Shut up, shut up, shut up!"

Cillian ran from the other side of the room and stood behind me, yanking my head back with a pull of my hair. Something cold nestled at the bottom of my neck, and I knew it was the blade of a knife he was holding. His eyes were crazed, unfocused, lost to the here and now, and I relished in every single moment of it.

That's right boys. I want to see you fall apart. If I am going underground, I am taking your sanity with me.

Well, what was left of it.

"Cillian," Kieran started in a calm voice, and I could see him in my head, trying to be the reasonable one in this situation. But there was no reasoning with a person when the blood-lust takes over their body. There were no words you could say to bring them back to the land of sanity.

I knew it, I knew it very well, because I couldn't even count on the fingers of one hand, how many times I've been in the same situation. How many times I couldn't see anything else, but the object I had to kill. It wasn't about the job, it wasn't about what the Syndicate wanted, it was always what I wanted.

And I wanted to see them dead. I wanted to see their blood seeping from the wounds inflicted by me. I wanted to hear them scream, because if you were so fucked up that they would send me after you, you deserved the worst ending ever known to humankind.

This broken son of a bitch that held me down, he was the same. It was as if we were cut from the same cloth, and I always wondered why it was that I fell for his brother, but not for him. Kieran was the light, he was always the proper one, the kind one, the one that wanted to save everyone around him, but Cillian...

Cillian just wanted to see everybody burn. He wanted them dead just as much as I did. Oh this wonderful look in his eyes. His hatred for me was almost palpable, almost visible, and I wanted to play with it. I wanted to have fun with his pain, because there was no better way to break somebody's mind than to play with what they'd lost.

"Awww, you brought my favorite, Cillian," I choked out, my voice breaking from the strain in my neck. "I didn't know you loved me that much."

"Shut the fuck up, you psychopathic bitch."

"But, Kill," I pouted, "I'm not the only psychopath in this room."

"Cillian." I felt Kieran's presence in front of me, but Kill was too far gone to listen to his brother. He started pulling my hair lower, and the blade slowly started cutting into my skin. Blood broke out of the wound, and I could feel it trickling down my chest, onto the shirt I wore. It's such a bummer really, I actually liked this shirt. It was a bitch trying to remove blood from light-colored clothing, but maybe I could ask K where they bought it.

"Let her go, Kill."

"She has to die."

His chest was rising and falling in fast intervals, and I could see his pupils, enlarged, the black almost eradicating the brown of his irises. I knew what excitement was when I saw it, and this one was excited to kill me.

I knew it because I always felt the same. Those couple of minutes before I dragged my knife through their bodies, before I removed the safety of my gun and shot them between their eyes, those minutes were filled with excitement —my heart racing inside my chest, my breathing going erratic, my hands almost shaking from what would come.

It was addictive, it was fulfilling, and only fools would say they didn't feel it before taking another person's life.

"She will die, but we need her first."

Oh, they needed me. How beautiful was that, huh? Cillian's crazed eyes never left mine, the promise of hell on earth in them, the promise of terror.

"Come on, Kill. You know you want to push that knife deeper. You want to see the blood gushing out in rivulets."

"Shut the fuck up, Ophelia!" Kieran yelled at me, and I really wanted to see his pissed-off face. "Cillian—"

"Word of advice, though." I lowered my voice. "You might want to move the knife a couple of inches to the left. It's really beautiful seeing somebody bleed out from their carotid artery."

"Cillian," A hand landed on his shoulder, and the heat from Kieran's body seeped onto mine, as he stepped over me, his legs on the sides of my hips. "Step away, Brother."

"I want to see her lifeless eyes—"

"And you will." *Jesus fucking Christ, could they be any sappier?* "Take the knife away, Kill."

But we were just getting started. Don't take the knife away, I almost came from merely the pressure it had on my neck.

"Kieran." The idiot holding my hair finally looked at his brother, his voice shaking and the little show was over. God fucking dammit. I was finally enjoying it, and Kieran had to barge in and stop all the fun.

He lifted the knife, and I finally swallowed, my neck

cramping from the position he held me in. Cillian stepped back, leaving Kieran on top of me. Oh, I actually kind of liked this position. Him on top of me, me at his mercy… How far would he go to get what he wants?

"And now you two can kiss," I taunted. A hand landed on my cheek, sending my head flying to the other side. I tasted the blood in my mouth, and slowly turned my head back, clashing with Kieran's furious eyes. He grabbed my face, digging his thumb into the wound on my cheek. It finally started healing, but with his punishing grip, I just knew it would reopen again.

"You think you're so smart, so ready to die, huh?" The vein appeared on his forehead, a telltale sign of the level of anger he was currently on. Well, fucking finally. "The knife at your throat would be a merciful way for you. No, baby girl, you don't deserve mercy. You deserve to be tortured, broken, and fucked for everything you did."

"You mean all of my deepest desires will come to fruition?"

"You're a crazy bitch, Ophelia." He leaned down, our noses touching. "But you already knew that, didn't you?"

"Takes one to know one, baby." My tongue darted out, licking over the seam of his lips. His eyes darkened, the grip getting stronger, but that hitch in his breathing couldn't be mistaken for anything else but the desire he still had for me.

I started chuckling at the confused look on his face, the pain flowing through my body, but it was a welcoming distraction.

"Okay, okay," Tristan spoke up, pulling us from our reverie. "Can we start or are we going to waste another hour?"

"Hand me my knife, Tristan," the asshole in front of me instructed, still stabbing his thumb into the wound on my cheek. The pain was pulsing through the left side of my face, blood coating my cheek, but I wasn't going to show him how much it hurt. He didn't get to have the privilege of knowing me in that way. Not now, not ever again.

I couldn't move my head, but the shuffling of feet, the silent *tap-tap-tap* on the concrete floor, told me we were about to start.

Really, really start, and I couldn't wait to see what exactly they wanted from me. I mean, besides the fact that they wanted to kill me for the crime I never committed. I was curious to see if they actually improved their torture skills.

God knows, they majorly sucked four years ago.

The tearing of fabric, the chilling sensation on my skin, and the tip of a blade touching my body as Kieran slashed through the shirt, leaving me exposed to them. *Fucking shit on the rollercoaster, there was no saving this shirt now.*

"Nice bra," he grinned.

"Oh, thank you very much. Tristan bought it for me." The smile disappeared quicker than it appeared. "Would you like to take it off?"

"Oh, birdy, birdy, birdy." He patted my head, annoying the shit out of me. "If I wanted to take it off, I wouldn't be asking for your permission."

Of course, you wouldn't, you sick fucking fuck. My throat closed from the emotion coursing through my body. A conversation I had not so long ago played in my mind, and the only thing I wanted in that moment was to cut off his balls, and make scrambled eggs with them.

"Tell me, birdy." *I fucking hated that nickname.* "Are you still in contact with daddy dearest?"

Ah, of course. I should've known.

"None of your business, darling." I smiled, even though the only thing I wanted was to smash his skull.

"Are you sure about that?" He dragged the blade of the knife between my breasts, tracing the fabric of my bra. "I think not. I think you should tell us everything you know about Syndicate."

"And tell me, Kieran, why the fuck would I do that?"

"Because you owe us." He stood still for a moment, before moving to my left arm, going over the snake tattoo there. The one we got together. "Because you owe me for all the shit you put me through."

"Oh, I put *you* through shit?" *Calm your fucking titties, Phee.* "Well excuse me, but I'll—"

Before I could finish my sentence, a searing pain shot through my arm.

"Motherfucker!" I screamed, only to be welcomed by the smile on his face. I turned and saw the gash over the tattoo, blood already dropping to the ground. Funnily, pain was a welcome distraction from the murderous thoughts bumping around in my head.

He fucking destroyed my tattoo.

"Fuck you, Kieran!"

"You already did that, and I didn't hear you complaining when my dick was rearranging your insides." Somebody snickered behind him, but his focus was solely on me, smearing the blood on my arm. "I will ask you again, are you still in contact with your father?"

I started laughing, the sound echoing around the room. "And I will tell you again, none of your business."

Another hit to my cheek, then he pulled my head back into the position, holding my hair.

"We can do this easy way, or the hard way. It's' your choice."

I spat at him. My blood mixed with saliva decorated his face, trickling down his cheeks. He grabbed my throat, squeezing harder than Tristan did, and I started gasping for air.

Show me your fucked-up, baby. Show me how far you could go.

"Hard way it is then." Black dots danced in front of my

eyes, yet I could clearly hear the clinking sound of a knife hitting the ground. So, no more knife party? Such a shame.

"I... will," I wheezed, "enjoy this."

He ignored me, spreading the blood from my cheek, over my lips, a faraway look in his eyes.

"Heat up the iron, Cillian."

"K—"

"Now, Kill."

The noise in the background was completely lost to me, as he twisted the middle finger on my right hand, pulling it into an unnatural position. The bone cracked, the ligaments tearing, my stomach roiled, the urge to puke strong as he pulled the bone from its natural position.

I bit on my lip, refusing to scream for him.

"Answer the question, Ophelia." He let go of my neck, only to pull me closer to his face. "You look beautiful in red. Maybe we can put you in a red dress when we send your body to your father."

"I look beautiful in everything. Too bad it wasn't enough for you."

This time, a fist connected with the right side of my face, and a buzzing sound started in my head. My ears were ringing, my head was pounding, and my eyes couldn't focus on his face anymore. This would be a headache from hell, if I managed to survive this night.

"Where is your father hiding, Ophelia?"

I had a feeling I was under water, drowning, sinking... Another hit.

"What is Project X?"

Stupid, stupid, stupid.

Something hot pressed against my collarbone, and a scream tore from me, my skin burning under the pressure.

"Where have you been all these years?"

A tiny moment of relief flooded through me, as he removed the scorching iron, only for it to get pressed into the other side, pulling another scream from me.

"You can burn in Hell, Kieran," I gritted through my teeth, and the pressure of the iron increased, his full body weight pressing down on me. It felt as if my shoulder would fall off next, or the iron would exit on the other side. My, my, they wanted to know everything about Syndicate. Color me surprised, but I thought that Theo already shared everything there was to know about our family. I guess Papa didn't really trust him, and it was probably driving Theo mad.

"We are already in hell, baby girl. You put us here." He removed the iron, throwing it to the floor. "You made us this way, and now you gotta pay the price."

"You have no idea what hell really is, Kieran. You have no idea how it feels like to be ripped from the inside and stitched back together. You walk around with your woe-is-me attitude, but the only real pain you ever experienced was Ava's death."

"Don't you dare mention her name." He pressed into the wound on my hand, and my eyebrows scrunched in pain.

"Why, K? Is it because you failed her? How did it feel seeing her lifeless body there, huh? How did it feel being ripped apart by your biggest fear? The loss of somebody you love, somebody you wanted to spare from this world. I would also want to kill every person that ever hurt my sister."

He flinched at my words, confusion and a flicker of fear painting his face. That's right K, I would kill every single person that laid a single finger on Maya. That was one of the rare things we had in common.

"I won't ask you again." He stood up, masking all of his emotions. "Where is your father?"

My middle finger stood in the funny position, and seeing where my eyes went, he crouched and took a hold of it. His eyes connected with mine, and in the next second he pulled the said finger down, straight down. They say that once you hit one nerve ending, it travels to the rest of them in your body. I could feel that broken bone in every single part of my being. I could almost picture the fucked-up state my bone was in already.

He pressed on it, squishing my hand between his and the wooden armrest.

Don't you fucking dare scream.

And I didn't. I didn't scream, but that obviously didn't sit well with him.

"Last chance, Ophelia."

"Fuck you!" My right eye was closing, swelling from the punch he gifted me with. "Even if I did know something, I would never tell it to a Nightingale. You are nothing but a sad excuse of a man, looking for answers in all the wrong places."

His expression became blank, and he turned his back to me, pulling my attention to the other two, who no doubt were just waiting for their turn. With swift movements, he faced me again and his fist connected with the other side of my head, sending me into a dark abyss.

Motherfucking son of a bitch.

15

KIERAN

Cillian paced the length of the room, giving me a fucking headache, while I crouched in front of the chair Ophelia was strapped to. I could hear Tristan's voice somewhere behind me, arguing with somebody, but I was too focused on the knocked-out hellraiser to pay attention to whatever he was saying. There was an ongoing battle inside of me —one side didn't give a fuck she was in this position in front of us, her head hanging, and blood seeping from the cuts on her hand and her cheek. The other side, that was the side I needed to silence.

That side wanted me to pick her up, and save her from this place. It wanted to heal the part of her that pushed us all into insanity.

"Is this what madness feels like?"

Her words from that night, from the fucking night that started changing everything, kept repeating in my head. Is it, is this madness?

We fought so much against it —against our families, our upbringing, everything that was making us this way, and for what? Only to end up in the same spot, if not, the worst one. I sometimes had a feeling that I was going on as a broken record, repeating over and over again how much she destroyed us, but I did the same.

What would've happened if I were stronger, smarter... What could we have been if we managed to escape all those years ago, instead of staying and trying to fight? They made an assassin out of her, a coldhearted, psychotic assassin. And I... I didn't even know who I was anymore.

Was I a killer, a son, a lover, or was I just a lost man, trying to find his place in this sick world?

I stood up and walked toward her, fighting the urge to touch her, to make sure she was still alive. Even with the slow rising and falling of her chest, a clear indication she was still with us, I just wanted to hold her. Motherbitch, this is exactly what I didn't want to happen.

I didn't want to feel anything toward her. I didn't want to love her. I didn't want to care if she lived or died, I just didn't want to have this suffocating feeling inside of me, drowning me, pushing me deeper.

Like a weight sitting on my chest, that's what it felt like. As if somebody placed ten thousand pounds on me, and I carried it. I carried it well, but I didn't want to do it anymore. I just wanted this fucking feeling to disappear.

I wanted her to disappear, to be gone. I needed to be free of this hold she had on me.

"Why, Phee?" I murmured. "I just want to fucking know, why."

She was unconscious, unresponsive, but this was the only time I would even dare uttering these words. This woman, this beautiful, broken, sadistic woman in front me, she fed on other people's emotions.

Good and bad.

"Kieran." Tristan's voice penetrated through the haze,

through the pain my mind was putting me in. I turned only to see the tightness around his lips, and a worried look on his face.

"What happened?"

Ophelia thought Tristan was the weak one, when in reality he was the strongest. He was the only one whose mind didn't get broken with everything that happened. The only one who could keep all of us in touch with reality, and the only one who had enough patience to deal with all of the administrative things I simply didn't want to do.

I was the leader, that was correct, but only because I took it upon myself to be the one who decided who lived and who died. I didn't want that shit on my brothers, no matter how much we fought. The two of them already suffered enough with Ava's passing, and everything our father was throwing at us. This was the least I could do.

He held the phone in both of his hands, his skin becoming pale with every passing second.

"What the fuck happened, Tristan?" My patience was running thin and knowing that he usually wasn't the one to worry unnecessarily, his whole demeanor was creating sinister thoughts in my mind. Was it our mother? Did something happen to her?

"We have a problem."

"What kind of a problem?" Cillian asked, leaning on the wall behind Ophelia.

Tristan looked between the two of us, chewing on his lower lip.

"A big fucking problem, brothers."

I was going to kill them. No, oh no, I was going to torture them, and then I was going to kill them and send the pieces of their miserable bodies to their families.

"Fuck!" I threw the glass across the table, shattering it against the wall. "How in the ever-loving fuck did this happen?"

I focused my attention on Tristan, who kept walking back and forth with his hands wrapped behind his neck.

"I swear to god, Brother, if you don't stop pacing, I will tie you to the chair."

"I don't know how the fuck it happened," he threw back at me. "I don't know. It was supposed to be a smooth operation. Get the shipment from the bay, drive here and that's it."

"Then how is it possible, that Sons-of-fucking-Hades are currently holding the whole shipment of cocaine, our fucking shipment, if it was supposed to be as smooth as you're claiming it to be?"

I could already see his brain working overtime, trying to figure out how it happened. The focused look on his face, his eyes zeroed in on the papers in front of him, the map of the West Coast.

"I don't know. I think—"

"How?" I screamed. "Nobody knew, nobody but us. How is it possible that such sealed information could get to them, huh?"

He dropped down into the chair behind him, a look of disbelief on his face.

"We have a traitor in our midst."

"Don't be ridiculous." I pulled out another glass from the cabinet, pouring myself another two fingers of whiskey, and sat down, propping my legs on the table. "We would've known."

"Would we?"

Would we really? He was right, somebody was selling us out, but who? The men working for us here were our most trusted allies, each and every one of them handpicked by us.

Then it dawned on me. "What if Nikolai knows?"

"What do you mean?" My brother straightened up; a rare sight of fear visible in his eyes. Man, even saying his name out loud was like calling for the Devil.

"What if he knows about Ophelia?"

"Even if he knew about that, there is no way in hell that he could possibly know about routes we are taking for our shipments," he argued. "Besides, we don't even know if the two of them are still in contact."

"But think about it." I took the papers from him, lowering my legs down. "She would've been dead by now if he wanted her dead. Nobody walks away from Syndicate, not even family members. So why is she still alive?"

He kept quiet for a moment, tapping his fingers on the surface of the table. The map in front of me, the route they were supposed to take, it was all there. They weren't supposed to be anywhere close to the Hades territory. Why the fuck did they go through Santa Monica, when they weren't supposed to?

"Are you sure they had the same instructions?"

"Of course, they did," he exclaimed. "I handed these same maps and documents personally to Damien."

"Where were they intercepted?" They were supposed to take the shipment from the previous truck at Redondo Beach, and drive to Las Vegas, then through Utah and Colorado. Where the fuck did it all go wrong?

"They were almost out of Los Angeles when they got to them."

"So, they took the same route you mapped out for them?"

"Apparently so."

Fucking hell. I refused to believe it, but Tristan was right.

Somebody betrayed us, and once I found out who that was, they would wish they were never born.

"Can you get me the list of all the people involved in this? And I mean, all of them."

"What are you going to do?" He knew what I was going to do. I was going to question every single one of them until I found which one of them betrayed us to the enemy.

I already assumed that the men sent for this shipment were long dead. Sons of Hades never left anybody alive. I never met any of them, but the stories I've heard about their president sent fear crawling all over my skin, and that's saying a lot, considering I grew up the way I did with Nikolai as my godfather.

"I am going to find out which one of them thought it would be a good idea to play double agent."

I fucking hoped it was just a mere coincidence, and that Sons of Hades just ended up being in the right place at a right time, but if there was one thing this unholy life taught me, it was that nothing was coincidental.

Loyalty was everything to me, and I couldn't even grasp the fact that somebody would do such a thing and go behind our back. We fed them, we sent their kids to school, we gave them everything they ever wanted to have, and this was how they repaid us.

"How fast can you get everything I need?"

"Give me—"

"Guys." Cillian opened the door without knocking, halting Tristan mid-sentence. "I need you to come to the foyer."

He wore an angry expression on his face, his hand gripping the door with such intensity, his knuckles were turning white.

"What's going on?" I asked, but I wasn't too sure that I wanted an answer.

"I just need you to get your asses up, and get yourself to the foyer. Damien is back."

"He's alive?" The surprise in Tristan's voice mirrored my own feelings. They didn't kill him?

"Just fucking get up, and get going. It isn't pretty."

The urgency with which he spoke, the perspiration on his forehead, those were all the signs I needed to know that I wasn't going to like whatever it was that waited for us outside of this room.

"Fuck." I got up from my seat, with Tristan following my lead and walked after Cillian who didn't bother waiting for either one of us.

Walking down the stairs, I could see the grim faces of our guards. The younger ones looked ready to puke, the older ones ready to murder somebody, and I dreaded seeing what Cillian was about to show us. I couldn't see Damien once we reached the bottom of the stairs, but the impending doom I felt in the air was getting stronger and stronger with each step I took.

"Where is he?" I asked Cillian, who stood in the middle, his back facing me. "Kill?"

My brother turned to me, a fury I had never seen before dancing in his eyes. Tristan's footsteps echoed through the foyer as he joined us in the middle.

"Where is Damien, Kill?"

The energy in the room was suffocating, rotten, sending the sick feeling into my stomach. Cillian kept quiet, staring at me, then at Tristan, both of us in the dark about what was going on.

"Kill?" Tristan asked quietly. "Do you mind telling us what is going on here? You said Damien is back. Where is he?"

Without a word, my twin brother stepped aside, and my eyes zeroed in on the box perched on the top of the small table in the middle of the foyer. I didn't have to be a genius to know what the dark, red color decorating the bottom of it was. I took a step forward, but I wasn't really there.

I often heard about out-of-body experiences, and this whole

moment felt like one. I could feel my body moving, but my mind was solely focused on the box in front of us. The room echoed with each of my steps, the soles of my shoes hitting the white marble. The deafening silence of the room felt suffocating, as if everybody held their breath to what was about to come.

And I knew… I fucking knew what was inside, but it was as if my mind had a hard time catching up with the situation at hand.

"What's inside?" I asked, my eyes focused on the brown lid with a red X colored on the top.

"Open it."

"But what's—"

"Just fucking open it, Kieran!" Cillian yelled out and came to stand on the opposite side of the table. Tristan kept his distance, but I could feel his eyes on us, the nervous energy buzzing around us.

"Okay." I took ahold of the lid, my hands almost trembling from the anticipation. Cillian gripped the edge of the table, his eyebrows scrunched together. He already knew what was inside, hell, half of this room already knew.

I pulled the lid up and an unmistakable stench of blood infiltrated my nostrils. Living the way I was living, and doing the things I was doing, there was almost nothing that could take me by surprise.

But this… This monstrosity sitting in this box, this was a whole other level.

What was once blond hair, was now colored in red. Damien's lifeless eyes stared at me from the bottom of the box. Their vibrant blue diminished by the death that came to him. His face was purple and red, and I could only imagine the terror he went through with the Sons of Hades.

"Sadistic pieces of shit," I whispered. Even in death his

expression was a terrified one. His left cheek was missing, the muscle structure hugging the bones visible all the way from his eye to his jaw. What disturbed me the most was the branded sign on his forehead. The three-headed beast with their teeth on display and the quote I saw once before.

Only once, but it was enough to haunt me for the rest of my life.

Tempus Fugit, Memento Mori.

"Time flies," I started reading out loud. "Remember your mortality."

"*Remember your mortality, Kieran. We all have to die one day, and it is up to us how we chose to spend this life.*" That was what Ophelia once told me. Remember my mortality.

"There is a letter for you," Cillian started, still staring at the box. "Here." He pulled it out of his pocket, handing it to me.

I turned it around, seeing my name in a clear, white script on the backside. The envelope was black, sealed with their insignia. The three-headed dog, Cerberus.

Tristan came closer, gagging at the sight in front of him.

"What the fuck?"

I tuned him out, I tuned them all out, as I started tearing through the paper, and pulling out the letter addressed to me. I rubbed my eyes, the words getting blurry, and focused back again on it.

Dear Kieran,
It's been a long time since the last time I saw you. How have you been? I've heard you reallocated your whole operation to the mountain side. Good for you, really, really good.
Do you remember that time your crew came to Las Vegas, and slaughtered half of my club? No? Well, let me refresh your memory, my old friend.
It was summer, three years ago, when you decided to snatch our

territory away from us. When your soldiers raped our women, killed the kids playing in the clubhouse, and slaughtered half of my men. Oh, wait. Wasn't it just after we granted you the right to transport your drugs through our territory? Well, my old president granted you that. If it had been up to me, I would've cut your throat and fed it to my dogs the moment you stepped anywhere near us.

You, my friend, bit the hand that fed you. You spat on the trust we gave you.

Your greed, your infinite need for more took away innocent lives, so I took away something from you. How is your daddy dearest? Still alive?

What about your mommy? Damn man, those dresses of hers... Phew, I can almost imagine her completely naked.

Now I took something from you, and a little bird told me this was your main shipment for the quarter. What a surprise, right? I'm not sure if I should even be negotiating with you, or with your father, but I guess I could try. No?

I really loved hearing the screams coming out of your man here. He shared some interesting information with me, so how about this?

You have five days to get yourself and your brothers to Las Vegas, or you will never see this whole shipment or your mommy dearest. My men took quite the interest in her, and I must say —she looks absolutely dashing for her age. Hell, she might be a good addition for one of my dance clubs. Does she like knives? Her cream-colored skin would look beautiful in red. What's the color of your blood? Is it darker or lighter? Is your mother's the same?

Oh, man, I'm getting hard just thinking about it.

Anyhow, you know what I want. And what I want, I always get —one way or another.

I truly hope you'll be ready to give me everything I need in five days, or, well, we both know the consequences. There is an old Cathedral on the outskirts of the city - Saint Angelle's Cathedral. I hope to see you there at 5 pm.

Oh, I almost forgot. I hope the blood didn't stain your furniture too much. It's really grueling getting it out.

With all my infinite love,

Storm.

Was my eye twitching? Yes, yes it motherfucking was.

The box went flying to the ground, blood splattering all over the floor and our guards avoided it as if it were poisonous.

"Fuck!" I screamed, scrunching the letter in my hand. "Fuck, fuck, fuck." I pushed the table to the ground, the crashing sound ringing in my ears.

"K." Tristan took my arm. "Calm the fuck down."

I fought him off, pushing him away and started pacing from one end of the room to another.

He had our mother.

That motherfucking psychopath had our mother, and I fucking knew he would do everything he mentioned in the letter, and so much more. The only other person I knew to be that deranged, that cold, was sitting knocked out in our basement.

But she was the devil I knew.

Storm was the one I had no fucking clue about.

"What did it say, K?" Cillian asked carefully.

What did it say, he wanted to know? I started laughing. "I'm going to kill him with my bare hands."

"Okay, I agree, but what the fuck happened?"

"He has Mom." I turned around and looked at both of my brothers, their faces paling momentarily. "He took her with him, and he wants Las Vegas back. He wants his territory back."

I could feel the rage simmering inside of me, and I knew my

brothers felt the same. My brothers and I, we never went after other people's families. That was one thing we could all agree on, and one oath we swore to uphold.

Those men were never supposed to attack his club, but our father issued orders we weren't part of. And this was where it got us.

And he fucking took one of the most important people in our lives. She wasn't perfect, but she was ours. She was the last connection to any humanity we had. The last person we tried to keep away from this mess.

"What did you just say?" Cillian asked slowly, each syllable carefully pronounced.

"What you heard. Storm kidnapped our mother, and he wants us to meet him in Las Vegas in five days, or he would…"

I couldn't even finish that sentence.

"He would what? Kill her?" Tristan approached slowly, the turmoil of emotions playing all over his face.

"No." I felt dizzy. I felt sick. I was fucking angry. "He won't kill her. He will use and abuse her body, destroy her soul, until she begs him to die."

"What do you want us to do?"

In this moment, Tristan reminded me of Ava —always the coolheaded one, always trying to understand the situation without emotions involved.

"What do you think?" I retorted. "We are going to mother-fucking Las Vegas."

16

OPHELIA

Something was burning.

I slowly opened my eyes, only to be met by Cillian's crazed ones, a cigarette between his lips, smoke billowing around his face.

"Good morning, princess."

What in the hell happened? My cheek was throbbing, and there was something probing in the back of my mind—a memory, an onslaught of events that took place before.

Motherfucker, Kieran knocked me out cold.

I tried to move my hands, but the sharp pain traveled all the way to my shoulders. It took me a moment to clear my head and actually take in my surroundings.

I wasn't sitting anymore. My hands were tied above my head, holding my full weight, as my legs dangled above the ground. The whole right side of my face hurt like a bitch.

"Fuck off, Cillian."

"Oooo, so feisty." He chuckled. "I hope you're ready for the next round of games."

"What, are you going to tickle me until I confess all my sins? I'll pass."

Something cold pressed against my stomach, and the Einstein in front of me looked like a Cheshire cat, a satisfied grin plastered on his face. Am I going to get bored again?

"Oh no," I gasped. "You got a gun this time. Oh my, what am I going to do now?"

"You're such a good little actress, aren't you?"

"My God." I faked the tremble of my lower lip. "Please don't hurt me, Cillian. I'll tell you everything. Every single thing you want to know."

"Oh yeah?" Our heads were on the same level now, with me hanging and him standing in front of me, pressing the barrel of the gun into my stomach. "Are you going to confess?"

"Please, Mr. Cillian." I almost barfed at the amount of crap flowing from my mouth. "Please don't hurt me."

"I like that. You begging me, you at my mercy."

"Oh yeah," I cooed. "Why don't you come closer?"

I wasn't really sure if I should be laughing at this whole situation or crying for him. Once upon a time, I would've felt bad for him. I would've even tried to help him, because Cillian was what I refused to be.

I refused to be someone unable to accept who I truly was. Even after all this time, there was a struggle within him. He was still trying to fight it, trying to lock the other part of him in a box, so that he could suit the needs of other people around him.

He stepped closer, our noses bumping, our breaths mixing together. His pupils dilated, and I did what any sane— or well, insane —woman would do. I pressed my lips to his, pushing as far as I could. He should've pushed me away, should've punished me for my little, stupid act, but he did neither of those things.

Cillian kissed me back.

He fisted my hair in his hand, tilting my head back, and licked over the seam of my lips, urging me to open up. With the gun pressed between the two of us, he started kissing me harder, our tongues battling for dominance.

Kiss.

Bite.

I bit his tongue, pulling a growl from his chest, and it was like looking at a wild animal, being released into the wilderness. He pressed the gun to my temple, pulling the safety off, but he didn't stop devouring my mouth.

Push and fucking pull, that's what the two of us were. Now I regretted it even more for never going after him and instead choosing his brother. Holy fucking hotness on two legs, this fucked-up psycho could kiss.

Unfortunately for me, the same tingling sensation I felt whenever Kieran kissed me was nowhere to be seen. My mind was still very much aware of everything, but it felt good. It felt too good to be stopped, so I used all of my strength and enveloped my legs around his waist, grabbing the ropes with my hands.

The pain ricocheted from my mangled finger, but even that couldn't deter me from getting to what I wanted to have.

"Fuck," he murmured against my lips, as I started rubbing myself on the bulge in his pants. My skin was on fire, and I needed him to remove my panties and the bra that felt like a heavy weight holding me down.

"Take it off," I instructed between kisses. "Take your pants off."

"What if I don't want to, birdy?"

"Don't fucking mess with me right now, Cillian. Take. Your. Pants. Off."

I bit his jaw, soothing the spot with a kiss. Whatever was on his mind before this obviously disappeared, because in the next moment, the belt hit the ground and I untangled my legs from him, as he started unbuttoning his pants.

Kinky son of a bitch didn't wear any underwear.

He picked the belt up, and I could see the condom in his other hand.

"Do you always carry condoms around the house?" I asked, to which he grinned, the boyish expression throwing me off guard. Who the fuck was this person in front of me?

"Maybe."

My bra went flying in two different directions as he tore it apart with his hands, and my underwear quickly dropped to the ground, tangled with his pants. He left the gun on the ground and swiftly grabbed my hips, squeezing tightly. Goosebumps broke all over my skin as he started tracing circles with his thumbs, slowly moving between my breasts, the cold metal on his belt, following their lead.

"Are you sure that you want this, birdy?"

God fucking dammit, don't be sweet on me.

"Kill," I moaned as he circled over my nipples. "I'm begging you."

"I need to hear those words."

His cock nestled against my stomach as he lowered his head and kissed my neck.

"I just want to fucking feel something, Kill," I cried out. "I need to feel something else besides this shit inside me, tearing me apart."

His lips trailed from my collarbone, over the burned skin there, pain and pleasure mixing together. He pulled my legs up, wrapping them around his waist, and started the slow descent toward my pussy, spreading the lips in his path.

"We need to get you ready, birdy."

"Just fuck me already."

"Tsk-tsk." He placed a kiss on my cheek. "Not so fast."

He pinched my clit, and started sliding his hand toward my opening.

"Fuck, Ophelia. You're already wet."

"Yes." I tilted my head back as his lips moved from my cheek to my neck, and back to my lips. Before I could even take my next breath, he pushed two fingers inside, my back arching immediately, my breasts rubbing against his shirt.

The friction felt good, like a sweet oblivion, combined with the slow strokes he was assaulting me with. I started protesting as he removed his fingers, but in the next moment, something hard landed on my neck, and a clicking sound told me it was his belt that he tied around my neck.

There was no sound, not a word uttered between us, as he dropped my legs, ripping the foil of the condom packet off, and putting it on his hard cock. Goddamn, and all of the saints.

He stroked himself, and I don't know what the fuck it was about men pleasuring themselves, but it evoked something primal inside me.

"Kill," I protested. In a blink of an eye, he was holding me up, and slammed inside.

"Holy fucking shit!"

He didn't wait for me to adjust to his size, and just like the animal he was, and just like the fucked-up person that I was, he started fucking me with slow, punishing strokes, hitting all the right spots. His other hand pulled at the belt he secured around my neck, and the pain from the injuries I had, the strain on my neck, his hooded eyes looking at me as if I were something to be held and not something to be destroyed, were driving me insane.

"Faster," I urged. "I need you to go faster."

The belt tightened, and I clenched around him more and more, his own eyes closing from pleasure. I held onto the ropes, the metal pole above my head squeaking with each move he made, fucking rearranging my insides.

"Kill!" I gritted through my teeth, and he dropped the belt, only to hug me closer, plastering me to his chest. With this position, he pistoned inside, my screams drowned out by his lips on mine.

"Do you want to come, birdy?" he purred against my lips. "I can feel you squeezing my cock."

"Oh God." My eyes rolled to the back of my head, the black dots appearing in front of me. "Holy fuck, holy fuck, holy…" I trailed off, but he was relentless.

He started slowing down, and just before I could protest, the shackles holding my wrists unlocked, and he pulled us to the ground, with me straddling him.

"I want you to ride me, Ophelia."

I could feel the throbbing of his cock inside, my heartbeat going crazy, and I leaned down, pushing his shirt up, revealing his strong abs. Oh fuck me sideways, he had a motherfucking V there.

I let my legs drop to the sides, and I started lifting myself up and down, sliding on his length, as he held my hips, letting me set the tempo.

"Oh fuuuuck," I drawled as he started hitting a new spot inside my pussy. The tightening in my lower stomach became harder to ignore, and I started pushing myself faster. He stopped me, flipping me over onto my stomach and lifting my ass in the air.

"Spread your legs," he commanded, and my God… That tone did something to my insides.

I spread my legs further, completely unprepared when he slammed inside again, slapping my ass cheeks with every new onslaught.

"Are you close, birdy?" He leaned down whispering in my hair, increasing his pace, "Because I really need you to fucking come."

"Fuck… yessss."

"Come on, Phee." He was a man possessed, and if it wasn't for his hands that held me above the ground, I would've ended on the floor already. He sneaked another hand toward my clit, and the pinching and rubbing he started, were the triggers I didn't think I needed.

"Fuuuuuck!" I screamed and was pretty sure half of the house heard me, but I couldn't give a fuck at that moment. I clenched around him as my orgasm tore through my body, the tremors wracking me.

"Oh. My. God." He pushed inside with a few more strokes and pulled out, warm liquid hitting my back. I turned my head to see him stroking himself, coming all over my lower back and my ass.

Cillian seemed hypnotized with the sight in front of him, and reached down to smear the cum over my butt cheeks, a small smile playing on his face.

At this moment I almost forgot my own name, not to mention anything else, and he seemed to feel the same. I felt sleepy, sated, and just about ready to hit the bed.

"Are you okay?" he suddenly asked, and I wanted to curse him for the sweet demeanor he was suddenly showing toward me. I had no doubt it was just the aftershocks of the orgasm. He wasn't his brother, but it just made it harder, knowing what the future held.

I still had to do what I needed to do, and Cillian was one of the last people I wanted to hurt further.

"My, my." A clapping sound came from behind us, and I dropped to my knees, covering my boobs with both my hands as Kieran came into the light. "You two made quite the show there."

"Fuck off, Kieran," I bit out.

I wasn't sure if I hated the look of indifference he wore, or if I appreciated him not showing any emotions. Cillian kept quiet next to me, slowly collecting his pants, and picking up the used condom from the floor, stuffing it into the pocket.

"Is this a thing now? Should I call Tristan as well? Maybe you'd like to fuck him too."

"Maybe you should." I smiled at him. "I have to try all of the Nightingale brothers before you take away my life. It's only fair, isn't it?"

He took his phone out, and I halfway expected him to take a picture of me like this, naked and on the ground, but he instead started talking to Cillian, ignoring me.

"Did you tell her already?"

"Nope." Cillian shrugged. "I was too busy fucking her."

"Tell me what?"

Kieran walked to the chair in the corner of the room, retrieving the shirt lying there, and threw it at me.

"Well, we are going on a trip." His eyes kept flickering between Cillian and myself. If I didn't know better, I would say there was a tick in his jaw. Oh, poor baby, he was actually jealous.

Didn't he know that having somebody's body was the easiest thing to do? It was the soul that you had to earn, and a heart to win.

"What kind of a trip?"

"We're going to Vegas, birdy."

17

KIERAN

The bartender wanted to cut me off, but did I listen to him?

Of course not.

The amber liquid in my glass was almost the same color as her hair, and I couldn't stop staring at it. These last couple of days were pure hell, fucking torture. Having her so near, and knowing she was as far as she could get was killing me slowly.

Knowing she wasn't going to come out of this alive was another burden I had to take, but it had to be done. Fuck, if only I could turn off my heart, this would all be much easier.

If only I could forget what her lips tasted like, what her skin felt like, I would be able to go through this unscathed, with my mind intact. I needed to get myself out of this misery, because allowing myself to even think about my feelings for her was a recipe for a disaster and the probability of me screwing this whole operation for her would be almost certain.

And Storm.

Motherfucking Storm Knoxx.

I was going to kill him myself as soon as we got our mother away from him. Tristan called our father yesterday, letting him know what was going on, and he confirmed her disappearance. They couldn't figure out when or how, but nobody had seen her for over five days, and that asshole, our sperm donor, didn't think to tell us.

Well, he was another asshole I was going to kill, and the list was just growing longer.

I almost killed my own brother when I saw him with Ophelia. Fucker knew I was falling down this rabbit hole of feelings and regrets, and he just went ahead and fucked the only person I ever loved.

Seeing her give herself to him, seeing her enjoy it, I finally understood how she felt all those years ago when she found me with Cynthia. What the fuck had I been thinking? I screwed up the best thing I had for pussy that meant nothing to me.

And all because I couldn't handle everything that was going on around me.

I couldn't handle Ophelia gradually turning into a psychopath, my sister marrying a man I didn't want her to marry, our father pushing us further into the business, Cillian spiraling... I just couldn't handle any of it.

"Do you know what the best way is to screw up your life, Stephan?" My words were slurred, but fuck if I cared at that moment. The bartender who couldn't be older than twenty-one looked at me skeptically, and I couldn't blame him. I was pretty sure I was a sight at that moment.

"No, sir."

"You fuck over the girl you love more than your own life, because you are a pussy."

"Sir?"

"Have you ever been in love?"

"Can't say that I have, Mr. Nightingale."

I laughed as he started eyeing me slowly, probably ready to call security to escort me to my room. Hell, if I were him I would've escorted myself out of here three hours, and two whiskey bottles ago.

"Trust me, you don't wanna be. It is a recipe for broken heart, and an eternity of messed-up feelings."

"Um..."

"Pour me another one." I chugged the rest of my drink, and dropped the glass on the bar.

"Sir, I really think you should head back to your room."

Maybe he was right, but not to my room. An idea popped up in my head and what a brilliant one it was. She already fucked my brother, so what was the worst thing she could do after that. My heart was already upstairs in her room, so why not the rest of my body?

"You know what?" I stood up, almost falling off the chair in my drunken stupor. "I'm alright, I'm alright." I straightened myself up before he could even come around the bar. "I am going to go back, and I hope you have an amazing night."

I didn't wait for his response, and started heading toward the main lobby and the elevators leading to our floor. These lights were way too bright. I would have to talk to the team here to change them.

If I couldn't get drunk in Vegas, what was even the point?

"Good evening, sir." A bellboy appeared in front of me. "Do you need any help?"

Did I need help? Of course, I needed fucking help, but he couldn't give me what I needed. What I needed was to go back in time and fix all the shit I did to her. I needed to save my sister, take her far, far away from Croyford Bay and Ophelia.

Hell, maybe if I hadn't fucked up like I did, I wouldn't even have to take her away. Ophelia would still be mine; we would be married by now, maybe with a kid.

"Sir?" He was still standing in front of me, waiting for a response.

"No, thank you. I just need to go to my room." I passed him, crossing the lobby.

They couldn't have made these elevators in the lobby directly, but they had to put them inside another hallway. Why did we acquire this hotel again?

Oh, right, the money was too good to pass up the opportunity.

Well, what the hell, maybe we did do something good. I pulled my key card from my pocket, and tapped it on the console as soon as I stepped inside, and pressed the button for the tenth floor.

To do it, or not to do it?

To go to my room or to go to hers?

Go to hers.

But I shouldn't. I really, really shouldn't. I tried checking the time on my watch, but I couldn't understand the numbers. Was it broken? Shit, I really liked this watch.

She gave it to me on our first anniversary.

It couldn't be fucking broken.

The ding of the elevator pulled me back to the present time, before my mind could drown me in memories I didn't want to have anymore, and I stepped outside, seeing our guards stationed in front of all our rooms. Two were in front of her room, and I started laughing because we needed two bloody guards to contain her.

Such a hellfire, such a spirit.

Instead of going to the end of the hallway, I stopped in front of her bodyguards, their postures going rigid.

"Mr. Nightingale." Both of them nodded.

Why did everybody insist on calling me Mr. Nightingale? That was my father's name, the way he liked to be called.

I was just Kieran. Not Mr. Nightingale, not sir, just Kieran.

"Is she alone?"

If Cillian ended up going to her room, I was going to strangle him right here and right now. I didn't give a shit that he was my brother. That scene in the basement was enough to haunt me for the rest of my life.

Nobody touched her but me. Nobody brought her pleasure but me.

Not anymore.

"Yes, sir."

"Unlock the door for me please. I need to talk to her."

They looked at each other, and then at me, contemplating my request.

"I said, open the door."

"Sir, we don't think it's a good idea."

"You're not being paid to think," I growled. "You're paid to execute orders, my orders, so open the fucking door."

Another second passed before one of them pulled the key out, and pressed it against the key reader, opening the door.

"We will be here, sir."

I nodded and pushed between them, entering the room.

My brothers and I were in the suite at the end of the hallway. Her room was much smaller, and as the door closed behind me, I froze in place seeing her sleeping on the bed, her back turned to me. Her amber hair was sprawled over the pillow, and my eyes started cascading from her head, toward her shoulders, and the back, all the way to the swell of her ass in those shorts.

She was fucking magnificent. I was a fool for coming here, but I couldn't stop myself.

My need for her was always bigger than anything else, and there was no place for sanity where she was involved.

She was crazy, but so was I. The difference was, I was crazy about her, and she was crazy for everything else.

I removed my suit jacket, letting it drop to the floor as I

sauntered toward the center of the room. The bed dipped beneath my weight, and she stirred in her sleep, turning toward me.

The infinite color of a sky I could always see in her eyes, connected with mine, and a small furrow in her brow showed her confusion.

"What are you doing here, Kieran?"

I brought my hand up, gliding it over her hair, ignoring her question.

"Kieran?"

I thought this was going to be easier. I thought hating her for what she did would exorcise my demons and salvage my soul, because what I did could never be forgiven. She didn't know everything that happened after we broke up, and I hoped that she never found out.

What I did to her sister was unforgivable, and I was a fucking hypocrite trying to destroy her now when I wasn't an innocent party here. None of us were innocent, but the two of us, we deserved a special place in hell for all of the gruesome things we did.

For all the orders we followed.

"If you're here with another one of your fucked-up games, you can let yourself out and let me sleep."

"Shhh." I placed my finger on her lips, feeling the softness below. "I don't wanna talk, Phee."

"Are you drunk?" She propped herself up, and I let my hand drop from her hair. "Of course, you are. Jesus, Kieran, did you drink the whole distillery tonight? You reek of it."

"I'm sorry."

She was vividly taken aback by my words, and started inching closer to the edge of the bed, away from me.

"Please don't go." I pulled her closer to me. "I just wanna hold you, just for one night. Just this one time."

"What the hell, K?"

I hugged her to me, burying my face in her hair. If I could, I would've taken her away a long time ago. Maybe If I was stronger, I would've been able to save her, to save us. But I was late, so fucking late, and in a blink of an eye, she became a monster I had to destroy.

But not tonight, no.

Tonight, she was my Ophelia. She was the little girl chasing after us with Ava. She was a woman who stole my heart, and the one I wanted to spend the rest of my life with, no matter how miserable I was.

Tonight, she was an angel I needed. If I had to pretend that everything that happened was just a bad dream, so be it.

"Please, Phee," I pleaded with her. "Please. Just tonight."

She gradually relaxed in my arms, and I knew I had what I wanted.

A sweet dream.

A bitter fantasy.

I was always going to be hers, I knew that. Even when the last breath leaves her body, I was still going to be hers. Nobody else ever came even close to her and what we used to have. Nobody ever would.

"Okay." Her voice felt like a caress on my skin, and in that moment, nothing else mattered.

None of the things she did, the monstrous things I did. Not even the fact that we pushed each other over the cliff.

None of it.

I dropped down onto the mattress, pulling her with me. There was no fight left in her body, and this felt like one of those nights we spent together before our world burned down.

"I am sorry, Phee." I gripped her tighter, pulling her closer. "I am so fucking sorry for everything."

I could feel her stiffening again, but I wasn't letting her go.

"What are you sorry about, K?"

Could I tell her? Should I tell her?

No, I needed this now. I needed her to pretend it was just us.

"I fucked it all up. I wasn't strong enough, wasn't smart enough to withstand everything that was going on."

"It's okay."

"No, it isn't." She dropped her leg over my hips, straddling me. She reached the nape of my neck with her hands, playing with my hair, and it was as if nothing ever happened.

But it did.

I did something bad, something really, really bad, and she would never forgive me if she ever found out.

I cheated, I lied, I destroyed an innocent life because I couldn't stand up for what I believed in.

"I hope you'll be able to forgive me one day, Phee. I hope one day, you'll understand that everything I did, I did it for Ava and you. I never wanted to hurt you."

She kept quiet, continuously playing with my hair. And just before my eyes closed down, alcohol and exhaustion pulling me under, I heard her voice in the dark.

"I could never forgive you, Kieran."

18

KIERAN

Four Years Ago

W *hat have I done?*
What the fuck have I done to us?
I've been hiding in my apartment for the better part of the last four days, and I still couldn't wrap my head around the fact that she was gone.

Ophelia was gone, and I was the one to blame.

I always thought she would end up being the one to push me away, but no, I did it all by myself. Our picture stood on the table in front of me… She was smiling, and I was looking at her as if she was my whole goddamn world.

And she was, she still is, so why the fuck did I do this? Why, why, why? Why did I allow my mind to take me to the darkest of places and betray her like that?

I had no excuse for breaking her trust, breaking her heart. Fuck, I didn't just break hers, I broke mine as well. And that look on her face as she left the apartment… that look would haunt me for the rest of my life.

I knew she wasn't joking when she told me to run. I fucking

knew she would react like this. In Ophelia's world there was no place for forgiveness, only vengeance. In her head, forgiveness wasn't something you could ever earn, and once you lost her trust, there was no going back.

It didn't matter if you were her blood, her lover or her friend. Her revenge was always the same —ten times worse than what you did to her.

And I definitely wasn't a person she loved anymore. It was all there, written in her eyes. She hated my guts.

Maybe if I drank myself into a stupor, I would forget I broke both of our hearts. It was tempting to break this glass in my hand, and just cut my veins open. It would hurt less than what I did to us.

It would hurt less than this suffocating pain in my chest, this turmoil in my head. Maybe I should do it. Maybe I should just leave this world. Because the world without her wasn't the world I wanted to live in.

And she would never forgive me.

She would never forgive me for this.

I wish I knew why I did it. Why I cheated on her. Maybe if I knew, I would be able to explain and ask for forgiveness. Maybe... Maybe she would understand.

Yes, that's right. If I figured out why and what pushed me to do it, I would be able to talk to her, to make her understand. It wasn't me; it was my mind playing tricks on me.

Cynthia was just there, willing, and I didn't know how to deal with this fucked-up shit we found ourselves in.

I grabbed my hair as if that would relieve me from the mess brewing in my mind.

I had a feeling my head was about to explode. The alcohol, my father pushing for things I didn't wanna do, the fact that I lost the only good thing in my life, it was all creating a hurricane there, and I didn't know how to stop it.

And where the fuck was my phone?

I tried getting up from the sofa I parked myself at, but I underestimated the amount of alcohol I drank, and plopped down like a sad sack of shit. Pathetic. That's what I was. Fucking pathetic. A weak, fragile man... No wonder she never really trusted me with everything that was going on with her. I wouldn't be able to take it.

I wouldn't be able to understand all that she was going through, because I was scared. I was scared of the darkness inside her, I was scared of the uncertain future both of us had, I was scared for my family, my brothers and my sister.

I was fucking terrified this world would consume us both, and what we used to be, would be just a memory.

"Fuck!" I yelled at no one and nothing in particular, or maybe at everything. Maybe I yelled at the unfair hand of destiny all of us were dealt.

I reached for the bottle on the table, only to find it completely empty. Brilliant, just fucking brilliant. Now I had to get myself to the kitchen and find another one. I didn't even know when I drank it all. I mean, it wasn't that late.

I looked at the watch on my right hand, but the numbers were blurry, unrecognizable. Shit, did I break my watch as well?

Wait, I just got an idea.

I should go to talk to Ophelia. Yeah, that's right.

I should get my ass up and go and talk to her. She needs to listen to me. She had to hear what I have to say. I needed to tell her how much I loved her, and that Cynthia didn't mean anything to me. That's right.

I should do that.

Pushing myself off of the sofa, I stumbled into the table in front of me, knocking the empty bottle on the floor.

Fucking idiot.

The shards of shattered bottle went flying all over the floor, and the same thoughts entered my head. What if I wasn't good enough anymore? What if she never forgave me? Why won't I just end it all?

It would be so easy, so fast.

I crouched down and took the closest broken piece of glass into my hand. Funny, wasn't it? All of us are always trying to keep it up, to keep the pretenses, this whole life, but we all end up broken. Just like this bottle.

Just like I was.

A small cut, just the length of my vein. I rolled the sleeve of my shirt up, exposing the skin on my underarm. It was there already, pulsing, transporting blood, keeping the life I didn't want to keep. Nobody would miss me.

At least there would be one bastard less to taint this world, because I knew that this was only the beginning. These killings I did, these orders I issued, these were just the beginning of the never-ending cycle I was a part of.

I loved dreaming about a day when I would be free of this —these shackles, all of this pain, all of this guilt I was feeling and couldn't let go. I killed bad men, but I also killed the good ones.

The innocent ones who had families waiting for them at home.

The ones who just happened to be at the wrong place, at the wrong time.

One cut wouldn't mean anything, right? It wouldn't bring them back, but at least I wouldn't be here anymore. I was so tired of all of this —of fighting this filthy world from consuming me.

Ophelia.

Ophelia.

Ophelia.

Would she miss me? No, probably not. I was lying to myself, but I knew she would never forgive me.

What was stopping me?

I pressed the shard into my skin, the other end biting into my hand. I wondered how much I would bleed. I hoped my brother would be the one to find me, and not my mother or my sister.

There was a small sting as I pressed harder into my skin, but it wasn't taking away the pain from my head. I could still hear everything in there. I could still feel the water pulling me under.

Drowning.

Choking.

Screaming.

I stopped for a moment. Should I write a letter? Should I maybe explain why I did what I did? Maybe I could write one letter to my family and the second one to Ophelia?

No, no, no.

There was no stopping now.

The clear reflection of the glass started getting red, as my skin finally broke and the weirdest sensation came over me. I felt free.

My cheeks were getting wet, and I realized I was crying. But I wasn't scared. This was the first time in many years that I didn't feel any fear. I felt absolutely nothing.

I started moving my hand, the shard cutting deeper into my skin, the blood slowly pouring out. Yes, this is it. This was the euphoria I needed.

This was…

My movements were halted with the loud banging coming from the front door. No, no, no, they couldn't stop me now. I was finally going to be free.

I started gliding the glass over my skin, as the voice I never wanted to hear again echoed through the apartment.

"Kieran!" There was more banging on the door. "Open the door, Son. I know you're in there."

My father. The bane of my existence. He wanted to stop me. He wanted to destroy what was left of my humanity.

"Open this fucking door, Kieran!"

I kept sitting on the floor, not even moving a muscle. But maybe I should, get up that is. I could get rid of him and get back to this.

Yeah, that's right. I could do that.

I picked myself up, throwing the used shard below the sofa, and rolled down the sleeve. Blood seeped into the dark material, and I hoped he wouldn't be able to see it. Not that he would ever care.

Trudging across the room toward the hallway and the door, I started tucking my shirt in my pants, and ran my hands through my hair. I had no doubt my father would have something to say about my physical state, but he could fuck off into the depths of hell for all I cared right now, because all of this would soon be over.

Soon I won't have to ever see him again or hear his ridiculous demands. I would finally be free.

I opened the door, my eyes clashing with the same dark ones. The ones I kept seeing in the mirror every day. I was the carbon copy of daddy dearest, and I wondered when he became such a ruthless man. When did he stop caring for his family, and start thinking only about his own personal gain?

Disapproval.

Anger.

Of course, those were the only emotions visible on his face. This was the man who never showed compassion, never cared about what we really wanted. He never once asked me if I was okay with everything that was going on, never stopped to see how all of this was destroying Cillian. How scared Tristan was, and how much damage we were causing to Ava.

No, the only person he ever cared for was himself. I sometimes thought he had so many kids just to make sure there would be somebody left to continue the Nightingale bloodlines. You know, in case the other ones ended up dead, which was highly possible.

Well, don't worry, daddy dearest. I was about to fulfill your wishes.

"You look like shit," he sneered, but his behavior wasn't anything new. I couldn't remember the last time he praised me for anything I did.

"Good morning to you too, Dad."

"Evening, Kieran." He shouldered his way in, leaving me at the door. "It's fucking evening, and you smell like you bathed yourself in a sea of whiskey."

"Now that would be fucking awesome, wouldn't it?"

He was scanning the living room with me stumbling behind him, when the uncanny thought of bashing his head on the glass table in front started infiltrating my thoughts. It would be quick, a little bit messy, but I would be doing a good thing for the first time in my life.

"I need you to do something for me."

The blood on the carpet would be impossible to get out, but I could do with some remodeling.

"There's a girl outside." He turned toward me. How would it feel to see the life leaving his eyes? "Are you even listening to me, Son?"

I shook my head, trying to rid myself of these thoughts.

"Sorry, Dad. I guess I drank too much."

Yep, that was me —a disappointment of the year.

Disgrace of the family.

I could never do anything well enough for him.

"You're such a fucking mess, but I guess you'll be okay to do this job. After all, how hard is it to fuck somebody."

I took a step back, shocked by his words. "You want me to fuck somebody?"

"Did you become deaf as well, or just dumb?" He walked toward the sofa chair in the corner and sat down. "Yes I want you to fuck somebody, but this one is special. I need you to break her in for my buyer. She's a bit of a spitfire, and I need her pliant. I can't have any returns, and I don't want her buyer breathing down my neck."

"Dad, I can't—"

"Bring her in!" he yelled, not even listening to me. He wants me to wreck somebody for his sick games. Sex slaves? What the fuck were our families thinking?

The sound of feet shuffling had me turning around, and what I saw made my blood run cold. Maya Aster, Ophelia's sister, stood between the two guards with a terrified look on her face. Her brown hair was disheveled, and the clothes she wore weren't fitting. No, they were hanging on her frail body. My alcohol-induced mind was racing with questions. Wasn't she in Europe, or some shit like that?

Her hands were shackled in front of her, and her eyes kept flickering between me and my father.

"Kieran," she whispered, almost inaudible, shock and confusion mixed in one. "Kieran! Oh my God!" She tried moving toward me, but the two monkeys on her sides held her in the same spot.

"Let go of me, you fucking assholes!" She started wrestling with the two of them, and as the light started hitting her face in different angles, I could see the bruises on her cheeks and on her neck. Even her arms were filled with purple and blue markings. Ophelia would be devastated if she knew where her sister was.

"Well, I will leave you to it, Son." My father tapped me on my back, and started walking toward the two mongrels and Maya.

"Dad, I can't do this. It's Maya! I just… I can't."

He turned to me, that calculating gleam in his eyes.

"It's better Maya than Ava." He grinned. "Don't you think?"

Did he just… Did he just insinuate what I think he did?

"You fucking wouldn't." I took a step closer, fury like no other taking over my body. "You wouldn't put Ava through this?"

"I won't if you do what you're asked to do."

Motherfucking son of a bitch.

He would do that to his flesh and blood, to his own daughter?

"Well," he chuckled. "Have fun, my boy. I will send somebody in the morning to take her back. And be careful, she's a feisty one."

With one last look at Maya, he and his goons disappeared, leaving me with a scared-looking girl. What the fuck was I supposed to do now?

Refusing to do this would cost Ava her freedom, probably her life. But doing this would destroy even the slightest chance of ever getting back with Ophelia.

What do I do?

What do I do?

What do I fucking do?

"Kieran," her soft voice called out, and I realized I was no longer standing on the other side of the room, but in front of her. "Please, Kieran. Please let me go."

She pleaded, and if it wasn't for what my father told me, I would. I would've let her go, I would've helped her, hid her, told Ophelia… But I couldn't.

I couldn't do any of those things, because it was either her or Ava, and no matter how much I cared for Maya, how much I loved Phee, I couldn't subject Ava to this. I couldn't damn her soul for Maya's sake.

"Are you gonna let me go, Kieran?"

She looked so hopeful, her eyes sparkling with unshed tears. The same color of the eyes I betrayed just days ago, and I was going to do it again. I was going to destroy her family for the sake of mine.

I was going to shatter her sister to save mine.

"Kier—"

"No, Maya." I inched closer, masking my emotions. "I am not going to let you go."

"But… You and Ophelia… You can't!" she screamed. "You can't do this to me!"

Ocean blue, crystal blue, they almost looked the same.

"You have to help me," she cried out. "Please, please, please, Kieran. Help me! I can't live like this, I can't—"

"Shhh." I pressed a finger to her lips, grabbing her arm with my other hand. "It'll be okay."

"Nooo," she wailed, but her tears weren't important right now. Nothing was more important than my sister, and this was the question of life or death. Besides, Nikolai would for sure take his daughter out, he would help her.

"Don't do this, Kieran!" She struggled in my hold, as I started pulling her toward the bedroom I used to share with Ophelia. Was I going to fuck her sister in the same bed I professed my love to Phee?

"Kieran!"

"Shut the fuck up!" Maya's head flew to the other side as my palm connected with her face. "If you shut up, this will be over faster than you think."

Her whimpers were tearing at my chest, but I couldn't stop now. I wouldn't stop.

This was for Ava, and one day... One day, Ophelia would have to forgive me.

For a moment, she stood still as a statue, looking at the bed in front of us. Her eyes never met mine, but she was Ophelia's sister, and those fucked-up minds of theirs were always cooking something. Always thinking about the way out.

"Why don't you remove these?" She held her hands up, her handcuffs rattling against each other. "Then we can get this shit done."

"I don't think so, Maya." I laughed. "Do you really think I'm that stupid?"

"No, I—" she stuttered.

"Get on the bed."

"But, Kie—"

"Get on the motherfucking bed, Maya." I threw her frail body on the bed, and she landed on her back, her legs spread. "That's good."

"Kieran, no!"

"I said," I gripped her jaw in my hand, pressing on the bones there, "to shut the fuck up. Didn't I?"

One lone tear rolled down her cheek, and then another one, and another one, and another one, until her body started shaking with the strength of her sobs.

Just turn it all off, Kieran. Turn the guilt off, push through this and you will be okay.

"Stop crying, for fuck's sake. It won't help you."

"Please," she mumbled between her pressed lips. "Please, Kieran. I will disappear."

"Too late, Maya."

"Please." She tried pushing herself up, but I pushed her down, holding her by her throat. "Please don't do this to me, Kieran. Think about Ophelia, think about what you're going to do."

"Ophelia?"

Her eyes were blue. So, so blue, like the Mediterranean Sea in the middle of July.

Blue.

Ocean.

Ophelia.

"Ophelia," I choked out, and it wasn't Maya I was seeing in front of me. "Ophelia, you came back."

Her smile was blinding, but the watery trail left from her tears made me feel like the biggest asshole on the entire planet.

"I am sorry," I kissed her cheek. "I am so sorry, baby girl. I promise I will make everything better."

"Kieran," she sobbed. Why was she sobbing? "Please…"

"I will make you feel good, Phee. I promise."

She lost so much weight in the past couple of days. As I pulled her shirt up, revealing the soft swell of her breasts, I could see her ribs protruding, her stomach sinking in.

"You need to eat, baby. You need to eat, otherwise you'll get sick, and I don't want you to be sick."

I would make her feel better. I would.

This was my chance to make everything better, this was what I was asking for. I unbuttoned my pants, letting them drop to the floor, and started doing the same to the shorts she was wearing. Why was she wearing shorts? It was cold outside, she could get sick.

"I am sorry, baby."

I started kissing her neck, as I pulled the shorts from her hips, dropping them to the floor, next to the bed. Shivers erupted over her skin, and I kissed my way from her collarbone to the valley between her breasts, dropping one hand in her panties.

"We will be happy, Phee. I will make you so happy, so, so happy. You'll see."

"Kieran, please."

"Shh, baby girl. Shhh."

My lips locked on hers, urging her to open up, but she wasn't returning my kiss.

"Let me go, Kieran!"

"No, no, princess. No!" I pulled her underwear down, taking my cock out, slowly stroking myself. Her eyes were so blue, so brilliant, I could always get lost in them. "You're mine. You will always be mine, no matter what. We will always be together. Kieran and Ophelia, against the world."

"Kieran, I'm not—"

I shushed her with another kiss, pulling her lower lip between my teeth. She whimpered as I nestled my cock against her clit, slowly rubbing from her opening to the hood of her pussy.

Pulling the cups of her bra down, I flicked my tongue over one nipple, the little bud hardening beneath my touch. Kneading the other breast, and giving it the same attention, I sank my teeth in her neck, swiftly licking the spot I'd bitten and kissing her sweet spot.

"You like that, baby?"

She kept quiet, but that was okay. I had her. She was mine again, and this time I wasn't letting her go.

"Please, don't do this. I'm begging you, Kieran."

I ignored her pleas, because I knew Ophelia. She always liked to play hard to get, but I knew better. I knew she wanted this as much as I did. She wanted to be here with me, to be devoured by me, and to have everything go back to normal.

I spread her legs further, and slowly sank into her heat, my eyes rolling into the back of my head as all of the nerve endings in my body woke up from the grip she had on my dick. She yelled out, and I pushed deeper, reveling in her sounds.

She was enjoying this, she loved this, and I was the luckiest man on the entire earth.

"No, no, no…"

"Yes, baby, yes. Feel this, feel us."

"Kieran, please. I'm not—"

"No more talking, Ophelia. Just feel us." I started moving, in and out. Slowly at first, savoring the moment. This beautiful connection we had.

"I love you, baby." I sank all the way in, before pulling out. "I love you so fucking much, Phee."

I moved her hands above her head, holding them there. My girl loved being tied up. She loved being restrained. She was struggling in my hold, trying to pull herself up, but I held her down.

"Tell me you love me, baby." I buried my face in her hair and whispered in her ear, "Tell me you can't live without me."

I increased my pace, her walls clenching around me. I wasn't going to last long like this, because she was tight. Too tight.

"Tell me, Phee." I pulled her hair, exposing her neck and started leaving bites there. "Tell me, tell me, tell me."

"Kieran," she cried. "It hurts."

"Enjoy it, baby. We are together again. Together, forever."

"I can't." She started shaking her head, evading my lips.

I released her hair, pinching her nipple between my fingers. A moan escaped from her mouth. See, I knew she loved this.

Pulling her legs up over my shoulders, she opened up more and I started drilling in, my balls slapping against her ass.

"Do you love me, Phee?"

"No, K—"

I slapped her, and placed my hand against her mouth, the other one holding her nose, stopping her intake of breath.

Muffled sounds erupted from her, but I kept going, holding her like this.

Pretty little masochist, I didn't know she had this in her. So compliant, so mine.

"Do you love me?" I released her as a coughing fit erupted from her.

"Tell me!" I roared, and I could feel my balls tightening. "Tell me, Ophelia."

"Yes!" she finally fucking yelled. "I love you, Kieran."

"That's right, baby."

"I love you so much."

"Yes, yes, yes." I gripped both of her legs, my pace increasing, my orgasm inching closer and closer. "Are you close? Please tell me you're close, baby, because I need us to finish together."

"Kieran—"

"Come on, Ophelia." I rubbed her clit. She tried closing her legs, but I wasn't letting her move them from the position on my shoulders.

"No!"

"Baby, I'm close. I'm so fucking close," I grunted. "Give in to me!"

I pressed harder against her little bud of nerves, and the eruption I was waiting for happened right in front of me eyes. She threw her head back, the walls of her pussy clenching around me, pulling my orgasm out from me.

"Fuuuuuuck," I shouted as my cock started spurting inside her, milked by her tight heat. "Fuck, Ophelia. Fuck, fuck, fuck."

She trembled, her legs shaking, and when I opened my eyes, it wasn't Ophelia in front of me. But their eyes, they had the same eyes.

Oh my God.

"What have I done?" I tore myself away from her, stumbling over the clothing on the floor, and plastered myself to the wall. "Maya."

Her eyes were focused on the ceiling, not a single sound coming from her. My blood was smeared on her face.

"I'm sorry." I dropped to the floor, trying to remind myself why I did this. For Ava, everything I did was for Ava. Why did I feel like this then?

"I am so fucking sorry."

I rubbed at my face, expecting a retribution, a sound from her, but she just kept staring at the ceiling, without saying a word.

19

OPHELIA

Present

Were monsters born, or were they made?

I've had this question running through my head for quite some time, and yet, I still didn't find an answer. Was I born with a fucked-up mind, or was it the circumstance in which I was brought up that shaped who I am today? I was almost certain I wasn't born like this.

On the days when the air felt thicker, and I could feel her here, with me, I could still remember what it felt like just being a normal teenager with Ava. I could see us strutting around Croyford High, going from class to class, talking about such insignificant bullshit, it almost made me puke right now. I wasn't a monster then.

I was just a kid, a normal teen with ridiculous problems.

And the biggest one of them all was, would Kieran ever see me as anything else but his sister's friend? If I could, I would travel back in time and warn seventeen-year-old Ophelia to run. Just take Ava and run away.

Save Kieran from the monstrosities he was going to commit.

Just take all of them away, far, far away.

I wasn't born a monster. I wasn't born filled with hatred, filled with all this pain, with this need for vengeance. Fairytales usually start with "Once upon a time", and once upon a time I was a happy girl, and then they ruined it.

Bit by bit, day by day and year by year, they were killing me slowly. These three brothers sitting in the car with me, these three monsters, they were pawns just like I was, but then they became the executioners. Each one of them became what they promised they wouldn't be.

Each guilty of something, but only one of them deserved what was coming for him.

Kieran took my heart and stomped all over it, and I would've forgiven him. I would have, because I loved him so much. Because I thought he was the best thing to ever happen to me. But then he took my soul and ripped it all apart.

The knowledge I gained, the things he did, it fucking shattered me, and for that, he was going to pay.

These three idiots thought they had me where they wanted me. The poor, little souls didn't know that they were actually puppets in my show.

Fear doesn't last forever, but they should've held onto theirs. They should've remembered who I was and what I stood for. They underestimated me, and each minute spent with them was another minute I learned something new.

The Nightingales were broken.

Lost.

Disorganized.

Fighting.

I would use all of their weaknesses for my own gain. My act of fear, me trying to run away, they were so easily fooled. These last couple of days with them told me more than I needed to know.

They were an easy target, a disheveled mess. And here I thought my whole mission would be much harder.

They should've killed me on the spot —severed my limbs, cut the head off the snake, and burned my remains. But these three idiots thought they'd be able to get additional information from me.

Thinking that I had any useful information about the Syndicate was going to be their destruction. I hadn't talked to my father in years, and I was glad for it.

But I guess that Theo wasn't much help to them either.

Papa still didn't trust him with the business and for that I was glad. I was happy that the slithering snake wasn't getting what he wanted. That's another traitor I would have to deal with, another asshole nobody would miss.

I always imagined Theo to be adopted, with only Maya and myself being the real Aster's. Unfortunately, that sack of potatoes really was my brother, and the DNA tests we all did were the proof of that.

Nightingales on the other hand, they were just pestilence I needed to get rid of. It was so easy getting inside their heads, and their weakest link was sitting right next to me.

Tristan Nightingale.

Kieran was at the wheel of the car, while Cillian sat on the passenger seat with his feet propped on the console in front. It was such a shame he didn't want to allow himself to truly live.

He and I, we were kindred spirits, and I knew Ava's death destroyed the last pieces of sanity he had. It destroyed mine as well, but I learned to control my demons.

I learned to tie those bitches up and be their master. I couldn't allow myself to be reckless anymore, not if I wanted to live.

Tristan shuffled in his seat, leaning between the front seats.

I looked through the window deciding to ignore all three of them. The games were just starting, and unbeknownst to them, they weren't the masters.

I was.

But I would allow them to think differently, at least for now.

Kieran hasn't said a word to me since last night. He wasn't in my bed this morning, and it pained me to say that I slept like a little baby with his arms enveloped tightly around my body.

I refused to acknowledge the fact that I still wanted him. But what I wanted and what I needed to do were two different things, and Kieran stopped being the good guy a long time ago. The audacity he had, coming to my room and asking for my forgiveness.

I knew why he was asking. I knew what he was asking it for, but I wasn't going to give it to him. He didn't deserve it.

I cracked my neck, my eyes zeroing on Kieran's neck, and I could almost imagine the moment I was waiting for ever since I found out what this idiot did.

Of all the things I knew he was capable of, this was the one thing I never even thought he would do. And he dares to ask for my forgiveness?

Too late, buddy, too fucking late. Whatever the reason for his betrayal was, I didn't wanna hear it.

Destroying somebody else's life because you were a pathetic piece of shit was a big no-no in my book, and me being me, I really didn't have a lot of no-noes.

It was rather simple with me— don't be a traitor and don't rape women.

This buttercup violated both.

"Turn right here," Tristan instructed him, and I didn't even notice when we started driving through the sketchy neighborhood.

One-story houses were lined up on both sides of the street, but there were no people outside. There were no kids playing around. The few cars I saw didn't belong to this side of the town. Range Rovers, one Maserati, and four motorcycles were the only vehicles I saw, and I knew they didn't belong to the occupants of those houses.

"How much longer?" It was Cillian this time, the irritation in his voice almost palpable. His forefinger tapped on the door in an inconsistent rhythm, and I started humming, creating a melody in my head.

Thump-thump thump. Thump-ta ra ta thump.

"We're almost there, so calm your fucking titties."

Kieran sounded irritated, and I would be as well if I had to be confined in a car with brothers I didn't trust and a woman he once loved. Truth to be told, I didn't even know why I was here with them. They could've easily let me be at the hotel, but the paranoid shitholes had to keep their eyes on me at all times.

I mean, I was crafty in hostage-type situations, but I wasn't the Incredible Hulk. I couldn't exactly break out of these handcuffs and go all "Ophelia, smash" on their asses. Not that I didn't want to.

"There it is," Tristan whispered to them, and I leaned forward and saw what they were seeing. "Saint Angelle's Cathedral."

Ooo, spooky.

I had no idea what exactly we were doing in Las Vegas, but the nervous energy the guys were emanating told me it wasn't for the sheer fun of it. Besides, whoever was meeting them here and chose this place was a fucking genius.

The gothic-looking cathedral at the end of the road looked like something that came out of the world of *Edward Scissorhands*, and with the dusk settling on the city I had a feeling one of Tim Burton's characters would just jump out of somewhere.

Was this whole trip messing with my initial plan? Yep, it definitely was. But I wasn't worried. The when and where didn't exactly matter, because the execution of my plan was coming, one way or another. Would it be in their house or somewhere on the side of the road, it really didn't matter.

What mattered was that I had to keep my mouth shut and hope Theo would appear at one point as well. That one was more my personal vendetta than the actual orders. I wanted to carve his heart out and feed it to the dogs. Maybe stab him a few times so that he could know how it feels having somebody you know killing you slowly.

"Do you see any of their guards?" It was Kieran who asked as we slowly approached the entrance of the cathedral. I craned my neck and looked outside, only to see a mean-looking blond guy at the entrance standing all alone.

The leather jacket he wore hugged his body tightly, and I didn't need him to be naked to know that this guy's muscles had muscles. But the fact that I could climb him like a tree wasn't what called my attention.

No, I could swear I saw this guy before. I just couldn't remember where. But this guy, whoever he was, oozed danger from every pore in his body. I couldn't take my eyes away from him, the way he commanded the space. As we started exiting the car, me behind Tristan, more guys wearing the same jackets appeared behind him.

That's when I got a better look at the insignia on the back of their jackets.

Motherfucking son of a bitch. English wasn't creative enough for all the curse words running through my head right now, because these three fucking idiots messed with Sons of Hades.

No, scratch that, because I wasn't worried that they messed with them, I was worried *he* would be here, and if my fucking life ends up looking like a Telenovela, I might stab somebody tonight.

The blond guy was scanning me from head to toe. Noticing it, Kieran positioned himself in front of me, leering at blondie. Perfect, K, now you were going to show your alpha side when we were probably targets of at least four snippers.

The clinking of the keys pulled my attention to Tristan, and he approached me slowly, removing the handcuffs from my hands.

"Don't try anything stupid, Ophelia."

He was scared.

Hell, I would be scared as well if I had to deal with Sons of Hades, and I didn't even know why we were here. Compared to them, I was a fairy godmother.

"Wouldn't dream of it," I murmured, shaking off the throbbing sensation in my wrists. Fuck, I hated these.

Kieran started walking first. The tension in the air palpable, you could almost cut it with a knife. Hell, I really didn't want to be here.

I had one very simple rule, and thanks to that rule, I managed to live this long in this world. Do not get fucking involved in shit that has nothing to do with you. And this right here, this had nothing to do with me.

So why the fuck did they have to bring me here? I didn't want to get involved, and what's more, I didn't want to see the other bastard who left me hanging when I needed him. Men were fucking trash, and right now I truly regretted ever trusting any of them.

"You're late." The blond giant chuckled as we came closer. "You know that he won't like it."

"I don't give a fuck if he likes it or not, Atlas," Kieran started. "He's lucky we didn't declare a war on your asses."

"But you would have to ask daddy dearest for permission first, wouldn't you?"

I chuckled.

I fucking chuckled, because holy balls on this man. He was right though. I was surprised the three of them could even go to the toilet without asking for permission first. I guess all those dreams about killing their father and taking over, were just that — dreams.

"Give me one reason why I shouldn't stab you in the eye right now?"

Oh, K was getting pissed, but I guess that whenever some-body dared to speak the truth, he got his panties in a twist. However, even I knew this was not a situation in which you could threaten a man who obviously had the upper hand.

"Because there is a person aiming just at you, positioned somewhere very close. So, if I were you, Kieran Nightingale, I would shut my preppy little mouth now, because Prez won't be this forgiving."

Fucking shit, being out of the Syndicate, I didn't even know who their current president was. Way to go, Ophelia. All those assassinations, battles, scars, and this is how you would end up dying —killed because of a cock war.

Truly magnificent.

"Should we head inside, Atlas?" Tristan, forever the peace-maker, asked while I kept quiet looking anywhere but at the men surrounding us. If I were to guess, there were at least three of them above us, probably ready to shoot on command.

"Sure," he answered and looked at me again. Recognition, the widening of his eyes, and I fucking knew. He was there that day. He was with them.

Just my fucking luck.

He opened the door, the creaking sound filling in the silence encompassing us, and entered without waiting for us. I admired him, actually.

We were taught never to turn our backs to our enemies, and this man, he just didn't give a fuck. Thanks to the three fuck-tards, we were outnumbered and in such a deep shit we were almost drowning, and they left their soldiers three streets away.

Who does that?

I would just like to know what kind of training these three took, because it was definitely different from the one I had.

The church was eerily quiet; the only sound was the clicking of our shoes on the marble floor that probably used to be white. Lamps were lit up on the walls, and I noticed that there were no chairs or benches inside.

This place was abandoned a long time ago, and while I didn't believe in God, I hoped that whichever force was there, it would allow me to die quickly if it came to that tonight.

The area where the altar usually stood was completely empty, but I had the feeling that the Saints painted on the windows of what once used to be a holy house, were judging us.

I mean, they had good reasons to judge us, but they could also fuck off. Where were all of the Saints, where was God when the first knife was placed in my hand and I was asked by my flesh and blood to condemn my soul to Hell for eternity?

Where were all the angels to save Ava and my sister, when they did nothing wrong in this lifetime? Where was this God when my nights were spent crying, begging, pleading to save us all from this misery?

They were nowhere to be seen, because they didn't care about us.

So, yeah, they could fuck off and take their judgy little eyes to somebody who cared. I fucking didn't, and I just wanted to survive this night.

I came this far, and I hoped I wasn't going to go out like this.

Killed in a church, well, cathedral— same shit, right? Satan's daughter slaughtered in the holy house. It would be the news of the century.

Cillian took a hold of my arm forcing me to stop, and before I could start a fight with him, my eyes zeroed in on Atlas at the bottom of the stairs, talking to somebody else.

Somebody hidden from us.

Black boots were the only thing I could see, before he stood up and looked at us. What were the symptoms of a heart attack, because I was pretty sure I was about to have one?

Clad in dark jeans and a loose Iron Maiden shirt, standing like a God of Death among mortals and wearing the scowl he didn't have the last time I saw him. Storm-fucking-Knoxx commanded the room with his sheer presence and no matter how much I tried to resist, I was sucked in.

Pulled under the water.

Drowning.

Drowning.

Drowning.

Another fucker I wanted to trust, yet couldn't. Another asshole who left me when I needed him. The shithead who pretended I didn't exist when I asked for his help.

He can fuck off too, along with all the deities, Nightingales and my own family.

I stepped next to Kieran, my blood fucking boiling at the mere sight of him. There he was, a masked expression on his face, his eyes raking over my body. Another fucking asshole who only saw that, my body.

He took a step closer, and another, and another, until he

stood face-to-face with Kieran, that cold, bored look pissing me off. He lazily looked at the three of them before settling back on me, moving from the initial bane of my existence toward the place where I stood.

"Hello, Persephone. We meet again."

20

OPHELIA

Four Years Ago

Why was I standing in front of a store I didn't know, in a town I've never been to, freezing my ass off?

Well, my beautiful friend thought it would be a good idea to go somewhere that nobody knew who we were to buy a fucking pregnancy test. It wasn't as if I didn't tell her already, I would go and get it myself and nobody would say a word. My father wouldn't care even if he knew, and Theo was too busy being an uptight prick to care if somebody knocked me up or not.

But nooo, oh no, she had to have her way and pull my ass here at the ass crack of dawn so that we could "catch the sunrise" and "go on a bonding road trip".

The only type of bonding I wanted to do for the last couple of days was the one where I stitched Kieran's mouth to Cynthia's pussy, so that they could be bonded for fucking forever.

I wasn't sure if I was sad, angry, heartbroken or murderous

anymore. Probably all of those, but one feeling remained the strongest.

Fucking murder.

To say that I was feeling stabby lately would be an under-statement of the century. Just yesterday Ava had to talk me out of going to Ventus City and having a "talk" with Kieran. Both her and I knew it would've ended up bloody.

And for fuck's sake, how long does it take her to buy a pregnancy test. She's been inside the store for at least half an hour, and the circulation in my fingers stopped working about fifteen minutes ago. Did I mention I didn't wear appropriate clothing for this time of year?

I was contemplating dragging her out, when the black motorcycle pulled up across the street, right in front of the store. Was I more interested in a man riding a bike than the bike itself? Maybe. Okay, most probably, but those thighs straddling the black machine had me thinking about a thousand ways in which he could be using them, and suddenly the ice-cold water I've been gulping down wasn't cold enough. The December air wasn't that cold anymore, and sweat settled at the back of my neck, regardless of the wind slapping me from both sides.

The town was overflowing with tourists this time of the year, it being the festive season and all, but even the annoying screams coming from a group of kids nearby couldn't divert my attention from the scene in front of me.

I could almost feel the rumble of that bike between my thighs; the way those vibrations would go through my body, the adrenaline I would no doubt feel… I was blatantly staring at the man as he turned off the ignition, and sat there for a second, staring at the store in front of him. He wore a leather jacket with some sort of a logo on the back, and I could only assume that he belonged to one of the MCs from the area. His face was hidden beneath the black helmet, and even from across the street, I could feel the energy emanating from him.

Danger.

Power.

Both of those things pulled at my insides, and I had the sudden urge to cross the street and talk to him. I wanted to, no, I *needed* to know him. The mere sight of this man calmed the storm raging in my head, and the only thought I had was seeing him, meeting him, and feeling that motorcycle between my thighs.

Well, a motorcycle and other things.

Kieran was just a back thought in my mind, and my sole focus was on this man.

My head snapped to the right side at the same rumbling sound, and I saw two more bikers approaching him. Surprisingly, seeing them did nothing to me. I admired their bikes, because God knew I wanted to have one myself, but there was no other reaction.

My eyes kept traveling to the imposing figure who decided to take permanent residency in my head. As soon as the newcomers parked behind him, they got off their bikes and started removing their helmets, and dear Jesus, Mother, Mary and Joseph.

If anyone ever asked me how I imagined the Princes of Hell looked like, well, voila. I'd point them in their direction.

All three of them wore identical jackets, all three of them dressed in all black. The blond man had his hair pulled into a bun, and even from this distance, I could see the array of tattoos gracing his face. The second one stood a couple of inches shorter than him, smiling at whatever the first one said.

When I finally looked back at the man that pulled my attention, our gazes clashed and I realized he's been watching me this whole time, while I've been too busy ogling the other two.

Pull.

Electricity.

That undercurrent of familiarity I felt toward him coursed through my veins, even though I knew I never saw him before. Then why was I feeling this way? Cars were passing between us, but the way he was looking at me, I had a feeling he could see my soul.

And for the first time, I didn't want to run in the opposite direction, because I wanted to see him as well.

"Where are you going?" I halted mid-step at the sound of Ava's voice behind me. I turned around and saw the confused look on her face, quickly realizing that I've been just a couple of steps away from crossing the street. "Are you okay?"

I started shaking my head, trying to get rid of the weird sensations coursing through my body. A quick glance to the spot where he stood told me he wasn't there anymore, and my heart squeezed at the mere notion that I missed my chance.

Oh, for fucks sake, Ophelia. Snap out of it, I chastised myself.

"Phee?"

"I'm fine." I smiled at her. "Did you get everything you needed?"

"Yeah," she answered skeptically. "Are you sure you're okay, though?"

"Yep, all fine. All good."

"Riiight."

I took a bag from her hand, opening it and seeing a pregnancy test inside. For the second time in just a couple of minutes, my heart squeezed painfully, understanding what this meant.

"Are you sure about this?" She laughed bitterly.

"Well, even if I wasn't, the baby is still there. I mean, if I really was pregnant."

"I know. Fuck." I rubbed my temple. "You know what this would mean for you and Nathan, right?"

"I do, but..." she stuttered.

"This is what you wanted. I know, trust me, I really do. And I will do everything I can to take you guys out of Croyford Bay and far away from our families. Even if you aren't pregnant, I think it's time for you to go."

"What do you mean? Why?" She took a bag from me, a frown forming between her eyebrows.

"I mean, we are both almost twenty-one now. Don't you remember the deal I made with my father?"

"Of course I do, but," she lowered the tone of her voice, "you think they would really make us go ahead with these weddings? You and Kieran aren't even together anymore."

Slice.

Slice.

Slice.

Just cut my heart in two, why don't you?

But I couldn't tell her that. Ava didn't know the full span of our breakup, and I would rather leave those details for myself. After all, it wasn't her fault her brother couldn't keep his fucking dick in his pants. If I ever heard another "but it was an accident" story, I was going to puke. Did he somehow stumble and his dick accidentally landed inside of Cynthia's pussy? Unbelievable son of a bitch.

"Ophelia?" My mind jumped back to the present time, and I registered concern shining from her eyes. "You're clenching your hands again."

"Fuck." I tried relaxing again, but the mere thought of Kieran was sending me into murderous rages these days. On top of that, my father was quite literally singing about the wedding I didn't want to happen.

How could I marry a person who stomped on my heart

when he fully knew how I felt about that whole thing? How could I pretend to be content with this constant control they had over my life?

"I'm sorry, Phee." She squeezed my arm, and the small gesture almost sent me into another fit of anger. I was familiar with anger, comfortable in its embrace. I just didn't deal well with other emotions. Especially the pity I could see written all over her face.

It was also something I hated seeing, despised it from the bottom of my heart.

My pulse skyrocketed as the rumble from before sounded again. The three bikers were back again, and he blatantly stared at me. *Again.*

"Ophelia," Ava's voice trembled. "Who are they?"

"I've no idea, but I'm about to find out."

"Ophelia." Her voice carried after me, but I was already crossing the street, heading straight toward them. Well, toward him.

This could be one of the worst ideas I've ever had, but I loved this imaginary line I walked every day, where I never knew if I would see the light of the next day. The adrenaline, the excitement, it didn't take me long to realize why I felt attracted to him. He might as well be a member of one of the MCs that wanted us dead, but I didn't care. Crossing that street felt crucial, and for whatever reason, my body listened to my gut.

He followed my every step as I dodged incoming cars and flipped a couple of drivers honking after me. The closer I got, the more I could see his face —high cheekbones, and those inquisitive eyes. My breath has been knocked out of me several times throughout the last couple of years, through my training and my assignments, but it never felt like this. As if someone was sitting on my chest, only it wasn't completely unpleasant. I knew danger when I saw it, and this guy... This guy should wear a neon sign on his chest, or better yet, his forehead. He leaned over the gas tank, patiently waiting for me. His hair was disheveled, slightly darker than mine, but not as dark as I initially thought.

It definitely wasn't black, thank you, Satan.

I was never the type of girl who gets tongue tied in front of a guy, but as I finally stood in front of him, two of his friends observing me, my mouth refused to connect with my brain.

"Hello, Persephone."

My heart thundered at the sound of his gravelly voice. It felt like a caress over my skin, over my soul, and I wanted to drown in it. His eyes raked over my body, and the flush creeped onto my face, no doubt making me look like a bloody tomato. What in the ever-loving hell?

Clearing my throat, I straightened my shoulders, and smiled coyly.

"Does that make you Hades?" The other two started laughing at my question, the sound muffled by the helmets covering their faces. Damn, and I really wanted to see their faces up close.

"Maybe." He got off the bike, towering over me. "But only if you're going to be my Queen of Hell."

Holy shit, the bluntness of this guy. I took a step back, and craned my neck to look at him. I knew this kind of a man. I was surrounded by them on a daily basis, but the ones I knew were never this straightforward. Never this imposing.

"I am already The Princess of Hell, so this offer isn't exactly appealing."

"Ah, Persephone." He pulled the strand of my hair and started playing with it. "Let me rephrase that sentence." He leaned down, inches away from my face. "You *are* going to be my Queen of Hell."

I gulped at our sudden nearness, intoxicated by his scent, by the sheer power emanating from him in spades. I loved Kieran, I still did, even after everything he did to me, but this... This familiarity I felt toward this man, toward this Devil, this was something else. It felt raw, animalistic, and I had the urge to throw myself into his arms, let him take me away.

"That's lovely, big boy." He laughed at my nickname. "But I think I'll pass. Besides," I took a hold of his hand, and removed it from my hair, "I don't need a king to become a queen. Twenty-first century and all that bullshit."

His hand grasped mine, and he pulled me closer to him, our upper bodies almost touching.

"That's fine, but what if I needed a queen to become a king?" His eyes were shattering walls I erected around my soul, inquisitive, curious. I felt both comfortable and uncomfortable with his nearness. I could feel the darkness in him. I could see it behind his green eyes. It was like a siren's song calling to me.

Kieran's light used to pull at me, or well, what I at least thought was light. But this here, this magnetism, it was as if we were in our own bubble, where everything else ceased to exist.

"Then you're looking for her in the wrong place, because I am not her." I extracted myself from his hold and came closer to the bike.

"I actually think you really are," he mumbled after me.

I ignored his remark and started gliding my hand over the leather seat, the insignia stamped on the side of the gas tank — the three-headed dog with its jaws open, and the name.

Sons of Hades MC.

Motherfucker. If my father caught sight of this, I'd be in the coffin and below the ground in a matter of minutes. Syndicate was bad, Outfit as well, but them... They made what we did look like a day in a kindergarten. Of course, I heard of them, who hadn't? How many times did our families warn us not to go to the West Coast, because that belonged to them? Me standing here with them was forbidden. A pure blasphemy, and I fucking loved every single second of it. Maybe it was my way of saying "fuck you" to all of the rules they were trying to impose on me.

"You like it?" His voice pulled me back to reality.

"I actually want to buy one, but I literally know nothing about bikes."

"You wanna try him on?" I whipped my head toward him at the double meaning in that sentence. "I mean the bike, hell-fire." He chuckled. "Though, I wouldn't be opposed to other things."

At this point, I wouldn't either. But before I could answer him, a female screech from behind me stopped all the thoughts I had, and an angry looking Ava stood there, just a couple of inches away from me.

"What the fuck, Phee?" I cringed at the fury coming from her. "What in the actual ever-loving fuck, my dude?"

"I'm just making friends."

"Seriously?"

She placed her hands on her hips, and I almost laughed at her. Unlike the rest of us, she looked more like an angry pixie, than a twenty-year-old woman.

"I told you I wanted to buy a bike eventually, didn't I?"

"This doesn't look like a bike shop to me?" She looked at the man standing next to me, but there was no reaction from her. "Hi, how are you? Would you excuse us for a moment, please?"

She came closer to me, took my hand, and pulled me away from them. Hades, or whatever his name was, laughed at us, leaning on the bike.

"Are you psychotic, you idiot?"

"Wait, is that a serious question, or—"

"Of course it's a serious question. What are you doing? You know who they are, you've seen their insignia."

"Yep," I answered cheerfully. "I sure did."

"Then what the fuck, Ophelia? What will Kieran think?"

What will Kieran think? Who gives a fuck what would Kieran think?

"Kieran can suck a dick for all I care." I pulled my hand back, and started walking backwards. "I'm going for a ride."

"Phee!"

"I know a place, not far away from here." I ignored her calls and started talking to him. "Is that tryout still on the table?" He looked at Ava and then back to me.

"Of course, sunshine. But here." He started removing his jacket. "It gets mighty cold on the back of the bike."

He stepped closer and enveloped me in the warmth of his leather jacket. Wasn't he going to freeze in this weather? It was way too big for my frame, but I never felt more comfortable in my entire life. He zipped it all the way to my throat, pulling my hair out and letting it fall down my back.

"T-Thank you," I stammered.

"Let's go, my queen." He took my hand. "Your carriage awaits."

He walked toward the bike, with me in tow, and only let go of my hand when he sat on it. My heart hammered in my chest as I placed my hand on his shoulder, and straddled the bike.

"Put your hands around me," he instructed, and I wrapped my arms around his waist. "Beneath my shirt, sunshine."

"What?"

He threw a glance at me over his shoulder. "My shirt isn't tight enough, and I need you to be safe. You could slip."

I groaned, "Fine." I lifted his shirt and traced the path over his back, toward his stomach. His abs clenched beneath my touch and a sharp intake of breath came from him. Here we were again, where everyone else disappeared around us. I could feel the strong abs on his stomach, the soft skin, and I spread my hands there, holding tight as he told me to.

"Okay." He cleared his throat. "Are you ready?"

I nodded against his back, settling myself there as if this wasn't the first time I was sitting behind this man. The vibrations of the bike tore through my body as he turned the ignition on, and with one last glance to Ava, we went flying down 7th Street, toward the hills.

~

T he sun was already setting on the horizon, but I didn't want to move from here. I didn't want to go back to the darkness waiting for me back home. The ocean looked so peaceful at this time of day, the red and orange streaks on the sky almost reflecting on the water.

Even the chill in the air couldn't move me.

He brought us to the eastern side of the city, and when I told him where to go, he seemed to know the way even without me instructing him. The area between my hometown and Marlow Heights was filled with cliffs overlooking the ocean, and I couldn't remember the last time my mind wasn't preoccupied with the next assignment, the next victim, the next life I would have to take.

Even when we stopped near the cliff, I didn't remove his jacket. Something about it being on my body calmed me, and he didn't mention it. I didn't know his name or what was he doing here, but I knew that his presence gave me the peace and comfort I so desperately needed at the moment, and that was all that mattered.

I used to read about this kind of connection with strangers, but I never truly believed in it. Yet, here I was, with a man I didn't know, having an urge to stay with him I couldn't explain.

It had been almost half an hour since we came here, and neither of us spoke. It was as if neither one of us wanted to break this comforting silence, this feeling of separation from the rest of the world. It was comforting sitting like this, just taking it all in. More often than not, we don't have time to slow down, to see the beauty around us. I know I never had time. It was easy falling into the endless darkness and getting stuck there. It was easy for our minds to play games with us, to tell us all of the monstrous things we did, but it rarely steered us into moments like these. The last three years didn't have enough of this.

There was always another shitshow I had to attend to, and moments like these were far and few between.

"I will forever be in love with the sky." I broke the silence between us, staring at the horizon.

"It truly is beautiful," he answered. But when I turned to him, he wasn't watching the sunset. He was looking at me.

His eyes seemed lighter, the sharp lines of his face highlighted in the sun. I inched closer, tracing my index finger over the dark eyebrow, feeling the scar there.

"How did you get this?" For a second there, he kept quiet, and I thought he wouldn't answer me. His eyes kept flickering over my own, zeroing in on the scar above my left eye. "I mean, you don't have to tell me."

I started retreating my hand, but he wasn't having any of that. He placed my palm on his cheek and pulled me onto his lap.

"My father had a temper, and serious drug issues. Unfortunately, he thought it would be alright to bash my head into the bedside table every time his drugs were running low."

My heart clenched painfully for him, and on instinct, I

kissed the spot as if it would somehow make it better. As if the fact that both of our fathers were sadistic assholes would disappear with that kiss. This sudden overprotectiveness I felt toward him was messing with my head, but I wasn't going to question it.

Live in the moment.

Take everything you want.

I wanted to kill his father, I wanted to kill my father, and I didn't understand how I could feel this way toward someone I just met. I didn't even know his real name, for fuck's sake.

"I'm sorry." I started retreating back when he cupped the back of my neck, keeping me in place.

"Don't worry about it. He can't hurt me anymore. No one can."

"Hades—"

"Storm. My name is Storm."

"Storm." I played with his name on my tongue, and his eyes closed at the sound.

"Say it again." He rested his forehead on mine, and looked into my eyes.

"Storm, Storm, Storm—"

The onslaught of his name was quieted with his lips on mine.

Claiming.

Wanting.

I opened for him, and he slipped his tongue between, battling with my own. The taste of him sent a rush to my head, and I knew I wanted this more than anything else in the world.

Fuck the Syndicate and all the bad things haunting me at night. Fuck Kieran and his cheating dick.

Now and here, this was what I needed. What I wanted.

"Oh God," I moaned between kisses. "More."

He pulled at my hair, exposing my neck to him. His lips

traveled from my lips, to my jaw, and lastly my neck, sucking at the spot just beneath my ear.

"Where have you been my whole life?"

"Here," I panted. "There, everywhere."

His other hand pinched my butt cheek and his lips again found a way to mine.

"I want to devour you until the only thing in your head is my name and everything I can do to you."

Oh dear God, yes please.

One thought started racing through my head. I wanted to leave with him. I wanted to disappear, go away. I wanted to dance with him in the moonlight while our demons sat waiting.

"Make it all go away," I moaned. "Give me everything you have."

"Come with me," he whispered against my lips. "We can leave now—"

"I can't." I wanted to. God, I wanted to leave with him. To leave all of this behind. I wanted to explore this crazy attraction, but he didn't know who I was. He didn't know about everything I would bring with me.

"Why?"

"There are..." I stumbled. "Things I need to take care of here."

"How long?"

"What?"

"How long do you need to take care of those things?"

I looked at him, trying to understand his question.

"Maybe a week."

"I'll wait for you. Here, in three weeks." *Another kiss.* "At this exact place." *Kiss.* "Promise you will come to me?"

"I—"

"You can feel this too, I know you can. I have never felt anything like this before."

"Storm—"

"No, listen to me." He cupped my cheeks. "The moment I saw you standing there, looking at us, I knew."

"You knew what?"

"I knew you were meant to be mine. You were meant to stand by my side."

I tried to find reasons to say no. I tried to remember Kieran, my family, Ava, but... After I got Ava and Nathan out of this mess, what was left for me here? Nothing but shackles they wanted to put on me.

This wasn't normal, and if he asked me a year ago, I would've said no. I would've told him to fuck off. But now.

I wanted this... whatever this was.

This insanity pulled at my insides, I wanted it all. I wanted to be devoured by him, and if that made me madder than I already was, so be it.

"Okay." I nodded.

"Okay?"

"Yeah, okay." I smiled at him, and a smile brighter than the sun itself etched itself on his face. "I'll be here."

"And I'll be waiting, Persephone."

21

KIERAN

Present

There were many people I didn't like. I guess it always came with the job I've been doing. But this guy, the infamous Storm Knoxx, I wanted to bash his teeth in and stomp all over his body.

Ever since he became President of Sons of Hades MC, he's been causing nothing but trouble. Their previous president was pliant, kept to himself and never went against what we wanted.

This one was the complete opposite.

Intercepting our orders, challenging us every step of the way, trying to regain territory that was no longer his, he was playing with fucking fire. I would've let it go, would've put up with his antics, but kidnapping my mother, now that crossed a line.

And for that, I was going to make sure he burned with the rest of his dogs. Seemed fitting, didn't it, because they all were nothing but a bunch of dogs trying to play in the big leagues.

Motorcycle Club, please. Give me a break.

As if they could ever have some sort of semblance as to what it meant to handle big business such as ours.

I was playing his game right now, but I wasn't going to give him what he wanted. I just needed to figure out a way to get my mother out of his hands and out of Vegas.

The stories I heard about him made my blood run cold. This was a man without honor, without emotions. He simply didn't care who got hurt as long as he got what he wanted. People used to say that we were monsters, but if they never had a chance to meet Storm, they didn't know what a real monster looked like.

I didn't like how close he stood to Ophelia. I didn't like it one bit.

And even more so, he seemed to know her. How in the fuck did he know her?

Did we fail to find out that part about her time away from Syndicate? No, that couldn't be it. We would've known if she were involved with them.

Besides, it wasn't admiration in her eyes. I knew that poisonous look, because I've been on the receiving end of the same many, many times.

Then how the fuck?

"Hello, Persephone. We meet again," the asshole started, and I wanted to wring his neck. Get the fuck away from her.

And why was he calling her Persephone? I hated not knowing things, and this right here was giving me a headache I really didn't need.

Ophelia took a step back, moving away from him, and a weird sense of satisfaction washed over me. Fucker looked good, and I knew girls always ran to his side. Our little spy told us that.

Well, that son of a bitch was good only for that, apparently, because he obviously didn't warn us about Storm's plan to abduct our mother.

For the first time since we took her, Ophelia's anger wasn't directed toward us. No, it was coming off in spades, and all of it was aiming toward Storm.

Goddammit, I needed to know how they knew each other. Did I miss something?

"I would like to say it's so good to see you again Hades, but I would be fucking lying."

There's my spitfire. I almost thought she became pliant or some shit like that, but no, she obviously still had it. The venomous look she was directing his way pleased me, but the cocky smile on his face made my blood boil.

The way he was looking at her... It was possessive, owning, there was so much yearning, and if I didn't know better, I would say that Storm really wanted her.

No, absolutely not. He couldn't get my girl.

She's not your girl anymore. My subconscious decided to rear its ugly head and remind me of everything that was not. Thank you very much brain. It's hard forgetting the shitshow our lives were thrown into, when my object of affection hated me more than I hated her.

Well, at least that's what it seemed like.

It was a bad idea bringing her with us. I just didn't want to leave her out of my sight because I knew what she was capable of.

Now that I thought about it, her and Storm were more alike than I wanted them to be. Neither one of them had mercy, and they didn't care who got hurt as long as they got what they wanted.

It was funny, really. I hated his guts, but I also admired him. He was always honest about who and what he was.

From the first time I met him when he just became president, he was honest about his intentions. My stupidity brought us here, thinking their MC wouldn't seek retribution for what our idiots did.

They were supposed to scare them, to get them away from this territory so that we could take over, but no, they had to kill all of those innocent people.

I guess that was what you get when you send brainless twats to do your job. Now I knew better, and that was why this time, the three of us were on the front lines of this war.

I fucking hoped this wouldn't end up becoming a full-blown war, because we definitely couldn't afford it. Between the Syndicate, the Albanians and the Cartel, we couldn't afford to have the Sons of Hades as our mortal enemies.

I couldn't stand the staring match the two of them were having anymore, and for some reason, no matter what transpired between the two of us, I still wanted to protect her.

I wanted to take her away, hide her, erase our memories and the past that haunted us.

I wanted to forget what I did, what she did.

What both of us were guilty of.

I took a step forward but Atlas, the ever-loyal dog of Storm, stopped me by placing a hand on my chest and pushing me backwards.

"What the fuck, man?" I started angrily, pushing his hands off of me.

"Boss's orders, Kieran. Nobody moves a muscle until he says so."

"Both of you can fuck off, right now." I pushed at his chest, and both Cillian and Tristan came closer, standing right behind me. "We're here, and we're ready to talk. Or are you going to continue behaving like kids with this whole, 'darkness is me' crap?"

A laughter echoed throughout the church, several of their

soldiers joining their leader in the cackling match. I turned to Storm, his dark stare already fixated on me. If Hell ever needed a new leader, they knew where to look.

He was standing right in front of me.

"Kieran, Kieran, Kieran," he started as he approached me. "That ego of yours always made me laugh. It was kinda annoying if I am honest, but it also made me laugh so many times."

"Fuck off, Storm."

"See." He cackled again. "Hilarious. Especially given the fact that you're surrounded, we have your mommy dearest, and yet, you still dare to give orders in my house, to my people, and even more, to me."

I looked at Ophelia who seemed to observe our interaction with newfound interest, and I couldn't help myself but wonder.

"Did you have anything to do with this, birdy?"

"Birdy?" Storm laughed again. "Oh God, you just made my night. Hell, you made my whole month."

"No, I didn't, you asshole. If I did," she smiled, "I would've told you so. I was never the one to hide my plans from you."

"How could I ever forget? You only failed to mention you were going to kill my sister."

She started advancing toward me, but Storm stepped in front, blocking her from me. The three-headed dog on his back glared at me, and I wanted to punch Atlas and remove her from Storm.

He took a hold of her arms and bending his head, he whispered in her ear. And whatever it was he said, she calmed down, her body going slack in his hold. I wasn't going to lose her to some biker who probably didn't know how to handle a gun like a real man.

But he does, you know that.

Oh fuck off, subconsciousness. Now wasn't the time to tell me what's wrong and what's right. He was an asshole. Period.

"How do you two know each other?" My curiosity was killing me. I had to know how it was possible that she seemed to listen to him, when she never ever listened to me.

I was never able to calm her down. She never went slack in my arms like she just now did in his. She never even allowed me to touch her in one of her fits of rage. My head would be flying off faster than you could say sex.

How in the ever-loving fuck was it possible that he managed to calm her down? What did he say to her?

"That's a long story," she mumbled as Storm stepped aside.

"Well, princess, you gotta tell me. We have the whole night, and I'm sure Storm wouldn't mind."

"Do you ever stop with the ridiculous pet names, Kieran?" the man in question asked, crossing his arms over his chest. "I am sure she has a real name, so why don't you use it?"

"Because if he used my name, he would betray himself." That little bitch. "Wouldn't you, Kieran?"

Boiling.

That was how I felt.

Fucking boiling.

"I swear to God, Ophelia." Storm seemed to freeze momentarily, looking at her and then at me. The confusion swirling in his eyes, and something close to realization visible there, but I didn't have time to ponder over it. Ophelia was the focus now. "If you had anything to do with this, I will—"

"You will what?" She came closer, leaving Storm behind. "Torture me, humiliate me, kill me?"

Her blue eyes were sparkling with something new. Something I hadn't seen before, and it wasn't anger anymore. It was excitement.

Like a newfound energy, she was glowing, and it wasn't thanks to me. Who was he to her?

"Do you see this?" She lifted her hand bandaged in the worst way possible. "This is the worst thing you can do to me. You couldn't even torture me properly. Poor little, Kieran."

"You little—"

"That's enough!" Storm roared. "We aren't here so that two of you can discuss all the ways in which you would like to torture each other. Not that I wouldn't like to see it. We are here to discuss serious things, and if you'd be so kind as to stop behaving like children, I will get to it."

Ophelia retreated back, and I hated the distance she was putting between the two of us. She seemed to trust standing closer to the Devil himself than me.

Why was that bothering me so much?

I already made peace with the fact that she had to die. We just weren't finished with her, but sooner or later, she would be gone. What I wanted didn't matter, because I couldn't betray my brothers like that.

They wanted to get their revenge. I wanted the same.

Then why was my heart constricting at the mere thought of her choosing somebody else over me? Seeing her with Cillian almost sent me into another fit of rage, but I knew why they both did it.

There were no feelings, no promises, and no calmness. This, right here, this was making me uncomfortable.

The familiarity with which these two behaved, her calm demeanor with Storm, it was eating me from the inside. What happened between them, and when?

"Are you calm enough to talk now, Kieran? Or do you need some milk with cookies?"

"Oooo, cookies," Ophelia squealed. "I love cookies."

The idiot smiled. This fucking shithead smiled at her.

"No need for cookies," I grunted. "We can talk now."

"Good." His gaze stayed trained on her, and she did the same. Look at me goddammit. Not at him, me.

"As you know, we have your mother—"

"Yes, we fucking know," Cillian started, finally showing some of those balls he always said he had. Fucking finally, brother. Thank you for all your support a couple of minutes ago.

"I didn't ask you, Cillian," Storm sneered. "I was stating a fact. When I ask you a question, or when I allow you to speak, you will know. Until that time, I am talking to your brother, not you, not your youngest, but Kieran. Understood?"

"You son of a—"

"Cillian." I turned around, stopping him from attacking Storm. "That's enough."

"But, Kieran—"

"No buts. Keep your mouth closed and let me handle this."

The way he was looking at me would bring a lesser man to his knees, but it wouldn't be the first time that my brother and I weren't in sync. You would think it would be opposite considering we were twins, but no.

Not the two of us.

I had a feeling we were more at each other's throats than in agreement.

"Please," I pleaded with him. "We need to keep calm, otherwise we might not see Mom ever again."

"Okay, fine."

I nodded and turned around to face Storm again.

"Thank you, mommy Kieran. Keep your kids in check and this might go easier than we both thought."

"Just get to the point, Storm."

I wanted to peel that smile off of his face, skin him alive so that everyone would know not to mess with the Outfit. The tattoos on his neck were begging to be presented to the world.

Spread somewhere with the rest of his filthy skin.

"As I was saying," he started walking back and forth, "your mother is with us, and she is safe. For now. Will she stay that way, depends on you boys?"

"What do you want, Storm?" I was getting tired of his little monologue.

"Well, that's a little bit tricky now. I knew what I wanted, but the rules of the game have changed."

I didn't like the gleam in his eyes as he looked at Ophelia and then back at me.

"Stop fucking around, Storm. What. Do. You. Want?"

"Why, I want the world, Kieran. But you can't exactly give it to me."

"Oh, for fuck's sake."

"I want her." He pointed at a shocked-looking Ophelia. "And I want Las Vegas. I want your goons out of this city, and I will release your mother. Unharmed, fed, healthy. It's up to you now."

Did he just... Did he just say he wanted Ophelia?

"Absolutely not."

"Kieran," Tristan hissed behind me. "Don't be a fool."

I ignored his remarks and focused on the demon in front of me.

"You aren't going to get Las Vegas, and least of all, her."

"Um, excuse me," Ophelia started. "The *her* you guys are talking about is standing right here, and I am nobody's toy to be sold, given, or whatever the fuck you idiots are thinking of doing."

"Shut up, Ophelia," I barked. "This doesn't concern you."

"Oh, I don't think so. This concerns me very much. And you," she turned to Storm, "who the hell do you think you are, huh?"

A collective gasp could be heard all around us, and I had to admit, the balls on this girl would never cease to amaze me.

She just challenged the most notorious MC leader in the United States, without blinking an eye.

"Do you really want me to answer that question, Persephone?" Here we go again with that fucking name.

"Kieran," Tristan hissed again. I turned to him, trying to ignore the staring match ensuing between Ophelia and Storm. "We need to think about this. Please don't be an idiot. She obviously doesn't know anything, and sending her with him would be a fate worse than death."

It would be, wouldn't it, but it would also kill me seeing her with him, even if he wanted nothing more than to break her apart.

"Shut up, Tristan."

"He's right," Cillian murmured. "We need to think about this, and we will. Tell them to meet us here tomorrow again, and we will give them our final answer."

"Absolutely—"

"Kieran," my twin growled. "Don't be a fucking idiot. This is our mother we are talking about. Don't make the same mistake of putting Ophelia before your family, because we both know she wouldn't do the same for you."

And that right there, ladies and gentlemen, that was what hurt me the most. The fact that I knew she would never do the same for me. I knew it. Fuck, I knew it for years now, but I never wanted to admit it to myself.

"Okay," I breathed out. "Fine. I'll do it."

But before I could utter the words meant for Storm, the doors of the church banged open, and three figures appeared basked in the glow of lanterns on the wall.

"Look what we've found, Prez."

I took a step closer, followed by Ophelia and my brothers,

and the last person I would've expected to see here stood in front of us.

"Theo?" Ophelia asked. "What the fuck are you doing here?"

Her brother grinned, struggling with the two bikers on his sides.

"Hello, guys. What did I miss?"

22

OPHELIA

Four Years Ago

"Ava." I knocked on the bathroom door for a third time. She's been inside for the last half an hour, and if she didn't get out in the next five minutes, I was going to break the door down.

"Are you okay?"

I was never an anxious kind of a person, but this shit was starting to give me anxiety. How long could it take her to pee, for fuck's sake?

"Aves, if you don't open this door, I swear to all that's holy, I will break it down."

They all thought I was crazy already. Breaking the door down would be the least psychotic thing I ever did.

"Ava!"

Alright, that's it.

Just as I took three steps backwards, ready to go "Hulk" on the poor door, she opened it up. Her head was bent downward, focused on the little stick in her hands. Who would've thought that little piece of plastic could change your whole life?

Well, I mean, you changed your life when you spread your legs and shit like that, but that was beside the point.

What was important right now, was the fact that she still didn't look at me.

"Ava?" I slowly came to her, trying to gauge her reaction to all of this. If she wasn't pregnant, I would be relieved because it would be one thing I didn't have to worry about.

If she was pregnant, well, I guess we could all buckle up and get ready for a ride, because I knew her, and I knew she would never get rid of that baby.

Especially if it was conceived with somebody she loved, and judging by everything she told me about Nathan, she truly did love him.

"Woman, if you don't start talking, I—"

"I'm pregnant," she whispered. "Holy fuck, Ophelia." She finally looked at me. "I am pregnant."

She started waving the stick in front of my face, and no matter how much I loved her, I didn't want to get the remnants of her urine on me.

"Okay, okay." I grabbed her hands. "Is that good? It's good, right?"

I didn't know how she would react to all of this. She seemed pretty reluctant the last time we spoke about this, but who knew, maybe she really was ready to be a mother?

I mean, she was already mothering me, asking me if I ate, if I drank enough water, did I sleep—of course I did none of those things properly.

Adulting fucking sucked, and when you were meant to be killing people for a living, having three meals per day, and drinking two liters of water took a backseat in your mind. It wasn't really important if you had a balanced diet. What mattered was that you didn't leave any fingerprints at the crime scene.

Now that was some important shit.

"It's amazing," she squealed, throwing herself in my arms. "Oh God, oh God, oh God, Ophelia. I am going to be a mom."

Yay for her, fucking shit for me. Don't get me wrong, I was really happy for her. But fucking hell, couldn't all of this happen at a better time? Ah Ophelia, of course it couldn't. This baby was happening, and you could suck it up and show some fucking emotions for a change.

"You're going to be a mom." I squeezed her to me. "Congratulations."

"And you will be an aunt."

An aunt? Oh fuck me sideways and six ways from Sunday, that kid was going to be screwed with me. I never thought about having kids, mine or anybody else's.

Being a mother never even occurred to me, least of all being an aunt.

I guess I could suck it up and be an adult for once. I just hoped she wouldn't think of leaving that kid with me. Because that, that would be a bloody disaster.

I was good with knives, locating arteries, torture techniques, handling a gun, but diapers, milk formula, and washing somebody's ass, even if that somebody was a tiny human, that shit terrified me.

What the fuck was I supposed to do if it started crying, huh?

"You're too quiet." She looked at me skeptically. "Aren't you happy for me?"

Here we go, the pouty face. How could I explain to my best friend that anything related to normal human interactions terrified the shit out of me?

"Of course I am." I started walking back to the room, with her following me. "I am thrilled for you. But there are other things on my mind right now, so I am a little bit distracted."

Yeah, other things, such as cutting Nathan's balls off and

feeding it to pigs. I wondered if he would be keen on seeing them in a meat processing machine.

"I know it isn't the best timing." She sat on the bed, crossing her legs. "And maybe I could've waited for a couple of years, but it's my baby, Phee. It's mine and Nathan's baby, and I already love him or her so, so much."

Fuck.

How was I supposed to shatter her dreams when she looked like she just won that special set of knives? Okay, scratch that. That would be me.

She looked like angels sang in her ear.

"I am really happy for you, Ava. But," I sat on the floor, our feet touching, "you know what this means, don't you?"

A somber expression took over her face, and I hated being the one to bring the bad news. Unfortunately, somebody had to, and if she were to stay alive, she had to face the facts.

Ava and Nathan couldn't stay here, and I think I knew just the way for them to get away. Or well, I knew a person who could help them disappear.

"We have to get away, don't we?"

"Yes. And I am sorry for saying this, but it has to happen soon. We can't risk anybody finding out about this baby, or even worse, your relationship to Nathan. There are things you don't know about our families, and I would like to keep it that way. But Ava, they are dangerous people. Hell, I am dangerous which is why I know what I'm telling you is the truth."

She sniffled, and I knew how much she hated being separated from her brothers. I guess even though I hated Kieran's guts, he was still her brother, and I was glad she had all three of them to protect her and support her.

Thanks to them, she never got entangled in the web of lies and darkness the rest of us did. I wished my own brother did the same for me, or even Maya.

Jesus fuck, I didn't want to ruin my mood further by thinking about my family. My lovely father still refused to tell me where my sister was, and Theo and his ignorant fucking ass could burn for all I cared.

He never gave a shit about the two of us, always thinking about his own ass. That was why I didn't feel guilty helping Ava to get away from him. That whole engagement was a nightmare none of us needed, and her misery wasn't something I wanted to look at for the rest of our lives.

"I know that what you guys are doing, aren't the nicest things." That's putting it mildly. "But I still love you, no matter what you do."

I wondered if she would still love me if I ever told her everything I did. Would she still think the world of me if she knew how many people I killed? How many families disappeared because of me, and how many kids lost their parents?

Would she still love me if she knew how many kids I killed, and I would do it again, because that was my job? It was who I was.

But I would never hurt her or people I loved. I would kill for them. They were the last ones I would ever hurt. Even Kieran, for all his faults, he was still somebody I loved. And those feelings didn't disappear overnight. I wished they did, but those little bitches stayed with me even after the shit he threw at me.

"Ava—"

"No, I know what you're going to say. I know you're dangerous, I know that very well. But I also know you would protect me and this kid with everything you have. You didn't think I fell for that stupid story of you traveling through Europe during that year you were gone? Come on Phee, you know me better than that. I know it had something to do with your father, the way you were behaving before, and my brother going crazy with worry."

Well, shit. I did think she bought it. I didn't want to explain where I was, and if I could, I would erase that whole period from my mind.

"Ava, there are things—"

"I don't know. Yes, I understand, and I don't wanna know. If keeping me in dark keeps me safe, so be it. I don't have to know. But I just want you to know that none of that shit matters. What matters to me is the way you are with me, and you've been nothing but supportive and an amazing friend. If Kieran didn't do the shit he did, you would be my sister."

That hurt, badly.

I had one sister, but I hadn't seen Maya in four years, and wherever she was, was unknown to me. That was another thing that ate at my soul, but I couldn't take care of multiple disasters at once. I had to focus on one Armageddon at a time.

"You know I'll try to do my best to keep you guys safe? I would give my life for yours."

"Shush your mouth. I don't want you giving your life for mine. If it ever came to that, I want you to promise me that you wouldn't risk yourself to save me."

Easier said than done, Ava. Unlike me, she didn't know where the monsters lurked. She couldn't defend herself, but if it made her feel better, I could lie.

Wouldn't be the first time.

"Promise me, Ophelia. Promise me you won't do anything stupid in order to save me."

God fucking dammit, she should've asked me to kidnap somebody, or some shit like that. I sucked at keeping promises, and this one was the one I would gladly break.

"Ophelia." She threw a pillow at me. "Seriously. No risking lives, and no reckless shit."

Was she kidding me—reckless was my middle name? Well, I mean, my other middle name.

"Okay, okay, I promise."

Liar, liar, pants on fire. The breath she was holding released out, and the calm energy she had earlier enveloped her.

"Now," she started again. "What the fuck was that shit today, huh? Don't you know who those guys are? Even I've heard about Sons of Hades, and they aren't somebody you want to get involved with."

Oh Ava, Ava, Ava. I wished I had her innocence and self-preservation skills. Unfortunately, I had none, and Sons of Hades weren't the ones I would be scared of.

Yeah, they could make you disappear, but they weren't the worst monsters I encountered. The shit I did, the ones they did, it was all the same.

We weren't the good guys, but we weren't the bad ones either.

I had to protect my family, and if that meant destroying somebody else's, so be it. I wasn't ashamed of who I was, not anymore. If I had to kill, maim and torture to get what I wanted and to ensure the safety of those I loved, I didn't mind. People did worse for lesser things, and family was important.

Even if I wanted to slice my own father at least five days out of seven, he was still my father. Even if I wanted to strangle my junkie mother, she was still my mother. Theo could probably die for all that I cared, but if Papa asked me to save him or to avenge him, I would.

"Don't worry about them, Ava. Men are like puppies. You show them some treats, and they come running."

"Those are not puppies, Phee. Those men are pit bulls, and they wouldn't mind ripping us apart."

"Okay, first," I lifted my thumb, "pit bulls are actually just big babies—"

"Aha, and I am chihuahua," she interrupted.

"Second of all," I lifted my index finger, laughing at her comparison, "don't worry about it." I stood up, walking to the dresser and looking at the picture there. It was two of us, fresh out of Primary School. We looked so cute together, and who would've thought we would be here. I never even dreamed about this.

"If you say so, but they looked terrifying."

"Did they hurt you when I left with Storm?" I turned around, trying to gauge her feelings.

"Well, no." She seemed to think about it. "They were actually quite nice, if I'm being honest. They even offered to take me for lunch while you two were doing God knows what."

"We were just talking." I laughed. "Besides, they'll be helping us."

"What do you mean?" A wary expression passed over her face, her eyes narrowing on me. "You don't mean—"

"Oh yes. I told you I need to get you out of here, and what better way than to do it with the help of somebody that powerful."

"Phee," she approached me, "I'm not sure if I like this very much."

"It's been decided, Ava. Storm will help to get us to the West Coast, and from there, you guys can decide to either stay with the club or live somewhere else."

"Are you serious?"

"Deadly."

She kept quiet for a second, before the widest fucking smile I've ever seen, spread across her face.

"I would tackle you on the floor right now if I knew you wouldn't bite my head off because I dared to hug you."

She was brimming with happiness and I felt the same. In some fucked up way, even being the way I was, I was happy when my people were happy. I loved seeing her like this—carefree, without that permanent scowl she wore for the last couple of years.

Things were finally looking good, and I knew it would only go better in the future. I just knew it.

"Okay." I eyed her. "You can hug me, but just for—"

I couldn't even finish the sentence before she threw herself at me, squeezing the life out of me. I could already see the headlines, *Ophelia Aster, Killed by a Hug.*

But if it was by Ava, I would allow it.

"Can you imagine our futures, Phee?" I could, almost. "My kids growing up far away from this cursed place, from this family. You having kids."

Okay, hold up, hold up. I never agreed to having kids.

"Uh—"

"Them playing together, us yelling after them."

Next thing, she would be telling me we lived next to each other, in those houses with white picket fences and our husbands as best friends.

"I can already see it, Phee. Two girls and two boys from each of us."

Was that my heart trying to get out of my chest? Oh shit, was this how a panic attack felt like?

"Can you see it?" She looked at me full of hope.

Oh I could see it. I could see me buying more knives for my collection, but I couldn't see myself with kids. That was never in the cards for me. I knew that from the time I came back from Siberia. This life wasn't meant for kids, and I didn't want to bring them into a world where they could end up dead because of who I was.

Nope, nope, nope.

It was one ginormous nope.

"Almost, Ava. Almost."

I couldn't shatter her dreams. We were different, her and I. Ava dreamed about white picket fences and having the love of her life with her. I dreamed about staying alive and being able to wash all the blood from my hair.

You know, priorities.

However, if my saying I could see us growing old together calmed her, I could live with that.

"But, back to the plan. Nathan is out of town, correct?"

"That's right. He shouldn't be back until the day after tomorrow."

"Okay." I pondered. "Okay, that could work. Storm left me his number, and I'm going to tell him to have everything ready for the day after tomorrow. Tell Nathan to meet us at the Old Theater on Wednesday, at eight p.m."

"I got it." She nodded. "Old Theater, Wednesday, eight p.m. Anything else?"

"Yes. Please don't pack everything. Just something light. We will be buying you clothes once we reach Santa Monica. Leave everything behind, unless there's something you really want to take."

"Um..." She made a face. "What about my memory box?"

"Oh for fuck's sake, you can give it to me and I will take it. You will tell your father and brothers we are going out, and I'll pick you up. That way they won't assign any guards to you."

"What about your guards?"

I laughed thinking she was joking, but looking at her face, I realized she was serious.

"Oh shit, you really think I have guards?"

"Well, don't you?"

"Ah Ava, I am my own guard. Don't worry about that."

I looked at my watch and realized I was almost late for the meeting with my father.

"I gotta go now but remember, Wednesday, Old Theater,

eight p.m. Talk to Nathan tonight, tell him not to ask too many questions, and I'll talk to you tomorrow. Okay?"

"Got it. And Phee," she pulled me back just as I was heading to the door, "thank you."

"There's nothing to thank me for, Ava. I know you would do the same for me."

Now I just hoped we would manage to get out of this mess unscathed.

23

OPHELIA

Present

I s it possible for blood to boil, because mine definitely was.

The audacity that Disappointment 1 and Disappointment 2 had was pissing me off. What did the two of them think, that they could juggle me between them as if I was some sort of a toy?

What the fuck?

This was why I never trusted a man. I learned my fucking lesson when I placed my trust first in Kieran's hands and then Storm's. Both of them showed me I shouldn't have trusted either.

One of them betrayed me, the second one ended up being a cherry on the top of a shattering cake.

And now my brother had to show up. I was both elated and pissed at seeing him, because the fuckery ensuing around me was giving me a headache and dealing with his ass wasn't on top of my list today. Honestly speaking, I needed five days just to prepare myself for seeing him, because the urge to claw out his eyes was too strong to suppress.

The push and pull between Storm and Kieran, or how I liked to call it, the dick match, was a headache, and neither one of them was going to stop. I didn't know Storm well enough to say what kind of a person he was, but I knew men like him, and I knew he would turn Heaven into Hell to get what his soul wished to have.

And Kieran, that stubborn asshole wouldn't stop challenging him even if it meant every single one of us was going to die.

Stupid, that's what both of them were. Fucking stupid.

Their egos spoke louder than their minds, and that was the main problem I always had with men. They never thought about anything else but their own selves, and these two weren't the exceptions.

On top of this whole mess, because of course there was more, the attraction I felt toward Storm so many years ago was still here. When he touched me, I started burning. Skin on skin, I wanted to rid him of his clothes, and fuck him right then and there in front of everyone.

I wanted to punish him for turning his back on me when I needed him the most. Need, that was the right word for this. Maybe even obsession, but whatever it was I needed to get rid of it, because it would bring me nothing but more pain.

And those inquisitive eyes, they could still see my soul, and I fucking hated him for it. I learned my lesson already. I burned myself once trying to trust somebody else other than myself.

But there was no such thing as trusting them, was there?

I was all alone in this world, and hell, maybe that was how it was supposed to be. Maybe I wasn't meant to have another person walking with me through this hell.

Maybe it was for the best, because my heart couldn't take

another heartbreak—not from a lover, from a brother, sister, father or a mother.

I just couldn't take it anymore. I couldn't take the two of them throwing me at one another as if I were just a body, waiting to be claimed. I was so much more, and they couldn't see it.

I didn't want to be owned. I wanted to be respected, wanted to be equal.

Kieran couldn't give me that, and in some fucked-up part of my soul, that day I met Storm, I believed he could be the one to mend the broken pieces and pull me back together. But after all these years of being alone, after doing the shit I did, I now knew there was no such thing.

When darkness took over, it didn't just take over our lives. It consumed our souls. The darkness consumed our light, and another person wasn't supposed to pull you back together. It was my job, my responsibility, and it was stupid of me to think somebody else could do such a thing.

I was wrong and my father was right. He told me I was perfect the way I was, just before our lives took a turn for worse.

He told me I was enough, but I never trusted him because I didn't want to believe anything he said. I didn't want to trust him because he was the one that pushed me into this. What I failed to realize is that Papa loved me. With all his faults, all his shit, he actually loved me, and I fucked up.

If I survived this whole ordeal, I needed to make amends with him. If I managed to keep my part of the bargain, if I managed to do what I was asked to do, I would find him and I would apologize.

But first I had to survive the men-children going at each other's throats.

Theo's arrival halted all activity in the church, and we reluctantly retreated back to our hotel. I wanted to get this all done tonight, but Storm gave them one night to think about it all.

I wouldn't have given them even an hour, but that was just me.

Why the fuck did he want me?

He could've had me years ago, but the idiot failed. Okay, I might be exaggerating.

One of his pets failed, but I was still pissed off. He still pretended not to know my name, when we both knew better.

Persephone, my ass.

If he thought I would fall for that stupid act again, he had another think coming. He was the Devil, true, but definitely not Hades.

Hades would never leave Persephone how he left me. He never looked for me, I never heard of him looking for me at least.

Alright, I know, I know. I was a major bitch, and maybe it wasn't his fault, but I was pissed off. Currently, I was hungry, and the assholes never thought about feeding me once we came back. They all retreated to their rooms, with Theo throwing me dirty looks every now and then.

Patience, dear brother. You will get what you deserve.

I didn't have much time, and if I was going to do what I was sent here to do, I needed to find a weapon. A knife, a gun, a piece of fucking glass, anything. If they're giving me to him tomorrow, I had to act fast.

I wasn't going to be anyone's prisoner anymore.

I would rather die than have another man treat me that way. I couldn't do that again, I didn't want to live my life that way.

Not after everything I've been through.

I ran through what I saw in the church. There was only one visible entrance and exit in there, and with the amount of guys Storm brought, it would be tough getting out of there unharmed, but I had to try. Though, even if I did manage to get out of there, Kieran's baboons wouldn't let me get through.

Fuck.

The sudden knocking on my door scared the shit out of me, and I jumped out of the bed, preparing myself for another one of Kieran's antics. He's been getting creative lately, trying to make me remember what we used to be. Tough luck, I wasn't going to.

The door opened with a click, revealing the last person I wanted to see.

"What the fuck are you doing here, Theo?"

My beloved brother. Well, beloved was a grand word for what I felt toward him. Let me put it this way... If I saw him swimming in the ocean surrounded by sharks, I would throw some more blood on him so that they could finish the job faster.

The traitorous little leech had some balls showing up here. Papa didn't trust him, and obviously with reason. He was working with our enemies, licking assess hoping he could get something out of it.

"I came to see my favorite sister." *Oh, how touching.* "Is that such a bad thing?"

No, of course it isn't a bad thing, for normal families. The thing is, he was one of the fuckers that cost me my freedom. His love burned more than Kieran's ever did, and I never doubted that my hatred toward him only rivaled his toward me.

The little leech always thought he was going to inherit Papa's business, when it was never going to happen. Weak wolves were getting eaten by the stronger ones, or kicked out of the pack, and that's what he was.

A weak wolf. There was no power in his bones, and the only way he could get what he wanted was through lies, deceit and betrayal.

"You mean the only sister. I don't even know if Maya is alive."

"Oh, she's alive, somewhere." He chuckled. That mother-fucking son of a bitch. "How are you doing?"

"Cut to the chase, Theo. We both know this isn't a social call, and you couldn't give a fuck on how I'm doing. If you did, you wouldn't have gotten me kidnapped and tortured by the Nightingales."

I was letting him think that he had me where he wanted me —another fool underestimating me and everything I was capable of. I would've felt pity if I had it in me.

"You were always a 'straight to the point' kind of a person, weren't you, Sis?"

Oh, you have no idea. More, straight to the heart, but I didn't have my knives on me, otherwise he would've been dead five minutes ago, as soon as he stepped inside this room.

"I wanted to talk to you."

"Then talk." I had no patience for his little mind games. I also didn't have time, because I needed to find a way to get myself out of this mess. There was still a mission I had to finish, and while Theo's presence was an additional plus, I would have to deal with him when I had more time.

"Feisty." He sat on the chair next to the desk. "I love it. You're much more fun when you're like this."

"Theo." I rubbed at my temples. "I have no time, nor patience for you right now. If you have nothing smart to say, please get out of this room."

"Oh, Sis," he tsked. "That isn't a way to show love to your favorite brother."

"I said," I came closer to him, "get to the fucking point, Theo, or fuck off. I am fine with either one of those options."

His eyes widened at the proximity between us, and I felt

satisfied knowing that he still feared me. That's right leech, I could still kill you and I wouldn't need sharp objects to do so.

"Okay, fine." The fake smile he wore earlier completely disappeared, leaving behind the expression I knew very well. Leer. "I came to talk to you about that night."

Here we go, my time to play.

"I don't know what you're talking about." I smiled.

"Don't play dumb, Ophelia. We both know you aren't stupid. You know very well which night I'm talking about."

"Hmmm." I pretended to think about it. "No, not really. Enlighten me please."

"Stop playing, Phee."

Oh wouldn't you love that?

"I am not playing, my dear brother. I just don't know which night you're talking about."

"You know." He seemed uncomfortable. "The night."

"Ohhh, the night. You mean the night you betrayed me and decided money was more important than your own flesh and blood. When you decided killing my best friend and framing me was the way to go. Now I remember. How could I ever forget?"

How could I ever forget that he was the one who set me up? How could I ever forget being chained to the wall after Cillian and Tristan found me, cutting me bit by bit, letting me bleed out?

"I didn't kill her. I never even touched her."

"Oh really?" I stood in front of him, and leaned on the chair, my hands on the armrests. "I don't fucking believe you."

"I'm telling the truth. I swear."

"Well, excuse me, because I find that hard to believe."

"Look." He tugged at his tie. "I don't care what you believe or not. I need you to keep your mouth shut about my involvement there."

"And why would I ever do that?"

Not that I would ever use it for my personal gain. The Nightingales didn't believe it even after I repeatedly told them it wasn't me. So why bother now, when all I had left were bitter memories and a lifetime of regrets.

Besides, his downfall would be caused by me, and nobody else. I would be his personal executioner.

"Because if you ever say anything, I would make sure that Maya gets something worse than what she is getting now."

"Are you threatening me, Theo?"

He was fucking threatening me, when he knew how much I wanted to find our sister. Our father was tight-lipped about her whereabouts, always saying she deserved it. And if our father thought you deserved something and it wasn't death, it was a fate worse than anything I would ever put upon my worst enemy.

Wherever she was, it started with Kieran and his father, and no matter how much I tried, nobody knew where she was. Or they didn't want to tell me.

"I am just stating facts."

"No." I sat on the bed, getting away from him. "I think you're threatening me."

"Me?" He seemed offended. "I would never—"

"Cut the bullshit, Theo. You can remove the mask you are so diligently wearing on a daily basis. Or are you forgetting that I know what kind of scum you really are?"

The fake innocence with which he came with disappeared altogether, and I finally saw him for what he really was.

A fucking traitor.

That leering look on his face used to be directed at me so many times, I sometimes forgot how it felt having him look at me in any other way. As soon as I got initiated and started doing the jobs assigned by Syndicate, my brother changed.

He was always an asshole, but he never went out of his way to make me feel worthless. When our father started preferring my company over his, all niceties flew out the window. He became a person I couldn't trust, and I was young, thinking my brother would never betray me like that.

"Okay, Ophelia. I might be threatening you, but it's for your own good."

"My own good?" Was this guy for real?

"Yes, for you. Imagine the disappointment those three would feel if we ever told them what really happened that night. Tsk-tsk, you don't want them to feel like shit again. I think you did enough."

"I didn't fucking kill her. You know it, I know it, and the video clips from security cameras you so expertly erased that night know it."

"I don't know what you're talking about, Sis. Are you okay? Is your brain playing games on you?"

"Oh, you motherfucking—" I jumped up, advancing toward him, when he shuffled out of the chair, retracting closer to the door. "I don't need fucking knives to kill you. I'm going to do the job with my bare hands."

"Ah, ah, ah." He placed his hands in front of him, moving closer to the door. "Now, now, no need to get hasty here. I was just stating a fact."

I growled but before I could strangle him, the door opened revealing the two guards I knew were in front of my door.

"Remember what I said, Ophelia. Maya needs you."

With one last sickening smile, he exited the room, leaving me more furious than before.

Oh, I was going to enjoy killing him.

24

OPHELIA

Four Years Ago

My phone rang for the tenth time, but I didn't have the energy to deal with Kieran right now. I knew it was him. The first three times I denied his call he should've understood the message. I didn't fucking want to talk to him.

I never wanted to see him again, to feel this pain eating at my insides. He managed to do what even my father couldn't.

He fucking destroyed me.

Trust was a very important thing to me, and he just threw it away like yesterday's thrash. No, the time for explanations was long gone, and the only thing we were left with was the bitter taste of reality. He made his bed, and now he had to sleep in it.

I had better things to do, important people to save, and he was currently at the bottom of the list of people I cared about. Maybe in a few years, maybe in another life, but not now.

He screwed me over and I owed nothing to the traitorous little shit. I could almost hear his whiny voice, trying to trick me again that it was nothing. That Cynthia meant nothing.

What did men think, that just because emotions weren't involved it felt easier finding the one you love buried balls deep in another pussy?

I was trying to go over the plan for tomorrow evening, but my traitorous eyes kept glossing over, blurring the map in front of me. Fucking emotions, fucking Kieran, fucking Cynthia who kept messing with my life.

And why the fuck was I crying? That asshole didn't deserve my tears. He didn't deserve for me to even mention his name ever again.

Why did it hurt so much, that I felt as if my chest would cave in on itself? If this is what love felt like, I didn't want it. I didn't want any of it.

Ava told me that it takes time getting over somebody, but it shouldn't hurt this much. I was stronger, nothing affected me. Why couldn't I get over this?

Because love runs deep, but betrayal runs deeper.

Love, love, love, it could fuck off with the rest of the emotions I didn't want to have. It could burn for all that I cared, because it never brought me anything but hell. I thought loving Kieran would bring me some semblance of peace, that his light would work well with my darkness, that we would be happy.

Well, as happy as we could be in this fucked-up world.

But I was so fucking wrong. I wanted to hit myself repeatedly until I couldn't remember what it felt like to be held by him. Until the only memory I had of him was the picture of him fucking Cynthia in our bed.

God fucking dammit.

I swept at my cheeks, the wetness sticking to my hands. Why couldn't I stop crying? I was fine, I would be fine, and he will end up being just a bitter aftertaste of what could've been.

I was already tired, fighting myself from going after him

and bashing his head in, so when the phone rang again, I dashed toward the nightstand and answered on the second ring.

"Stop fucking calling me, Kieran!" I dropped the call. There was nothing he could say to make up for what he did.

Apologies wouldn't cut it out this time. Sweet little nothings he used to whisper in my ear wouldn't fool me this time. Did he really think I would be okay with all of this?

I threw my phone to the other side of the room, hitting the sofa. Too bad it didn't break. After tomorrow, he would never contact me again. He wouldn't dream of it, because I would end up being persona non grata for both his and my family.

But none of it mattered. What I felt didn't matter anymore, not that it ever did.

For the first time in my life, I knew what I had to do. I had to get out of here, and Storm was the answer to my prayers.

The fucking device started ringing again, and it was the last straw for me. I was going to strangle him.

"I fucking told you—"

"Ophelia," a voice I didn't expect sounded instead of Kieran's. I moved the phone away from my ear seeing the familiar number.

"Theo?" My brother rarely called me, and during the times he did, it was just to relay messages about meetings with my father. "Why are you calling me? We don't have another meeting for at least a month."

"I'm not calling you about a meeting."

"Why then?"

The rift between the two of us wasn't a secret, and the small chitchat most siblings had, died the day I came back from Siberia. He wanted our father's position, but my father didn't trust him. He was never the one he called for important jobs, never the one included in all the action, and he decided to behave like a spoiled little brat and redirect all of his resentment toward me.

Well, the feeling was mutual.

"Theo?" I asked again after a couple of seconds, since he decided to keep quiet.

"I am driving back to Croyford Bay." *Double shit.* I didn't want him here tomorrow evening.

"Why?"

"I received a call from Ava."

Ava? She never called him. She hated his guts more than I did, and that was saying something, considering that the little snake on the other side of the phone knew where Maya was. He just never wanted to tell me.

"Why would she call you?" I sat down, not liking the tone of his voice.

"Are you forgetting I am her fiancé?"

"Only in theory, Theo. Both you and I are well aware of that. She never wanted to marry you, never wanted to be anywhere near you, so why the fuck would she call you? What's going on?"

"She seemed distressed. Said there was somebody in the house with her. She was scared, Ophelia."

Scared? But there were at least two bodyguards with her. Why would she be scared?

"That's bullshit. There are guards with her, nobody could get in."

"No? They kept only one guard tonight, the rest of them are with Cillian and Tristan on a job." He let out a long sigh, before continuing. "Listen, I didn't call you to argue with you. Can you go to the house and make sure she's okay?"

"Why, you don't want to lose your golden ticket?"

"Ophelia, for fuck's sake, that's your friend."

"Yes, and if she was scared, she would've called me, not you. So why is that, Theo?"

"I don't fucking know," he barked. "I don't know. But can you stop being a bitch for one minute and check on her? The traffic is a bitch, and I won't be there for at least another hour."

I would do anything for Ava, no questions asked, but something in the way he was talking smelled fishy as hell. He was too nice, too concerned. He never cared about her safety, never even cared to check in on her and see how she was coping with everything that was supposed to happen.

Theo never put any effort into getting to know her. Maybe if he did, we wouldn't be in this predicament now, where I had to plan the best way to get her out of this town.

"Fine."

"Thank you."

"I was going to go there anyway, but since you asked so nicely—"

"You're such a psycho."

"Awww, thank you. I haven't heard such originality in a very long time. Did you come up with that nickname yourself?"

"Just..." the line started breaking up. "Get there, okay? Now."

What crawled into his panties tonight?

Unfortunately, all of my indifference fled out of the room the moment he hung up on me, and the unfamiliar sense of dread pooled at the pit of my stomach.

What if he was right and something was going on there?

Without another thought, I grabbed my car keys and ran out into the night. I just hoped Theo was pulling a prank on me, or that Ava was exaggerating.

I said it once, and I would say it a million more times— December had such terrible weather, and the position of our little town didn't help much. The openness to the Atlantic

Ocean meant that we were getting slammed by the worst possible wind during this period of the year, and my stupid ass kept forgetting to wear warmer clothes.

As soon as I got to the Nightingale Mansion, I noticed two things.

The guards weren't on their usual post at the gate, and the said gate was wide open, not a light in sight. That was fucking weird.

Okay, calm down, Ophelia. Just because nobody was here didn't mean that something bad was happening. Right?

I parked my car in front of the main door, turning off the ignition and trying to see if anyone was around. Logan Nightingale was a paranoid piece of shit, and two guards were always stationed at the front door, with the other two on the main gate.

Then why was it completely deserted, and why were none of the lights on the pathway on?

I slowly exited the car, slamming the door shut, and started walking toward the main door. The knife I strapped to my thigh felt heavy, and I prayed to every single deity that I won't have to use it tonight. I really wasn't in the mood for another attack, and least of all the one that could endanger Ava.

The door was unlocked, and I pushed it wide open, revealing an even darker foyer. A strong sense of deja vu hit me, the events of a night so long ago still fresh in my mind. The night my father took my innocence away from me, the night I truly saw who my mother was, and the night that man bled to death thanks to me.

The floor creaked beneath me with every step I took, and I gripped the handle of the knife, getting ready for the worst. I almost fell, stumbling over something on the ground.

It took me a minute for my eyes to adjust to the darkness, but even without a light, I could see what it was. Rather, who it was.

One of the guards laid in front of me, his eyes wide open, focused on the ceiling. I pulled my phone out, turning on the flashlight. The first thing I saw was the gunshot wound between his eyes.

Fuck, fuck, fuck, double fucking fuck.

My eyes scanned my surroundings, the training I had kicking in. Whoever killed him wasn't trying to rob the house. No. The bullet between the eyes was a clear indicator that whoever it was, absofuckinglutely knew what they were doing. Shit, the one time I needed to take my gun with me, I didn't.

I pulled my knife out of its holder and started walking deeper into the house, stepping over the guard.

He was already dead, and the only important thing was that Ava was okay.

The soft glow of light coming from the kitchen illuminated the hallway, and I started heading that way, hoping she managed to get to the panic room in the basement.

"Come on, come one. Just be okay."

With each step, my heart threatened to jump out of my chest. I hadn't felt like this since my first mission, and even then, it wasn't because I was scared for somebody else's life. It was because I knew I would enjoy it.

Now, this was my best friend, my soul sister, the other half of me. If something happened to her, there would be hell to pay.

"Ava," I whispered, but the reply never came. I couldn't hear anything but my breathing and my footsteps echoing in an empty house.

I could hear the dogs barking outside, but whoever made this mess seemed to be gone, or at least hiding.

My whole body froze when I reached the opening to the kitchen.

Her dark hair was spread over the floor, a complete contrast to the white marble below. The eyes that held so much joy just a day ago, were now closed, lost to me, because I knew that the pool of blood she was lying in wasn't something she could've survived.

A knife was sticking out of her stomach, the same stomach that held her baby. The baby she was so excited about.

It was all gone, lost. All her dreams, her future, all of those were sent to hell, because I knew that she was dead.

For a moment I stood frozen, my mind refusing to connect with my body and realize what was happening.

My best friend had been stabbed. She wasn't moving, her chest was still, not even a breath taken. What was that feeling in my chest? Was that pain or horror, because I felt as if somebody pulled a rug beneath me.

Our light was gone.

My senses kicked in and I ran to her body, dropping on my knees into the blood that shouldn't have been spilled. I pressed one hand to her stomach, trying to stop the bleeding, but it was futile.

"Ava, please, please, please." I sobbed into the empty space. "Please, stay with me."

Pushing her head backward I pressed on her pulse, trying to find even the smallest beat. For a moment there was nothing, and the scream tore from me, the anguish taking over my whole body.

"Ava!"

I started shaking her body, thinking it would bring her back.

"Ava, you can't leave me. Please." I pressed harder on her neck and felt a small beat answering my prayers. "Yes, yes, stay with me. Just stay with me."

I moved higher, right above her chest, positioning my hands on her chest.

"This will hurt, but I promise I won't let you go. I won't let you die."

I started pressing on her chest bone, trying to make her heart beat faster, trying to bring her back to life. The redness on my hands was taunting me, mocking me and my attempts, but I wasn't stopping.

"Twenty-seven, twenty-eight, twenty-nine," I counted each compression, "thirty."

I pushed her head back, opening her mouth and breathing into her. Once, twice, but her chest only lifted when I breathed in.

"Come on, Ava." I started chest compressions again, when a crack sounded around us, and I knew I broke at least one of her ribs. "I'm sorry, but you will feel better. You'll see. You'll be better."

My vision was getting blurry, but there was no time to wipe away the tears spilling from my eyes.

"Fifteen, Sixteen, Seventeen, Eighteen... Please, Ava. Please."

Another crack, and another bone broken.

She'll be fine. She'll be fine.

"You'll be fine, Ava. Everything will be just fine. You will grow old, and you'll have four children. You will pester me for the too many cigarettes I'm smoking, just please. Breathe for me, please breathe."

Her pulse spiked up, but it wasn't enough.

Maybe... Maybe if I removed the knife. I could do that. I should do that.

What did they say on the first aid course, to remove the object or not?

God fucking shit, I couldn't remember. Should I remove it or leave it in? What was the better option?

A small movement of her chest gave me hope, and I stopped chest compressions, hoping she could hear me.

"Ava." I shook her body. "Can you hear me? Everything is

fine, Ava. Everything is fine. You just keep resting your eyes, okay? I will help you."

Sobs rocked my body but I didn't have time to stop. No, no, no, there was no time. She had to live, she just had to.

I eyed the handle of the knife again, and before I could talk myself out of it, I pulled it out. The blood gushed out in rivulets, adding to the already expanding pool around us. I pressed harder, trying to close it with my hands, but it still spilled over my fingers.

No, it couldn't spill over. It had to stop, just stop.

"Ophelia? Oh my God."

I was so focused on Ava, that I didn't hear the approaching footsteps, and when I turned around, a pale Tristan stood at the doorway, his eyes flickering from me to his sister.

"What have you done?"

What have I done? I tried to save her. Oh God, I hope we still had time.

"What have you done, Ophelia?"

Why did he sound so angry? He should be helping me. He should call an ambulance. I couldn't keep pressing on this wound forever. But she was alive, I felt her heartbeat. It was there, she would survive this.

"Tristan, can—"

"What the fuck did you do?" He strode to us, and in a second yanked me away from her, the knife I was holding clattering to the ground. Another pair of hands pulled me up, and a fury I had never seen in Cillian's eyes met mine before he slammed me against the wall.

Tristan started talking to Ava, but I couldn't hear what he was saying. What was happening? Why aren't they calling an ambulance?

My eyes closed down from the pain, as Cillian slammed my head on the wall, holding an elbow to my throat. Small, black dots started dancing around his head when I opened my eyes, and I couldn't understand the look in his.

There was so much rage. I had never seen him this way. Why was he pinning me to the wall? I just wanted to help. I needed to help her.

I struggled against his hold, but the pressure he had on me just increased, a vicious expression taking hold of his usually calm face. Was he... Was he mad at me? I wanted to tell him I tried to save her. I wanted to tell him there was still a pulse, but I couldn't talk as he started cutting off my intake of breath.

"Kill... Cillian," I muttered, but the thunderous expression only increased with every attempt I made. What was his problem?

"What the fuck happened here?"

Theo. He would help her, that's why he was here. Everything will be okay.

His gazed slammed to me, and if I wasn't so drained, I could've sworn I'd seen a satisfactory smirk taking over before he masked it again, feigning concern. No, he wouldn't. Not Theo.

"How could you, Ophelia?" Cillian snarled. "She was your best friend. She would've done anything for you."

How could I what? I was starting to lose my footing, and if it wasn't for Kill holding me up, I would've ended up on the floor. Why was he holding me up like this?

"How could you kill her?" There were unshed tears in his eyes, and it took me a second to grasp what he just said. They thought I killed her.

No, no, no....

I started thrashing against his hold, grabbing his hands, trying to push him away from me. I needed to explain. It wasn't me. How could they think I would be able to do such a thing?

"No, no," I tried talking, but the fist that connected with my cheek sent my head flying to the other side, the throbbing increasing.

"Shut your filthy mouth." He grabbed my chin, squeezing painfully. "I knew you were a psychotic little bitch, Ophelia, but I guess I never really knew the lengths you would go to satisfy your craving for blood."

But it wasn't me—I wanted to scream.

"Cillian—"

"Do not say my name." He breathed harshly. "Don't ever say my name, or any of our names. This time you sealed your fate, and this time I will be the executioner. Not you. And this time, your daddy dearest won't be able to save you, because the moment you stabbed my sister and let her bleed to death was the moment you sealed your destiny."

I wanted to argue, to shout, to tell him it wasn't me. I always loved Kieran's brothers, especially Cillian. I knew what it felt like when your mind played games you didn't know how to play.

And he was always kind, always understanding.

But this Cillian standing in front of me... this Cillian had so much hatred in his eyes, and the target was me.

"Let me explain," I screamed out. "It wasn't—"

But I didn't manage to say what I wanted to say because in the next moment something stabbed me in the neck, and the reality I was trying to hold on to started slipping away, sending me into the darkness.

25

KIERAN

Present

My mother used to say that mornings are smarter than evenings, and to try and sleep it off before coming up with a decision. But what was I supposed to do if I couldn't sleep the whole night?

I kept talking myself from going to her room, knowing that whatever I had to say to her would end up in another screaming match. I couldn't bear her looking at me with so much hatred anymore. I was a fucking hypocrite, because I did the same.

Problem was, I didn't know anymore if I loved her or hated her. Did I want her dead or did I want her safe? Seeing her with Storm yesterday brought something out in me, and I couldn't shake this feeling that I had already lost her. But I wanted this, right? I wanted her to suffer for what she did to Ava.

She killed my sister, but something inside of me was screaming. There was a flicker of doubt playing in my mind, and it didn't matter how much I wanted to believe everything my brothers were telling me about that night.

Did she really kill me sister?

Now that I thought about it, it didn't make any sense.

Why would she kill her? Ophelia was deranged. The things she did to other people were insane, but she was always so protective of Ava. She didn't even want to tell her what our jobs were. Then why would she kill her?

"Are you ready to go?" Cillian sat across from me, stealing the croissant that remained untouched on my plate. In the moments like these, I allowed myself to remember us as brothers who loved each other, who protected each other, instead of this hatred that consumed our entire lives. He seemed calm, collected, but I knew that there was a thunderstorm brewing behind those dark eyes.

I snickered at myself.

Thunderstorm.

Storm.

That motherfucker.

I knew what both Cillian and Tristan wanted. They wanted to give Ophelia away, because they both knew it would be her eternal damnation. The way Sons of Hades behaved toward their females was deranged, vicious, primal, and I shuddered even thinking about it.

Or at least that's what I've heard.

She would be broken, beaten up, utterly destroyed if not killed, but I couldn't bring myself to agree with that decision, even though I knew it was the best course of action we could take.

We would get our mother back, and Las Vegas could fuck itself if it meant not losing another member of this family. Father would be furious, but if he even attempted to lift his ass from that leather chair he was so comfortable in, he would've known our mother was missing. He would've tried to help us, instead of telling us to deal with it on our own.

"Kieran?" Cillian asked. "You seem lost in your thoughts. What's bugging you?"

Was I that obvious?

"Nothing." I shrugged. "Just thinking about all the things I wanna do to Storm once we get Mom back."

He seemed to contemplate it for a moment, crossing his arms over his chest.

"Are we giving him Ophelia?" he asked carefully, and I hated how well my brother knew me. It didn't take a genius to realize how uncomfortable I was with the mere notion of giving her to that monster.

We were monsters, we were terrible, but we would've granted her death sooner or later. That fucker would keep her alive, keep her suffering.

"Kieran?"

"Sorry." I tried shaking off my traitorous thoughts. "Yes, we are."

The gleaming smile I haven't seen in a very long time took over my brother's face. His eyes shined with the newfound light, and I knew this was the right decision, even if I didn't feel like it was.

"I'm glad you finally saw the reason." Isn't that right? "If you're done here, we should get going. Tristan already picked Ophelia up, and they're waiting in the car."

Fuck, I wanted to talk to her before heading out. I wanted to try and understand for one last time what happened that night, but now we didn't have time.

It felt as if we never had enough time.

Cillian stood up before I could overthink the whole situation, and I followed his lead, heading to the basement parking and what I knew would be one of the hardest days of my life.

In the light of the day, the church we met in yesterday didn't seem as eerie as it first looked to me. Unlike yesterday, two rows of bikes were parked in front, and I knew Storm brought reinforcements.

Today, I let Cillian drive, and I used the opportunity to sit next to Ophelia, even if it meant I would just be dragging out my own misery, I had to feel her next to me. She never once looked my way, focused on the outside. If you asked me what would be one supernatural power I would like to have, I would tell you mind reading.

I wanted to know what was dancing around her head, what she felt, and if everything I was told was true. But none of it mattered, and as we came closer to the main entrance, I could almost feel her slipping further away.

Away from me, far away from my reach, and she wasn't the only one to blame.

So much misery between us. I would never forgive her for what she did, she would never forgive me for what I did. I hoped she would never find out.

The monstrosity I committed wasn't a murder, but it wouldn't matter in her mind. She would always see it as the worst thing I ever did, because I hurt somebody she loved.

The opening and closing of the front doors pulled me back from my reverie, and I somberly followed suit, stepping on the sidewalk next to Tristan. Ophelia was pulled out by Cillian, but she didn't struggle. She seemed to accept whatever was coming for her. But this hellion was always a devil in disguise, and if I learned anything over the years I spent with her, it was that she always had something up her sleeve.

I just needed her to behave until we took our mother away from here. What she did afterwards wasn't my business, even if my heart constricted at the mere thought of leaving her here.

The second car pulled behind ours, and a smiling Theo exited, as if we were walking into a party and not the beginning of a war.

"You guys look gloomy." Jesus fuck, why didn't I get rid of this guy? He was a pain in the ass, and even the information he was providing us with wasn't sufficient to have him around. But my father kept him with us, arguing that having an inside man in Syndicate, even if it was Theo, was better than nothing.

So the idiot stayed.

Everyone ignored his remark, and the five of us walked toward the front door, keeping Ophelia between us. The doors opened even before we could reach them, revealing a smug-looking Atlas.

He was another person I wanted to kill, and it had nothing to do with the little stunt he pulled yesterday. No, this man was one of the closest people to Storm, and I knew he did some sick shit for his president.

Atlas was an enforcer, and enforcers never did cute jobs. Cillian was ours, or at least he used to be before I pulled him out and convinced our father to give him a break. But this one, I could see it in his eyes, in the way he was observing everything around him. That calculating gaze, he was dangerous.

"Finally. Are you always late, or is it on purpose?"

"Fuck off, Atlas," I snarled, but he laughed, stepping aside and letting us in.

"Do you know any other words, or is that the best you can do?"

I ignored his taunting and instead focused on the man standing at the altar, his back to us.

"You're late," he said, slowly turning to us. His eyes zeroed in on Ophelia, raising my hackles.

"So I've been told."

"You know," he jumped over the steps, and closed the distance between us, "I admire you, Kieran. I really do. You're trying to do what's best for your family, to protect them, and I do the same. If the situation were different, we could even be friends."

"In your fucking dreams."

"Ouch." He feigned hurt. He was the puppet master, the devil. He loved to play games. This was just another one. "You hurt me, but that's fine."

"Let's get down to the business, okay?" I was impatient, sick of everything going on around us, and I just wanted this nightmare to be over. "Where is our mother?"

"Nuh-uh, not so fast." He stood in front of me, not paying attention to the rest of the people behind me. "Do we have a deal?"

Did we have a deal? Was I going to hand Ophelia over to him? I couldn't care less about Las Vegas, but she was mine.

She was mine even when she didn't want to be mine, and in this or another life, she would always be mine, no matter what.

"I-I," I stuttered. The nervous energy was zapping through me, the expectant look on his face tearing through me.

"Kieran," Cillian hissed behind me.

"Yes?" Storm asked. "You what?"

I looked back, focusing on Ophelia, but she wasn't looking at me. She was looking at him, and something akin to fascination was visible on her face. Please, baby, just look at me. Show me I shouldn't do this.

Show me you still love me.

But she never did. She ignored me, ignored everyone else and kept looking at the man I wanted nothing more than to kill. Because of her, I failed to protect my family once, but I wouldn't be making the same mistake.

She hated me, didn't want to be near me, fine. I would grant her what she wanted the most.

"Ophelia is yours," I announced without taking my eyes off of her. She slanted me with a furious look, but there was no usual remark. There was no bitchiness, just the fury emanating from her eyes.

Theo pushed her forward into my embrace. I hugged her closely, holding her head to my chest. Dropping my head down, I whispered in her ear, "You're free now, birdy. But I can't wait to see you begging for mercy when Storm gets done with you."

"Kieran," she stood on her tiptoes, reaching my cheek, "go to fucking hell."

She kissed my cheek followed with a smirk on her face and I pushed her away, toward the man I knew would break her soul.

After all she did, she deserved nothing less.

Ophelia landed right in Storm's embrace, and as he took a couple of steps back, pulling her with him, I couldn't help myself but wonder if I did the right thing. The smirk on his face irked me, but what unsettled me most was the protective stance he took once she was with him.

Gone was the man that just wanted to attack. No, the way he positioned his body, he was protecting her. And then it hit me—he really wanted her. Somewhere along the way, they met each other, he knew who she was, and this wasn't going to be torture for her.

If there was one thing I knew about men like Storm, it was that they protected those they cherished with their life.

He looked at her, and the cold mask of indifference cracked a bit, showing the human beneath the monstrous façade. That soft gaze, the way he touched her hair, it was obvious.

So fucking obvious, and we were blind to it all.

He looked at me, our eyes locking on each other. It was an eerie sight to see. He lowered his head, leaning into her. I couldn't hear them, but I could see the look of surprise on her face—an elation, satisfaction, and finally determination. Her lips moved and a smile spread across his face before they both turned to us.

"An eye for an eye, Kieran," she said.

In a blink of an eye, bikers I didn't see before gathered behind them, pointing their rifles at us. Ophelia straightened up, standing tall, next to Storm.

"Did you really think I was trapped with you, Nightingales?"

My brothers and Theo shuffled behind me, the nervous energy radiating off of them in spades.

"Did you really think I would've allowed you to kidnap me, you fucking idiots."

"What are you talking about?" Cillian asked. "You were kidnapped."

"Oh, poor Cillian," she chuckled. "I knew your thirst for revenge would destroy the remaining brain cells. I am sorry to disappoint you, but I knew you would do just this. I knew my lovely brother would use the first opportunity to sell me out, and you would use it. You couldn't see what was happening, and you didn't see the enemies that gathered on the edges of your empire, waiting for you to fail. And you did. You failed gloriously. Because while you were busy hating me, I was busy trying to figure you guys out. And you know what I found out?"

Motherfucking bitch.

"You are falling apart. I told you once, a long time ago, don't underestimate me. And you did exactly that."

Storm placed his hand over her shoulders, and between her telling us she was willingly kidnapped and him staking his claim on her, my heart beat rapidly. My palms were sweaty, and if I ever saw an ambush, then this was the classic one. Why didn't I bring our guards inside?

I still didn't understand any of this. Why was Storm doing

this? Why was he helping her? It couldn't have been only his interest in her.

"Phee," I started, trying to reason with her, but the venom in her eyes stopped me from going further.

"I think it's time for us to finish this. What do you think?" She looked at Storm. He smiled at her. The first real smile I've ever seen from him, and if that didn't destroy the last ounce of hope I had that this would end differently, nothing else would.

"Sons of Hades," he turned to us while talking to his team, "let's fucking finish this."

Before they could start advancing toward us, I pulled my gun out and shot the first one in the chest.

"Not without a fight."

And that was when all fucking hell broke loose.

26

OPHELIA

I *nat.*

It was the Albanian word for malice. The same word Storm whispered in my ear.

The same word Agon, the leader of Albanian mafia, gave me when he sent me on this assignment. I wasn't the person that made correct choices. The mistakes in my life kept piling up, but the biggest one was getting involved with the Albanians.

I owed them my life.

But this was my chance to be free, and I took it. And after Agon told me what Kieran did, I didn't even hesitate. I just didn't think he would hire somebody else to help me. No, scratch that. I didn't think he would send Storm to help me.

I should've known. The interest I thought I saw in Storm's eyes was just a pretense, and I again allowed my foolish heart to believe he truly wanted me. But none of that mattered because I had a job to do. A freedom to earn, and my feelings for Storm wouldn't stand in my way.

I had a sister to save, and people to kill.

This was the breaking point for all of us, and I couldn't wait for it to happen. I've waited for years. I've kept quiet, lived in hiding, running away so that all of them could live their lives without the constant reminder of me. I went through hell and crawled out, only to find out about the monstrosity the one I loved committed.

But not anymore, never again. I would never again lower myself for the sake of those that betrayed me. We could've been perfect, but we ended up tragic. We ended up messy, and there was no going back from this point.

We all made our beds and now it was time to sleep in them. I thrived on insanity, I lived for it, loved its darkness, and it took me a long time to realize that I wasn't the problem.

They were.

They fucking threw me into the darkest pits and refused to acknowledge me, when all I wanted, all I needed, was just a little bit of love, and a little bit of understanding. It was so easy framing me for something I never did, so easy to throw me away like I never meant anything at all.

Maybe I didn't.

Maybe I was just a marionette. Just another puppet, another person manipulated by others, so that they could get what they wanted.

More power, more money, more control over the things they craved.

I was fucking sick and tired of men controlling our world, of controlling every step I took.

Smile, Ophelia, stand tall, Ophelia, don't hold the knife like that, Ophelia, take a smaller gun, Ophelia, it suits you better... Kill them, Ophelia, gut them like animals but don't feel anything because feelings have no place in this world.

Be a machine, Ophelia. Be a living and breathing destruction, and you would be rewarded.

I was never fucking rewarded. I was just left to my own devices, to my own insanity, because I didn't really matter.

I had to admit one thing, though. I should fucking thank my father for making me this way. I should thank him for making me see who wanted me for me and who couldn't stand to see what I became, because if people couldn't handle me at my worst, they sure as hell didn't deserve me at my best.

All the blood spilled, all things we went through, they all led us here, to this final resting place, because most of us wouldn't be leaving this church alive. Suitable, wasn't it? A perfect place to die and descend.

Maybe in death we would find the peace we couldn't find in this life, but I sure as hell wasn't dying until I could see the lying piece of shit that shattered my soul and took everything from my sister, dead.

I wasn't afraid of dying, I never really was. If heaven and hell really existed, I already knew where I would end up. Hell itself couldn't be worse than this hell on earth, because living in this nightmare was the one thing I would never wish even to my worst enemy.

All of these men that only thought with their cocks, their fucking egos, their never-ending craving for more, they were the ones that made us this way. I knew Kieran wasn't always a monster, but sometimes you needed to choose what kind of a monster you became. I was a killer, possibly a psychopath, but I made no excuses.

I killed, I maimed, I tortured, and I would do it all again if it meant protecting those I cared for. But I would never hurt those I was supposed to protect, and that was the main difference between Kieran and me.

They all swore that family meant everything to them, but that was such a bunch of bullshit. They didn't care who they had to hurt to get what they wanted. If they did, I would know where my sister was, and this fucking idiot looking at me with fear in his eyes would have told me what was happening that night he destroyed every single chance of us ever getting back together.

No, fucking scratch that.

He sold his humanity, the trust I had in him, all for a chance to win over a person he hated more than I hated my own father. He had years to come clean about what he did, he could've found me.

He also had years to accept the fact that I didn't kill Ava. I was framed for a monstrosity I never committed, but I guess that's what I got trusting the wrong people.

And that slimy piece of shit standing behind Kieran, my own brother.

My flesh and blood chose to side with the enemy, not only betraying me, but the whole Syndicate. And I could bet he thought he would be able to get out of this.

Well, that was the show we wouldn't be watching, because this time, I would be showing him who I really was. He spent so much time hating me for things I wasn't even responsible for that he forgot what a weak little shit he actually was.

The sound of a gun going off threw me off balance, and as one of the Storm's guys fell to the ground, it felt as if time stopped. Something cold landed in my left hand, and I turned to the side, only to see Storm placing a dagger in my hand.

How did he know?

I looked at it before meeting his eyes, and the same feeling like the day that we met resonated through me.

Familiarity.

Connection.

Home.

But I couldn't dwell on all of that right now. No matter what he felt like to me, I couldn't forget what he failed to do. I guess that at the moment I decided to choose the one I didn't want to kill in cold blood, and if that meant Storm, so fucking be it.

The doors of the church banged open, and six guys I knew from Kieran's group of bodyguards, filtered in, rushing to his side. Well, the snake brought his little reinforcements. Good, it was starting to get boring.

Sons of Hades stood in place, some of them looking at their fallen brother, and some sending murderous looks to the Nightingales.

Buckle up, buttercups.

I didn't wait for any of them to move before I started running toward the small group guarding my brother and his masters. Just like a dog, he listened to everything they said, everything they wanted, and he thought he had freedom.

Stupid.

I gripped the handle of the knife harder, and before the first bodyguard's fist could connect with my face, I dropped to the floor, kicking his legs. The bigger they are, the easier they fall.

This one dropped like a sack of potatoes with a little umph coming from him.

From the corner of my eye, I could see Storm's guys going head-to-head with the rest of the guards, one of them on Cillian, and the other two with Theo and Tristan.

I couldn't see Storm, but I also couldn't see Kieran, and I didn't have to be a genius to know those two were at each other's throats.

The shithead on the floor grabbed my ankle, pulling me to the ground. The dagger clattered next to me as I landed on my back. The guard crawled over me, pinning my hips to the ground.

"I've been wanting to do this for days," he sneered. With both hands in the air, he fisted them together and they started descending to my face.

Ah, shit.

I maneuvered my head to the side, his fists connecting with the floor. The knife laid next to his leg, and I grabbed it, stabbing it into his leg. A scream tore out of his chest, as he started moving backwards, slowly releasing me from his weight.

I pulled myself upward, reaching for the handle sticking out of his thigh. Tearing it out of his flesh, the blood started gushing out, and before he could compose himself, I jumped up, rushing to his backside.

"You aren't the only one with homicide on his mind, darling."

I grabbed his hair as he thrashed, trying to move away from my hold. But it was futile, they all should know that. The blade of the knife connected with his neck, and I pressed harder, cutting through his skin, through the tendons of his neck, the sound of his skin separating, music to my ears.

His cartilage started crushing under the pressure of the knife, and the choking sound from his mouth, followed by the blood dripping down his chin, seemed like a fucking opera to me.

It was art, really. Van Gogh would've made a painting out of it.

As his body hit the ground, the pooling blood started expanding around his body. Weird, I didn't even cut the artery.

I guess it wasn't just that the big ones fall easier, it seemed that they bleed more as well.

I looked around at the total and utter chaos happening around me. Kieran and Storm were wrestling on the floor, but Storm seemed to have it under control. I just hoped he wouldn't kill him before I had a lovely little talk with him.

After all, he was my task, my bounty, and I swear, if Storm harmed him before I could, I would shoot him in the ass. I didn't give a shit he was larger than me.

The fighters that caught my attention, however, were Theo and Atlas, and I didn't like the scene unfolding in front of my eyes.

Atlas was on his knees, his face bloodied, one of his eyes already closing up, and my fucking brother stood above him, the barrel of the gun pointed at him. I didn't know Atlas, but I remembered Ava's words. He was nice to her that day, charming even, and that was more than I could say for my brother.

Wiping the blood on my pants, I moved the dagger to my left hand, and started heading to them. Atlas was Storm's brother, and looking at the situation we were in, they were helping me to fulfill what I came here to do. So excuse me if he meant more to me than the blood I shared with my brother.

I collided with Theo, knocking him to the ground, as the bullet shot out of the gun. I didn't have time to see if it missed Atlas, I just hoped he had enough time to dodge out of the way before it was too late.

Theo knocked me off, sending me a foot away from him, but this time I wasn't giving up.

I was tired of his taunting, tired of his mind games, and the hold he had on me. If he wasn't going to tell me where Maya was, well, he was going to die with the rest of them today. There was no love lost between us, just good old hatred.

Such a shame, really. We would've been an amazing team, because for all his faults, my brother had a brilliant mind. He was never much of a fighter, but the way he was handling things... I guess you had to have it in you.

I didn't.

I couldn't go behind somebody's back just to accomplish my shit. But I guess that it wasn't too different from killing people, was it now?

I crawled back to him before he could get up, and latched on his leg, pulling him back to the ground.

"Get the fuck off of me," he shouted, trying to rid himself of my hold.

"How does it feel, Theo?" I turned him, sitting on his stomach. "How does it feel being helpless?"

My fist connected with his cheek, and a small whimper erupted from him.

"How does it feel," I pulled him by the lapels of his jacket, "to be at my mercy?"

"Sis—"

"Oh, now I'm your sister?" I punched his other cheek, his head flying to the other side. "I am your sister only when you need something from me. Only when you have something to gain, and I have everything to lose."

"I didn't," he whimpered.

"Don't fucking talk unless I ask you to talk."

The tie he wore looked tempting, and I pulled it up, closing the knot around his throat, pulling it tighter.

He started gasping for air, and I laughed at the expression on his face.

Fear.

Fucking fear, and I couldn't even remember how many times I wanted to see just that.

"Oh, you can't breathe?" I snickered. "Poor little Theo. You don't seem afraid enough to me. Let me help you with that."

I pushed him to the ground and squeezed his throat, feeling the larynx beneath my palm.

"Does it feel good, Theo? Because it feels amazing to me."

"I-c-can't—" he wheezed.

"Awww, you can't breathe." I moved back, removing the knot from his neck. "Here, this should help."

The coughing fit erupted from him, and the small satisfaction I felt over his helplessness was short lived, because I wanted more.

I wanted to see him bleed just how I bled. I wanted to see him fucking chained to the wall, just like the Nightingales chained me the night somebody stabbed Ava. He watched, knowing it wasn't me. This motherfucker said nothing.

I didn't know it then, but I understood now.

He knew who it was, and he was protecting them.

"Who killed Ava?" I asked him, but the smirk on his face told me everything I needed to know. He wouldn't tell me shit. "Tell me!" I pulled him up, before slamming his head on the floor. His eyes closed on impact, a moan following suit. He sounded like a little bitch.

I guess I shouldn't have been surprised.

That was what he always was—just a little bitch.

"I swear to God, Theo."

"I will never tell you." The motherfucker laughed at me. "And you can't do anything to me to make me talk. No amount of punches will make me talk."

Clueless little monkey.

He thought he would survive me.

"Oh, darling." I grinned and leaned down to his ear. "You aren't walking out of here alive. You wanted to know how psychotic I was? You gave me that nickname, Psycho Ophelia. Remember?"

I pulled myself back, looking into his eyes. And would you look at that, the slightest tremble of his chin, the frantic look, he finally understood what was coming for him.

"What? Did you think I was going to let you live after everything?" I laughed at him. "You know better."

"Ophelia, please—"

"Oh, now you're begging me. How funny." The dagger in

my hand felt heavy, and I knew what I needed to do to finish this once and for all.

"Please... I didn't know."

"Oh, you knew. I know that you knew. You knew who killed her, just like you know what happened to Maya. Where is my sister, Theo?"

"Phee—"

"Stop stalling. Where. Is. Maya?"

He turned his head, looking at Kieran and Storm, and I followed his gaze, seeing Storm holding Kieran in a choke hold.

"Don't worry, Brother. You won't be the only one leaving this place in a body bag."

"I don't know where she is. I don't. You have to trust me," he pleaded. "I'm your brother. Your family. You can't kill me."

"Blood doesn't make you family. It means nothing to me. You mean nothing to me. After all the shit you pulled, you should know better."

"But—"

"No, shut up for once, and let me talk." I patted his hair, moving the wayward strands from his forehead. In another life, he would've been a loving brother who helped me through all of this, and I would be a sister he wanted to have. Maybe each of us would be that person the other one could trust with their life. I would ask for him when things went wrong because my brother would've been my protector.

But unfortunately, we were the wrong brother and sister in this life. Maybe it was the blood running through our veins that couldn't allow us to be normal. But then again, what was normal anyway?

"You are going to die, darling." I started humming the melody our mother used to sing to us when we were kids. "You are going to die, and I will be the one to kill you."

He started struggling, but I pinned one of his hands above his head and slammed the dagger through his palm, to the wooden floor. The crack of his bones, followed by his scream echoed around us, but I couldn't allow him to escape.

He used to carry a knife inside his jacket, and this time was no exception. I pulled the small swiss knife out, and started playing with the set, while he panted beneath me.

"Let's see," I pulled the smaller looking blade first, "what should I do first? Should I carve your skin off, bit by bit, until you tell me who killed Ava? Or should I pull your eye out with this little piece until you tell me what happened to Maya and where she is?"

"No, please—"

"Shhh." I grabbed his chin in my hand, halting his movements. "It won't hurt too much. Just a little bit, you know? Unless you tell me everything I want to know."

"Go to fucking hell!" He spat in my face. "You'll never get anything out of me."

I wiped my face before pressing harder on his.

"Very well then." I pressed the small blade on his cheek and started carving out a small piece of skin. He was thrashing, grabbing my hair with his other hand, but I was relentless.

There, he looked perfect now. As ugly on the outside as he was on the inside.

"Where is Maya?" I left the meat of his cheek hanging and pressed my forefinger into the bloodied mass beneath. The screaming, the struggling, it was all futile. "Tell me, and I might even let you go."

"Never!" he shouted.

"Your choice." I started pulling the chunk off of his cheek, moving it toward his ear, and with it, additional skin.

That's right, brother. Just scream for me.

"No, no." He took a hold of my hand, "No more. Please."

"Will you tell me what I want to know?"

"I can't." More like he didn't want to. "They will kill me."

"And I won't?" *Was he stupid?* "As I said, your choice."

I pressed the blade to his other side, shaking his hand off of me.

"Mexico," he suddenly shouted. "That's all I know. She's somewhere in Mexico. That's the last thing I heard."

"Mexico?" What the fuck was she doing in Mexico?

"Yes, yes," he cried. "Please, just let me go."

"Hmm, Mexico." I pondered over it for a moment. I didn't have anybody in Mexico right now, but I could ask Cole. He always had my back, and I could give him a visit, see if he knew anything.

"Ophelia?"

"Shhh," I pressed the blade to his mouth. "I'm thinking."

But what if she wasn't there anymore? Or worse, what if this little shit was lying to me?

"Are you lying to me?" I looked at him.

"No, no, I'm not," he mumbled against the knife on his lips. "You have to believe me, Phee. I would never lie to you."

"Seriously, Theo?"

"I'm not lying!" he exclaimed. "I'm not."

Huh, maybe he was telling the truth. Which meant that I had to finish this shit and get to the next one. Time was fucking ticking, and I wasn't leaving Maya alone. Not anymore.

I already failed her once, and I wasn't going to do it again.

"Okay, I believe you."

The breath he was holding whooshed out of him, and his body went slack on the ground. I knew that no matter what I did, he would never tell me who killed Ava. I wasn't too scared. With or without him, I would find a real culprit behind everything.

"Thank y—"

Before he could utter another word, I slammed the knife into his eye, the small, red handle sticking out. I could write poetry about this.

A few little gasps left his body before his body went slack. Blood coated his face, and the small sense of relief rushed through my body. One down, three to go, and the next one was in this room.

I was so lost in what I was doing, that I didn't even notice the moment Storm and his guys tied the Nightingales up and killed the other guys.

I pulled the dagger from Theo's palm, and started walking toward Kieran, who was on his knees, right in front of Storm.

27

KIERAN

She looked like an avenging angel, standing in front of me, holding the knife covered in her brother's blood. There was no trace of the girl I used to know.

The girl I loved, that loved me.

This person standing here was a stranger, and I guess I was to blame for it all.

I abandoned her as well, just like everybody else. I didn't listen to her, and it was too late to ask for forgiveness.

She wasn't my Ophelia anymore, and it cut deep. I thought I lost her four years ago, but in reality, this was our breaking point. This was the end of us.

But maybe I could try. Maybe she would listen, and she would see I was still the same person that loved her. Maybe she could forgive me for everything I did to her in the last couple of days, and everything my brothers did.

But she killed Ava.

No, I wasn't sure if she killed Ava. I wasn't sure about anything anymore—about my family, hers, who was pulling strings, and who was the puppet here. I wasn't even sure why we were seeking vengeance anymore. Was I doing it to appease my brothers, or was it my own agenda trying to get back at her for breaking my heart?

But that wasn't how this story went. I was the one that destroyed her, and if she ever found out about what I did to Maya, she would never forgive me. Why, why was I such a mess that night?

No, focus, Kieran. I couldn't change what happened then, but I could change how our future looked.

Mine only existed if she was with me. These four years, I was just breathing, but I wasn't living. I was a corpse without her warmth, without her touch, without her smile.

"Ophelia—"

"How does it feel being on the receiving end of somebody's revenge?" she interrupted before I could speak. My hands were tied as I kneeled in front of her.

The Ice Queen.

The Assassin.

And no matter what, she was still the woman I loved.

"How does it feel knowing that this is the end for you?" She crouched, our eyes on the same level. "Do you still feel power-ful, Kieran? Or do you finally understand what's going on?"

No, I didn't understand. But it didn't really matter now, because the only thing I wanted was for her to remember who we used to be.

"Do you remember that night Ava died?" Another slice over my heart, because that was one death I would never get over. "Are you finally going to listen to what I have to say? I mean, not that you have much choice, but you know, really listen."

"I wasn't in Croyford Bay that night."

"I know you weren't." She started playing with the dagger, the point of it on the floor, while she turned it around with her hands. "Which is why it hurt me so much more when you accused me of something I never did."

"But they saw you—"

"They saw me trying to save her!" she roared. "Cillian and Tristan saw me trying to stop the bleeding after I removed that knife. My knife, might I add, the one that went missing three weeks prior to that night. They saw me doing CPR on her, because there was still a pulse. She was still alive when they arrived, and if any of you idiots had listened to me," she looked behind me, right at my brothers, "she might've survived. But no, you had to let emotions take control over your body, and instead of helping me, you pushed her deeper into the grave."

"Phee," I tried, but she instantly placed the tip of the blade beneath my chin, lifting my head.

"It's my time to talk, Kieran. You had your chance, and you blew it."

"Okay."

"Good." She removed the dagger from my face, holding it in one hand, with her arms on her knees. "The reason I went to your house that night was because Theo called me. That motherfucker told me that Ava called him and sounded upset."

"Why would she call him?" I was confused. Ava hated Theo, and if there was one person she tried avoiding as much as possible, it was him.

"Now you're getting it. He was the one that helped me escape after you left me to die in that basement cell. He was the one who knew who really killed her, and instead of chasing the murderers in your lines, you were so focused on me that you never even realized what was happening right under your nose."

"But we found your knife. It was the murder weapon."

"Right, the one I just told you was missing." She stood up, looking down at me. "When I arrived there, her guard was already dead. When I saw her in the kitchen, she was already almost dead. She was stabbed by somebody else, not me."

Were we really that blind?

"You were chasing the wrong person, and all this time, you had one traitor in your midst. Did you really think that my father didn't know Theo was working with you? He just probably didn't care because that slimy toad never knew even half of what was going on in the Syndicate."

"But then, who killed her?" If it wasn't Ophelia, it had to be someone who knew our routine.

"I don't know, but I am going to find out."

"That's bullshit," Cillian attacked from behind, but was it? Was it really bullshit, because the Ophelia I knew never shied from accepting the things she was guilty of? If she really killed Ava, she would've said so. But looking at her, the way she behaved, the way her pain still shone through, I finally understood.

She really didn't kill my sister, and my pain, my anger, the need to take it out on somebody, anybody, made me betray her in the worst way possible.

What was I thinking accepting the things without relevant proof?

We were wrong. We subjected the wrong person to the suffering she didn't deserve.

"Ophelia, I am sorry."

"Your sorry means nothing to me." She pulled my hair, exposing my neck. "Your sorry can go to fucking hell. You're only sorry because you ended up here. The excuses, apologies, none of those will cut it this time."

"Please, listen to me."

"I am done listening to you." She leaned in. "I am tired of men telling me what to do. I am tired of men taking whatever they want without any consequences."

Did she... Did she know?

"You take our innocence, our sweetness, and until you turn it into something ugly, you never give up. But when that happens, you throw us aside, like yesterday's trash, looking for a new toy to play with. Isn't that what you did, Kieran? You took everything I was, and when what I became wasn't good enough, you decided to dip your dick into somebody else. Somebody I hated. But you did something else as well, didn't you?"

No, she couldn't know. Nervousness I had never felt before, rushed through my whole body. My hands started shaking, and the night I wanted to forget, the one I wanted to erase from my memory, started repeating in my mind.

Glass.

Cut.

My father.

Maya.

The worst thing I ever did in my life was taking what wasn't mine to take. I raped her. I fucking raped her, and if Ophelia knew... No, she didn't know. If she knew, I would've been dead by now.

"Phee," I started, trying to remind her of who we were. "Do you remember your seventeenth birthday?"

She let go of me, taking a step back.

"Do you remember how excited you were to get all those presents, and how you pretended to be serious every time I was in the room? Do you?"

Her eyes frantically looked from me to Storm, but she finally focused on me before replying.

"What does that have anything to do with this?"

"It has everything to do with this, because even though you tried to hide it, I knew you liked me. And you know what, I liked you too. I liked you so much that I would've tried to take the stars from the sky, just for you, just so you could keep smiling in that crooked way of yours."

She took a deep breath, and dropped to the floor, sitting crossed-legged.

"And when they announced our engagement, I was thrilled. I was also terrified, because how could someone like you, ever love someone like me." I took a deep breath, before continuing. "I hated what they did to you, what they made of you, and for the longest time, I tried to change that. But there's no changing it, is there? This is who you are, and I was too stupid to accept it, and for that I'm sorry. I am sorry I wasn't there when you needed me, when the darkness was too much to bear. I am sorry for being confused by my own grief that I never saw yours."

"Kieran," she whispered.

"I needed someone to blame because it was easier blaming you than blaming an unknown person. And Cynthia," she started shaking her head, but I didn't stop, "she was one thing I never should've done. I hurt you so much, and I am so, so sorry. For everything I did, for everything I didn't do. There are so many things I want to change, but the past is in the past, and we are here, in the present."

She finally looked at me, and hope blossomed in my chest at the cracks in the façade she erected around herself, because that girl, the one that used to smile at me, she was still there.

"Phee." I reached for her hands with my tied ones. "Stop this madness. I believe you; I really do. And Cillian and Tristan will too. Just come home, Phee. Come back to me."

I thought she would move back, she would get away from me, but she just sat there, staring at our joined hands.

"Please, baby girl, please. Let's leave this madness behind. Let's start anew. Only you and me. Far away from this mess, from this insanity. I don't care what you did, but I can't spend another day living with this pain eating at my insides."

I pulled her closer, our knees touched.

"I need you by my side. I just want everything to be normal, for us to be who we used to be."

"Kieran, we can't."

"No, I refuse to believe that. We can, we still can. God, don't let what we had go to waste."

"But you did it first," she said. "You threw us into the flames, and now you expect me to run to you, when all you did was run from me. You were the one that destroyed us, not me. You destroyed us."

"No, no, that's in the past."

"But that past," she wiggled her hands out, "is what shaped us. You, me, your brothers, my family. Do you really think I can just get over everything? Just like that. Just because you asked."

"No, but we can work on it." God, please. I am begging you. Let us work on this. Just give us another chance, and I promise, I will never betray her like that again. And I will help her find Maya. I will even tell her everything that happened. She has to know. "Just come back to me."

"I-I can't."

"Yes, you can. Please, Ophelia."

"No." She shook her head. "You couldn't handle me then, and I am sure you won't be able to handle me now. I am not who I used to be, Kieran. I am not the girl you remember. That naïve little girl doesn't exist anymore. She's gone, and you and your family helped push me over the edge."

"Please, baby. Just, let me in. Let me in and I'll show you how good we both can be."

"Ophelia," Storm started, interrupting us. The way he looked at her still bugged me, but her attention wasn't on him anymore, it was on me, and I felt victorious just seeing it. "You gotta hurry up. The rest of their guards will be here soon, and my guys are injured. We need to get out of here."

The shadows descended over her eyes with every word he

spoke, and it was as if everything I just said didn't mean anything. The same cold mask she always wore reappeared again, and I was losing her.

I was losing her, and I didn't want to lose her. I couldn't let her go, no matter what. So I used the last thing I hoped would bring her back to me.

"I love you. I still do. I always will, and no matter what, nothing will ever change that."

"Stop it."

"No, I need you to know that I still love you, and even if you don't love me, I can be patient. I can wait, but just please, come back to where you belong. And you belong with me, you always belonged with me."

28

OPHELIA

Chaos.

That was the perfect word to describe the two of us. A perfect chaos, a sweet destruction, complete desolation of our souls. How could I kill him without killing myself as well?

"Do it, Ophelia." Storm broke through my thoughts.

No, how could I kill the light of my life? I did this to us. I brought us to the brink of insanity. I killed the innocence in him, but I couldn't take his life as well. I thought I could. I thought that maybe, just maybe, I would be free of this life, of these memories, of these demons that haunted me for years.

Seeing him like this, kneeling in front of me, beaten, broken down, destroyed... I couldn't.

"I-I can't." I dropped the knife to the floor, both Tristan and Cillian following my movements. There was so much hatred, so much destruction in all of us, when would it stop?

When the fuck would this madness go away?

When did it start? Was it with our families, or was it with us?

"I can't... I can't, Storm."

Theo's lifeless body laid on the other side, his eyes wide open, staring at me. I felt no remorse seeing him like that, just like he didn't feel any remorse when he destroyed my life.

But Kieran… This man—his only fault was loving me. His only fault was thinking that the monster had a heart big enough to change what it really was. His only fault was trying to do what his father told him to do.

He always thought I could be better, I could be kinder, sweeter… I just never told him I could never be what he wanted me to be. I tried. My God, I tried so hard.

But the two of us, we were wrong for each other. Two opposites colliding at every step of the way, but we never met each other in the middle. Positive and negative atoms attract each other, but ours were never destined to function.

Ours were destined to destroy, and that's what we did.

We pulled all of the good things from each other, leaving behind two souls so numb that no amount of love could fill the void. We were wrong, so, so fucking wrong, and I wanted to scream at the world for putting him in my path.

I wish I never met him. I wish our families never worked together and I never met his sister. I didn't deserve his love.

I didn't deserve him.

"Ophelia," Kieran croaked. Tears I refused to drop before now gathered in my eyes. His bloodied hand reached for mine, entwining our fingers.

Red, all I could see were red streaks. What the fuck did I do? What did I do to him? What did I do to us? Oh God.

My chest was squeezing, my heart felt like it might explode. I broke us. I fucking broke us and I knew there was no going back after this. Why didn't he tell me what happened then?

"Ophelia," he whispered again, "look at me."

I started shaking my head, my tears falling free onto the

floor between us. Everything else ceased to exist. Storm, Tristan, Cillian, Atlas, all of them… They weren't here anymore.

"Please."

The emotion in his voice choked me, the pain in my chest intensifying with each new breath.

"Ophelia!" Storm barked behind me, his voice sounding closer than before. Oh God, what did I get myself into? What did I get my heart into?

"Phee." I looked up, my eyes colliding with the mess I created. What happened to the boy I used to know? I was such a fucking hypocrite. I lied to him, brought him to his knees, and I wanted revenge. For what?

For him having too much love for me? For the way he cared for me when nobody else gave a shit? For every single time he cleaned my wounds, every kiss, every touch… Who was I really hating?

"I am so sorry," I croaked, pulling myself closer to him. "I am so fucking sorry, Kieran. So, so sorry. What did I do? What did I do to you? I can't… I can't do this."

"Phee." His hand traveled over my cheek, and he brought our foreheads together. "Phee, Phee, Phee…"

I clutched his hands with my shaky ones. I couldn't look at him. I couldn't see everything he still felt for me, even after everything I've done.

"Do you have any idea how much I love you?"

"No, Kieran—"

"Because I do." He kissed my nose, my cheek, "I love you so much. I will always love you, and it doesn't matter if it's in this life or another one. You will always be mine and I will be yours."

"Kieran." I gripped his hair as if it would keep him here with me. As if it would transport us back to the time where it was only the two of us, without all the sinister plans killing our happiness.

"Nothing and no one can take that away from me. Not my father, Storm, not even you, baby. Because it will always be here." He pulled my hand to his chest. "My heart will always beat for you, and even when you can't see me, I'll always be there."

"Stop it." I tried pulling away from him. "You can't love me. No one can love me."

"Phee—"

"No, no, no!" I screamed. "You can't love the darkness. You just… You just can't. You never could, and it was fine—"

"I always loved your darkness," he cut me off. "I always yearned for your darkness because you were the only one who could understand my demons. You were the first person I thought about in the morning, and the last thought before I fell asleep."

"Please—"

"No, you have to hear this, okay?" He pulled me closer, so close, our chests were touching. "You need to hear this, because you have to forgive yourself. You have to learn to let go, Ophelia."

"I could never let you go."

"But you'll have to. Baby, you have to."

"Ophelia, we need to get going. The rest of their guards are going to be here soon," Storm's voice penetrated through the little bubble we created. "If you're going to do wh—"

"Give me five fucking minutes," I threw back at him without moving an inch from Kieran. His hair was coated in blood and cuts marred his face, but instead of looking like a demon, he looked like an angel. I was just too stupid to ever realize that.

"I want you to know," I fisted his shirt, "that you were

always enough. You were always more than enough, but I was the fucked up one."

"Ophelia—"

"No, no, let me finish." I took a deep breath and continued, "You were always the light to my darkness, and I am sorry I took it away from you. I am sorry my demons couldn't dance with yours. All the lies, all the pain, I didn't keep it away because I couldn't trust you. I wanted to protect you from myself. I wanted you to live, safe from everything that I was, that I still am."

"Baby—"

"I am broken, Kieran. I was probably broken even before I got involved in all of this. I just never realized that. There is this emptiness inside of me, this black hole eating away at my insides, and I don't know how to stop it from spreading to everything I love. It'll swallow me whole, and I don't know how to stop it."

"For fuck's sake, can you just get on with it?"

Storm was pacing behind me, but I had to have this.

"Baby girl…" Kieran trailed off. "I forgive you, you know that?"

"I know." I nodded. "But I never asked for your forgiveness."

I enveloped my arms around him, inhaling the scent of blood, sandalwood, and everything he was. He exhaled, as if the calmness took over, and I squeezed my eyes shut at the pain ricocheting through my body. I pulled myself into his lap, entwining my legs around his waist, clinging to him like a monkey.

"It's okay, Phee." He rubbed my back. "It'll all be okay."

But nothing would ever be okay.

Nothing would ever be okay, because I gripped the dagger I was holding. Sobs wracked my body, but I had to do this. He and I, we could never exist in the same world, and one of us had to go.

No matter how much I loved him, I could never forgive him for everything he did to Maya. I could never forgive him for throwing me aside, as if I never meant anything to him.

I screamed and I cried for him, but he never came.

They chained me like an animal for the crime I didn't commit. You don't do that to the person you love. This hatred, this pain, it was eating me alive, and I had to be free.

I wanted to be free of him, of these chains he still had around my heart. Maybe I would have to kill myself in the process after all.

Because this could only end up one way.

I pulled back and claimed his lips—one last time, one last memory to haunt me for the rest of my life. He opened for me, and I could feel a small smile playing there.

He thought we were fine, he thought it was all forgotten.

I don't trust you anymore.

He loved me.

I can't stand even looking at you.

He hated me.

What have you done, Ophelia?

He ripped me apart.

I want to see you bleed.

And now, I was going to rip his heart out.

With my lips pressed to his, I gripped the dagger harder and slammed it into his chest. He ripped away from me, shock, fear and lastly pain, written all over his face. He started reaching for the handle protruding from his chest, but I beat him to it, pushing the dagger deeper. Dark, red blood gushed from the wound, his mouth opening and closing from the shock.

"Ophelia?"

I pulled it out as he fell to his back. There it was. Pain, so much pain in his eyes, and it wasn't from the wound.

"You forgave me," I leaned over him, "but I never forgave you."

"Nooo!" somebody screamed, and it sounded like Cillian. "Kieran!"

"Shut him up," I said to no one in particular.

"Why?" Kieran whispered, blood pooling from his mouth. "I thought—"

"You thought all was good and we would drive into the sunset together?" I sat on his stomach, the blood freely flowing from the wound now. "Why, you're asking? Because you never apologized for making me the way I am now. Because you never apologized for the destruction you caused Maya—"

"Ophelia—"

"It's my time to talk, darling." I smiled as his face paled, and I knew he had minutes to live. "When were you going to tell me that you raped her? When were you going to tell me that you fucked my sister while she begged you to stop?" I leaned down, placing my elbow at his throat. "When were you going to tell me that you betrayed me long before that night?"

"I-I didn't—"

"You didn't think I would find out? I always find out. Always. I loved you so much, so goddamn much, but you never wanted to set me free. You were just like him, my father."

"Phee," he coughed. "Please."

"I would've changed myself for you. I would've abandoned this world, and for what? For a lying piece of shit who couldn't keep his dick in his pants. I would have forgiven you everything, but this, destroying my sister... My sister, Kieran! I could never forgive you. For chaining me up like an animal without an opportunity to explain myself—"

His breathing became labored, and the dark of his eyes I used to love so much, was slowly fading away.

"Look at me." I took his chin in my hands. "Look at the devil when you're dying. I want to be the last thing you'll see." I kissed him one more time, my lips coated in his blood. "I want you to know who killed you."

"Love." A hand dropped on my shoulder, pulling me back into reality. I turned from my past and looked at Storm. "We need to leave. Now."

"Right."

I took one last look at the person who once upon a time meant everything to me. A person who destroyed me, destroyed my life and took away everything good and bright I ever had.

"I will see you in Hell, darling." I pulled myself up. His hand shot up, grasping at mine. I knew he couldn't hurt me anymore, at least not physically, but that look, that smile he once again plastered on his face. That bloody, sinister smile, it could open another wound, another can of worms.

"You finally did it, baby girl." I frowned at him. "Your darkness finally swallowed us whole."

"Ophelia!" Storm yelled from the other side of the room, waiting with Atlas.

"I'll see you on the other side. Hell will be a beautiful place for the two of us."

I shook his hand off of me, and started running toward Storm. My heart was screaming at me, but we both knew this had to be done. This part of my past had to die, and even if it meant an eternal war, I had to do it. I destroyed us both, but he pulled the trigger.

"What about the other two?" Storm asked as soon as I reached him. "Atlas could easily take them out."

"No," I started. "They weren't the target. Their brother was."

"Are you sure?"

I wasn't, but Cillian and Tristan didn't have a target on their heads. Kieran had to die for more reasons than one. In any other situation I would have eliminated all the targets, but these two… These two were already broken enough and the destruction they would bring to themselves was already enough.

"Yeah, I am sure."

Just as we started walking out of the church, a voice boomed through the air.

"Ophelia!" I turned around only to see Tristan kneeling over his brother's body, and Cillian facing me. "I will find you, and I will kill you."

His words were poison, an eternal damnation, holding a promise of retribution. I smiled at him, stopping completely.

"I am counting on it."

29

OPHELIA

I t was done.

It was finally done.

I was going to be free. My part was done, and I hoped as hell that *they* would keep their word. I just killed him. I killed my past.

But I thought I would be happier. He cheated on me, raped Maya, and threw me to the wolves, never trusting in me. Why did my chest hurt? Why did my eyes keep watering when I brought justice? I killed the traitor. He deserved this. He deserved even worse, but I didn't have enough time to torture him how I wanted.

I didn't have enough time to show him what real pain felt like, because what he thought was painful, was nothing to me. At least, not anymore.

But I wanted to cry. I wanted to scream, and I didn't know if I was happy or sad.

Was I ecstatic? Was this how it felt?

Because I didn't feel good. I felt empty, drained. I was so tired, so, so tired, and I just wanted to sleep for days on end, but I didn't have time for that.

I had to find Maya. I had to save her from wherever she was.

Or if she didn't need saving, I needed to see it with my own eyes. I couldn't abandon her now that I had even that small clue.

She was in Mexico, or at least, she used to be. I just hoped she was still there because it would be a hell trying to find her otherwise.

I lost the concept of time inside, and as soon as I stepped outside the church, following after Storm, I was surprised to see the darkness. It was already past sunset.

Storm, Storm, Storm, that was another mess I really didn't have time for. Another shit thing I didn't want to deal with because I had more important things to do.

If I could, I would rip my own heart out and bury it somewhere far away from here, because feelings, love, that weird connection to another person, that was a recipe for disaster.

A faster way to die.

Nope, he could go to hell as well.

The car we came in was parked in front, but if I had to guess, the keys were still with Cillian, and that was one confrontation I didn't have the energy for right now. Atlas was sitting at the bottom of the steps, head bent, shoulders slouched. My brother got him good, and for a moment there, I thought I was too late. I still didn't know if he got shot when that gun went off, but he was alive.

Everything else could get patched. Life, not so much.

"Are you okay?" I asked him as I moved closer to him. His blond hair was disheveled, spatters of blood clinging to the ends. To be honest, I was pretty sure I looked like the demon bride myself, but there was no mirror to confirm my suspicions. I chanced a look at my hands.

My bloodied hands.

The hands that killed so many and would kill so many more.

But maybe once I found my sister, once I took her somewhere safe, somewhere far away from our families, maybe then I could rest.

Maybe then I could just be Ophelia. Not an assassin, not your regular psychopath.

Just a girl living her life.

Was it possible? Probably not. But I could always hope, and one thing I learned over the years, is that hope never dies. I would cling to that fucker until there was nothing else left, because most of the time, that was the only thing I had.

"Ophelia," Atlas started, and I realized he'd been talking this whole time. I zoned out—again.

"Sorry, I just... went somewhere else."

A soft smile touched his lips, and under the cloak of night, his injuries didn't look that bad. Apart from his closed eye and the bruises forming over his face, he didn't look that injured. I wouldn't want to be him tomorrow morning, though. He's going to feel like shit.

As a matter of fact, I wouldn't want to be me tomorrow either. There was a bump forming at the back of my head, and I didn't even want to think about the other parts of my body that have been hit, punched and almost shot at. Though this was probably one of those times where I could say "you should see the other guy".

"It was nice seeing you again, but I gotta go now."

He turned his whole body to me, wincing at the same time, and I could only imagine the state of his ribs if he had difficulty doing this small movement.

"Where are you going?"

I looked up, seeing Storm observing us quietly. Where was I going? As far away from here as possible. If I got the opportunity, I would haul my ass to Uganda or one of the other countries where they wouldn't be able to find me.

But I had to talk to my father first. After I found my sister.

"I don't know. Somewhere." I looked back at him. "Anywhere but here."

"You could stay." He shrugged. I believed him, I really did. I might not have been the best judge of character in the past, but Atlas seemed to be one of those people who really meant what they said. Besides, I didn't have any reason not to believe him.

The man almost got a bullet between his eyes because of me. Helping me do what I needed to.

"Yeah, I don't think that's a good idea."

"I don't think you have a choice," he snickered, looking behind me. I could feel his presence. How could I forget the way he made me feel, even if it was only for one day? I wasn't questioning it then, but I was questioning it now.

Desire, love, attraction, those were the things that brought me where I was now. Those were the things that fucked me over once, because I trusted blindly. I loved with such ferocity, and I thought the other person loved me in the same way.

And it wasn't only Kieran.

I loved Ava, Cillian and Tristan, I even loved my father and my mother, and look where it all got me.

The only person that deserved my love now was Maya. The only one that probably needed me was her, and after so many years running away from who I was, from what happened to her, it was time to face it all.

This was just the start of everything I was gonna do to those that wronged me. Logan Nightingale was the next bitch on my list, but there was an order of things.

There were things I had to do first, and my personal vendetta against him and the rest of his monkeys would have to wait.

"I always have a choice, Atlas. They caged me before, but I won't allow anybody else to do the same again."

I turned, meeting Storm's impassive gaze. It was as if he flipped a switch, and the protective stance he had toward me while we were in the church just evaporated. I guess I wasn't the only one good at pretending.

He was as well.

"What do you want?"

I had no patience for men that wanted to control every aspect of my life. He could take his whole Alpha demeanor and shove it up his ass. I didn't want it.

"I hear you're leaving. Or well, planning to."

"Yes, and?" I passed next to him and started walking down the sidewalk, toward the second car Kieran's guards came in. "I didn't know that I needed your permission."

In a blink of an eye, my back collided with his front as he pulled me backwards. My heart, my stupid, traitorous heart, fluttered from his nearness, and as he curled one hand around my neck, I wondered if I got more than I wanted this time.

"Let me go."

His thumb grazed softly against my pulse, and I knew he could feel my heart beating like crazy.

"I don't think you really want to go, sunshine." His lips grazed the shell of my ear before his teeth bit down on my earlobe. "I think you want to stay."

His proximity, the soft touches, the biting, caused shivers to erupt over my skin and I hated my body for betraying me in these moments. This wasn't supposed to be happening, goddammit.

"Storm, let me go."

"I can't."

"Why not?" I was out of breath, and I blamed him for it. My hormones could go and fuck themselves.

"Because you belong to me, Persephone. Don't you remember what I said?" He lowered his voice, the husky tone like a feathery touch on my skin. "I need a queen, and you are a perfect candidate."

"Fuck off. I don't belong to anybody."

"But your body disagrees with you."

It does. It wanted to stay with him. My body wanted to let him have his way with me, to press harder on my neck, to show me what I've been missing. But just before I could succumb to my deepest desires, I remembered something else.

The day I came to Santa Monica.

Two days after I ran away from the Nightingales. The day his guys told me to fuck off and that their president didn't want to see me. The day I needed him the most. I needed somebody on my side, and he did what every other male in my life did.

He abandoned me.

So fuck him and fuck what my body wanted. I was my own master. I belong to no man, to no place.

I threw my head backwards, slamming into his face. His grip on me loosened, and I used the momentum to dash to the car. I had to at least try.

Unfortunately, luck was never on my side and before I could even open the door, my head got slammed onto the roof of the car. The impact knocked me out, sending me into the infinite black void.

For fuck's sake.

Not again.

.

COMING SOON

Do you want to see what will happen next?
Pre-order the second book
in The Rapture Series: **EQUILIBRIUM**
Pre-Order Here

ACKNOWLEDGMENTS

When people say that they needed a small army in order to publish their book, handle the things and whatnot, trust me, they aren't wrong. I was lucky enough to find my tribe through this process, and this book wouldn't be here if it wasn't for them.

To my Stephanie, my Momager, the first person that read this book. And when I say that, I mean, every single version of this book. Thank you for believing in me and this series. For freaking out over these characters, and all the plotting at three a.m. For kicking my ass whenever self-doubt would creep in, and telling me that I can do this, and that people have to get this book. Thank you!

Elisabeth, my keychain, my Tinkerbell. You were my voice of reason, and I am so grateful I managed to snatch you. Thank you for loving these characters as much as I do.

To Kenia - thank you for all the late-night talks. I will forever be grateful for our video calls, and the love you've shown for this book.

Laura, your love for Phee really took me by surprise. Thank

you so much for being a part of my Beta team, and helping me through this process.

There is one very special person I've met halfway through this book. My Daddy Rachel. You've no idea how grateful I am for every single piece of advice you've given me. Thank you for being you, and for listening to my rambling and reassuring me that things will go as planned.

My beautiful Street Team, my Queens of Carnage. You guys have rocked this game, and I am thankful to each and every one of you for sharing your love for this book. For being there, cheering me up, and hyping this book. Keep rocking!

Maggie, my absolutely fabulous Editor. You've no idea how much you've helped me. Thank you for all your suggestions and advice for this book. It wouldn't look this pretty if it wasn't for you.

To music. For always being there, keeping me afloat and helping me shape this book, this whole world into what it is today.

My amazing reader's group, The Reid Cult. You guys have been my safe zone during this whole thing, and I can't even tell you how happy I am seeing you all so interested in this book. Thank you for supporting me and being there for me.

My mom. My beautiful, strong and fierce mom. Thank you for helping me accomplish my dreams, and for always cheering me up. I wouldn't be the person I am today if it wasn't for you. One day, I hope I will be half a woman you are today.

My little, not-so-little, brother, Dino. The strength you've shown over the years, your positive attitude, overcoming all the obstacles that life has put on you, has helped me to finally start working on my dreams and on things I want to have. You are my real-life Baby Hulk. Thank you for always hyping me up, and for being the best brother I could've ever asked for.

And last, but not least. To readers. Thank you so much for giving this book a chance, and for giving me a chance. I hope you enjoyed it and I hope you loved Phee and this beginning of her journey as much as I loved writing it.

ABOUT THE AUTHOR

L.K. Reid is a dark romance author, who hates slow walkers and mean people. She's still figuring out this whole "adult" thing, and in her opinion, Halloween should be a Public Holiday. She has a small obsession with Greek Mythology and all things supernatural. Music has to be turned on from the moment she wakes up, all the way throughout the day and night.

If she isn't writing, she can be found reading, plotting upcoming books and watching horror movies.

Sign up for my Newsletter

The Reid Cult - L.K. Reid Group

Printed in Great Britain
by Amazon